More praise for
WANDERING STAR

"Rarely does a book come down the pike as colorful and so thoroughly entertaining.... The principals in this rousing drama are fascinating, believable and thoroughly human."
—*Fort Worth Star-Telegram*

"A thoroughly convincing picture of its time and place and some characters with whom readers will readily identify. The author worked hard to get his history right ... [and] he sets down the results in a style readers will enjoy."
—*The Amarillo News-Globe*

"[WANDERING STAR] draws effectively on our shared senses of history and myth.... We know how it feels to be Tom, torn between a too-rigid sense of good and bad, and we're powerless to resist the tug on our archetypal heartstrings."
—*Booklist*

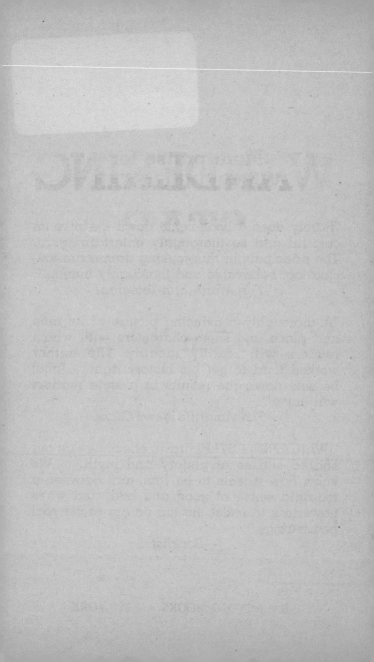

WANDERING STAR

Steven Yount

BALLANTINE BOOKS • NEW YORK

All rights reserved under International and Pan-American Copyright Conventions. Published in the United States by Ballantine Books, a division of Random House, Inc., New York, and simultaneously in Canada by Random House of Canada Limited, Toronto.

Library of Congress Catalog Card Number: 93-47467

ISBN 0-345-39437-2

Manufactured in the United States of America

First Hardcover Edition: May 1994
First Mass Market Edition: May 1995

10 9 8 7 6 5 4 3 2 1

This book is dedicated to my mother and father,
sisters and brothers, wife and son,
who have sustained me throughout.

ACKNOWLEDGMENTS
I owe thanks not only to my family, to whom this book is dedicated, but to Robert and Linda Nowotny, who assisted in the conception and execution of this tale; Peter Miller and Jennifer Robinson, who would not rest until it was printed; and to those rare and venerable friends in Austin, Texas, and Western North Carolina—particularly the extended Draco tribe—who made even the most wearisome times more fun than I deserved.

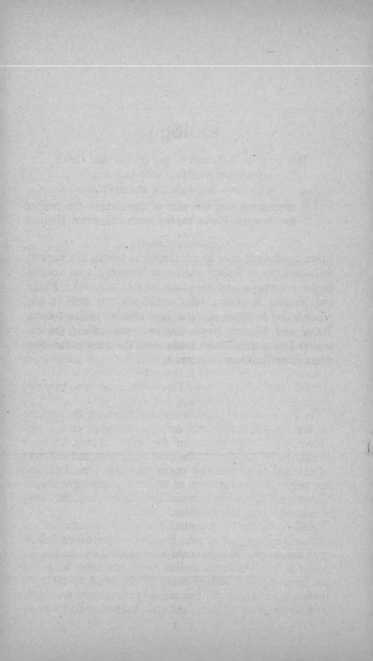

Prologue

Nineteen ten was the year of the comet—the year of the drought. I was twelve years old when Halley's Comet first appeared in the early morning sky of the Texas Panhandle, but I feel my life truly began that year, since everything I'd seen and done up till then didn't amount to a handful of sand compared to those short, remarkable, chaotic few months when damn near the whole town of High Plains, Texas, waited for the world to end. It didn't. But to my mind the whole twisted experience was summed up by a Doc Moss observation, an insight that might well serve as the town's epitaph. In the heat of the struggle for High Plains's soul, when the forces of restraint were looking for encouragement, reason to believe that the town could right itself, Doc could offer none. Doc said, "Folks won't be reasoned out of a hole they dug in dread."

To my everlasting sorrow and bemusement, the validity of that statement has held up over the span of my life. However, in the defense of the good citizens of High Plains, Halley's Comet is the most portentous and enduring of celestial omens, trailing centuries of fearsome lore, and the pulpits and newspapers of the town made quite certain that no one ignored its passage. It was their duty, they said. It was also good for business.

Still . . . it was the twentieth century, the American Century, and time to put archaic European superstitions behind us. I believe High Plains could have ignored this cosmic intruder if it had come at another time—any other time. But we were a town and citizenry predisposed to taking a plunge into the calamity that can only result from an unholy coincidence of time, place, and circumstance. And I venture

1

that there are scant few towns that would acquit themselves
more nobly if forced to endure in one brief season a rancor-
ous prohibition campaign, a searing drought, and a doomsday movement. Stir in the contribution of a top-notch,
hell-roarin', jackleg evangelist and you have a guaranteed
recipe for bitter affliction.

And we were in transition. In 1910 the Panhandle of
Texas—that vast godforsaken stretch of flat-ass grassland
that nobody wanted for so long—was slowly filling up with
dirt farmers and ribbon clerks. Only thirty-five years had
passed since the Comanche had reigned over the millions of
acres of prairie called the "Great American Desert" by a
disinterested eastern public. But after the Civil War, cattlemen began casting covetous eyes on the limitless grazing
land, and the U.S. Army was dispatched to secure it. The
Comanche were quickly defeated and quarantined on reservations; the buffalo that had sustained them wandered only
in the night sky and in the smoke of the campfire. Five million buffalo were killed in a decade, clearing the plains for
cattle.

The Texas cattle drives, the backbone of the cowboy
myth, lasted less than twenty-five years, pulling up well
short of the turn of the century. When the huge cattle
ranches, some of a million acres and more, proved unprof-
itable, they were broken up into sections and sold to settlers
attracted to the greatest expanse of cheap farmland in the
Southwest. While the repeating rifle, barbed wire, and the
windmill made settlement of the Panhandle possible, cheap
plentiful land made it inevitable. Land prices were so reasonable that the immigrants chose to ignore the lack of sur-
face water, the absence of trees, and the constant wind.
Although yearly precipitation was only marginally adequate
for farming, the settlers put their trust in God, their cash on
the barrel head, and prayed for rain and the railroad. The
rain was immutable—the railroad responded to the cash.

The first settlements of any size in the Panhandle were
the rowdy cow towns of Mobeetie and Tascosa, but they
were civilized out of existence when the railroad passed
them by. Towns sprang up overnight alongside the freshly
laid tracks, and the new citizens eagerly embraced the trap-

pings of respectability; churches and schools elbowed the saloons and brothels to the outskirts of town and beyond. Working desperately to put distance between their frontier past and the promise of the twentieth century, the new body politic mounted a brutal attack on John Barleycorn. By 1910 prohibitionists had managed to ban alcohol in virtually the entire Panhandle.

Blind Mule, a settlement named by a drifter who observed that only such an animal would consent to live there, avoided extinction by attracting a railroad and, at the behest of the railroad, changing its name. Blind Mule became High Plains through a near-unanimous referendum by those citizens inclined toward democracy and sober enough to vote. The townfolk could not, however, vote away their boisterous past or venal inclinations, and the original Blind Mulites resisted all entreaty to reform.

Blind Mule/High Plains became the last holdout against the Panhandle's stampede to decency. Vice survived, but by a fast-diminishing margin as upright settlers supplanted fading pioneers, and at the expense of peace and civility in the town. Combine this sorry state of affairs with a year-long drought that busted the fall harvest and threatened the spring wheat, and you've got a powder keg groping for a spark. The spark was, ironically, an innocuous ball of ice, gas, and dust that happened to be carousing through the neighborhood on its seventy-six-year orbit of the solar system. It was a natural phenomenon that a whole lot of people took personally.

The genesis of the High Plains tragedy, as near as I can make out, is rooted in an archetypal belief common to the inhabitants of the third planet from the sun in a nondescript solar system in the western spiral arm of the Milky Way galaxy: the belief, remarkable in its audacity, that *their planet is the center of the universe*. Befitting this lofty position, their individual souls have become the focus of a cosmic battle between Good and Evil, Creator and Destroyer. That's a lot of responsibility for flesh and blood, and occasionally these folks lose their perspective. In High Plains, Texas, in 1910, they lost it in wholesale lots.

It was only from the vantage of over half a century of

hindsight that I first attempted to chronicle these events that changed every life they touched as well as the course of the town. The arrival of Sam and Rebekah Adams to High Plains on the same star-crossed train as the evangelist, Brother Nicholas, introduced me to people and circumstances that made my sixty-year newspaper career not only possible, but inevitable.

The bulk of this manuscript was written some thirty years ago, but, spurred by the pale and impotent incarnation of Halley's Comet in 1986 and the death of the last of the principals involved in my history, I find no reason to withhold this account any longer. Most of what I will relate to you is what I remember, some of it is what I was told, and some of it is culled from the newspapers of the time. It is the truth as far as one man can know it, which is, of course, not the truth at all.

Chapter
One

I recall walking well back of the wagon so the rolling cloud of dust kicked up by the mules would miss me. I had intended to ride to the depot, but Shad and I had argued about something—there being acres of contested ground between a contentious young white boy and a stubborn old black man—so now I wasn't about to give him the satisfaction of asking for transport. My pride was an onerous piece of baggage at age twelve, which would not tolerate admitting error, doubt, or weakness to an adversary. Even an adversary that passed for a friend most of the time.

When the train whistle blew in on the north wind, I pulled my coat collar up around my ears and smiled at the thought of all the people in New Town who, jarred out of their sleep, would be cussing it. The train was often late, but three hours stretched everyone's tolerance. As I walked up the middle of the street, I spotted another breach of the peace. A temperance banner—PROHIBITION OR BARBARITY: VOTE NO!—had worked a tie loose from its mooring in front of the *High Plains Citizen-Advocate* and was flogging itself mercilessly in the wind. If the noise bothered anybody, you couldn't tell it: not a soul stirred or a light flickered that I could see. These folks sure knew how to waste the best part of the night. You might just as well be spending time in a graveyard as in New Town after ten o'clock.

I ran ahead of the wagon for the last fifty yards, just to show Shad that riding would only have slowed me down, and reached the station before the train pulled into sight. The usual crew of a dozen or so—half workers, half loafers—were standing around lying and complaining to each other. The workers had to be there, so they did the

5

complaining. The loafers expected no freight and greeted no passenger; they just waited for whatever mystery and romance might roll in on the train. These were not men who were easily disappointed.

I spoke to the Carter brothers—Jap and Shorty—who were standing next to their horse-drawn cabs. Both hotels sent buggies to the train on the off chance that they might pick up a paying lodger. It wasn't uncommonly cold for February, but the Carters were shuffling around and blowing on their hands as though it were the worst norther of the year. That probably had more to do with the waiting than the weather. If cold was the problem, they could have gone inside and warmed themselves at the stove.

Old Zack Hart was wrestling a baggage cart across the platform and telling anyone within earshot about that legendary cutting horse he'd owned some forty years back that was so fast and agile it could "cut fly shit out of black pepper." Since everybody there knew the story word-for-word, they just nodded and stared down the track like sailors searching for the first glimpse of land. Zack cut his story short when he caught sight of me.

"Hey, Wingnut!" Zack yelled, in a voice that sounded like a man churning a handful of gravel. My ears burned at the nickname, but I ignored him. "Tom Greer, get your ass over here," he shouted again.

I took my time walking over so he'd know I didn't have to come at all. I called to several folks by name and talked about the weather—cold—and the chance of snow— somewhere between slim and none. Zack was working in his shirtsleeves; he was too damned ornery to acknowledge the cold.

"Put your back behind this, boy," he ordered as I climbed up the platform. The cart was stuck in a hole between two planks, and he couldn't budge it. It wouldn't have been any trouble for him except that a day or so before he had fallen onto the depot stove and burned his right hand. He had a dirty rag tied around it, more, I suspected, so he wouldn't have to look at it than for therapy. I lifted the cart, pushed it to one side and waited for him to thank me. I should have known better.

"You two here to meet that editor-feller?" Zack asked, nodding toward Shad, who sat ramrod straight in the wagon. Because he had loaded and unloaded every train in and out of High Plains since the track was laid, Zack figured that everything that happened at the depot was his business. I set him straight.

"Maybe I am, maybe I ain't," I said, jumping off the platform. "Can't see it's any concern of yours."

The train was pulling in, so I moved around to the passenger drop. I should have known that the old man wouldn't give up the last word that easily. He shook his head and spat a half wad of tobacco on the platform; the other half settled into his beard. "It's a damn shame that Langston can't manage no better than a snot-nose boy and a nigger to meet that feller," Zack yelled. "But I 'spect it don't matter no longer than he's gonna last in this town."

The train had barely ground to a stop before the passengers started piling off. A haggard-looking woman followed three scrappy little kids off; she looked as if those brats had ridden her all the way from Kansas. Running and jumping around the depot and screaming like banshees, they reminded me of bird dog pups released from a pen after a winter's confinement.

A couple of drummers staggered off next. You could spot them a mile away: loud voices, flashy suits, and big wicker sample cases. Stumbling off to the side of the depot, they killed the dregs of a pint of Farragut whiskey—known far and wide as "Firegut"—and broke the empty bottle against the platform.

A tall, broad-shouldered man, who I took for a German farmer, and his wife cut a wide berth around the peddlers. She wore a white hat and had a shawl wrapped so tightly around her face that she reminded me of one of those mummies out of *Harker's Tales of Horror*, a dime "thriller" that had made the rounds at school and the poolroom.

Cowboys with saddles, farmers in misshapen suits, and weary women and children filled up the platform and waited while Zack hauled their gear from the baggage compartment. I was eyeing everybody hard since I didn't know this "Sam Adams" from Adam's off-ox, but nobody there looked like a newspaper editor. There was a short, skinny little fellow dressed in black who appeared to have missed enough meals to qualify, but his mouth was pinched so tight at the sight of those drunken drummers that I marked him off. I'd never seen a printer who would begrudge a man a drink, or shy away from one himself.

The train was empty, and I still didn't have a suspect. Nearly everyone was coupled up, and Langston hadn't said a word about Adams having a wife; newspapermen could rarely afford the luxury. I glanced over at Shad, hoping for some direction, but he appeared content to let me sort it out myself. Shad hadn't moved or spoken since we got there, and his face didn't reflect the cold or the impatience I felt. He looked so damn superior sitting up there that I felt like chucking a rock in his ear. Instead, I walked up to the little man in black and asked him straight out. "Are you Sam Adams?"

He couldn't have been more than an inch or two taller than me, and when he turned around, we stood nearly nose-to-nose. But his eyes . . . those eyes belonged to someone about six-foot-six and three hundred pounds. The pupils were large and black and sunk deep under a hedge of wild, heavy brows. His eyes held me so that I couldn't turn my head, couldn't even blink. I felt kind of swimmy-headed and panicky, like when you try to fight your way out of a bad dream. It was like staring into a deep, dank cave.

"Are you looking for me?"

I spun around feeling confused and stupid and angry enough to spit in a tiger's eye. In the adolescent mind, it is often a short and fluid step from frustration to anger; for me it was a greased downhill slide.

The speaker was the fellow I'd pegged as a German farmer. Besides being too healthy-looking for a trade that seemed to attract the pale and tubercular, he didn't look particularly smart. His face wasn't ugly, but it was set up sort of off center. Not the product of a malicious artist, but an inattentive one: his nose and mouth looked like they had been borrowed from two passing strangers. But his expression was friendly. If he'd been hard-looking, I'd probably have had more sense than to yell at him.

"If you're Sam Adams, I'd like to know where the hell you been? I've been bustin' my ass tryin' to find you."

There wasn't much he could say to that since he had been on the platform all the time, but I felt better now that I had control of the situation. His eyebrows rose a notch, and his attention shifted off to my right. I followed his gaze and discovered the prettiest woman I'd ever seen in my life; she stood with her mouth open in surprise, staring at me. The shawl had covered her face before, or I would have spotted her a mile away in a dust storm. She was even prettier than Callie Shanks had been three years back when she came straight off the farm to work in Derby's saloon.

But this lady was perfect, and I remain at a loss to describe her form and grace. It's easy to recount imperfection or excess in the human form, but beauty defies metaphor. Her eyes were blue and her hair was yellow. If you care to conjure up images of robin's eggs or new-mown wheat on a June morning, have at it. The best I can manage is to say that when Rebekah Adams was in sight, it was everything a strong man could do to tear his eyes away from her. At that moment I knew that she was the loveliest woman I would ever see. I also knew that my mouth had once again proved to be my gravest enemy. I was thankful when Adams spoke; it pulled my chestnuts out of the fire.

"I *am* Sam Adams," he said pleasantly. "And this is my wife, Rebekah." Taking her arm, he led her the couple of steps to where I was staring at the platform and turning red. His huge hand swallowed mine when we shook. I muttered my name without looking up into his face.

In deference to the lady, I took my hat off and bent forward quickly from the waist while pulling my right foot back slightly, just like my Mama had taught me. When Miss Rebekah smiled at me and nodded, the book that she held in her left hand tumbled to the platform. A King James Bible. Sam Adams and I bumped heads when we both scrambled to retrieve it. By then Shad had walked up beside me, and he spoke his piece.

"My name's Shad. Mr. Langston Harper sent me and the boy down to pick you up and take you back to your place." The black man made a move toward the suitcases. He was

as surprised as I was when Adams stuck his hand out to
shake.

"I'm Sam Adams."

I had no insight into the customs of the people of Kansas, but I knew for a fact that I had never seen a handshake
between a white and a black man in High Plains. I also
knew that Adams was going to have a treacherously tough
row to hoe in this town, even without shining up to the colored folks. And it got worse:

"And this is Rebekah," Adams finished.

Then *she* shook Shad's hand. I took a hurried look
around the platform to see who was watching, and was
grateful that everybody seemed to be tied up in their own
business. I grabbed a suitcase and headed for the wagon,
hoping to break up the cozy little tea party before everybody in town noticed. "Better get the wagon loaded," I
shouted over my shoulder as I stepped off the platform.

Shad and I tossed the suitcases on the flatbed as Adams
and Miss Rebekah walked back to claim their trunk. The
drunker of the drummers—it was a close contest—leaned
against the depot and waited impatiently for his merchan-
dise case. He couldn't resist a few ill-chosen words of
counsel to Zack. "Be careful with that trunk, Methuselah,
or I'll take a razor to you myself." The drummer winked at
his buddy, and they shared a little, dried-up, sour kind of
laugh.

The drummer was referring to an incidence of fashion
that I have always found curious. During and immediately
after the Civil War—or "The War of Aggression Against
the South," as Doc Moss called it—it seemed that most
full-grown men, including every U.S. president from 1860
to 1897, wore a beard. But one of the first concessions to
civilization and town life in the West was submission to the
razor. Zack Hart was the only working man in town sporting chin whiskers on a permanent basis. He did so, I suspect, out of habit, out of convenience, and to show
everybody within an eyeball's reach that he did not—and
never would—give a damn.

CRASH! The drummer's case bounced off the platform,
and the sound of broken glass rattled across the depot and

down the empty street. Zack slid the chest in the general direction of the salesman, who could only manage an empty threat. "I'm reporting you to the president of the railroad, you . . . goddamn savage!"

Unfortunately, Miss Rebekah's trunk lay directly between the two antagonists, and she caught the drummer's profanity full-bore between the eyes. She winced on impact. Adams stared the drummer into a hasty retreat inside the depot, then took his wife's arm. "I suppose, Rebekah," he said, as he walked her back toward the wagon, "that we're going to have to accustom ourselves to a certain . . . earthiness while we're here. We'll get used to it, I'm sure."

She shouldn't have to, I thought angrily. I felt like kicking the drummer's ass personally but managed to talk myself out of it.

By the time Shad and I had tossed the trunk on the wagon, Miss Rebekah had collected herself. "I'm fine, Sam," she reassured him. "It's just the long ride. And the way he said that, in public, I was surprised. It was silly of me."

Knowing that profanity was the preferred dialect spoken around a railroad, I tried to hurry our departure before the lady was exposed to further abuse. As we climbed onto the wagon, the skinny little fellow in black—the one who had stared me down—walked up to the wagon. He had a bad limp that I hadn't noticed before. "Do you know where I can find an inexpensive boardinghouse?" he asked.

Adams allowed that it was his first night in town and passed the question on to Shad with a glance. "They's cheap rooms down in the Bowery." Shad spoke straight ahead without bothering to turn his head.

"Can I ride with you?" The little fellow's question was addressed to Sam Adams, who again deferred to Shad. I sincerely hoped that Shad would tell the fellow that there were several hack drivers within spitting distance who would be happy to take him anywhere in town, that was how they made their living. For my part, I had rather ride shotgun on a hearse than share the back of the wagon with that ghoul. But no one asked my opinion.

"The mules won't mind," Shad said. But nobody asked them either.

The little man threw his suitcase onto the wagon and used the wheel to climb in back. He introduced himself loudly, as if addressing the universe. "I'm Brother Nicholas."

Damn! Just what we needed, with this town already rode to death with churches and preachers. Adams turned to shake hands or introduce himself, but Nicholas was pawing through his suitcase with his back turned. Apparently he wasn't concerned with anyone else's identity.

Miss Rebekah sat between Shad and her husband, giving the gossips more ammunition, and I took a place in back, facing away from the preacher. New Town was stone quiet and dark, but there was enough moonlight to read the banners and posters that hung from storefronts and stretched across the road. As we rolled up the street, Adams read a few of them in a deep, melodramatic voice. "Demon Rum Must Go!," "Vote Decency—Not Whiskey!" and "Save Your Children: Vote No!" He whistled in admiration of the huge streamer that stretched across the street: "Temperance Revival—All Week—Right Reverend William Jacob Presiding. Topic: Saloons Versus Salvation!" Adams laughed, but his wife sort of nudged him and shook her head. Since I couldn't remember a time when the town wasn't in the midst of a prohibition campaign, I didn't understand his amusement. That was everyday language around here.

Adams turned back to speak to Brother Nicholas. "High Plains appears to be bracing up for a knuckle-busting liquor battle, Brother."

Nicholas shook his head grimly. "This town has come to the crossroads. It can join in the march to Godliness and Prosperity, or it can follow Satan's path into the everlasting torments of Hell."

Adams shook his head as if impressed by the scope of what had appeared to be a simple local-option liquor vote. "I take it you're leaning toward the godly route," he said.

"I've been sent to play a part in all this," Nicholas intoned. Adams's irony was lost on him. Nicholas pointed to the Bible that rested in Miss Rebekah's lap. "It appears that this young woman has a similar mission. Are you Baptist?"

She shook her head. "Episcopalian. My father is a deacon."

Nicholas turned to Adams. "And you?"

"I'm a newspaperman," Adams confessed.

Nicholas's look of contempt indicated that his answer was sufficient to condemn Adams to the hottest corner of Hell. We rode along in weary silence until snatches of an off-key song came drifting in from the north. About twenty yards ahead of us a wagonful of railroad men—I knew them all by name—pulled out from between two buildings and into the middle of the street. They were singing a bawdy version of "Buffalo Gal" at the top of their lungs and passing a demijohn of whiskey around while their skinny little mule pulled the wagon unsupervised on a meandering route. The brakeman's red lantern was suspended on a pole behind the wagon, and I swear it looked like it was winking lewdly at us. When the carolers got to the part where they described their designs on the "Buffalo Gal" when she finally did "come out tonight," Sam Adams made a request.

"Could you give them a little room, Shad? They're having more fun than I care to listen to."

Brother Nicholas was more direct. "Drunken pigs," he snorted.

Shad pulled his mules to a halt in the middle of the dark street, and Adams jumped from the wagon to stretch. When he rolled his head back, he caught his first conscious glimpse of a prairie sky. He whistled again as he scanned the heavens. "You can see to the far side of forever out here."

Miss Rebekah had been sagging noticeably since we left the depot, but she perked up now. "It's so clear . . . beautiful."

Since I had never been more than twenty miles from this spot, I took the night sky for granted, but Miss Rebekah's admiring tone caused me to appraise it with a new eye. On the Great Plains you can extend your arms parallel to the ground and observe the horizon from fingertip to fingertip.

On that winter's night, you balanced stars on those finger-tips.

Adams was busy getting his bearings. He looked to his left, then directly overhead, then straight down the street, naming a star or a constellation at each juncture: "Polaris ... Cassiopeia ... Pegasus. Rebekah, can you see those four stars that look like a square?"

You couldn't miss the excitement in Adams's voice as he continued. "Just below it there's a point of light with a cloudy tail behind it. Right above the horizon." It wasn't very bright, but I found it. Adams's voice was triumphant. "That's Halley's Comet!"

I'd heard the name before, maybe in the newspaper, but I didn't know anyone in town that gave a damn about it. It was still a long ways away and dim, and it didn't come out till early morning, when respectable folk had been abed for several hours. Most of the people up this late had their eyes—and often their hands and knees—on the ground. Mrs. Hardy, my schoolteacher, had mentioned something about a comet coming, but it was just after lunch, and I was settling into a good nap. It was nothing to lose sleep over. Not back in February.

It excited Miss Rebekah, though. Her face lit up and her voice rose when she turned to explain. "Sam and I looked for it one night in Wichita, but the city lights were too bright." She shook her head in amazement, and yellow hair fell from under her hat. "The stars out here are so close, I feel I could pick a handful for a necklace."

My heart beat faster just watching her smile and talk. Not everyone was charmed; Shad was inscrutable, and Nicholas impatient. "That wagon is gone now," Nicholas said. "We can continue."

Adams climbed aboard, and Shad nudged the mules into motion. There was a perceptible edge to Adams's voice when he addressed the preacher. "I'd have figured that a man of the cloth would be concerned with the workings of the heavens. That's your territory, isn't it?"

I don't know if Nicholas resented the question, or if he always spoke as though he were instructing an inattentive schoolboy, but I recognized the tone. "The souls of men are

my responsibility," the preacher said testily. "I leave the firmament in the hands of the Lord." He turned away, folded
his hands in his lap and concluded: "The fate of High
Plains is my mission now."

Miss Rebekah elbowed her husband just as he started to
reply; she wasn't up for an argument. Adams relented and
occupied himself by reading aloud two of the larger banners that lined the street. "Whiskey: Scourge of the Prairie!" and "Chase the Plague from High Plains!" He shook
his head in disbelief and spoke to the silent streets. "This
town doesn't appear so all-fired sinful to me."

Shad smiled for the first time all night as he guided the
mules off the main street. Once shorn of the protection of
the buildings of New Town, the lights and noise of the
booming settlement raced across the three hundred yards of
prairie and struck me like a boot in the chest. Selective
memory is a gift and curse that I had managed to hold on
to well into adolescence. Just as I had easily ignored the in-
evitability of discovery and punishment when I locked that
cow in the courthouse, or when I "borrowed" R. N.
Barkley's prize mare to ride in the Founder's Day Parade,
I had conveniently erased from my memory the existence
of the "other" side of town. In my desire to spare the beautiful and modest Miss Rebekah further mistreatment, I had
managed to block from my mind the fact that she was going to have to come face-to-face with the area that was
commonly—often proudly—called "Gomorrah on the
Plains."

"What in the world . . . ?" was all Miss Rebekah could
manage.

"It's the Bowery," Shad explained. "It's where the town
started out before everybody run off to squat around the
railroad."

The destiny of the Panhandle, and much of the western
United States, was dictated by the railroads. Towns that
were bypassed withered and blew away and were replaced
by "jerkwaters" that sprouted beside the tracks like weeds
after a spring rain. So when the Prairie States Railroad
Company announced its intention to lay track through Blind

Mule, Texas, the townspeople rejoiced. The settlement had been left without benefactor when the U.S. Army pulled out of Fort Steele, and had struggled by as a two-bit cow-town layover between Amarillo and Fort Worth. But the place was dying and everybody knew it. Only a railroad could save it. There were conditions, however: first, the name must be changed. The railroad decreed that High Plains sounded like a destination that would attract responsible immigrants, and the ex–Blind Mulites agreed. Secondly, the Prairie States announced that the tracks would not run directly through the town but several hundred yards north, across land recently purchased by a Fort Worth millionaire, Mr. R. N. Barkley. The citizens accepted the revised plan with little complaint since the railroad's legal majesty was as readily acknowledged as its inclination to graft. (It was once rumored that a railroad track—possibly in Arizona, perhaps in 1905—was laid on a course uninfluenced by political pressure or bribery. The report remains unconfirmed.)

So High Plains became a town divided. Barkley offered cheap land to selected "decent" families from the original settlement and advertised relentlessly for new settlers. A vigorous respectable community—New Town—soon blossomed around the railroad tracks. It was peopled by the younger sons of midwestern immigrant fathers and the disenfranchised heirs of the unreconstructed South attracted by the cheap land, railway access, and boundless promise of a new life. Their tendencies were conservative, theistic, and prohibitionist. New Town quickly became the political and commercial center of High Plains, while Old Town (or the Bowery) languished a few hundred yards to the south and substantially further removed from the right hand of God. All the two sides of town shared was a common name— High Plains—and unlimited animosity.

The Bowery was left to house the majority of original Blind Mulites and maintain the saloons, gambling houses, and brothels that had been the town's livelihood since its founding. Bad feelings intensified with each passing year as the population of New Town grew in size and sanctimony, and the Bowery proved resistant to change or reform. The best elements of New Town carried on a continuous moral and judicial struggle to eradicate the ulcer on its southern border, but the Bowery, like the appetites it slaked, was implacable. It endured.

And right at that moment the Bowery was wound up tight even by Saturday night standards—it being the last of the month and the cowboys' payday. As Shad's mules pulled us closer to the raucous streets, Miss Rebekah asked a question, though she must have feared the answer. "Are we going to live down there?" Her voice was a whisper.

"The newspaper office be right in the middle of it," Shad said.

The answer deflated the lady visibly; so Adams put his arm around her and whispered encouragement. I assume that he told her that their residency in the Bowery was only temporary, that they would move to New Town the first chance they got. The promise was one she would now share with every decent woman living in the Bowery. Brother Nicholas wasn't disappointed at all, but showed a malicious enthusiasm at the sight of sin, glorious and abundant. "Saloons, gambling halls, brothels. A world of vice such as revolted Old Testament prophets." He cackled with sullen delight.

As we approached the main street, I saw that all six saloons were doing turnaway business, with the overflow being picked up by several empty stores that sold whiskey on payday, holidays, or whenever there was loose money floating around. Drunken cowboys and farmers whooped and bellowed as they roamed aimlessly and stumbled over the uneven wooden sidewalks. Some danced shambling waltzes, keeping time to the rinky-tink rhythm of player pianos that leaked from cracked windows and open doors. A quick survey of the alleys revealed at least three bareknuckled fights worth watching had I been in different company. I took a quick reading on Miss Rebekah's reaction to all this. Her face was expressionless and her eyes remained riveted straight ahead; she was working hard to ignore the lurid carnival surrounding her.

We caught up with the wagonful of railroad men just as they were greeted by half-clad courtesans hanging from the windows of Maude's Parlor House. The brakeman's red

lantern was blown out and kicked over as the men stumbled
over each other to take advantage of the only town in a
hundred-mile radius with legal liquor and open prostitution.
The Bowery harkened back to the days of Mobeetie and
Tascosa, when towns were founded by soldiers, cowboys,
and gamblers, and the women tough enough to make a living off of them. When those two towns went belly-up, the
Bowery fell heir to their less respectable citizenry. It was a
way of life fast dying in the Panhandle, but to a twelve-
year-old boy it was exciting and glamorous. Up until that
night.

As we passed the Panhandle Prince Saloon, a cowboy,
motivated by the boot of a bouncer, stumbled into the street
and steadied himself on the neck of Shad's mule. Our
wagon stopped and the cowboy raised his head, only to be
blessed with the vision of feminine perfection sitting stiffly
between Shad and Sam Adams. The cowboy, I'm sure, felt
compelled to express his admiration by the noblest, most
cavalier sentiments that reside in the male breast. His
choice of words, however, was unfortunate.

"Gawddamn!" he hooted. "What cloud did you fall off
of, Miss Angel?" He shook his head and rubbed his galled
eyes to convince himself that the comely spirit was not a
whiskey mirage. "Whichever house you gonna work at, I
wanna be first in line."

Miss Rebekah nearly fainted. Shad took the reins, but the
cowboy didn't loosen his grip on the mule till I scrambled
down and kicked hell out of his shins. He took a roundhouse swing at me while hopping around, but another shot
to the ankle left him cussing into the dirt.

The newspaper office was only a few buildings away,
and Shad had already tied the wagon when I caught up.
While dismounting, Miss Rebekah stepped on the hem of
her dress, and the ensuing rip could be heard far down the
street. Adams, once again, attempted to comfort his wife,
but I could see she was worn thin and fading fast. The appearance of the newspaper office surely wouldn't cheer
anybody up; the wind rattled the open door and shook the
burlap sack that didn't quite cover the broken window in-
scribed HIGH PLAINS MESSENGER.

Brother Nicholas showed no reluctance to confront a landscape filled with drunks, brawlers, and all form of peril for the righteous. "Where's the boardinghouse?" he asked Shad.

Shad didn't bother to run around, he just pointed a finger down the street. Nicholas jerked his suitcase off the back of the wagon and limped resolutely into the bacchanalia. I felt well rid of him.

Taking a suitcase in each hand, I followed the couple into the office. The place was a shambles: the floor was littered with old newspapers and rubbish, and the walls, windows, and doors cried out for paint and repair. The bedroom and kitchen probably looked every bit as bad, but I had no intention of finding out. Shad lit a kerosene lamp then threw the burning piece of paper into the wood stove. "Here's some cow chips and coal for the fire." Shad shook a bucket next to the stove. "They's a two-holer in the back." That news did not seem to cheer Miss Rebekah as I thought it might.

"We're much obliged, Shad," Adams said. He shook Shad's hand again.

"Mr. Langston's in Amarillo lawyerin'," Shad said, pausing at the door. "He say he'll be around in a day or so."

Adams got busy inspecting the printing equipment while Miss Rebekah sat down in the only chair in the room. I was anxious to leave too, but I knew that I had to say something, apologize somehow. "I'm real sorry about everything . . . the Bowery . . . this place . . . what I said at the depot. . . ." My head slipped to my chest as I spoke, and I edged to the door.

Miss Rebekah stood up and Adams put his arm around her, in support as much as affection, I figured. "This has been a tough night for all of us, Tom," Adams said. "But Rebekah and I are going to get a good night's sleep and start fresh in the morning. If you want to give us a hand, come by tomorrow and we'll put you to work."

They both managed to smile, and I felt a whole lot better. "Good night, folks," I said, opening the door.

"Will you be all right out there?" Miss Rebekah's concern was genuine. I imagine that she felt that the battlefield at Gettysburg was safer than the Bowery streets. I tried to put her mind at ease.

"Heck, ma'am, this is my home. I'm as safe and happy as a pig in—" I stifled the instinctive curse. ". . . slop."

I could still feel her smile well after I had closed the door behind me. Usually on payday Saturday I'd stay up for another hour or two hanging around the saloons or watching the fights, but it had already been the longest night of my life. There was much to consider.

I snuck back into my house, taking great care not to wake my mother, and lay awake thinking for a long time. As I drifted off to sleep to the sounds of Bowery discord, I remember hoping—damn near praying—that the people of High Plains would realize just how important it was to have a second newspaper in the town.

Chapter
Two

"**S**on, it's time to stop playing with that food and eat it," my mother instructed as she finished her own trencherman breakfast. "There's many a child in China who could live for a week off what you throw away."

I was absentmindedly chasing a poorly fried egg and a thin piece of side meat with a crust of biscuit, hoping that it might disappear without my having to swallow it. Mama believed that an egg had to be fried until it harbored no trace of liquid yolk. "Runny eggs," I was constantly reminded, "don't stick to your ribs."

I had told Mama that I wasn't hungry, but the likelihood of my leaving the house without a "good, hot breakfast" was as remote as my chance of avoiding church on this, or any, Sunday morning. I was eager to hightail it over to the *High Plains Messenger*, but the obstacle barring my heathen path was profound.

Red-haired and nearly six feet tall, the "Widder Greer," as she was known throughout the county, packed formidable will and bulk and cast a long shadow over a young boy who desperately wanted an identity separate from, and usually antithetical to, his mother's conspicuous piety. Though robbed by the Spanish-American War of a husband to reform, my mother had been blessed with a single son, an obvious heir to the counsel she dispensed reflexively. My father existed for me only as a stern example and a photographic icon displayed in Rough Rider uniform in our parlor.

"Now, finish up and put on your Sunday coat. I'll not have my son looking like a ragamuffin in front of the whole congregation."

21

I forced a shiver and a cough. "Mama, I didn't sleep so well last night. I think I might be coming down with something—ague, maybe—it's going around. . . ." The lie was so feeble that as soon as it escaped my lips, I felt the cold, rough church pew pinch my rear end.

Mama rested her palm on my forehead briefly. "You're all right, just need some fresh air and exercise," she said as she cleared the table. "When I was your age, I'd have had the cows milked, chickens fed, eggs collected, and pigs slopped before I walked the three miles to church every Sunday—"

"—up the north side of a mountain, in the middle of a hailstorm, during an Indian raid," I added under my breath as I retrieved my Sunday coat. Hoping to avoid inspection, I walked quickly toward the door.

Mama caught me by the arm and spun me around. "Stand up straight, don't slouch," she said, straightening my shirt and buttoning my coat. "You're a handsome boy," she sighed, licking her hand and attempting to smooth down my cowlick, "but you need to pay more attention to your appearance. Maybe if you keep your cap pulled down, your ears won't look so big."

When she stepped back to evaluate the effect of her efforts, I saw that look—part exultant joy, part heartrending sadness—and I knew what was coming.

"Give your mama a big hug," she said, gathering me in an embrace that threatened to pop my top shirt button and unlace my boots. I returned her hug, all differences for the moment forgotten. I was relieved that the hugging impulse did not wait to strike her, as it so often did, in public.

"Button up tight, it's cold out there," she instructed, pulling on her own coat and hat. With her hand on the doorknob, she glanced over her shoulder and shook her head in misery. "If anybody ever learned that I walked out of my house leaving a sinkful of dirty dishes, I'd never be able to hold my head up in this town again." She pushed me through the door. "Let's go, let's go, we're gonna be late."

After church, I changed clothes and spent most of the afternoon running errands around town for the Adamses while they tried to scrub the newspaper office into habitability. The last thing I expected or wanted to see when I walked back into the office with an armload of clean rags was my mother covered in soapsuds, washing the walls. Mama had apparently learned of the new Bowery citizens at church and had wasted no time in offering advice and elbow grease to her new neighbors. Although she normally frowned on Sunday labor, the Widder explained to Rebekah and Sam, the state of the newspaper office was so wretched as to constitute an offense against righteousness, and thus justify bending the Sabbath prohibition. The Widder was widely known to greet newcomers with a fruit pie and an offer of any assistance that could rightly be expected of a Christian woman. Our house had long been a refuge for alienated young women or children between permanent homes. Every stray dog in town knew our back door.

Mama was instructing Sam and Miss Rebekah on the confused spiritual state of the town as I quietly dropped my rag bundle and retreated, unobserved, from the office. I unilaterally declared my day's work done and cut a path out of there. I could see that Sam Adams would like to have done the same. I spent the rest of the Sabbath hanging around the Lamour Hotel listening to the old men argue, and then I played "Fox and Hounds" till dark with some of the guys.

"You need to eat every bite of this," Mama said as she slid the bowl of hot cereal in front of me. She pinched a piece of mold off a bread end before laying it next to my plate, pronouncing it "good as new." I ate quietly as Mama cooked, cleaned, and lectured. "I think she's about the prettiest and nicest young woman to come to this town in a long time. A hard worker too. She was going stroke for stroke with me on those filthy walls till she stepped in the soapy water tub and turned her ankle, poor little thing. It was nearly dark then and a good time to quit anyway.

"I can't say much for him, though. Kinda quiet and sorta funny-lookin' to have such a pretty wife. I think she coulda done better."

Mama stopped her cleaning and looked at the bare wall

for a long moment. "You just never can tell what two people see in each other."

Back to work. "I just hope he runs a good Christian newspaper, though I can't for the life of me figure why a town this size needs two papers. You can only have so many church services and club meetings."

"Coffee, please, Mama."

"You shouldn't be drinking this," she said, pouring me a cup. "It'll stunt your growth."

Mama cleared my dishes away and sat down with her coffee. "Rebekah Adams said you'd been a big help to them. She said you were a fine young man." Mama looked at me with concern. "I think you're drinking too fast, son. Your face is turning red."

Even a good cup of coffee—and to my knowledge Mama never made one in her life—would have been insufficient inducement to carry the freight of this conversation. I grabbed my coat and books and charged the door as though I couldn't wait to get to school.

Mama yelled the customary instructions at my back. "You be a gentleman at school, Tom. And remember: learn three new things! Three new things!"

But school wasn't in my plans. I bought a plug of tobacco at Hayes General Store, stowed my schoolbooks behind a dry goods counter, and struck off for the newspaper office.

Not much moved in the Bowery before mid-morning. Hayes opened for early business, and the restaurant in the Lamour Hotel served breakfast, but the economy centered on the night, so you could have the street pretty much to yourself till nine o'clock or so. A cold dry wind piled sand against a leftover cowboy who slept on the sidewalk, and peppered the two lean, mangy dogs that laid uncontested claim to the middle of the street. I felt about halfway lonely as I sat in front of the newspaper office whittling a mesquite branch into a slingshot, and moving only so far as necessary to catch the sun.

When the school bell rang, making my truancy official, I smiled. I didn't consider school intolerable so much as just boring. I'd show up most of the time, particularly in cold weather, but I didn't hesitate to skip if I got a better offer. My teacher, Mrs. Hardy, didn't seem to mind much—I was often more trouble than I was worth—and I never got so far behind that I couldn't catch up in a day. *Ray's Arithmetic* and *McGuffey's Reader* had precious little to do with my world, and there was never a time that I couldn't learn more from just the spillover of Langston Harper's talk or one of Doc's stories than from the best day I ever spent in a classroom. Mama had taught me to read before I even started first grade, but all that Horatio Alger stuff that they pushed on you—where "penniless young Jack" would save the millionaire's daughter and become rich and steadfast—just made me laugh. It was ridiculous, and I figured that there must be something wrong with someone that wrote stuff like that. Mama and Mrs. Hardy took it seriously, though; they really wanted to believe it.

"How long you been out here?" Sam Adams asked, stretching and yawning as he walked through the door.

I checked the sun. "About an hour," I allowed.

"You going to lend us a hand today?"

"Figured I might."

Adams walked to the edge of the sidewalk and stared up and down the empty street. "I think Rebekah is going to spend the morning cleaning the windows and floors," he said, turning to face me. "Your mother has kindly offered to drop by and lend a hand later on." He must have seen my jaw drop abruptly, because he smiled as he offered me an alternative. "If you'd like to come with me, I'll teach you something that every newspaperman has to know."

"How to get the news?" I responded.

"No," he said grimly. "How to sell advertising."

When Adams struck off to the north, I tried to straighten him out. "I hope you ain't figuring on selling anything up in New Town."

He nodded and kept on walking.

"Forget it. Barkley's got that business sewed up tighter'n an old maid's snatch."

He kept walking. "Where'd you learn to talk like that?" he asked.

Hell, I'd worked long and hard, studying with the Mas-

ters to absorb vocabulary, timing, inflection. And, if
pressed, I likely would have modestly admitted some native
talent for the dialect. I continued, "I tell you, you're just
lopin' your mule up there. Ain't nobody gonna buy a damn
thing." I stopped walking.

He continued straight and hard toward New Town. I followed from a distance. I wanted to be around when he
found out who was right.

The streets of New Town were hopping and buzzing and
doubtless had been for several hours. Whereas the Bowery
was just now taking its first halting, hungover steps into the
new week, these ambitious New Towners hit the ground
full tilt on Monday morning. Storekeepers bartered, barbers
clipped, and bankers gouged as the citizenry moved with
intent and direction. Wagons drawn by horses and mules
shared the street with an occasional motor car, although
horseman and driver were each still a trifle skittish in the
company of the other. The sidewalks were crowded and
most of the benches occupied, so I decided to go over and
sit under my tree while I kept an eye on Sam Adams.

The sorry, stunted, dried-up excuse for a poplar tree I sat
under was one of two dozen that lined the street in a measured row, and it was far and away the scraggliest. When
the High Plains Civic and Gardening Club pulled all the
boys out of school two years back to plant them, I took offense at the idea of a gaggle of women planning something,
then pushing all the work off on a bunch of kids. So just
after I set my tree down into its hole, I tossed a double
handful of salt around the roots. I always made it a point
to visit my tree when I was in New Town.

Within an hour Adams had walked in and out of eight
different businesses. You could see from his gait that he
was wearing down from rejection. When he sat on the
bench in front of Reese's Bakery Shop and started scribbling in his notebook, I figured his spirit might be broken
to the point where he would listen to some good advice.

"How you doin'?" I asked, trying to avoid gloating.

Sam Adams didn't lift his gaze from his writing.

I pressed on. "If you're ready to go back down to the

Bowery, I can take you places that used to advertise in the *Messenger*. Up here—"

Adams's tone was sharp. "I'll spend the rest of the morning here. I'll leave when I finish what I've started."

I was ready to wash my hands of the bullheaded Adams until I noticed the approach of a figure so despicable that all other thoughts and intentions were chased away by loathing and anger. Bark Barkley was about a year older than I was, and from our first sighting of each other on the first-grade playground, we had assumed the attitude of owls and crows: all movement was prelude to attack. We fought less frequently now, both of us having grown large and bitter enough to inflict substantial punishment on the other. Our last battle, about three months back, left us both claiming victory but nursing wounds that required more than a few days to heal.

Bark walked directly toward us, and I braced for confrontation. When he stopped about six feet in front of our bench, I could tell that he hadn't come to throw down the gauntlet on these bustling streets. That wasn't his style; he preferred to attack from the rear with no witnesses save an ally or two to help him in case he lost the upper hand. The animus between Bark and me was well-recognized in town, and I was aware that a number of New Towners were finding pretext to remain close enough to our bench to witness any exchange of word or blow.

Though Bark kept his eyes on me, his words were aimed at Sam Adams. "You the guy that's gonna try to open up that two-bit paper down on the Bowery?" he demanded.

Adams raised his head slowly from his notebook. "Yes. And I'm the guy who is going to kick the ass of the next snot-nose kid who speaks to me in terms that he couldn't use in Sunday school. Do you understand?" Sam Adams looked from Bark to me. Apparently satisfied, he continued in a voice as flat as the landscape. "I'm going to edit the *Messenger*. Who are you?"

"I'm Richard Barkley, Jr. And my daddy runs the newspaper." Bark directed Adams's attention across the street to the sign: HIGH PLAINS CITIZEN-ADVOCATE—*Official Organ of High Plains City and Cody County.* The newspaper build-

ing was flanked by the First Cattlemen's Bank of High
Plains—R. N. Barkley President—and a custom-made shed
that housed the shiny 1909 Maxwell automobile owned by
the same man. Barkley also had a real estate office, an
insurance company, and a pretty young wife. There were
plenty of reasons, besides his misbegotten son, to hate
R. N. Barkley.

"My daddy wants to talk to you, *now*," Bark finished.

Adams smiled and shook his head. "Sonny, you run back
and tell your daddy that I've got business to take care of
now, but I believe that I could spare him a few minutes"—
Adams took a slow reading on the sun—"in about an
hour."

I laughed out loud, and there was a good deal of smiling
and nodding from the "audience," who did not even attempt to hide their interest. Bark stood there fidgeting, trying to think of something to say. He was used to people
jumping to attention when he tossed his father's name
around.

I added my counsel. "You run along to your daddy now,
sonny. We got work to do."

Bark's eyes narrowed. "Why ain't you in school, Greer
boy? Your mama is gonna wear out your skinny little ass
when she finds out you're playing hooky."

I was ready. "Don't fret yourself about it, Barkley. They
gave me the day off because I already knew all the Latin
they were going to teach today."

Several of our audience were in on the joke and laughed
out loud. Bark glared at me, and I thought he might charge.
Instead, he spun on his heels and took one angry step before nearly getting run over by a flatbed wagon. I could
hear him cussing the driver's paternity as he stomped back
to the newspaper office.

Sam Adams rose and started a slow amble up the sidewalk. "You boys don't seem to care much for one another,"
he observed.

"I wouldn't piss on him if his guts were on fire."

"What did you mean by that remark about Latin?" Sam
asked.

"Old man Barkley said the reason he took Bark out of

school was that he would never let his son go to a school that didn't teach Latin. Everybody in town got mad about that, so the old man had to write an editorial lying about it."

Even though I tried to steer the editor toward businesses where he could expect to receive the least abuse, his intention was to walk through every storefront in New Town. Adams didn't ask anyone to buy anything, and nobody volunteered, but he had an easy way with people and likely would be greeted pleasantly when he returned. I guess he figured that sooner or later he would wear them down and some advertising revenue would flow south to the Bowery. I gave up trying to tell him the odds against it.

"Is there anything I ought to know about R. N. Barkley before I enter the lion's den?" Sam asked as he walked toward his showdown at the *High Plains Citizen-Advocate*.

"Just cover your back," I said.

Adams smiled as he crossed the street.

"And after you shake his hand," I shouted at him, "be sure to count your fingers."

I crossed the street behind him and glanced through the window in time to see Adams casting a covetous look at the equipment that the newspaper's banner boasted of as the "Most Modern Printing Plant In North Texas." When he disappeared into Barkley's office, I walked around to the back alley where, if you stood on an overturned rain barrel and pressed your ear to the window, you couldn't help but hear the conversation from inside.

"Just what kind of newspaperman are you, Sam?" Barkley asked as he offered a cigar to the seated Adams. It was amazing how much Barkley resembled those short, fat cigars that he always smoked. He was over fifty years old and balding and—as my mother often said—ugly as a mud fence.

Adams refused the cheroot and dodged the question. "That's hard to say, Mr. Barkley. What are my choices?"

Adams's answer lacked the gravity that the question implied, so Barkley took another tack.

"I'm sure you know that a good newspaper can make or

break a town. Frankly, I'm glad to see that you're a young man with his eye on the future, and not one of those old ... muckrakers. They can empty a town faster than a tornado. No one wants to live in a town that hangs its dirty underwear on the courthouse square."

Since nearly all the "dirty underwear" in town had been soiled by R. N. Barkley, I found his modesty understandable. I ducked quickly when Barkley stood up, and after a few seconds slowly raised my eye to the corner of the window. My vantage was about three feet above head level and off to Barkley's right. When he moved around to the front of the desk, I could see both men fairly well. With obvious effort, Barkley planted his abundant haunches on top of his desk. He took off his glasses and shook them at Adams.

"What's your position on prohibition, young man?" Barkley's questions had become challenges.

"Can't say as I have one, Mr. Barkley. I figure every man should make his own decision on drinking." Adams wasn't giving any ground. Slippery as a catfish.

"Ordinarily I would agree with that, but right now the stakes are too high in this town for that kind of ... freedom." Barkley didn't seem satisfied with his answer, but he wasn't ready to give up the floor yet. "Did you come into town on the train?"

Adams nodded and Barkley barged ahead. "I brought that railroad to High Plains, and if this town votes 'Dry,' I'll have the Dallas-Overland laying tracks here to join up. The railroad wants clean, decent towns for their railheads, not ... frontier settlements."

That might have been what the bosses wanted, but I knew for a fact that the workers would rather sacrifice a blood relative at high noon on main street than give up the Bowery.

Barkley continued: "With the railhead here, I could pull the county seat away from Wishbone within a year. Do you know what county printing means to a newspaper, Adams?"

Adams knew. "Tax lists, court news, circulars, campaign advertising, broadsides—"

"Exactly! Enough printing for *everyone*." Barkley was

enthusiastic now. He relit his cigar noisily—the sound of a weasel sucking an egg. "The newspaper business is different out here, Adams. You can't make it on subscriptions. Half the people are broke, and the rest can't read. You won't even be able to scrape up meal money."

I could see Adams smile as he nodded toward Barkley's girth. "You don't appear to be living on a child's portion, Mr. Barkley."

The round man laughed and patted his stomach. "I don't make a dime on this paper, and that's the God's truth. It's just an expensive hobby. I do it for the town."

I nearly fell off my barrel at that lie, and from what I could see of Adams's face, he knew better too. Barkley continued in a voice too friendly to be trusted.

"Sam, I want you to know I'm not your enemy. A good weekly with local news, church reports, some humor—it can make a place for itself in High Plains."

"I see," said Sam Adams, rising to leave. "So long as I write about church socials and two-headed calves, we'll get along just fine. But I would be well-advised to stay out of politics. Isn't that about the size of it?"

Barkley laughed again, then attempted to smooth over his ham-fisted proposition. "It's just a matter of facilities and resources, Sam. Daily papers can handle the hard news while weeklies lend themselves to social—" Barkley could see that he wasn't getting anywhere with that line, so he resorted, as is a rich man's habit, to his wallet. "Here, how much is a year's subscription to your paper?" He waved his money clip at Adams.

"One dollar a year."

Barkley reached for a bill, but Adams shook his head and turned toward the door. "Don't bother, Mr. Barkley. I extend a year's enlightenment to all my competitors."

The smile that rose to my lips was cut short by a thud and the immediate panic of falling. The first thing to hit the ground was my back, and then my head, leaving me dazed and breathless as heavy blows poured upon my head. I was able to cover my face partially with my left arm, but my right was pinned at my side by the body astride my chest. After what seemed like a thousand blows, I managed to twist my body enough to give me some leverage when I pushed off with my right leg. I did not unseat the son of a bitch on my chest, but I unbalanced him enough to get my right arm free and throw one desperate punch that connected with my tormentor's face. My wrists were grabbed and my arms were pulled up beside my head and pinned by a force I had no hope of dislodging. I opened my eyes long enough to see the huge right fist of Bark Barkley raised and ready to descend on my naked face. I turned my head to the right reflexively and waited for the blow that I assumed would maim me for life.

That blow never fell. The weight on my chest was lifted and my arms released in the same instant. I rolled over on my stomach, and when I opened my eyes, I saw Sam Adams swinging Bark Barkley by the seat of the pants and the scruff of the neck. Leon Jackabee, Bark's stooge and the thug who had pinned my arms, started running from the alley, hoping to escape while Sam had his hands full of Bark. Sam tossed Bark like a sack of feed into the path of the fleeing Leon, and they both hit the ground in a tangle of arms, legs, groans, and abject pleas for mercy. Then they skittered away on all fours, roaches escaping a massive boot.

Sam helped me to my feet and knocked some of the dirt off my clothes. "Are you all right? Let me see that eye." He led me to a water pump and washed my wounds with his handkerchief. It was all I could do not to cry out. "How do you feel now?" he asked.

I took a couple of deep breaths. "I'm all right," I said, still shaking from rage and fear. "Let's go get those sumbitches—"

Sam caught me by the arm. "Oh, no. Not today," he said. He turned me toward home. "It's a small town; you'll get your chance." He put his hand on my back and gently guided me forward. "Let's eat lunch, rest a bit, and then you can show me around the Bowery."

Chapter
Three

It was mid-afternoon before Sam Adams walked out of the *Messenger* office to canvass the Bowery. I was sitting out front of the Lamour Hotel watching the "Raglars" play dominoes and argue as they soaked up the welcome sunshine. At one time or another nearly every man in the Bowery would stop by to play or offer advice, but four men—the Raglars—could be depended on to anchor the game regardless of time or location. Zack Hart and Shorty Carter would be there if there was no train to meet, while Doc Moss and Old Joe Clark were even more constant.

Although the Raglars would never recognize a "leader," you couldn't help but notice that Doc Moss was rarely interrupted during even the most passionate of discussions. Doc had given up his medical career—a practice that dated from service with the Confederacy at the Battle of Sharpsburg—several years back when his palsy had gotten so bad that everyone in his office flinched each time he picked up a needle. A weakness for laudanum, which he had controlled admirably when shouldering medical responsibilities, had begun to carve sizable chunks out of his year. By 1910, Doc had settled in as a full-time philosopher and often remarked that the pay was about the same as medical work but the hours were better.

After a hard winter spent in the crowded general store or the drafty blacksmith shop, the Raglars didn't mind pushing spring a bit to get outside. They'd catch the morning rays on the benches in front of the general store and switch sides of the street when the sun crossed the yardarm. In the summer the order was reversed to avoid the scorching heat. Since they could all tell a good story and knew everything that happened in town, I used to spend a good deal of time in their company. They didn't mind a boy hanging around as long as he kept his mouth shut and would run the odd errand.

"Yonder comes that editor-feller," Zack Hart observed in his low, rumbly voice. He laid a domino down on the game of Moon. "Reckon how many of them advertisin's he sold up in New Town?" Everyone snickered since they all knew the answer.

"Do you think this Adams might amount to something, Tom?" Doc asked, peering over his glasses. I was rarely consulted on any subject, and when I was, it was invariably by Doc.

"It wouldn't surprise me, Doc." I muted my enthusiasm to enhance my credibility. "He's stubborn and tough, and he didn't take no bullshit off Barkley this morning, so I'd say he stands a chance." I spit tobacco to underline the gravity of my judgment and glanced around to judge its effect. Almost everybody nodded.

Shorty Carter had an opinion; I never knew him to be lacking one. "Wouldn't bother me if he stayed awhile, his wife bein' so easy to look at and all. You know what I mean?" The remark made me a little angry, but Shorty was over sixty years old so I let it slide by.

Sam waited up when he saw me running toward him. "You ready to meet some people who can do you some good?" I asked.

He nodded and followed me across the street to Big Mike Manahan's blacksmith shop. Mike put down his hammer and ran his hands over his sweaty biceps before drying them on his apron. The Irishman always cut the sleeves out of his work shirts, and opinion varied as to whether it was for the sake of function or vanity. To my knowledge nobody was ever fool enough to challenge him on it, but personally, if I'd had arms like that I would have rented a shop window to display them.

Adams and Mike engaged in the brief test of strength that often attends a first handshake between two strong men, and then exchanged respectful nods. Big Mike took off his apron and leaned against the forge, appraising the editor with a cocked eye. "It appears you've done a spot o' work in your time. What is it about this town that interests you?"

"Adams is taking over the *Messenger*," I said.

"Pity," Mike said, reclaiming his apron and hammer. "I hope they didn't hit you for more than a week's rent."

"Adams is different—" The heavy hand on my shoulder silenced me.

"I didn't come to High Plains because I like the scenery, or the climate, or anything else I've seen so far, but I'm getting damned tired of everybody packing my bags and throwing them on the train. I'm not expecting to make a fortune here—"

"There's no fear o' that—"

"—but from what I've seen of Barkley's operation, this town could use a decent paper, and I'm not leaving till they've had a chance to read one."

Mike smiled as he hammered out a windmill fitting. "And him with two days in town and ready to chase Barkley off the prairie. Well, God be with you, for you'll need the ally."

When Mike laid his hammer down next to me, he noticed my split lip and black eye. "Have you been scrappin', Tom boy?"

I nodded.

"Fought honorable and won, I trust?" he said.

I nodded again and was glad the subject dropped. Adams was bent on leaving, but when he turned around, he caught sight of an object that he couldn't resist. In the corner of the shop, resting alone and horizontal on a rack made special for it, Big Mike's forty-five-ounce baseball bat demanded attention. Adams whistled low at the sight. He probably saved himself a broken arm when he asked, respectfully, "May I?"

Mike nodded.

The editor removed the bat gently, and Mike stood by as proud and protective as a new father. "She's 'Katey Dailey.' Had the wood shipped from New York. White ash. Turned her myself. You could drive railroad spikes with her," Mike smiled grimly, "if you had nothing to live for."

Adams looked real comfortable hefting the mighty stick, and the air was soon thick with memories of home runs swatted and strikeouts pitched. Within five minutes the two men were fast friends. Mike was like that; if he took to you, he'd plead your case at the gates of Hell. Since the occasion seemed to demand potent spirits, Mike suggested we adjourn to Derby's Silver Dollar.

You couldn't miss the Silver Dollar since it was the only place of business in High Plains—north or south—that was painted front, back, and both sides. Inside, Derby's was even more impressive: a forty-foot hand-carved bar was paralleled by a solid brass foot rail, and a full-length mirror covered the wall behind the bartender. Flanking the mirror were two voluptuous nude paintings—one standing, one reclining—that had inspired cowboys and farmers, and at least one young boy, for years. Derby's was the only business in the Bowery sporting a piano player rather than a player piano.

Derby had turned up in High Plains the winter of 1907 with a surfeit of capital and a dearth of past. Virtually all the local gamblers shared some history in Tascosa, Fort Worth, Colorado City, St. Louis—the towns west of the Mississippi where sporting men gathered—forming a loose but knowledgeable fraternity whose paths crossed frequently, usually intersecting in the hip pocket of a drunken rancher or a trail-rich cowboy. These speculators knew each other on sight or by reputation and had connections running back to New York or Baltimore, and west to the Gold Coast. Still, nobody knew Derby.

Before Derby turned his first hole card in High Plains, he bought the old Lucky Star, gutted and remodeled it, turning it into the finest sporting house in the territory. With roulette wheels, Klondike cages, faro, seven-up, and poker tables out front, and a back room where business leaders could swap high stakes in privacy, the Silver Dollar provided honest dealers and a level of peace theretofore unknown in the Bowery. The "upstairs" was honest, clean, and monitored weekly by Doc Moss—his last remaining medical duty.

Although shorter than the average man who walked into

his saloon, Derby carried himself big. He dressed and spoke with considerably more style than his clientele, but it was widely assumed that he was coiled tight and wouldn't hesitate to shoot or cut if occasion arose. It never did, to my knowledge; there were churches in town that tolerated more violence than the Silver Dollar. Though everyone in town knew that Derby carried a small pistol in his vest, I knew no one who had ever seen it. The scar on his right cheek was rumored to be a souvenir from a shooting back East—or out West, or up North—but Derby never said. He kept his history and opinions under the round hat anchored to his balding head. If he confided in anyone, it would have been in Belle, who "managed" the eight women who worked upstairs. But she was as tight-lipped as he.

As the four of us stood at the bar and watched Belle shine shot glasses, Derby challenged our proposition. "Gentlemen," he said coolly, "explain to me, one, why will this venture succeed where so many have failed? Two, how will it increase my profits? Three, how will any investment that I make be any more sensible than throwing money up a wildcat's arse?"

Tough questions. Fortunately, Belle had a vested interest in advancing our case. "You don't just advertise for *more* business, Derby," she said as she pushed her curly red hair away from her face. Her hands stayed busy, unsatisfied. "You advertise for *better* business. Lord knows the girls would sure appreciate a better breed of customer."

"The lady's right, Derby," Adams agreed. Belle smiled and nodded, appreciating the confirmation and the promotion. "People will know they're stepping into something special when they come here. They'll spend more money, feel good about it, and act like gentlemen to boot."

Mike reminded Derby of his priorities. "And how many times have you said you'd back the devil hisself if he bumped heads with Barkley? Here's your chance, 'cause Sam Adams is here to stay. He's a ball player!"

"I'll take a month's worth of quarter-page ads, and I want to see them before printing," Derby said quickly. "Tack a subscription onto that. I'll pay you when the first issue comes out and in advance thereafter. Bell, give us three whiskeys."

Mike rubbed his biceps in triumph and said, "Sam calls hisself a pitcher. Claims he struck out Ping Bodie in a exhibition game in Kansas."

Derby's eyes brightened at the prospect, but Sam quickly disclaimed, "I don't play anymore," he said. His voice was that of a man speaking of a dear friend, just buried.

"Throw your arm away?" Derby asked.

Sam shook his head.

"Lose your stuff?" Mike continued.

"No."

Belle recognized the symptoms. "Get married?"

Sam nodded assent as Derby and Mike shook their heads in pity. In the Panhandle of 1910, baseball had roughly the same respectability as, say, bear-baiting or cockfighting. Nobody much minded if the school kids played it, but High Plains society viewed ownership of a baseball glove by a grown man as scarcely more honorable than possession of a full set of burglar tools or a running iron for changing cattle brands.

Belle set up three shots of whiskey on the bar. Mike and Derby eyed the amber liquid with appropriate lust, but I noticed some hesitancy in Sam Adams when the three men raised their glasses.

"To the success of the newspaper," Derby toasted. "Mike, take Sam to every bar in town, and point out to the gentlemen who run them that Derby thinks it's a fine thing to have a paper in the Bowery again."

We were about to leave when a female voice shrill enough to shatter a beer mug rained down from the landing above the bar.

"Miss Belle, Daisy won't get out of bed and help with the cleaning. She says she's got the grippe and don't have to." It was Callie Shanks. She was only half dressed, and I felt a tug down in my privates that excited and scared me.

Derby gave Belle a hard look like he did whenever upstairs business spilled over into the saloon. Belle passed the abuse along in a tone that startled everybody in a hundred-yard sweep. "You tell that chippie she better get her ass out of that rack in one second, or I'll see to it that she never does business with the One-Eyed Worm in this town again."

Callie backed away from the railing as if it had just burst into flames. As she stood momentarily frozen, like a deer startled by a sudden light, I studied her. My heart sank at the toll three dissolute years had taken on a countenance and nature of pastoral grace. Doc Moss had spoken the sad truth several months back, when he said, "Callie's face is getting so hard you could strike a match on it."

Belle shrieked an afterthought. "And put some goddamn clothes on before you walk out in front of decent people."

Callie streaked down the hall like a scalded cat. Belle must have noticed the look on Adams's face, because her pale skin flushed slightly. Her voice returned to the human register as she raised the liquor bottle.

"Would you gents care for another shot of tanglefoot to help you on your travels?" she asked pleasantly. She filled three glasses, assuming that nobody turned down free liquor. The men knocked down their shots, but Adams seemed to lack the enthusiasm usually associated with free-flowing whiskey. Must be a beer drinker, I figured.

We hit four more saloons before the setting sun convinced Adams that he'd better cut trail back to the newspaper office. Each establishment had purchased an advertisement and subscription and had offered a complimentary drink to help launch the new endeavor. The editor and blacksmith were feeling no pain as the three of us walked up the Bowery street and approached a small group of hecklers circled around a powerful voice.

Standing on the raised sidewalk, within spitting distance of Maude's Parlor House, Brother Nicholas was making his inaugural address to about a dozen of the Bowery's finest cross-toters. "How long, I ask you, will you choose to carry the burdensome cross of intoxicating liquors that leaves you with empty pockets, rotted stomachs, and aching heads while profiting the bartender, the pimp, the usurer, the foreigner, the gambler, and the white slave procurer? You must turn away! 'Look not upon wine when it is red. For at the last it biteth like an adder and stingeth like a serpent.' Proverbs twenty-three–thirty-one.'"

Mike nodded his head in fervent agreement. "If a man offered me a drink of wine, I'd slap his face." The fruit of the vine, held in low esteem by Bowery men, was considered fit only for old ladies and immigrants.

We stopped to listen long enough for Sam to take a few notes, but I was ready to move along until Brother Nicholas turned his attention to a second bulwark of Bowery commerce. Pointing a bony finger down the sidewalk toward an aging prostitute and a sawed-off cowhand, Nicholas shouted, "There you have the unnatural and obvious product of a liquor-soaked town: a common whore, who both guzzles the poison and exploits other users in the congress of debauchery that cheapens and condemns even the most righteous citizen who must walk the same street."

The cowboy, who couldn't have stood as much as five and a half feet tall, was a stranger to me, but the prostitute was Mabel Joy. An old-timer by the profession's standard, Mabel Joy had managed to maintain some humor in a calling that commonly ground gaiety to dust long before youth was spent. Likable and competent, she had moved into administration and recruitment—likely the talent she was plying at that moment—as she had aged and only occasionally entertained clients.

Neither the cowboy nor the concubine seemed to take offense at Nicholas's disparagement, but the preacher pressed on. "Imagine the shame this young boy's mother must feel knowing that her son has fallen prey to—"

Before Nicholas could finish his pronouncement, the cowboy had taken several quick strides, pulled a revolver from beneath his coat, and placed the barrel rather gently against the preacher's left temple.

"What did you say about my Maw?" the cowboy demanded.

There was a statute against carrying a gun in town, but it was widely ignored as long as you kept your weapon concealed and didn't use it often or against anyone who mattered. Sheriff Alonzo Coffey couldn't fathom why such a ban existed and couldn't imagine life without a sidearm, so innocent blood had to be spilled before he would take action. Even so, there hadn't been a six-gun killing in High Plains in years, most serious shooting being done by purposeful men wielding shotguns usually directed at the small of an enemy's back. But no temporal law was going to rescue Brother Nicholas at that moment, as the wee cowboy pursued his mother's vindication.

"Nobody runs down *my* Maw, Preacher. She's worth ten of you, and if she was here right now, she'd be the one holdin' this gun ready to blow your head into the street. Now you take hit back."

The preacher and the cowboy were very close to the same height and build and were the smallest full-grown men in sight. Their stunted profiles contrasted sharply with the tall, ample Mabel Joy, and the scene resembled, at least to me, a grammar school play, supervised by a distracted teacher that had gone woefully awry.

The silence that followed the cowboy's demand was understandable since I would wager that few men could have uttered a word if placed in the preacher's predicament. But Brother Nicholas's voice did not quaver as he stared straight ahead, separated from eternity by only a few ounces of pressure on what was likely a hair trigger.

"I had no intention of insulting your mother, young man. I was only demonstrating the depths of depravity that every mother's son is capable of—"

"Not *my* mother's son!" the cowboy shouted, cocking the pistol.

Everyone stood silent and motionless—everyone except Mabel Joy who had probably seen more guns pulled than any five men in the crowd. "Aw, hell, Travis, that preacher don't know no more about your maw than a pig knows about Sunday. Come on inside here and I'll have Maude set you up with one on the house. Any gal you want. Come on and have a couple drinks and a poke for free."

Travis looked tempted, but having gone to the trouble of pulling and cocking his gun in front of a crowd, he knew he'd look like a damn fool if he didn't get some compensation for his effort. He jabbed Nicholas's temple with the gun barrel.

"Take hit back, Preacher."

"I truly regret any slight, real or imagined—"

"I said TAKE HIT BACK!"

"I take hit back," Nicholas said quickly.

The cowboy holstered his weapon, tipped his hat to the ladies in the audience, and slapped Mabel Joy on the rear as they entered Maude's. The folks in the crowd shook the tension from their bodies and quietly started on their separate ways when Brother Nicholas jumped right back into his spiel.

"This demonstration of outlaw thuggery will not silence me any more than stoning stopped the Old Testament prophets. Since time immemorial—"

Sam, Big Mike, and I shook free of the crowd and headed back toward the newspaper office. Sam Adams shook his head in amazement. "That preacher must feel a powerful urge to take 'The Word' to the people. If I had come so close to meeting my Maker I'd be tempted to hitch a ride on the first thing with wheels leaving this town."

"There is no lack of courage in mad men," Mike grunted. "And who might that little preacher be?"

"Calls himself Brother Nicholas," I answered quickly. "He came in on the same goddamn train as Adams."

Sam Adams stopped me in the middle of the street. "Let's get something straight right now, Tom." He wasn't angry, just dead serious. "My name is either Mr. Adams or Sam. Got that?" I got it. "And if you speak one word of profanity around my wife, I will kick your ass till your nose bleeds. Understand?"

I looked to Big Mike for some help, but none was forthcoming. I nodded my agreement to the conditions, and we continued up the street. I was angry at being brought up short like that, but it didn't last long. Within a stride or two, we were comparing our recollections of the Brother Nicholas drama as Sam wrote down the things we agreed on in his notebook.

When we reached the *Messenger*, the blacksmith peeled off toward the boardinghouse where he stayed. The two men had consumed about half-a-dozen whiskey shots apiece, but they were big guys and neither seemed to be the worse for it; their steps remained true and their tongues unthickened as near as I could tell.

I checked from the window to see if Mama was still haunting the newspaper office before following Sam inside. I was amazed; the place was spotless. Miss Rebekah, her back to us, continued scrubbing the back wall, but the room was clean enough for the Queen of England to take high tea in.

"Rebekah, this place looks . . ." Sam searched for the word, "clean! You must have slaved like a Turk all day."

Miss Rebekah beamed as she laid down her rag; she was beautiful even in a dirty apron and with hair in kerchief. She smiled at me and said hello, then took off her apron to hug her husband. "Thank you, kind sir," she said. "Did you sell any advertising today?"

"I surely did, and some subscriptions too." Sam lifted her off the ground in an embrace.

Miss Rebekah stiffened then pulled back from Sam. Her face clouded and her voice twisted in accusation. "Sam, you've been drinking."

Though I was surprised by her reaction, I was shocked at his response. "I had no choice," he defended lamely. "They drank a toast to the newspaper."

She turned her back on him. "How could you?"

"It was only a couple drinks," he lied. "It's nothing to worry about, Bekah."

I slipped out of the door when their backs were turned and collected my thoughts on the way home. I was shocked and disappointed by the performances of both Adamses. What kind of woman would raise so much hell over a few drinks? She sounded like one of those dried-up old hatchet-faced WCTU women that made speeches up by the courthouse. And what kind of man would stand there and take that sort of nagging, and then lie on top of it? By age twelve I had heard countless discussions on the proper relationship between men and women, and I'd fully expected the Adamses, in whom I had invested a good deal of time and hope, to conform to my ideal. The courageous man and beautiful goodwife had, in the space of a minute, transformed into gutless milksop and shrewish fishwife.

Maybe it had something to do with coming from Kansas; everybody knew how crazy those people were: they'd outlawed liquor over thirty years ago and were making serious noises about giving women the right to vote. By Bowery consensus, the last proposition was tantamount to enfranchising barnyard animals.

I would have to ponder on the situation for a while, and maybe talk to Langston or Doc about it to get another slant.

Chapter
Four

I ran down the street dodging man, horse, and dog, threw open the *Messenger* door and shouted, "Sam! Come to the courthouse. Langston's defendin' a chicken thief, and he's drunk as a fiddler's bitch!"

I hadn't gone by the newspaper office for several days after the liquor brouhaha and probably wouldn't have that morning except that Langston Harper had staggered off the train just in time for Gem Scott's trial. Most of Langston's trials were worth sitting through, and when he came to court with a bag on, you could depend on a good show. I'd been looking for a way to reinsert myself into the Adamses' life, and this trial was as entertaining a diversion as was likely to happen by.

Sam was sitting on a wooden crate fishing metal type slugs out of a bucket of gasoline and scrubbing them down with a wire brush. He seemed glad to see me, and even happier to get out of the office. The courthouse was in New Town; a distance we covered at a gallop with a minimum of discussion.

It was too early for spring planting, and the bulk of equipment repair and general maintenance that occupied ranchers and farmers through the winter had been completed, so nearly any amusement in town would draw male spectators. Court, being free and public, was good diversion and also offered the convenience of being beneath the dignity of respectable women. It was common sentiment that had the bailiff served cheap liquor, court would have been perfect.

Wishbone, the county seat, handled all the big cases, but they graciously allowed us to judge our own thieves, whores, and grifters. Blind Mule had been the original county seat before Wishbone slipped a cold deck in on us six years back when they imported and registered one hundred Mexicans as Wishbone residents. After Wishbone won the countywide referendum challenging our primacy (by eight votes), they got all the Mexicans drunk and took them back to wherever they came from. Their brick courthouse supplanted our stone building, and nothing but bad blood had run between the two towns ever since.

Sam and I leaped up the high courthouse steps three at a time. I had to shove the door hard just to get inside. After I elbowed us a place to stand against the back wall, I surveyed the gallery. The room was packed tight as a tick—everyone male and white except the defendant and a handsome Negro woman who sobbed quietly in the front row. I could see her neat, flowered bonnet bob rhythmically into a saturated white handkerchief as a torrent of tears rolled off skin as luminous as polished copper.

I cussed to myself when I saw that the proceedings were nearly over; the prosecutor, Ray Mitchell, was talking directly to the jury. Mitchell was the kind of oily rascal you always seem to find hanging around the Halls of Justice. In Doc Moss's words, "They had to run Ray Mitchell off from Crieder's Funeral Home because he kept stealing the pennies off the dead men's eyes." Predictably, he had political ambitions.

"Everybody in town knows Gem Scott is a chicken thief, known it for years," Mitchell intoned. "And I don't have to remind you that it was only a few years ago in this part of the country that it was common practice to exercise some 'stretched hemp justice'—a little party with 'Ol' Jack Ketch'—with a chronic thief like Gem Scott. But those days are gone, and we're all glad of it." Mitchell didn't sound that glad.

"Now Mr. Clement believes"—Mitchell nodded toward Jack Clement, sitting stone-faced at the prosecution table with his two large cretinous sons at his side—"and I believe, and I think you'll all agree, that Gem Scott is one darky that needs to be taught a hard lesson so that he'll never consider stealing another chicken. Six months in jail might convince him that crime doesn't pay in High Plains, Texas. Anything less would only encourage him to repeat his misdeed. And we all know how the example of unpunished crime spreads among that element of our society who will seize upon our seeming weakness as evidence that our will is insufficient to stop the rape, murder, and miscegenation that will surely follow. Like the defenders of the Alamo, it is time to draw a line in the dirt with our swords.

"I thank you kind folks for your time and attention."

The good men of the jury nodded their heads in agreement as Mitchell slid back to his seat. I glanced over to the defense table where Gem Scott sat, shaking his black head from side to side as if there were no hope of even living the day out. When Langston made no effort to rise, Judge Abernathy prompted him. "Mr. Harper?"

Langston shook his head as if being awakened from deep thought . . . or sleep.

"Your summation," the judge reminded.

The lawyer rose slowly and walked toward the jury. I heard Sam's low whistle when he caught his first glance of Langston's court apparel: a long Prince Albert coat that rode over California white breeches which tucked into the finest pair of gloss-shined high-heeled boots around. Tall and lean with graying hair, Langston was considered the handsomest man in town. His face was patrician thin, with cheekbones so high and distinct as to have been stolen from the bust of a Greek god. His reputation as a rake was unparalleled in the Panhandle, and tales of his exploits were legion and legend.

Langston seemed somewhat surprised when his short unsteady walk was terminated by the jury box. There was some nervous laughter in the courtroom that quieted as soon as the lawyer began speaking. "I was just in . . . sort of a . . . reverie, about how our lives are ruled by habits and cycles . . . traditions and rituals." Langston steadied himself on the jury box and talked quietly in a voice that bespoke unstudied breeding in every syllable. For the first time since our arrival, the room was silent. "Here it is spring again, and just as sure as the vernal equinox brings hope and vigor to the fine citizens of High Plains, you can bet your Aunt

Fannie's farm that we're going to put ol' Gem Scott on trial
for stealing Jack Clement's chickens."

The jury and gallery shared a hearty laugh. A single rap
of Judge Abernathy's gavel restored silence, and Langston
continued. "It's become a ritual, but it's one that we need
to examine closely. Six months of a man's life is at stake
here.

"Let's see . . . Mr. Clement says he *tracked* Gem down
and found him rubbing his stomach over a pile of chicken
bones while cooking yet another chicken over a fire. But
you folks must remember that the night of February twenty-
first was cloudy—we were all hoping to get some rain out
of those clouds. And there was no moon out at all. Check
your almanac. Heck, Kit Carson would have had a tough
time tracking down a herd of buffalo on a night like that."
Langston smiled and shook his head in wonder. "Much less
one skinny little colored man.

"What happened, I suspect, was that Mr. Clement noticed that he might be a pullet or two short—it would be
hard to tell since he owns so many—and he made a beeline
for ol' Gem's place to see if his old nemesis might be picking his teeth with a chicken bone. And sure enough he was.

"But Gem says that he raised those chickens, and he
was cooking them outside because he'd just had an argument with his wife"—Langston winked knowingly at the
jury—"it happens in the best of families, gentlemen, and he
figured that a chicken dinner might help his disposition.
And it did too, you see, because Gem was cooking that second chicken for his wife."

At this point the Negro woman in the gallery let out a
low mournful wail that chilled the marrow in my bones. I'd
seen Gem around town for years, but I didn't know he had
a wife. Of course, nobody really tried to keep up with the
matrimonial situation out on the Reservation—the black
settlement southwest of the Bowery. Langston let the
court's eyes rest on the handsome Negress before continuing.

"It was a peace offering to get them over their little
dispute. But the first thing Gem knew, here comes Jack
Clement and his two big ol' sons waving guns and threat-

ening his life. They say he confessed right on the spot. I
don't doubt that. If I'd been ol' Gem, I would have confessed to being the Grand Wizard of the Ku Klux Klan if
they had demanded it."

The laughter in the court had a grim edge to it now.
Langston turned away from the jury box and rubbed his
head for several seconds. When he addressed the jury
again, the humor and camaraderie in his voice had changed
to a confessional sincerity.

"But this whole case is a lot bigger than whether this
particular colored man stole those two chickens. You've got
to try to put this all in perspective. Gem, here, has spent his
whole life being told what he *can't* do by people whose authority resides only in the fact that *they* are the descendants
of Noah's son Japeth, while Gem is the descendant of Noah's son Ham. When Noah cursed Ham because he saw his
father drunken and naked, he doomed generations of Negroes who are guiltless of *any* sin.

"If Gem were the wisest man in this town, he couldn't
be mayor or doctor or judge. If he were the best businessman, he couldn't own a store or run a bank. He can't even
walk the streets of this town after dark.

"I am not proud of the fact that I belong to a race that
persists in the humiliation of another, and I am sure that we
will all have a great deal of explaining to do when we are
called upon to account for our sins. As you know, we *all*
will be."

While Langston let that thought sink in, I glanced around
the room to gauge the reaction. The spectators and jury, almost to a man, listened in silence with downcast eyes. Sam,
who was writing like crazy in his notebook, and I were
among the distinct minority unmoved by the threat of the
"Final Judgment." Maybe it didn't bother me so much
since my mother had spent the better part of my life threatening me with tales of the diabolical tortures that awaited
boys who stayed out late at night, consorted with wicked
company, and skipped school and church. I didn't doubt
that there was going to be a price to pay, but I couldn't see
it coming due for a considerable time yet. Besides, I put a
lot of stock in deathbed repentance. Over at the prosecution

table, I could see that Jack Clement wasn't impressed with Langston's argument either; his expression left no doubt he still craved his pound of flesh.

Langston continued: "I don't know if Gem stole those chickens—none of us knows for certain. But if he did, it was because he was driven to it by people like you and me. And if I were in his situation, my anger would be deeper and my crimes more heinous than the one he has been accused of. Remember, we're talking about a couple of twenty-five-cent chickens here."

Langston ran both hands through his thick gray hair and gave the jury time to think about the numbers: six months and fifty cents. Resting his hands on the jury box, he made his final appeal.

"I'm afraid that too often we think of the law as a means of punishment. But in its best and noblest form it can be an instrument of justice and mercy. I hope that you folks can find it in your hearts to send forth one of life's unfortunates with the words that Jesus spoke in the Book of John: 'Neither do I condemn thee. Go and sin no more.'

"Thank you."

As Langston slowly walked back to the table, the court was silent but for the soft cries of the Negro woman. Everyone was hesitant to move or speak, and Langston was seated by the time Judge Abernathy tapped his gavel. "The jury will retire to consider the verdict."

The men talked quietly among themselves as they walked toward the jury room. They reached a verdict before they got to the door. The foreman, a local layabout and occasional ranch hand called Oscar, led them back. He seemed in a hurry to get the decision off his chest. "Judge, we've decided that ol' Gem ain't guilty—or not so guilty that he oughta be throwed in jail over it."

The judge construed Oscar's muddled verdict as "not guilty," and then adjourned the court. A number of folks walked up front to shake Langston's hand and rub Gem's head before filing from the courtroom into the midday street. On the other side of the room Jack Clement made no effort to conceal his low opinion of Ray Mitchell's prosecutional efforts; the few people left in the courtroom were treated to a display of profanity that would have impressed the crew of a whaling ship.

The place was nearly empty when Sam pocketed his notebook, and we moved up to the front. Just as I was about to introduce editor to lawyer, Jack Clement pushed past me and leaned on the defense table. He shook his fist in Gem's face.

"Nigger," Clement snarled, "if you ever step onto my land or touch another chicken of mine, I'll make damn sure it's the last thing you ever do."

I've never seen color drain from a man's face as fast as it left Gem's. I thought he was going to pass out. As the two lummoxes that Clement called sons pressed in closer, the old man turned his wrath on Langston.

"I've had a bellyful of you, shyster. Anything I lose from now on comes out of *your* ass." Clement banged his hand on the table, and then stalked out of the courtroom.

I couldn't find my voice. Gem and Langston didn't appear to have anything to say either, so Sam stepped into the breach. "Congratulations, Mr. Scott." Sam's voice was even and controlled.

Gem nodded but didn't raise his head high enough to see Sam's outstretched hand. Langston, distractedly stuffing papers into his briefcase, was clearly shaken by Clement's threat.

"That was a brilliant summation, Mr. Harper. I'm Sam Adams."

Langston stood up and the two shook hands. "Thank you, Mr. Adams. I intended to stop by the *Messenger* today, but Gem's predicament demanded attention. Excuse me for a moment please."

Langston waved me over to his side. "Do me a favor, Tom." He pressed a silver dollar into my hand and nodded toward the Negro woman who sat alone and dry-eyed in the gallery. "Give this to Miss Lizzie and tell her that I'm going to need her in Amarillo on Wednesday of next week."

Damn! I should have guessed it. It was just the sort of thing that Langston had been accused of for years. Gem raised his head high enough to smile at the woman, but she refused to meet his gaze.

"Mighty handsome woman," Gem said. "I'd be much obliged for an interducin', Mistah Langston." Langston ignored the request.

After delivering the dollar, I found Gem entering his second plea of the day. "Mistah Langston, you know I got no money, but if I get some, I'll bring it to you straightaway."

"Don't worry, Gem," the lawyer said. Langston had regained his composure, and his wink implied conspiracy. "Just bring me a couple frying-size leghorns the next dark of the moon."

Sam and I gladly accepted Langston's offer of a ride back to the Bowery. His carriage and sorrel horse were as fine as any in town, and I often had the pleasure of viewing the world from that elevated perspective. I ran errands for the lawyer when he was in town, made sure his horses were fed and watered if he got hung up at a bar or parlor house, and kept him apprised of what happened when he was gone. I was also the driver of last resort on those occasions when the lawyer was so deeply into his cups that navigation was impossible. Unfortunately, he had an enormous capacity for alcohol, so I rarely touched the reins.

Sam and Langston swapped small talk as we rode down the main street of New Town. They had friends in common back in Wichita, which was evidently how they had come to an arrangement about the newspaper. It was all news to me. I had no idea that Langston was from Kansas, and had never heard him mention the state with anything but contempt.

"How's Jim Mast getting along?" Langston asked. "I haven't seen him in twenty years or more. Since he turned bad and started hanging with that newspaper bunch."

"Doing fine, near as I can tell. Still writes the toughest editorials in the state," Sam replied.

Langston tipped his hat to two ladies passing on the sidewalk. They seemed both flattered and embarrassed; it was a common reaction.

"He seems to think you'll make a good editor," Langston said. He offered Sam a pull from his flask. Sam refused.

"There were times that I wondered about that," Sam said.

"I often had the feeling that Jim Mast wanted me to be more . . . political."

The lawyer smiled and nodded toward the Lyric Theatre. The Baptist Church and the High Plains Lyceum and Literary Club were cosponsoring another version of *Ten Nights in a Barroom*. He pointed across the street, where three men were hanging a new banner instructing the citizenry to: DESTROY THE MAD DOG "DRUNKENNESS" IN HIGH PLAINS. "Around here," Langston said, "there's no alternative to becoming 'political.' "

Sam nodded grimly. "It's a paradox, isn't it. Flat land as far as you can see, but no middle ground in sight."

The words had barely cleared Sam's mouth when a motor car pulled out from between two buildings, charged our carriage and startled the sorrel. The auto swerved before impact, running up on the Western Union sidewalk. Langston did a fine job of calming the horse, or there would have been whiskey, blood, and gasoline all over the street. He even had time to tip his hat to the car's passenger, Mrs. Lily Barkley, and receive a smile in return. R. N. Barkley shook his fist at us as he rocked his car off the sidewalk. The Maxwell sped away in a cloud of dust and gas fumes.

After Langston and Sam finished the cussing demanded by the situation, the editor asked the obvious question. "Is that Barkley's daughter?"

"That's his *wife*."

Sam's expression indicated that he wanted some exposition on how this beautiful woman got tied down to that plug-ugly.

"I knew Lily from Fort Worth." Langston smiled at the memory. "She was the loveliest of the 'soiled doves' in a town that was waist-deep in commercial promiscuity. After Barkley finally worried his first wife to death, he married Lily and moved here where he could be the fattest frog in a small pond." He shook his head sadly as he guided the horse south toward the Bowery. "She deserved far better."

The Bowery was moving at about half speed, which was normal for early afternoon. All four Raglars were on display in front of the hotel: Old Joe and Zack were hunched over a game of checkers, while Doc and Shorty sat quietly, conserving their strength. When Joe caught sight of Sam, he couldn't resist hurrahing him a little.

"Hey, Mr. Editor!" Joe shouted, in a voice capable of offending the recently interred. "I growed me a turnip looks just like Teddy Roosevelt! Will you put it in your paper?"

We got a laugh out of it, but Zack was unimpressed. "Sit down, you damn fool. All turnips look like Teddy Roosevelt."

Sam yelled to Joe that he could bring it on by the office, and he would take a look at it. As Langston was unloading us at the *Messenger*, Sam asked the question that I suspect had been on his mind all day.

"No offense intended, Langston, but you don't appear to be the newspaper type. How'd you get into this business, anyway?"

"By chance," Langston stated flatly. He took another long draw from his flask. "I won the equipment from a printer who chronically overestimated the potential of an inside straight."

Sam smiled and nodded. "Anyone so improvident as to believe he can make a living editing a newspaper should never touch a deck of cards." Sam ran his hand over the sorrel's muzzle. "We appreciate the ride."

"I enjoyed the company. When do you figure to have a paper out?"

"Monday, with luck," Sam said. "And I changed the name. You're speaking to the editor of High Plains's newest weekly: *Plain Talk*."

"Sounds promising to me." Langston nudged his horse into motion. "That is surely the last thing anybody expects from a newspaper in this town."

Chapter
Five

Mama spun around and assumed the bearing of a high sheriff addressing a suspected felon. "I don't think you chewed that last mouthful thirty-two times. You know that's the key to proper digestion and good health. I suspect that's why you've kept that cough for the last week."

It was Saturday lunch, and I was doing my best to finish the meal before Mama sat down at the table, where she could accurately gauge my mastication. Ever since Mama had bought Dr. Horace Fletcher's *The ABC of Nutrition*, our meals had come to resemble tedious arithmetic lessons. Sometimes weeks would go by without reference to Fletcher and his disciples, John D. Rockefeller, Thomas Edison, and Henry Ford, but any sign of illness—either hers or mine—would reintroduce this wearisome therapy.

"Finished, Mama," I said, jumping up from the table and scraping the remains from my plate into the scrap bucket. "I've done all my chores. Can I go now?"

Casting a sharp eye about the kitchen, she noted that the ashes had been hauled from the stove, the coal bin filled, water bucket replenished, and the floor swept—tolerably well. "Where are you going?" she asked, sitting down to her meal.

"Thought I might try to find some odd jobs. I need a little something for the offering tomorrow." True enough, I figured. You never could tell when a nickel of mine might find its way into the collection plate.

"Reverend Poovey is doing some work on the pews down at the Lutheran. He could certainly use some help."

"I might stop there," I allowed, with a thoughtful and pi-

ous nod. Unlikely, though. The good reverend invariably
paid off in promises and parables.

"I've heard that you're spending a good deal of time at
the newspaper," she said.

"I stop by when they got work."

She shook her head. "There's nothing wrong with newspaper work, I suppose, though it seems like a lot of people
who get mixed up in it are looking for the . . . wrong side
of life. It's good to learn to spell and write properly, but
you need to know what's worth writing about."

Edging toward the door, I waited for the first lengthy
pause that might permit escape. Mama, of course, was familiar with the tactic and knew to make her point swiftly.
"I just believe that you might profit more from Mrs. Adams's example rather than her husband's. So, if you're going to spend time over there, try to pay more attention to
her words and actions than his. Do you understand?"

Boy, howdy, did I understand.

"Mama," I said, feeling both pleased and sincere in reassuring her, "I promise to do exactly that."

I had done odd jobs for nearly every business in the Bowery, but I'd always made an effort to avoid newspaper
work. Only as a last resort did I subject myself to the uncertain pay and tedious labor endemic to the print trade.
Every incarnation of the *Messenger* had needed a "devil" to
do the thousand dirty, thankless jobs, and there was always
some gullible kid who would fall for the promise of fifty
cents a week for "an hour or so after school and maybe
some Saturday work." I never knew one of those guys to
work less than plantation hours for any more than slave
wages. But none of those boys was granted the inestimable
pleasure of sharing time, space, and breathing air with
Rebekah Adams; I would have followed her down into a
coal mine.

After she finished her household chores, Rebekah would
help us with *Plain Talk*. Although hopeless with machinery,
she knew grammar backward and forward and could spell
like an old maid schoolteacher. On a few bright, rare occa-

sions those first weeks, Rebekah and I even had the office to ourselves.

"I bet you were glad to get out of Kansas," I said as I removed the platen from the printing press. I was cleaning the press while Miss Rebekah scoured the type case. Sam was out, still chasing down advertising for the first edition. News generally came looking for you; advertising demanded spirited pursuit. "From what I hear, the best part of living in that state is leaving it far behind."

Miss Rebekah was sitting on a wooden crate with a pan of hot, soapy water at her feet. Outfitted in a housedress and apron, her hair swept up and held by a scarf, she still looked prettier than any other woman in town on her wedding day. When she shook her head, a lock of yellow hair fell across her forehead. "I think your sources may be prejudiced, Tom. There are many things about Wichita that I enjoyed, and I'm sure I'll miss." (As I write this I recall that Rebekah Adams had the slightest of lisps, so slight that to record it on these pages in twelve-point type would be to overstate its presence. In fairness, I must ask the reader to occasionally imagine a gentle "th" where an "s" stands, but only where its substitution lends gentility and charm.)

By the way her voice trailed off at the end, I could tell that Miss Rebekah's "missing" of Wichita had already begun. Kansas, to my mind, was a state run by Carrie Nation and a battalion of hatchet-wielding women anxious to dissect anybody who uttered a cussword, spat on the sidewalk, or even considered having a little fun.

"Miss what, exactly?" I asked, just to keep her talking. I didn't expect to be convinced.

"Art, music, lectures. I used to go to the museum every week, on Thursday. I'd go right after lunch and spend most of the afternoon looking at the paintings and sculpture. They had paintings from the sixteenth century and sculpture from the Greeks and Romans, back before the birth of Christ. Then I'd go by the city library and see what new books had come in, and usually end up spending the rest of the afternoon in the reading room with magazines and newspapers." She laughed lightly, the tinkle of a chandelier on a summer breeze. Leaning back in her chair, she tilted her head up and to the right. "Sometimes I would be late for dinner and Daddy would be angry. But not *really* angry. He just wanted our days planned down to the last minute."

"We got a library," I said quickly. I wanted her to know that High Plains took a back seat to no town in cultural matters. "It's up in New Town, but they have to let you use it even if you're from the Bowery. Some of the mothers got together and cleaned out Jackabee's old tannery, and everbody gave books they didn't want anymore. They must have dozens of 'em with covers and all the pages inside."

"I'll have to visit there soon," Rebekah said, smiling with a grace incapable of condescension. As she struggled to insert a newly cleaned drawer into the type case, it got wedged, then fell heavily on her foot. It must have hurt, but she just laughed and limped back to work.

I wiped off the drawer and placed it in the type case, probably making a show of my strength, which was not insubstantial for a boy my age and size. Miss Rebekah was humming what sounded like a church song, but one that I was not familiar with. I used the clue to keep the conversation going.

"You a big churchgoer back in Kansas?"

"Oh, yes. My father and I were very active. I played the organ for the worship service. I heard that there is no Episcopal church in High Plains. Is that true?"

"Yep, but we got one of every other kind. If you want to play the organ, though, you'll have to go to the Catholics."

Rebekah smiled and shook her head. Not an option. While I was searching for another question, a loud unmistakable voice penetrated our office and our thoughts.

"Sounds like Brother Nicholas is summoning his flock," Rebekah said, as she limped across the room to close the door. "Every time I look out the window, it appears that his tribe has increased."

"Yeah, Preacher Simon of the Baptists is gettin' real nervous. You see, they're both workin' the same side of the street: whiskey, gamblin', sinful women. Ol' Simon has been tryin' for years to get Maude's House closed down. He says if you got a house of iniquity like that with liquor and depraved women, it almost always leads to dancin'."

Rebekah laughed, although I could tell she had tried not to. "Sam told me about that harrowing experience where the cowboy held the gun to Brother Nicholas's head."

"It didn't slow him none. It weren't but a day or two later that Nicholas showed up at our school with a bunch of angry parents, raisin' the devil cause he heard that one of the teachers read *Aesop's Fables* and *Grimm's Fairy Tales* in class. Our principal ran them out of the building." I laughed at the memory. "It was a real show. Ol' man Hurley hobblin' down the hall swingin' his cane, and ol' Nick bobbin' and weavin', threatenin' hell fire and damnation."

"There seems to be no end of diversion in this town," Rebekah said. "This is quite a different world than I grew up in. I spent a great deal of time in church. I was the secretary; I wrote up all our news and delivered it to the *Wichita Union*. That's where I met Sam."

I didn't particularly want to hear about that, but there was no stopping her.

"He was the city editor, and every time I walked in the door, he would drop everything to take my article. Fires, murders, political scandals—everything would wait while Sam checked over my little article on who sang the hymn solo, or whose baby got christened, things like that.

"It took him months before he finally asked me out. After that we would go to the theater together, to the museum, walking in the park. He was so sweet and shy."

She had gone kind of dreamy on me, so I tried to change the subject. "If Kansas was so wonderful, why did y'all decide to come way out here?"

"Daddy and Sam didn't get along. In fact, they hated each other. And Sam wanted to edit a newspaper . . . so we left." She was looking down at the pail of water, and I could see a small furrow of concern crease her brow. It looked alien, misplaced on her milky skin. "I'm sure it will all work out for the best, no matter how it seems at first," she said.

"You got any brothers and sisters?"

"No, it's just Daddy and me. My mother died in childbirth."

Damn! I scrubbed and oiled the track that the press slid on, trying to come up with a subject light enough to clear the air of the longtime misery that had haunted Miss Rebekah's last answer. It took only the presence of Sam Adams at the door to restore her; she was on her feet and in his arms before I could blink twice. I excused myself, though no one noticed, and took a walk around the Bowery to knock the edge off my jealousy.

Sam and I spent the rest of the day, and many others, breaking down, fixing, and reassembling the antiquated equipment that Langston Harper had sold to Sam dirt cheap. Our George Washington hand press was a fine piece of early Americana that had probably performed admirably when it reported the election of Andrew Jackson in 1828, but somewhere on its odyssey from New York to High Plains—perhaps during its years of military conscription in Georgia during the Civil War—it had picked up a few idiosyncrasies. Invariably, they showed up when we were behind and couldn't afford the luxury of spending hours jury-rigging a part.

Sam Adams had the right disposition for this type of work: he was even-tempered and seemed to enjoy working fifteen-hour days and seven-day weeks. He worked longer and harder with less complaint than anyone I've ever known. Back in those days there was no such creature as a lazy newspaper editor.

Once Rebekah and I learned enough to be useful, a work pattern emerged. Sam was the editor; he wrote all the copy. Either Rebekah or I would take his scribbling over to the type case—situated under the southern window for maximum light—where we extracted the metal type, placing it into the composing stick. A full stick, holding about ten column lines, was then transferred to a long narrow metal tray—the galley. When the galley was filled, a "proof" was run off to check accuracy and legibility. The corrected type was then secured into a rectangular iron chase, and small wedges of wood were inserted to keep the type in place. This preparation work was done on top of a large, flat marble slab called an imposing stone. The press was old and cranky, the type worn, and the galleys and chases bent or chipped from decades of use, but the imposing stone was virtually indestructible. It could be depended upon to stand up under any natural disaster short of an earthquake. The stone's durability was a necessity since replacing it was expensive and time-consuming.

The chase, with a full page of type, was placed on a sliding track on the bed of the press. A roller was used to ink the type—my job—and a sheet of clean newsprint was lowered on a platen (or press) by pulling a curved lever. The printed page was then extracted and replaced with a fresh sheet of newsprint, and the process repeated for the better part of a day. It was meticulous, repetitious, and boring work, and I'll admit that on occasion I would look with envy at R. N. Barkley's Hoffman Off-Set Lithographic Printing Press. But I reminded myself Barkley's men were little more than machines themselves; they never felt the reassuring "tug" of the platen contacting the typeface that changed a clean sheet of newsprint into a page of newspaper. Even after half a century, that righteous sensation burns like a warm coal in my memory and muscles.

The writing and page composition went on all week, and we printed on Monday—the only day that Barkley's *Citizen-Advocate* didn't. *Plain Talk*, a four-page, five-column, twelve-by-sixteen-inch weekly in ten-point (long primer) type, was usually on the streets by nightfall. Unwilling to sully my hands with the crass, commercial end of the profession, I recommended a couple of guys from my school as newsboys to hawk the paper on the street.

We didn't get our "salutatory" issue out till noon on Tuesday. Since we didn't have much news—other than the Gem Scott trial and Nicholas's confrontation with the Wee Cowboy—Sam wrote a couple of long features. One was on a bloodless knife fight at the Panhandle Prince between two ferocious but clumsy "assassins," the other on the coming of Halley's Comet. The first piece was a raucous parody of combat, and the second made light of the superstitions that historically had followed the comet. The comet lore was news to me, and, judging from the public response, to almost everyone else in town. We softened the impact of the saloon advertisements by inserting ads for nearly every business on both sides of town. Sam figured that the merchants might be grateful enough for the free plug to pay for a follow-up. Very few were.

I had taken a copy of *Plain Talk* across the street to where the Raglars were resting in the sun. So after we finished cleaning up the office and sent the paperboys out, Sam and I walked over to get the definitive Bowery review of our effort. Doc was reading the last of the comet article to Zack, Shorty, Joe, and a few assorted loafers.

" 'If your luck is running thin, and your wife is moody, or the weather is too hot or dry, or just plain "wrong," blame it on the Wandering Star—Halley's Comet. Folks have been doing just that for over two thousand years.' " Doc took off his glasses and folded the paper as the half-dozen listeners nodded their appreciation.

"What do you think, Doc?" I asked, wanting to hear it from the horse's mouth.

Doc, in the tradition of old men everywhere, was miserly with praise. "Not so bad," he said slowly, "for a first edition."

"Good piece on the knife fight at the Prince," Old Joe Clark said. Several heads nodded.

" 'Course it ain't gonna win you no friends in New Town," one loafer offered. More silent agreement.

I could see that was all the discussion we were going to hear, but I was glad to get it. That was as much enthusiasm as I'd ever heard this bunch show for a newspaper. Sam appeared, if not pleased, at least comfortable with the reviews, and he settled down into an empty chair. He was bushed after working through most of the night.

Old Joe delayed the domino game by ceremoniously unwrapping a pack of Fatima cigarettes ("A Picture of a Popular Actress in Every Pack"). Every eye was on him as he slowly extracted a card and jealously guarded its identity from the group.

"Who'd you get?" Shorty asked anxiously.

Joe savored the card for a moment, then displayed it for everyone to see. "Lillian Russell," Joe declared with pride. Everyone was impressed.

"Let me see it," Shorty said, reaching across the table.

Joe recoiled like a man protecting a firstborn child. "Are your hands clean?"

Shorty's hands hadn't been clean since he fell drunk into the horse trough last October. "Yeah, yeah, they clean," Shorty confirmed. He wiped them on his filthy pants to appease Old Joe.

Joe passed him the picture, and Shorty's hand trembled as he gazed down with wonder at the high-busted figure of the most famous actress of the day. Eventually the card passed around the circle.

Sam whistled when he got his peek. "No disrespect to the Almighty intended, but I think I'd have to agree with Mark Twain when he said that more men had rather see Lillian Russell naked than see the Second Coming."

Everyone in this group obviously sided with Mark Twain. The card was passed around twice before Joe reclaimed it and stuck it in his otherwise empty wallet. When the domino game restarted, Sam and I slipped back across the street to await further critical and economic reaction to our first edition.

Chapter
Six

The newsboys had managed to sell about half the five hundred issues that we had printed, and Sam had them give away the rest. We nearly broke even—a victory indeed on a first edition—and the editor was in good spirits when I reported to work after school on Wednesday.

"What did you learn today?" Sam asked, offering his usual greeting. Generally, he used my answer as a springboard for discussions that often lasted for hours and could stretch across days. In school, I memorized dates of wars and practiced penmanship; my education began when I walked through the door of the newspaper office.

"Mrs. Hardy told us all about the Revolutionary War, how George Washington and Jefferson and ol' Ben Franklin rose up against the King of England and set us free," I said, tossing my hat, coat, and books in a pile in the corner. "Miss Rebekah got the day off?"

"She had to pick up some cloth and thread in New Town." Sam grunted as he laid his shoulder up against the type case. "Can you give me a hand with this?"

I helped him turn the case to where it picked up the afternoon sun a little better. We were edging up toward the spring equinox, and Sam didn't want to miss a minute of the lengthening day.

"Did Mrs. Hardy mention anything about the economics of the Revolution?"

"Economics?"

"Money. About the taxes and trading policies."

"Money didn't have a thing to do with it." I was certain of that: Mrs. Hardy hadn't mentioned it, and there wasn't anything in our book about it. It annoyed me when Sam would ask me what *I* had learned, then turned around and contradicted me. "We were fighting for our liberty, like Americans always have, always will."

"You can start setting up page two. The column headline should be in twelve point, pica," Sam reminded me as he went back to work at his desk. "I appreciate what Mrs. Hardy is saying, but bread and property are easier for most people to understand than liberty and the pursuit of happiness. When historians write of 'Principle' and 'Justice,' it is usually a good idea to check and see whose hand is in whose pocket, whose ox is being gored."

"Well that ain't the way it was with the Revolution. It was a clear case of being oppressed by King George and the Redcoats and standing up to them. The next thing you're going to try to tell me is that the South shouldn't have seceded from the Union, or that they did it for money."

Sam didn't say anything, but I didn't like the look in his eye. We worked quietly for a while until I got bored. "We collected some plants today and took them to Mr. Hurley to identify. He knows a lot about plants and rocks and things."

"Is he the science teacher?"

"He's the principal, but ever' once in a while he'll stop by the classroom and talk to us. Sometimes he forgets what he's saying, and he makes Mrs. Hardy uncomfortable, so we don't see him often. At the end of the year, when we go out to the canyon for our picnic, he tells us about how old it is, how it was formed. He says it took hundreds of thousands of years. 'Course nobody believes it."

"Why not?"

"Because the Bible says the whole world was created four thousand and four years before Christ. That means the whole shebang can't be more than about . . . six thousand years old."

"Where did you get that figure? Four thousand four B.C.?"

"Everybody knows that. Nine A.M., October twenty-sixth, four thousand and four B.C. Heck, I missed it on a history test one time. Had to write it a hundred times on the blackboard."

It was a good while before Sam responded. I was about ready to change the subject.

"Have you ever heard of the theory of evolution, Tom?"

"How's that?"

"It's from a book called *Origin of Species*, by Charles Darwin. He—"

"Oh, yeah," I interrupted. "Preacher Simon did a long sermon on it once. He talked about where this Darwin said that men came from apes, and how ol' Darwin's kinfolk might have been monkeys, but the preacher's dear old sainted mother sure wasn't. Everybody got a big hoot out of it, and I think Simon would have liked to have preached on it some more, but nobody around here could take it serious enough to make it worthwhile. That Darwin's from England, ain't he? It's a good thing we broke away from that bunch."

I was still laughing when Sam turned away from his desk to face me. He was serious as a gut wound. "It's not that simple, Tom. What Charles Darwin said was that hundreds of thousands of years ago, maybe millions of years ago, human beings and other primates, like apes, shared a common ancestor. The apes branched off in one direction, and man, because he had more capacity for change, and met his challenges differently—he developed a larger brain and a better thumb, and started walking upright, and talking—man was able to adapt to different situations while the ape was content to stay in the jungle and eat whatever he could gather."

Sam was picking his words carefully, so I knew he wasn't joshing me, but I couldn't believe that he could be taken in by a cock-and-bull story like that. I knew a lot of people who had funny ways—Zack Hart talked to his own personal Indian ghost, Jap Carter swore that Frenchmen ate snails and snakes *and liked them*—but I'd never run into anybody that believed that man had started out as a monkey. I didn't like the sound of it.

"Were Adam and Eve a couple of apes?" I demanded.

Sam leaned back in his chair and rubbed his eyes. I'd bet that he regretted sticking his hand into that snake hole, but he was in up to his elbows and had to make his case or admit defeat. I figured I had him on the run.

"If we're going to discuss things like this, you're going to have to keep your mind open and be willing to consider ... points of view that you're not familiar with and that might contradict a lot of what you've been told. I won't tell you anything that I don't believe is true. I won't try to fool you, or try to convince you. It's up to you how much of it you choose to believe. Agreed?"

"Suits me." I said, knowing I had an ace in the hole. "Does Miss Rebekah believe in this evolution stuff, or does she believe in Adam and Eve?"

Sam had to stand up and walk off that question. "I think Rebekah believes in both," he said slowly, "and tries not to see the conflict. She has to work her way out from under her father's prejudices. We all have to live with contradictions—"

"Not me. I'll bet if she had to choose, she'd take Adam and Eve."

"You're probably right."

"Well, once you've convinced your own wife, you and I can talk about it again."

Sam smiled and nodded, but I felt that I'd won the argument. Sam was always straightening me out, and this once I had thrown the last punch. Sam went back to his desk while I basked privately in my victory. It wasn't long before I got bored and asked him a question about Napoleon, and we talked about the French Revolution for the rest of the afternoon, our disagreement forgotten. That was the thing about Sam: he didn't feel as though he had to win every argument. Sam Adams knew that he had time on his side.

The folks that we talked to in the Bowery seemed to like *Plain Talk* well enough, but it was Thursday morning before we got the official New Town reaction. I was sorting type—"throwin' in," in the printer's vernacular—before heading off to school, while Shad tore out rotten boards from the back wall with a sledgehammer and crowbar. When a blow from the hammer rattled the small framed picture of Mark Twain that hung over the type case, Sam nearly broke a leg rushing to its rescue. He moved the photograph to the safety of his desk, where it stayed.

When the *Citizen-Advocate* hit the door, I raced outside to retrieve it. A paper had been delivered free of charge every morning since Sam and Barkley had their talk. Sam had made out like a rustler, swapping a four-page weekly for a daily eight-pager.

Sam paced the floor as he read out loud from the front-page editorial. The piece started off pleasantly enough: Barkley welcomed the new paper into town and complimented us on the "neat" appearance of our layout. He then expressed his unflagging belief in that primary American principle, "Competition," which had made this nation, state, and town the paradise that it so clearly was. He stated flatly that the town of High Plains was large enough to support two newspapers, and that the citizens would be the beneficiaries of any contest between the two. However . . .

The second part of the article was written with a pen dipped in vitriol. Barkley ripped us for carrying ads for saloons and other businesses with "highly questionable" reputations, as well as for our "unhealthy interest in the social and commercial life" of the Bowery. He called Gem Scott's acquittal "a miscarriage of justice perpetrated by a silver-tongued mountebank on an unsuspecting public." Sam's parody of the knife fight at the Panhandle Prince was decried as "exploitation of criminality, better left to the courts than to cynical journalists."

Sam was nearly sprinting across the room as he read the summary paragraph. " 'This glorification of the baser elements of this fine town does no service to High Plains or its citizens. It is our hope that future editions of *Plain Talk* will reflect better judgment and more social responsibility than this initial effort. However, we hardly expect it from a newspaper that is owned body and breeches by Langston Harper.' "

Miss Rebekah had walked in from the kitchen and listened at the doorway. She was pale with shock and indignation. "That's just horrible," was all she could manage.

It didn't surprise me a bit. "I told you that sonuva . . .

gun would attack his own grandmaw if she ran a newspaper."

"There's more," Sam said. "Barkley says that due to the 'inflammatory nature' of *Plain Talk* and the 'potential for violence' that it has introduced, he has asked 'my friend the governor' to dispatch a contingent of Texas Rangers to monitor the prohibition referendum."

Sam leaned wearily against his desk and tossed the *Citizen-Advocate* into the trash can. " 'Inflammatory?' I said that every man should 'search his heart and vote his conscience.' I want to keep *Plain Talk* out of this, at least until we get a foothold. I don't want the existence of my newspaper to depend on the outcome of a liquor vote. And why in God's name does he want to call in the Texas Rangers?"

No one had any answers. The miserable silence was broken finally by Shad's laconic prophecy. "That's like invitin' gasoline to a fire."

Shad's remark made no sense to me, and I had no trouble ignoring it, as I did most everything he said. It would take some bitter exposure to the Rangers and a closer reading of history before I was to realize that by the first decade of the twentieth century, the Texas Rangers had outlived their usefulness. They had served a worthy purpose back in frontier Texas when they were often the only "law" separating the settlers from marauding bands of Indians, Comancheros, and assorted outlaw gangs, but those days were long past. Like the "gunslingin' sheriff," the "Injun scout," and the "stagecoach bandit," the Texas Rangers were vestiges of the past, as alien to High Plains as gunfights in the street and buffalo massacres. But the Ranger legend persisted, fueled by the human need to lay claim to a legacy more romantic, a lineage more noble than bleak reality testifies to.

In 1910 the Rangers persisted in employing the same violent tactics in breaking labor strikes and monitoring elections that had served them so well on the frontier. Since their brutality was most often directed against those people on the margins of Texan society—Mexicans, Negroes, strikers, and petty lawbreakers—the Rangers managed to main-

tain their grip on the hearts and minds of the masses. But
as the population grew and the duties of the Rangers
brought them into increased contact with the man in the
street, many citizens came to dread the sight of the once revered lawmen. Within a decade of our prohibition referendum, the estate of the mighty Texas Rangers would plunge
to the point that they were stripped of all law enforcement
responsibilities and restricted to ceremonial functions.

But the Rangers had never visited High Plains, and the
city fathers were proud to welcome these icons from the
glorious past. Their first assignment was the maintenance of
order on the final night of Reverend Jacob's Temperance
Revival. The good reverend had been heckled on occasion
during his lectures, and while it didn't bother him personally, the celebrated evangelist explained, he greatly resented
the insult to his Bible, his God, and his Cause. The Rangers
assured him that he would speak uninterrupted on his last
appearance. Come hell or high water.

Chapter
Seven

"Sowing in the morning, sowing seeds of temperance,
Sowing in the noon and 'neath the evening sky,
Waiting for the harvest, and the time of voting,
There will be rejoicing, Texas will be dry.
Texas going dry, Texas going dry . . ."

The town band was doing its feeble best to maintain the tune to "Bringing in the Sheaves," while the Baptist Women's Choir sang the hastily revised words. Mama and I heard the discordant music a good hundred yards before we reached the hallowed assemblage in New Town, but that wasn't why we stopped in the middle of the street.

"Are you sure you washed your face?" Mama demanded. "This looks like ink." She touched her handkerchief to her tongue and rubbed my forehead vigorously. "Since you started working at that newspaper, no amount of washing can get you clean."

As folks hurried past to claim prime positions at the revival, Mama ignored their greetings and continued the humiliating public grooming. "Hold still, now. Every decent person in town is going to be there tonight, and I don't want you looking like an orphan." After she had rubbed till skin gave way to bone, the walk and the sermon resumed.

"I want you to stay close to me and pay strict attention to what Reverend Jacob has to say. It may not seem important now, but it may save your life—and your everlasting soul—when you grow up and face the temptation of strong drink. Oh Lordy, look at the size of that crowd. I knew we should have left earlier."

I had managed to avoid the previous meetings, but I'd

seen Reverend Jacob on the street several times; he looked like he'd just stepped down from Mount Sinai with the Ten Commandments under his arm. He was huge in form and manner, with a long mane of white hair, eyebrows thick enough to conceal small animals, and a voice that rattled glass from one end of town to the other. The "Drys" knew they had a good horse to ride, and they were pulling out all the stops for the final night, including the appearance of the legendary Texas Rangers.

After the first night's crowd had nearly busted the seams of the town meeting hall, the subsequent rallies had been moved into the street. The unusually mild weather, widely interpreted as a sign of Divine Favor, lured people in from as far away as Wishbone, Bramlett, and Skankton. The Bowery was heavily represented by people drawn to free entertainment regardless of content. All had come to hear the preacher who spoke of the tortures of alcoholism—not from a pontifical distance, but from tragic experience.

Reverend Jacob was the last of a breed. He spoke of the agonies that he had *personally* endured while in the clutches of the Demon, and he proclaimed it in a voice that left your flesh ripped and bleeding and your eyes scalded by the River of Fire. The melodramatic approach had flourished in the nineteenth century but had lost ground steadily to the latter-day crusaders who could boast of *never* having tasted the Devil's swill. The ebullient Billy Sunday—an ex-professional baseball player so patently an authority on decadence—continued to dominate the Midwest tent circuit, bodily dragging the semicontrite up the sawdust trail to the altar, but his was a triumph of charisma. While each region of the country still seemed to support one "Hellfire-and-Brimstone" crusader, the movement's future belonged to the pious, not the penitent. The "new" prohibitionists preferred a saintly paragon to a scarred veteran.

When we pulled up at the last rank of the gathering, Mama spotted the familiar bonnet of Clara Clark. The crowd was at least two dozen deep in front of the speaker's platform, and Clara was about fifth rank, center. Mama, undaunted by the scores of obstacles between her and her destination, plunged into the crowd, dragging me behind by the arm. Luckily, the folks weren't packed tight yet, so you could still move among them if you didn't mind the dirty looks and muttered aspersions. Mama's grip relaxed momentarily, allowing me to break away and head straight to the front.

The band and the choir were roped off in front of a platform that was twice the size of any I'd ever seen. It was jam-packed with town officials, church leaders, and heads of various civic groups. Banners hung above the chairs so everyone could distinguish the Methodist contingent from the Knights of Pythias and the Odd Fellows from the Disciples of Christ-Campbellites. Someone had enough sense to seat the Women's Christian Temperance Union on the opposite side of the platform from the Anti-Saloon League; although they presented a united front against liquor, they fought like rats and ferrets over women's suffrage. The antagonism was personal as well as institutional; Edna Pringle and Ray Mitchell, the prosecutor, were the leaders of the respective groups, and neither could tolerate even the blighted sight of the other.

Under their tattered Stars and Bars ensign sat three Confederate-clad veterans, each of whom I'd seen stumbling through Bowery streets regularly, desperate for a taste of the poison they publicly decried. Civil War veterans wielded substantial political power, and the obvious inconsistency between their private appetites and their public posture was a common and accepted hypocrisy. Hell, half the people on that platform were drinkers, had been for years and would die that way. But they all knew that you couldn't get anywhere in High Plains politics or society without attacking liquor. The people down in the Bowery didn't take the duplicity personally; they just trusted these pharisees to do the right thing when the time came to cast their ballots. Thus far enough of them had, and the liquor continued to flow unimpeded.

I walked past the booths where the WCTU ladies sold their pamphlet "The White Ribbon" for a dime. They would give you a copy if you signed up as a member, and most of the folks took the cheap way out. Another display had posters of "Old Popskull" and "Whiskey Stomach,"

showing the ruinous effect of alcohol in such lurid detail
that the men in the booth had no one to talk to. Represen-
tatives from both the Gatlin and Keeley institutes were
there advertising their alcoholic "cures." All in all, it was a
right interesting carnival.

I took a hasty step back when I bumped into Brother
Nicholas, who stood front row, dead center, staring straight
ahead at the platform. The crowd had begun pushing in, but
the preacher had a good two feet of room around him, and
nobody seemed inclined to challenge him for it. Although
a newcomer in the crowded prohibitionist field, Nicholas
had picked up a small, sturdy following, and some respect
from clergy and laity alike for the courage he had shown
down in the Bowery. The established preachers, except for
the jealous Simon the Baptist, had ignored Nicholas after
determining that he was not actively raiding their flocks.
The ecumenical consensus was that Brother Nicholas was
welcome to any or all of the drunks, gamblers, and whores
he could reclaim from Bowery dissipation. Nicholas hadn't
taken his shot at the big time in New Town yet, but we all
knew he would have to make his move soon since the referendum was fast approaching.

"Call out ol' Reveren' Jake and see if he kin scare us up
some rain. We need that worse'n religion."

I recognized the bullhorn voice blaring from the middle
of the crowd as Pocky's—a verbose fellow who worked
down at the stockyard. He was loud but sometimes funny,
so people usually didn't mind his comments. The remark
referred to Reverend Jacob's former occupation in
pluviculture. Around the turn of the century William
"Cloudburst" Jacob had serviced the Southwest as a rain-
maker. The drought of '03 and '04 had driven him into
temperance evangelism, a profession where results were
less objective. The career move was a natural since bom-
bast was the cornerstone of both endeavors and sincerity
was unnecessary in either. The rainmaking industry had survived Reverend Jacob's defection and endured in the area
for many years afterward.

As I wove my way through the crowd, looking for Sam
and Miss Rebekah, I made certain to remain safely behind

my mother's voice, which rose distinctly above the low hum of the expectant assemblage. My heart sank when Mama's words revealed the unfortunate Rebekah's fate.

"It's the Gospel truth, Mrs. Adams. You can ask Clara. I have a perfect right to be up on that stage. I've belonged to every group up there that takes women. I started most of them. It's envy, is what it is. Isn't that right, Clara?"

She had a point. Mama had laid the foundations of virtually every club and association accessible to High Plains womanhood (including the WCTU) as well as half the churches; yet she presently belonged to none. Her singular attributes—steadfast conviction, boundless energy, the guts of a highwayman—were indispensable in the creation of a movement, but, just as surely as you cannot execute a successful revolution with anarchists, you cannot sustain a movement with revolutionaries. Mama's certitude, recognized as indispensable in raising money and recruiting membership, was soon viewed as intractability, her intensity regarded as a threat to the stolid equilibrium of a functioning institution. The Widder had always been proud and perceptive enough to quit before being drummed out, and by that time she was generally disappointed and bored with both membership and motivation. And there was always another cause beckoning: new, immediate, unfocused. In the spring of 1910, however, she was adrift between crusades and frozen out of the biggest game in town.

After Mama had finished belittling everyone on the stage, she lit in on my case. "Mrs. Adams, I want you to know how much I appreciate your influence on my son, Thomas. I've tried my best to raise the boy up in a Christian atmosphere, but this town being what it is . . ." Mama hesitated. When I heard that catch in her voice, I knew what was coming. "Ever since his father died, God bless his soul, I've—"

As I scrambled through the crowd, I knew that Mama would be detailing the hardships of raising a boy without the help of "the finest man God ever breathed life into."

My father was killed fighting with Teddy Roosevelt at San Juan Hill. I didn't remember him at all, so I never really grieved, but I always felt real low when Mama talked like that. It was as if there were a part of me that I could never touch, that would always be missing. Though dead, my father's presence was constant. Once, he had appeared in a dream, and with a single stern and disapproving look had warned me off the profligate course that I had been steering. It was the most harrowing moment of my life. And it had worked—for almost a week I was the paragon that my mother knew she'd always deserved.

At age twelve I had little tolerance for sorrow or indecision. It didn't help, I suppose, that I was one of the smallest boys in my class and had a set of ears that were connected at right angles to a none-too-handsome head. "Wingnut" was the nickname that I outlived by fighting every boy in school who uttered it.

My disposition did not improve when I emerged from the crowd and ran smack into Bark Barkley. He was talking to his daddy just off to the right side of the stage. As soon as we made eye contact, we both knew we had no alternative to confrontation; walking away would admit cowardice. I quickly scanned the area for the sight or scent of Bark's henchman Leon, and was relieved when I didn't find him.

When R. N. Barkley climbed the steps to the platform, Bark and I approached each other. My heart raced and my fist clenched as we closed to within four feet—I knew that standing within striking range before battle lines were drawn would invite a sucker punch. I'd seen Bark employ that tactic many times.

"Greer boy, I'm surprised to see you out in public without Adams to protect you. You could get hurt coming up here alone."

"Alls I have to do is stay out of alleys where a couple of rats can jump me from behind. Where's Leon at, Barkley? It took two of you last time, and I'd a still stomped your ass if you hadn't run away."

A circle of boys gathered instantly, and I heard whispers of "Get him, Tom," and "Whip that bastard good, Tom." The boys would ensure a fair fight once the first blow was struck.

I pointed to the alley between the bakery and the barber

shop. "Let's find out what you can do when you fight by yourself, Barkley."

"TOM GREER!"

I had taken only one step when the voice boomed from above and behind me. The circle of boys disappeared instantly. I swung around, trying to keep both adversaries in sight, and prepared to repel attack from either flank.

R. N. Barkley loomed high above me, leaning over the railing at the corner of the speaker's platform. His face was distorted with rage as he shouted down. "Tom Greer, if you so much as touch my son, I'll have you locked up for the rest of your life. And you better get rid of that knife you pulled on Richard or I'll have Sheriff Coffey confiscate it and run you out of town!"

Knife? What the hell? I searched for words to express my outrage when the appearance of a wagonful of the biggest, hardest-looking men this side of the state prison pulled up within six feet of me. There would be no fight tonight.

"It's the Rangers!"

The word went through the crowd like a dose of salts through a tall Swede. I joined the stampede of gawkers, a number of whom had abandoned choice viewing spots in front of the platform to get a closer look at the legends come to life. Every boy there had read the rag-eared dime copies of *Big Jim Duke—Texas Ranger*, and *Texas Charlie, the Boy Ranger*, which were passed paw to paw through the school till they disintegrated from use. But none of us had ever seen a Ranger in the flesh.

Those guys didn't wear badges; they didn't need to. Each had a rifle or a pistol, some had both, and they were all at least six feet tall with two measuring half a foot above that. The only man in town who regularly wore a sidearm was Sheriff Lon Coffey, and he never used it. The Bowery was full of guys who could remember when Billy the Kid showed up in Tascosa or when Bat Masterson shot his first white man at Mobeetie. I was raised on those stories, knew them by heart, but this was my first head-on encounter with "the Old West." There were only six of them, but they filled up that wagon, and the crowd took a long step back when they unloaded. The Rangers didn't say a word to anybody, just fanned out into the crowd and stood quiet and hard as chiseled marble ... waiting, watching.

The wind was getting up like it always does around dusk, forcing one of Reverend Jacob's flunkies to make several passes before successfully lighting the twelve kerosene-soaked torches that ran around the perimeter of the stage. They could have strung electric lights across the stage—they'd had electricity in New Town for years—but Reverend Jacob was adamant about using the torches. He knew what he was doing: the torches enveloped the platform in a mystic corona that emphatically separated the speaker from the groundlings. That stage was the closest thing to a huge flaming chariot that anyone in High Plains was ever likely to see.

A few stragglers still wandered up, but everyone who was really serious about the meeting was ready and had been for thirty minutes or more. I finally found Sam and gave him a rundown on everyone on the stage. I knew them all except for a tall, thin guy who seemed to be drawing a lot of attention. The prune-faced old lady standing next to Sam said that he was Reverend Jacob's "associate," and turned her nose up at our ignorance of the sainted personage in our midst. Sam and I expressed our contrition by referring thereafter to the associate as "Skinny."

The band had switched from "Texas Will Be Dry" to "Lay Hold on the Lifeline," but the singers were out of breath, fading fast, and looking for relief. That fact was duly noted by the most vocal members of an increasingly restless crowd.

"You better bring that preacher out, cause that lifeline is frayed and ready to break!"

Pocky was regaling the folks about ten yards off to our right. Most everyone laughed at the remark, but when I saw the crowd burst apart, I knew something was wrong. Nothing but trouble moved that fast.

Sam and I followed in the wake of the disturbance, and both of us saw Pocky get knocked off his feet by a tall, redheaded Ranger. If Pocky was able to get up, he had enough sense not to; the Ranger's rifle butt had put a couple more dents into a face that smallpox had already played hell with. Everyone was stunned by the sudden violence, but all murmurs of disapproval were met with a defiant glare and the raised rifle. Several other "protesters" scattered through the crowd were similarly silenced as the Rangers dragged Pocky off feet first and tossed him, like a sack of potatoes, on the back of their wagon. It was over in a heartbeat, and the redheaded Ranger moved back into the crowd. Sam was as amazed as I was, as everyone was, but he quickly began getting the names of the people beaten and arrested by the peace officers.

Pretty soon the Rangers' wagon was full, and the crowd was quiet as a graveyard. Only the folks on the platform showed any life, and they looked downright desperate. It was sundown and past time for the circus to begin, but Reverend Jacob was nowhere in sight. R. N. Barkley was holding forth stage center. He yelled angrily at Jacob's associate (Skinny), then banished him from the stage with a melodramatic wave that evoked the image of a nickelodeon father ordering his despoiled daughter and her illegitimate child into the snow. Skinny hightailed it down the street in an awkward, splayfooted gait, his back rigid as a post, definitely a man with a mission. Since Sam was busy talking to witnesses, I decided to play a hunch and follow the guy. The show couldn't start till Jacob came anyway, and everything about ol' Skinny looked wrong.

Chapter
Eight

Skinny busted through the front door of the Gatewood Hotel like he was raiding the joint. The room clerk followed him upstairs with all the dispatch his seventy-year-old legs could recall, and by the time I got inside, I could hear the pounding and yelling overhead. When I peered around the staircase, I saw the room clerk trying to insert the key while Skinny beat on the door. The key was dropped and retrieved twice before the pair finally fumbled the door open and fell into the room. I walked right in behind them like I owned the place.

I found Skinny bent over the body of a handsome, square-jawed, silver-haired man. The Right Reverend Jacob was lying dead . . . drunk on the floor, a bottle of Rosemont Rye next to his heart, where his Bible belonged. I laughed out loud then scrambled out before Skinny could get his hands on me. I couldn't wait to give Sam the news. It was my first scoop.

As I searched through the crowd, dodging the pockets where Ranger persuasion threatened well-being, I heard Edna Pringle doing her level best to encourage the crowd to sing the Women's Christian Temperance Union anthem, "Where There's Drink, There's Danger." The people apparently didn't know the words, didn't like the song, or didn't want to risk attracting Ranger attention, because they surely weren't singing. When I broke the news of Jacob's fall from grace, I thought Sam was going to hug me. We watched as Skinny, visibly laden with his cross of miserable information, slowly climbed the platform steps. The town notaries jumped on him like chickens on a wounded June bug. After a flurry of pecking and wing flogging, Skinny escaped from the stage with his dignity in shreds but his hide intact. Miss Pringle broke out of the pack and addressed the gathering.

"Ladies and gentlemen, brothers and sisters," Edna began in her strident screech, "we've just received word that Reverend Jacob has been stricken ill and will be unable to speak tonight. We will all pray for his recovery." Sam and I winked at each other. "In Reverend Jacob's place, and I'm sure with his blessing, I will speak to you on a subject very dear to my heart: 'The Effect of Ardent Spirits on the Texas Family.' "

A discernible air of discontent passed through the crowd. These folks had gathered to hear Jacob rage about the depths of debasement and throes of despair of alcoholism, not to hear some dull Sunday school sermon by a fat old prude who didn't know beer from horse piss. What with the wind rising, the temperature dropping, and the general hostile feeling dragging on everyone anyway, a fair-sized portion of the crowd turned to leave. Edna Pringle attempted to seize the moment.

"In my capacity as the president of the first and foremost organization fighting the holy battle against intoxicating liquors, I have personally seen the tragic toll that alcohol takes on the family, and I declare that it is high time for this community to fall into lockstep with the rest of the Panhandle—"

"LET YOUR WOMEN KEEP SILENCE IN THE CHURCH, FOR IT IS NOT PERMITTED FOR THEM TO SPEAK!" Brother Nicholas's voiced boomed from the top step, stage right.

The multitude would have been no more impressed if the voice had emanated from Heaven. Nobody spoke, or even breathed, until Edna Pringle pointed her finger at the intruder and sputtered, "Will someone *pleqse* remove that man from this stage!"

The redheaded Ranger who had mauled Pocky was busy dragging a limp body to the wagon but dropped it in a heap when he saw that his territory had been invaded. Ray Mitchell also rose to repel the interloper.

Nicholas waved his Bible over his head and flinched not.

"As Paul instructed Timothy: 'Let the women learn in silence in all subjection. But suffer not a woman to teach, nor to usurp authority over the man, but to be in silence." Ray Mitchell and Ranger Red stopped in their tracks. They exchanged a What-the-hell-this-man-is-talking-sense shrug, and returned to their posts.

Miss Pringle, angry and confused, attempted to continue, but her voice was no match for Nicholas's deep, majestic tones, and it was obvious from whom the crowd craved instruction. Even the folks who had started to leave stopped and regrouped. It appeared that there was going to be a show after all.

Nicholas roared: "For too long the righteous have stood silently by as the drunken and depraved have spread their lethal spore. The locust have feasted on the crops harvested by our bleeding hands. No longer I say!" He moved to the center of the stage, forcing the WCTU leader to give ground. President Edna Pringle retired to her seat, defeated. "These jackals justify their cancer by telling us of the tax dollars that their deadly swill brings in. 'Woe unto him that buildeth a town by blood and establish a city by iniquity.' I say to you that these 'jag factories' do no more to increase the prosperity of a town than the ticks living off the lifeblood of a Texas cow make her give more milk!"

The crowd jammed in closer and stared up in wonder at the new revelator, who referred to neither note nor text. You could see Nicholas grow in stature and conviction as he fed on the energy that rushed in waves from the audience. "And to the saloon owner, the barkeep, and those who earn their putrid living by luring the workingman, the farmer, yea, the choirboy fresh from Sunday school; on these purveyors of maddening drink, these licentious profligates and itinerant libertines who grease the slope of the smooth, broad, downhill path to Hell, on *them* I call down the curse of Habakkuk two-fifteen: 'Woe unto him that giveth his neighbor drink, that putteth thy bottle to him, or that addest thy venom thereto, and makest him drunk also that thou mayest look upon their nakedness.' These shall be chastised with scorpions and plagued by adders!

"It is time to run these bloodsucking misery merchants

out of this town using every means in our power, every weapon in our grasp." The preacher moved to the front edge of the stage and screamed the phrase that became his marching cry: "THE SALOONATICS MUST GO!"

The reaction that followed those four words was amazing. The crowd went berserk, cheering and screaming and throwing things into the air as though they had all been struck drunk and rich in one fell swoop. They were ready to charge Hell with a wet hand towel. Nicholas preached on for another hour or better, but the course was set, the die cast with that short declaration. Sam and I shook our heads in amazement. I think we both felt at that moment that the citizens of High Plains were determined to hitch their fortunes to an express train bound for Bitter Conflict.

NEW STAR RISES ON "DRY" HORIZON,

shouted the Sunday morning *Citizen-Advocate* headline. The handful of cripples and shut-ins who had missed the revival were treated to a two-page account of Brother Nicholas's heroic performance, while the townsfolk who attended were encouraged to bask once more in the reflected glory of the "hometown" preacher—he was adopted overnight—who had rescued the temperance crusade from potential disaster. Nicholas was praised lavishly, the Texas Rangers were thanked for their "effective" crowd management, and the whole town was congratulated for a revival that both High Plains and God could be proud of. No mention was made of Reverend Jacob's inglorious absence or the nine bleeding citizens hauled bodily from the rally and banished to the New Town jail.

Although the revival piece claimed the front page, the story that ultimately gutted the town was festering back on page four, biding its time. The Raglars and four or five assorted loafers congregated in front of Lolly's Cafe, trying to ignore the chill in the air that negated a bright sun's promise. When Doc happened on that particular article, he was so impressed that he committed the supreme breach of Bowery etiquette: he interrupted a grim, grudge-bearing, no-holds-barred, four-handed game of dominoes. Four an-

gry faces—three, actually, since Shorty was taking a beating and appreciated the respite—stared up at Doc when he
spread the newspaper over the board. I was afraid Zack
might go for his knife, but cooler heads prevailed.

The top half of page four was covered with a drawing of
a menacing comet streaking across the sky, dripping war,
pestilence, and natural disaster over the earth. The article
was headlined HALLEY'S COMET TRAILS LEGACY OF CHAOS. I
peeked over Shorty's shoulder as the players and bystanders
huddled around the newspaper. We spent several minutes
just studying the illustration before Shorty asked Doc to
read it aloud.

The article was the most lurid piece of writing I'd ever
read in an era that plumbed the depths of yellow journalism. Noah's flood, the death of Julius Caesar, the fall of the
Roman Empire, and the bubonic plague that killed nearly a
quarter of the population of Europe were just a few of the
catastrophes ascribed to the "Celestial Assassin." According
to history, legend, and the *Citizen-Advocate*, you could expect natural cataclysm, revolution, famine, and war to rain
from the heavens every seventy-six years when the "Red
Dragon" scarred the night sky. Apparently the entire inventory of human tragedy and natural devastation could be expected to befall the planet Earth within the next two
months. The immediacy of the threat was driven home by
the assertion that the current drought coincided *exactly* with
the first sighting of Halley's Comet last fall. The article
concluded with a limp statement implying that though no
such disasters were expected during *this* visit, one would be
wise to keep his eye on the sky and a prayer on his lips
while the comet ruled the night.

"Sounds like folks might live forever if it weren't for
this comet," Doc said, closing the paper.

"This ort to give people something to talk about," Shorty
said.

"Damn fools," was Zack's only comment.

Predictably, there was a whole lot of talk around town
about the comet story. It was little wonder that after that
catalogue of calamity, a sizable number of readers paid no
attention to the impotent disclaimer at the end of the article.

The notion that the blame for the torturous dry spell could be affixed to a single cosmic malefactor was seized upon by a number of people eager to find a scapegoat. The majority, however, just considered the article a rather grim diversion.

It would take several weeks and a series of profane conjunctions before the seeds sown in Barkley's misguided essay began bearing chancrous fruit.

Chapter
Nine

The following morning, Monday, March 14, was the most glorious day to dawn in six months. By mid-morning the temperature was over seventy degrees, and the air was as still and restful as a warm bed. At recess I considered it only right and reasonable that I should declare a holiday for four or five of my buddies. By the time they missed us at school, we were swimming naked and free in the Red River.

The drought had shrunk the river up to where you could jump across parts of it, but we knew the one hole where the water would be deep enough for our purposes. Our swimming hole was east of the Bowery, past the old town graveyard, about a half mile short of the prairie dog village.

The sun had lured out rabbits and prairie chickens, which in turn drew a lot of attention from the redtail hawks and mouthy crows circling overhead. Scissortails and jays called from the cottonwood trees that grew along the riverbank and nowhere else for as far as the eye could see. The river was crawling with wildlife, most of which seemed a trifle slow after a long winter. Son Bob Suggs, my best friend, and a veritable assassin with his weapon of choice, managed to kill a quail with his slingshot. The rest of us worried hell out of the lizards and horned toads that wandered within a stone's throw.

We swam until we were completely given out, then lay on the bank and let the sun dry us off. I slept for a while and fished until the sun was getting low and never gave the first thought to anything except how good it felt to be exactly where I was. My newspaper work, school, and the punishment that inevitably awaited, were as distant and nebulous as the Hell that I had resigned myself to years before. My bliss was the exhilaration of the drinker who knew from bitter experience that grim and dire retribution would be exacted, but once liquor had touched lips, it was devil-be-damned till payment was demanded.

As we were putting on our clothes, getting ready for the long walk home, Son Bob innocently broached the subject that my mind had successfully avoided all day. "How much money they pay you for that newspaper work?" he asked as he buttoned his shirt.

Guilt swept over me in a wave. It was Monday, printing day, the day that my presence at *Plain Talk* was indispensable. Characteristically, my guilt mutated into anger, and I became silent and hostile. My friends knew me well enough to leave me alone while I finished dressing, and then I struck off on a hard trot toward town.

Standing under the back window of *Plain Talk* and listening, I hoped everything had gone so smoothly that my absence had somehow passed unnoticed. Not likely. Last week we had the paper on the street before dark, but I could tell from the tense voices and the banging around inside that things were bollixed up.

"That damn Barkley should know better. It'll sell some newspapers, but it's irresponsible journalism!" Sam's voice had an edge I'd never heard before.

Miss Rebekah's voice reflected concern. "Everybody's talking about it. Some of the women at the mercantile were scared to death. I tried to tell them that it has been coming around since before Christ was born."

But I could tell that the comet article wasn't the reason for Sam's anger; he had his own newspaper to worry about, and it should have been on the street hours ago. My only shot at forgiveness was that they might be so far behind that they would be happy to see me no matter how late I was. I decided to brazen it out. I walked around front and through the door, whistling as if nothing on God's green earth were wrong. When I saw their faces, my throat dried up and my head dropped to my chest. I don't know which was worse: his anger or her disappointment. I threw myself on their mercy.

"I'm sorry, Sam, I just forgot." I couldn't look him in the eye.

His voice was level but flint-hard. "There's no place in the newspaper business for a man who can't be depended on. We won't need you, Tom." He secured a chase of type on the bed of the press so tightly I thought it might break.

I was desperate. "You want me to deliver tonight? I'll do it for nothing—"

"No." Sam turned his back and drove a wooden wedge into the type with more force than necessary. "We'll manage without you."

I walked out the door and waited beside the window for a minute in case he changed his mind. I could hear Miss Rebekah's soft voice. "We're going to need someone to take these around . . ." She didn't finish the sentence, and Sam didn't bother to answer. The verdict was clear: my newspaper career was over.

As I walked home I got madder and madder. What the hell, I thought, I got along pretty damn well before Sam Adams ever came to this town, and I'll be here long after he leaves. He'd play hell getting help as good as me, and I'd be double-damned if I'd crawl back and ask for forgiveness for one little mistake. He'd only paid me fifty cents for three weeks' work, and I could make better money anywhere else in town. I must have been talking out loud and waving my arms around because a couple of drunks sitting on the sidewalk of the Panhandle Prince took turns mocking me. They laughed so hard that after a while it even got to me. I started feeling a little better and decided to sneak into the movie house.

I struck off to the nickelodeon, where they were running a scratchy old print of *The Great Train Robbery* to be followed by a talk by an ancient Rebel soldier who had served with Terry's Texas Rangers. I'd seen both movie and lecture before, but it was worth my time to see that gnarled old man shake his cane and cuss the "bluebellies" as if Atlanta were still burning and Richmond under siege. Afterward, if I had a mind to, I could drop by the poolroom for a couple games of eight-ball. I hadn't had much loafing time these last weeks, but now that I was a free man again, I might just as well start enjoying it.

The fickle Texas weather has a way of tendering an olive branch in one hand before smiting you across the bridge of the nose with the other. A norther blew in off the plains that evening, and the temperature fell faster than virtue on a Saturday night. When I dragged myself out of bed Tuesday morning, all that was left of spring was my sunburn. By ten o'clock the wind was vicious and the dust so thick that they let us out of school. We were all supposed to go home to be with our folks since it was prime tornado weather, but that was the last place I was headed. Mama sewed at our house during the day, usually surrounded by a gaggle of gossiping women. I always waited for the hen party to break up before daring to set foot in there. Mama alone was a full load; with an ally or an audience she could overwhelm.

Most businesses in town closed during dust storms, forcing the people who didn't care to stay home to search for company that they could tolerate for the better part of the day. As you might suspect, the bars did a booming business, and the parlor houses were jammed from midafternoon till breakfast. Fortunately, Hayes always kept his store open for the men whose age, sensibilities, or financial situation forbade the wild side of life. Since Hayes's was "respectable" and had the most secure tornado shelter in town, Mama didn't object to my spending the long, boring dust days there, so long as I came home in time for supper.

"Congratulations, Mr. Reporter," Doc Moss greeted me as I walked through the door of the general store.

"So you found the Good Reverend Jacob studyin' the bottom of his Farragut bottle, when he shoulda been ridin' the water wagon," Joe Clark offered.

"Rosemont Rye," I corrected, modestly. Sam had given me full credit in print for my scoop. Most editors would have quoted "knowledgeable sources," or none at all, rather than stake his paper's credibility on the word of a twelve-year-old. My entrance was also sufficient to ignite a roaring argument over the latest issue of *Plain Talk*. Under the banner "Texas Rangers Run Roughshod," Sam charged that the lawmen had gone to the revival expecting a riot, and when they didn't find one, they started one. High Plains would be better off policing its own elections, according to *Plain Talk*, and the Rangers should be restricted to riding in Fourth of July parades and "Wild West Shows." Sam included some filler about "long and proud tradition," but his recommendation was to get those guys out of town before they killed somebody.

There was much disagreement, and even I wasn't sure where I stood. Some rejected outright the proposition that the Rangers were anything less than heroes on horseback, and assumed that *any* action they took was warranted; others felt that this particular bunch of Rangers might be a trifle quick to anger, but that didn't reflect on the Texas Rangers as a whole; a final group—short in number, long in tooth—maintained that the Texas Rangers, like everything else since the Civil War, just weren't what they used to be. I have always found Texans to be exceedingly reluctant to abandon a reassuring myth.

But the Ranger controversy was not nearly as perplexing to Boweryites as Sam's refusal to take an editorial stand on prohibition. *Plain Talk*'s position that it was every man's responsibility to vote his conscience cut no ice with this crowd. What good is it, they demanded, to have a paper down here if it doesn't champion the single institution that nourished and sustained the community? Without liquor, the Bowery's likelihood of survival fluctuated between a Chinaman's chance and no chance at all. These folks couldn't understand how a man whom they all knew and mostly liked could be so wrong-headed on this issue.

It was a long time before I recognized Sam's shortcoming was one that is generally considered fatal for journalists, politicians, and religious leaders: he lacked self-righteousness. Sam believed a newspaper editor had no more right to tell people what they ought to do for their own good than a blacksmith or a barber. It was a quaint and noble attitude, but the nature of small-town politics was fast pushing the editor into situations that would not tolerate such equanimity.

Doc Moss had just begun to quote William Jennings Bryan's "Cross of Gold" speech word-for-word, and it looked like a good, hard, entertaining argument on "free silver" was developing when the door opened and the wind blew Lew Schekle inside. Once Lew started talking socialism and passing out copies of *Appeal to Reason*, I knew it was time to move on. Lew was an inept farmer who couldn't seem to hang on to anything except his belief in the Collective State and his burning desire to take the Word to the people. Mine was just the first of what proved to be a steady procession of departures, all driven away by an earnest man professing a reasonable philosophy in a manner that would provoke a saint to bloody violence. Zack said later that he suspected that the saloon owners had sent a carriage for Lew and paid him to break up the crowd at Hayes's. By four o'clock the Communist Manifesto had emptied the grocery store and filled the bars.

A slow, gray desperation settled over High Plains for two more days as the dust permeated every inch of the town. Finally the wind died down, and we spent the better part of Friday digging out and cleaning up. By sundown everyone was anxious to get outside and celebrate his emancipation from the elements. The beneficiary of this common will was the *final*—honest-to-God, no bullshit, may-lightning-strike-me-dead, *final*—prohibition rally of 1910. With the vote to be held on Saturday, there just wouldn't be time for any more.

The *Citizen-Advocate* was sponsoring the rally, and R. N. Barkley had organized it well, considering the dust storm and the serious schism that had developed in the prohibitionist camp. The Women's Christian Temperance Union and the High Plains Civic Club strenuously objected to the presence of Barkley's chosen speaker, the Reverend Brother Nicholas. They announced that they were holding a competing temperance meeting at the Campbellite church. Barkley knew the WCTU gathering wouldn't siphon off much of his crowd since the alternative event had gone unreported in the *Citizen-Advocate*, and the ladies had refused to notify or place an order for handbills with the *other* newspaper for fear of encouraging its infidel editor. Also, Barkley was sure that Nicholas would outdraw any speaker that the ladies could hire anyway.

Brother Nicholas offered other advantages as well. He was a local, so there were no train fares or hotel bills for the sponsor to pick up, and, amazingly, he asked for very little pay for his time and effort. Although Barkley wasn't about to force money on him, the preacher's asceticism must have made the banker uneasy; it eliminated a source of leverage that Barkley considered universal. Barkley exhibited something of a proprietary interest in Nicholas since he had "discovered" the preacher, given him exposure in print, and now presented him as the headliner and spokesman for the preeminent cause in town. It was obvious that Barkley saw Brother Nicholas as the man capable of wiping out the nest of vipers down in the Bowery. With the elimination of the quagmire to the south, Barkley envisioned an influx of solid, respectable taxpayers who would build a new, virtuous incarnation of High Plains. Railroads would beg for the right to lay track to the town, which would be declared county seat by acclamation. Then R. N. Barkley would be the governor in fact, if not in title, of the largest, richest, most respected city in the northern half of the state. If he turned a buck or two in this holy enterprise, well, he could tolerate that too.

The crowd for the Friday night revival was smaller and less enthusiastic than any that Reverend William Jacob had presided over the week before. Due to Jacob's public humiliation and the defection of the Women's Christian Temperance Union and sister organizations, substantial strength, both numerical and moral, had been sapped from the gathering. Then, too, the townsfolk were so glad to be freed from the captivity of wind and sand that they really couldn't muster the sort of righteous indignation that fuels the best revivals. Finally, and primarily, the indifference was a consequence of saturation; everyone in town had been liquored to death. The citizens were anxious to vote tomorrow and bury the issue for a while.

I suppose it should be mentioned that the presence of the

Texas Rangers vigorously patrolling the grounds and eager to enforce their bare-knuckled philosophy was sufficient in and of itself to lay a vise grip on spontaneity and participation. The lawmen had holed up throughout the dust storm in one of the Bowery's "blind pig" saloons, and the tales of their rank behavior were common knowledge. One Ranger had been treated for a gunshot wound, and another wore a patch over an eye that Doc Reeves couldn't guarantee would ever work again.

But Brother Nicholas had no trouble maintaining *his* enthusiasm and indignation on that final night of "The Great Prohibition Campaign of 1910." Tracing the temperance movement from the defeat of statewide prohibition in 1877 to the present day, Nicholas proudly reported that two-thirds of the organized counties in Texas were completely dry. Liquor was clearly on the run, its tail between its cowardly legs, and by sundown on Saturday, High Plains would chase the hydra-headed monster from its borders. That God would reward the town with the prosperity of the righteous was assured; that He would castigate the liquor fiend was manifest and documented.

"The story is as old as sin itself! Mankind cannot resist the temptations of the Devil, any more than Adam could resist the entreaty of Eve and the serpent. Ninevah, Assyria, and Babylon fell to drunkenness, and so shall our wicked civilization if we do not slay and gut the great succubus alcohol! For does it not say in the Book: 'Be not among winebibber, among riotous eater of flesh. For the drunkard and glutton shall come to poverty, and drowsiness shall clothe the man in rags!'

"*Who*, you should ask, profits? The saloon owner, the bartender, and the foreigners who own the distilleries, run the beer industry, who live in splendor off the wages of the wretches he enslaves. The foreigner who drinks as a family wine and beer with his meals, addicting *his very own children. HE* is at the bottom of this conspiracy!

"There are those who protest the involvement of the church, who contest the right of the town or state to regulate their drunkenness. They say it is 'a personal matter' and none of our business. 'Ridiculous and asinine,' I say.

Drinking is no more a personal matter than is murder or rape. Drinking involves politics, government, the church, schools, every part of the community. Every wicked redboned sinner who takes a drink in *my* town drags us all one fiery step closer to Hell. As Ninevah fell, so shall High Plains if we do not sink to the hilt our sword into the monster!

"The time is nigh! Tomorrow you fine people will decide the future of High Plains and the fate of your children. I know each of you will fulfill his Christian duty, and this town will be freed of the ball-and-chain that threatens to drag it through fiery Hell. To anyone who has doubts as to the righteousness of our cause, I trust that our merciful Lord shall demonstrate his will so powerfully that no one can deny it. His sign shall light the night and signal our course." The preacher waved his Bible over his head as the crowd cheered vigorously. Nicholas closed the rally and "The Great Prohibition Campaign of 1910" with a hymn. "Now let us join voices in 'Onward Christian Soldiers' and let us sing with the experience and with the understanding."

The crowd was in no hurry to get home to the same four walls that they had stared holes into for the past three days, so they milled around and visited with their neighbors for a while. I caught sight of Sam Adams walking back to the Bowery and considered running him down to get his opinion of the rally and tomorrow's vote. But I decided against it. He would need some help soon enough, and then he could come looking for me.

Chapter
Ten

I knew something was wrong even before I heard the shouts. I just didn't know if it merited leaving a warm bed in the middle of the night.

"Fire! Fire! Silver Dollar!"

I ran out the front door in my nightshirt. Our house was about sixty yards east of the Bowery main street, so there was a row of buildings between Derby's saloon and me. You couldn't see the fire from our porch, only its reflection in the sky, but the shouts increased in frequency and desperation.

"Derby's place! Grab a bucket! Fire!"

Then came the anguished sounds that turned my blood to ice. The screams of terrified horses cleaved the night air, a horrible keening such as only Hell should house.

I pulled on my pants and shoes and hit the street at a run before Mama had a chance to stop me. The cold air cut through my nightshirt, reminding me that a coat would have been handy, but I couldn't go back into the house. I knew every able-bodied man—and as many boys as could sneak out—would be there, and I wasn't going to miss it just because it scared my mama. Just about everything I did would have scared my mama if she had known about it.

I scrambled through the alley between two saloons but pulled up short when I caught sight of the spectacle at the far end of the street. In the few minutes that it had taken me to halfway clothe myself, the entire male population of the Bowery had turned out. Men with buckets, rakes, and shovels looked for guidance amidst the chaos. A number of women, including Belle and her "girls," stood on the sidewalk across from the burning saloon and shouted encouragement as the volunteer fire department clumsily wheeled the ancient two-man pump wagon into position and unwound the short hose.

The situation was critical. Derby's saloon anchored the southwest corner of the main street. The flames seemed to be confined to the near side of the saloon, but only a twelve-foot alley separated the Silver Dollar from Kerley's Livery Stable. If Kerley's went up, you could figure everything on that side of the street was lost since the buildings were old and packed together like cordwood.

I could see old man Kerley and his stable hand Ox trying desperately to lead their horses to safety. The animals bucked and reared and would not leave the stable. The horses could see the flames beyond the open gate, and wouldn't run toward them. Kicking their stalls, their handlers, and each other, the animals steadfastly resisted their salvation.

As I ran toward the fire, I could see a number of men fill their buckets at the water trough and race across the street to the burning saloon. They crowded each other at the trough and stumbled over one another in their haste. The nightmare quality of the experience was reinforced by the confusion of the eager volunteers, and much precious water was wasted before Derby took charge.

"Form a brigade from the pump! Give me six men with shovels for a ditch in back! Ten men wet down some sacks and beat out ground fire!" Derby shook his head and screamed to the heavens. "For God's sake, do something about those horses!"

Sam Adams charged from the newspaper office with the answer to Derby's prayer. A swift series of blows from Sam's sledgehammer and some rapid crowbar work opened a gaping hole in the back of Kerley's stable. The horses very nearly trampled their liberators as they fled out to the cold dark prairie. Within minutes every sledge in the Bowery joined the attack, and the stable was quickly leveled and hauled beyond the fire's reach.

I soaked an armload of feed sacks in the trough and joined the men fighting the grass fire behind the saloon. The elements worked to our advantage that night. There was virtually no wind—a most uncommon circumstance on the plains—and the season had been so dry that the prairie grass was sparse. If a couple of good rainstorms had established a thick mat, we would likely have witnessed a prairie fire sweeping south, burning uncontrolled. As it stood, about a dozen good men kept up with the ground fire while a half-dozen others dug a wide, shallow firebreak behind them. Within thirty furious minutes we had the perimeter secured. Two men were left behind in case of a flare-up, and the rest of us moved around front.

The firefighters worked to confine the blaze to the north side and ground floor of the saloon. Since the old hand pump could generate only a ten-foot stream of water, Derby's inside crew was charged with keeping the fire from reaching the roof. They raced along the second-story landing, stripping away burning boards from the side of the building and checking the spread of the fire upstairs. Sam Adams led a crew that took wood from Kerley's stable to brace up the weakened supports under the second floor. It was dangerous work, and I was chased away when I tried to help.

I grabbed a couple buckets and made the long run to the water trough at the north end of the street. In the distance I could see the men of New Town plowing firebreaks along their southern border. If the wind shifted, a grass fire would take only a few minutes to cover the ground between the Bowery and New Town. Of course, in the interim it would likely burn down the whole of the Bowery. The New Towners seemed willing to pay that price. Their shiny new fire engine hosed down their perimeter but made no movement toward the southern half of High Plains. A handful of citizens had come down to help us, but the majority chose to protect their investments rather than attack the fire at its source.

After several trips, I leaned against the north trough, gathering my wind for another run, when victory was declared.

"We've got it by the short and curlies now, lads," Big Mike shouted. "Every man bring one more bucket."

After delivering my bucket, I fell to the ground exhausted, my breath coming in long wracking gasps. When I finally lifted my head, I saw the street was covered with depleted bodies. I felt as though I had been captured in a Civil War photograph. There was no celebration, just a general sense of relief, coupled with a feeling that I had never known before: the bond of shared accomplishment among men pitted against a powerful enemy. It was success at the hunt, victory at battle. It was frightening and intoxicating.

I pulled myself over to a water trough, now nearly empty. The firefighters washed dirt and smoke from their faces and exchanged faint smiles and understanding nods. We agreed that if the blaze had been discovered a few minutes later, or if the wind had picked up or shifted, the Bowery would have been nothing more than a charred memory and a fifth-page item in *The Dallas Chronicle*. As it stood, Derby had lost one wall and a substantial portion of his ground floor, and Kerley had sacrificed his livery stable.

The women were offering hot coffee, biscuits, and gratitude to anyone who wanted them. As I sat down on the sidewalk in front of Lolly's Cafe, I was relieved to see that the two celebrated nude paintings had been rescued from the Silver Dollar and were in the possession of Miss Belle. She and her girls stood off to the side, now that the respectable women had taken control of the sidewalk.

"You did a man's work, Tom."

I looked up into the smiling face of Rebekah Adams. She handed me a cup of coffee and offered a blanket to put over my shoulders. I refused the blanket before I realized I was cold, then felt too embarrassed to ask for it. She rested her hand on my head briefly before she moved on. I had never felt prouder in my life.

Derby walked out of his saloon with an armload of hot liquor bottles. He passed them around freely, and the conversation warmed up. A local drunk named Harlow declared proudly that he was the man who had discovered the fire. He had been sleeping in the alley when the smoke woke him up. Someone corroborated the claim, so Derby passed the drunk a bottle for his exclusive use. That was doubtless the apex of Harlow's life: public recognition and a full bottle of top drawer whiskey.

Kerley was inconsolable about the loss of a big dun horse that had broken a leg in the stampede from the stable. "I don't unnerstan' why it had to be ol' Shadder. He was the best damn horse in town." Kerley moaned. "He had more sense than any friend I got." Kerley's best friend, Ox, muttered his agreement.

Everyone nodded in sympathy. Shadow was an exceptional animal from a species seldom blessed with intelligence. While a smart horse was rare, a good stable horse was very nearly unheard of. About a hundred yards out on the prairie you could hear old Shadow whinny in pain every time he set that bad leg down. We all knew that Kerley would have to shoot and bury him in the morning. A dozen men promised to help with the disposal of the horse and the rebuilding of the stable. And to a man they did.

I got a refill on coffee and walked down the sidewalk to where Derby was talking heatedly with a dozen or so firefighters. Derby's was the only opinion that counted, and he knew damn well that the fire's origin was arson, not accident. Having lost his hat an hour before, Derby distractedly ran his right hand through the few remaining hairs on his slick, sooty head as he laid out his battle plan to Sam Adams.

"I want a full-page goddamn ad for as long as it takes to catch the sonuvabitch. And posters on every column and post on both sides of town. I'll give a five-hundred-dollar reward to anyone who can give me the name of the bastard who struck the match. No questions asked. I don't give a damn about legal convictions or any of that horseshit. I'll weigh the evidence, and I'll set punishment." Derby didn't raise his voice, but no one in earshot questioned his sincerity.

Threats and projectiles filled the air when the High Plains fire truck finally arrived from New Town fifteen minutes after the last ember was drowned. I could hear Big Mike's inspired profanity—and a hailstorm of rocks—bouncing off the retreating fire wagon as I walked home to face Mama's wrath. That showdown never developed; she was still asleep when I checked her bedroom. It was all I could do to get my clothes off before I drifted into a proud and peaceful sleep under the shining star of Miss Rebekah's smile.

Even after a four-alarm fire, a few hours of sleep were sufficient for me—I never needed more than five or six back then. I was awake before daylight, and it was my intention to dress quickly, pick up a couple hard-boiled eggs and a wedge of corn bread, and be out the door before Mama got up. I should have known better.

Mama was drinking coffee at the table and reading a book when I entered the kitchen.

"Mornin', Mama. What you readin'?"

"Mornin', son. You're up early."

I opened the icebox. "I was thinkin' I might just take some food with me down to the courthouse. Get an early start."

"I'll fix you an egg." It was a reflex. She bent the corner of a page, closed her book, and started breakfast.

I sat down and opened Mama's book. *The Prophecies of Nostradamus.*

"Is there anything you need to tell me, Tom?" she asked as she poked up the fire in our stove.

Damn! How could she know?

"Yes, ma'am. There was a fire last night. The Silver Dollar Saloon burned down."

"Was anyone hurt?"

"No, ma'am. Some horses, but no people."

"And . . ."

"And I heard all the noise . . . and sorta went down there. To see if I could help."

Mama turned abruptly from the stove to face me. "You didn't try to fight a fire! You could have been burned! Killed!"

"No. They wouldn't let me near. I carried a couple of pails of water, was all. It was nearly over when I got there."

"Why didn't you wake me, and ask?"

"I was gonna, but you were sleepin' so peaceful, and it really weren't all that much a fire—"

"*Wasn't* that much a fire."

"Yeah, and I couldn't been gone more than a few minutes."

Mama set the plate in front of me. Her voice was more hurt than angry. "I don't want you leaving this house at night without telling me, you understand? And to a fire! I didn't worry and cry over you for twelve years so you could get burned up in a saloon fire. Don't you ever do that again! Do you understand?" She was near tears.

"Yes, ma'am, I promise."

"Eat your egg." She sat down with a cup of coffee for each of us. "And change your clothes before you leave the house. You smell like smoke."

Chapter
Eleven

Voting days were festivals in High Plains. The Masons, in full uniform and plumed hats, set up barbecue pits for the folks who would picnic on the square, or in the park, and spend the better part of the day in town visiting and shopping. Catchpenny games lined the street, and stores ran sales to take advantage of the crowds. H. W. Coffman's two inflated balloons soaring fifty feet above his drugstore—promising savings on everything you needed and most anything you craved—could be seen well out on the prairie.

The Bowery saloons were closed by law, but that locked only the front entrances; back doors were by nature contemptuous of propriety and swung freely for the thirsty. Although customarily indifferent toward elections, the Bowery turned out in force for liquor referendums. Like many another endangered species, they understood the difference between privilege and survival. People who rarely set foot out of the Bowery were ferried to New Town to exercise their franchise, then carted back to friendlier streets to be rewarded with a drink of whiskey.

As I approached the courthouse, I was surprised to see that handbills offering a five-hundred-dollar reward for the arsonist who started the Silver Dollar Saloon fire had been hung all over New Town. Sam must have stayed up all night running them off, and then nailed the posters up himself. The reward signs were the only counterpoint to the ocean of antiliquor propaganda that covered New Town.

In a regular election, you always saw a lot of hostility between rival camps about whose placards were hiding whose, and there was usually a sign so abusive or a partisan so vindictive that there was no alternative to a fistfight. Competition was heated and personal. Liquor votes were different: *all* the signs and spokesmen championed the prohibitionist cause. The Wets conceded moral authority and the propaganda campaign, choosing instead to invest their faith in that obscure area of the brain which, when activated by alcohol, convinced the human animal that it was, at least momentarily, better to be alive than dead. That primal reaction had been sufficient to ensure the development and continuation of fermented and distilled spirits throughout history and across geography for millenia upon millenia. Liquor would persist in High Plains, make no mistake about that; the day's vote would only determine accessibility and price. The distinction was crucial. If liquor was driven underground, to be dispensed by bootleggers out of the back door of gin mills, the Bowery as spiritual oasis for the cowboy, farmer, rancher, and, oh yes, the deacon and the judge, would cease to exist. A landmark and an era would lie trampled under the hobnail boot of gentility. Stripped of its lifeblood, the Bowery's denizens might just as well move to Oklahoma and take up vows of hypocrisy.

An army of prohibitionists had shown up at the polls to lend support to the righteous and discourage those considering the backslider's course. Waving their ensigns and shouting shibboleths at the arriving electorate, they lined both sides of the plank sidewalk leading to the courthouse. The WCTU and the Anti-Saloon League patrolled opposite sides of the walkway, standing cheek by jowl with every preacher in town and the leaders of prominent civic and social clubs in a picket line for rectitude. Brother Nicholas had arrived at the crack of dawn and staked out a prime spot next to the courthouse steps, directly in front of the No Electioneering sign.

Six Texas Rangers lounged on the high courthouse steps cussing, spitting, and making crude remarks about the ladies who waited for voting husbands. It is to my continuing shame and regret that I sat on the same steps and laughed along with them. I could not pass up the opportunity to warm my hands at the outer edge of the fire of Texas mythology. To insinuate myself into their circle, I offered up a schoolyard vulgarity that struck them as clever, and I was momentarily at one with the gods. Of this callousness, I can only ask for understanding and forgiveness from all women.

In my defense it should be understood that the twelve-year-old boy treads a slippery precipice, ever mindful that a misstep—a sign of weakness, a hint of ignorance or naiveté—will unmask him before the world as a poseur to manhood. The instinctive vulgarity of male adolescence is less a product of aggression than of fear, even awe, at the wondrous and terrifying mysteries of sexuality and the grim responsibilities of manhood. It is no more intended as an insult to women than whistling through a graveyard is meant to mock the dead.

A little after noon, I saw Shad's wagon pull past the courthouse. Actually I heard the whispers before I saw the abomination: Right out there in the open air, in front of God and half of High Plains, Miss Rebekah rode up front, seated between Shad and Sam. The whispers followed the wagon down the street to where Shad tied his mule up in front of the mercantile. As Miss Rebekah entered the store, Sam and Shad began walking the gauntlet of stone faces that led to the courthouse. Shad stared silently ahead, but Sam made a point of greeting all of God's lobbyists by name. In return he received grim nods and verbal reproof. Since Sam had remained neutral on prohibition, the Drys assumed he was an enemy.

The Rangers knew damn well he was an enemy. Their eleven eyes never left Sam as he walked to the polls. I heard folks whisper that this encounter was the only reason the Rangers had bothered to show up. They didn't give a damn whether High Plains went wet or dry; they weren't ever coming back anyway. They did, however, resent the hell out of a small-town editor trying to make a name for himself by attacking the Texas Rangers.

As I saw the showdown developing, my stomach turned over and a bitter iron taste filled my mouth. Shad was the only black man in town who voted, so I figured that his future was as grim as Sam's. I desperately wanted them both to turn around and leave. They didn't. They walked straight into the lion's den.

"Ain't this a helluva sight?" the tall, redheaded Ranger shouted. "The paperboy and his coon have come to vote."

Sam and Shad stopped at the foot of the steps and stared up at the cordon of lawmen who blocked their path. The battle line was drawn, and the non-combatants—the prohibitionists, the voters exiting the courthouse or waiting to enter—surrendered the field. No one said a word to discourage what was shaping up to be a mauling. I stood shaking on the top step and watched.

The Rangers were staggered about the steps, and as Sam moved to the right to avoid the man facing him, the Ranger with a patch over his eye filled the gap. Sam was again staring up at a large hostile man stroking a rifle butt. Patchy had something to say: "We don't appreciate the lies you been printin' in that rag of yours, and we sure as hell don't need no jayhawkin' peckerwood from Kansas to tell us how to run this state." Patchy spat off to the side when he finished his piece. He craved conflict.

Sam again tried to walk around the obstacle, but Ranger Red stepped in front of him. Shad stood at the bottom of the steps and didn't move a muscle as Sam took his hat off and wiped the sweat from the band. The editor appeared as calm as a man talking to a Sunday school class. "You gentlemen wouldn't be trying to stop us from voting, would you?"

"I'd rather stop you from breathing," Red hissed.

"Careful not to run roughshod on him, Red," Patchy growled, referring to Sam's headline, "he's liable to print it up in his little paper." All the Rangers laughed at that.

When Sam took another step forward, Red put his hand on the editor's shoulder, and then it was on. Sam threw a long roundhouse right that exploded on Red's nose; blood flew six feet in every direction. It was the best punch of the fight; it was the only one that Sam threw. Red hit the bottom of the steps on one bounce and laid in a heap while an avalanche of Texas Rangers fell on Sam. Once they got him down, the fight was over and the stomping began.

I hit a Ranger in the back with a flying tackle that rattled

my bones but didn't budge my intended victim. He grabbed
me by the scruff of the neck and the seat of the pants and
tossed me off the side of the steps onto the ground. It was
a long drop with nothing but a rock pile to break my fall.
Dizzy, scared, and mad enough to chew horseshoes and spit
nails, I stood up just long enough to fall on my rear. My
left wrist ached and throbbed as I crawled around the steps
just in time to see three Rangers haul a bloody Sam off toward the jail. Another Ranger was attending to Red, who
had managed to make it to his knees before toppling forward again. The last thing I remember before I passed out
was seeing Shad slowly climb the steps and enter the courthouse to vote.

"All hope abandon, ye who enter here." Langston Harper's
pearly tones echoed through the evening gloom of the New
Town jail before settling on the battered form of Sam Adams. The editor was sprawled in the corner of a barren cell
looking like Death on a three-day hangover. His white shirt
was now a couple of rags stained red from dried blood; his
face looked like an overripe cantaloupe that someone had
stepped on. I couldn't bear to look him in his good eye.

"Rebekah know?" Sam moaned through a mouth that
didn't move.

"I asked her to wait at home," Langston said. "I figured
you'd need some cleaning up before she saw you."

"How'd voting go?" Sam grunted. He managed to pull
himself up on the cell bars as the turnkey opened the door.
Langston steadied him before answering.

"The Wets won by sixteen votes. The Drys protested and
filed for another referendum in six months. Can you
walk?"

Sam nodded. "Bail?"

Langston spoke with the offhand cynicism of a man who
had spent his life dealing with the judicial system. "The
charges were dropped when the Rangers left town. No one
to testify."

Sam wobbled as he walked through the cell door.
Langston and I shored him up on both sides and pointed

him toward the street. Sam nodded to the sling and bandage that Doc had rigged up for my left arm. "What happened?"

I shrugged it off. "If that big sonuvabitchin' Ranger hadn't blindsided me, we coulda whipped 'em!"

Sam either laughed or choked, I couldn't tell which. But I could tell by the way he squeezed my arm that everything was jake between us. I was back in the newspaper business.

At the door, Langston took a long hard look at the New Town jail and offered the editor a particle of consolation. "I'd imagine it's hard for you to appreciate, Sam, but you're lucky they threw you in here. The jail down in the Bowery would back a vulture off a gut wagon."

As we staggered into the cold night, you could feel the contention in the air. A crowd had been massing around the courthouse steps for the last hour, and you could hear their anger rumble like low thunder down the street. After we loaded Sam into Langston's carriage, he pointed a shaky but determined finger toward the courthouse.

Brother Nicholas stood on the top of the steps and shouted at the two hundred surly people gathered in the street. "THEY HAVE CAST LOTS FOR MY PEOPLE, AND HAVE GIVEN A BOY FOR A HARLOT, AND SOLD A GIRL FOR WINE THAT THEY MIGHT DRINK!" Nicholas's voice boomed down from on high and echoed like a cannon in the rain. His performances at the temperance rallies had been dynamic but controlled. Now he was enraged. He stalked the top step and hurled down proclamations like lightning bolts on the heads of the mortals below. He spoke of the demons of Hell, and the vermin that was man. His pauses were filled with shouts from an audience that recognized a prophet who would lay bare his everlasting soul to save theirs. His message overwhelmed any restraint that intellect might counsel. There were no barriers between performer and audience: there was only the Message.

Nicholas screamed: "FAR MORE HAS BEEN LOST TODAY THAN A VOTE ON LIQUOR IN A SMALL TOWN IN TEXAS. THE LORD'S WILL SHALL NOT BE VIOLATED WITHOUT RETRIBUTION! AS GO-MORRAH AND NINEVAH AND BETH-EL WERE DE-

STROYED FOR THEIR DEFIANCE, SO HAS THIS TOWN SHOWN ITSELF INCAPABLE OF OBEDI- ENCE."

Nicholas's head dropped into his hands, and his knees buckled as if he had been struck from above. The crowd moaned as if it too had been smitten. Finally, Nicholas pulled himself upright, his face twisted by the enormity of his vision. Thrusting his hands into the air, palms to the sky, he roared the prophecy that ultimately would grieve every man, woman, and child in High Plains.

"IN SIXTY DAYS THE EARTH WILL PASS THROUGH THE TAIL OF THE GREAT COMET HALLEY. *THEN* SHALL THE SANCTUARY BE CLEANSED. 'THE DAY OF THE LORD IS AT HAND, AND AS A DESTRUCTION FROM THE ALMIGHTY SHALL IT COME.' "

Chapter
Twelve

Brother Nicholas's prophecy didn't roll over the town in a single, uniform wave. Like all popular movements, it advanced in fits and starts, picking up converts and momentum when fortuitous circumstance—natural disaster, social unrest, human tragedy—coincided with prediction or expectation. Since any cataclysm occurring on the planet constituted evidence, it is not surprising that documentation mounted on a daily basis.

With the whiskey question in abeyance for another six months, and the comet phenomenon yet to burst fully on the public consciousness, Nicholas gladly widened his focus of intolerance to include dancing, smoking and chewing, card playing, and moving pictures. All were unquestionably sins that demanded spirited denunciation, and the preacher gave each its due while reserving a deep, dark, rich vein of vituperation for "that clattering chariot of Satan," the automobile. Nicholas could launch a jeremiad of several hours, quoting the prophet Ezekiel exhaustively, on the intrinsic evil of the collection of nuts, bolts, and springs assembled for the express purpose of driving mankind straight to pyric Hell.

Brother Nicholas's primary logistical problem was solved the day after the liquor vote. Following a private meeting at Colonel Thaddeus B. Hedgman's palatial estate, the Colonel donated the use of an empty Bowery store to Brother Nicholas and his cause. The True Vine Church of Divine Salvation opened for business the following Sunday. It was conveniently located next door to Maude's Parlor House, by consensus the best bawdy house in town.

The Colonel's largesse shocked much of High Plains,

since the Civil War veteran had always proved resistant to
charitable solicitations, regardless of cause or purpose, and
had shown no interest in any town issue since the turn of
the century. Pushing eighty and attended full-time by a
nurse, the Colonel was an ancient and revered figure, but
one who rarely descended from his lofty front porch to the
dusty streets of High Plains. Hedgman owned thousands of
acres east of the Bowery, much of it bordering the river. He
was a self-made man who had amassed his fortune as a
U.S. Army procurement officer, traditionally a position of
trust that attracted the wiliest of freebooters.

When I inquired of the Raglars why a man like the Colonel would want to get hooked up with Brother Nicholas's
bunch, I received two plausible opinions.

"No way of knowin'," said Doc, as he dragged his knife
blade across his boot sole. "But it's not uncommon for a
man as rich and powerful as the Colonel is—or was, or
thinks he was—to confuse his death with the end of the
world."

Zack Hart looked at it from another angle. "I just, by
God, betcha the thievin' sonuvawhorehound is lookin' over
his shoulder and sees a lifetime of angry ghosts that he'd
like to buy off."

So Nicholas and his disciples shoveled out the storefront
and began the uphill task of convincing the townfolk that
they need make no plans that demanded more than eight
weeks to execute. Although the preacher's original prophecy had been witnessed by about two hundred people, all of
whom appeared convinced of its accuracy at the time, the
ranks of the faithful had fallen substantially with the next
morning's light. Unperturbed, Nicholas continued to preach
on a daily basis with a certitude that pulled in converts at
a slow but regular pace.

The elderly, the sick, the dispossessed, and those inclined
toward mysticism were the initial proselytes, but for those
first few weeks the town remained essentially unchanged
by prophet or prophecy. The most obvious difference was
apparent only to the drunken cowboys and overworked
prostitutes who were forced to share the early morning
streets with a group of true believers who craned their

necks to the sky, traced the comet's advance, and counted the days till Apocalypse.

I went back to work at *Plain Talk* the day after the liquor vote. Sam endured his injuries gamely while I displayed mine proudly, but it was a week before either of us felt whole. For several days our stumbling pursuit of news resembled a military retreat with the lame leading the halt. On Wednesday of the following week, I tangled with Sam. We'd been getting along dandy since our beatings, but we still had one coal of contention that burned low, waiting for a dry wind or a scrap of tinder to spark it.

I was working with Shad, framing up the back window and patching the wall while Sam set up a feature in the composing stick. It was Sam's nature to converse while he worked. He was curious about everything, and if you spent much time around him, he'd likely find out more about you than you'd had any intention of revealing. Sam and Shad had spent considerable time together, but the black man was tight-lipped and often hours would pass without response. However, it was the first time Shad had worked for Sam since the voting/beating, and he had something to say.

"Back in 'seventy-four and '-five, I was soldierin' at Fort Elliot, near Mobeetie—they called it Hidetown back then. We fought the Comanch' when they took to the warpath. The meat-hunters, you see, had killed off the buffalo, left the Indian nothing to eat. White men shot buffalo just to watch them die ... wouldn't bother with the meat or hide, just wanted to see something that big fall down and kick." Shad's voice displayed no emotion or judgment; that made it all the more galling for me to listen to. Since I was holding the boards that he was nailing up, I had no choice.

"The Comanch' called us 'Buffalo Soldiers.' Said they'd rather fight fifty whites than ten 'Buffalo Soldiers.' But man for man the Comanch' was tougher than anybody he fought. If they'd had weapons and food, they'd be kickin' up hell yet. Without the buffalo, we just starved 'em out.

"Sledge," Shad said. I passed him the big hammer, and he knocked out a section of rotten wall.

"I mustered out of the army in the spring of 'seventy-six

and hired out as a drover on the long drives to Sedalia and
Kansas City. Sixteen hours in the saddle and two hours of
night guard. I wearied of that, took to mule skinnin' around
Tascosa. That was around the time that the gamblers and
whores got run out of Mobeetie and dug in there at
Tascosa."

I'd known Shad all my life, and I'd never heard him say
the first word about his past. As the black man continued
his tales of greedy, vindictive "cattle kings" and back-
shooting "gunslingers," my resentment deepened. I hated
every word he spoke as he laid siege to my vision of the
Old West. The Texas Ranger fiasco had been a harsh blow
to a boy raised on the heroes of nickel paperbacks and the
romantic memories of boastful old men, and there was certainly no room in my Texas Frontier for Negro Indian-
fighters, oppressed redskins, or cowardly and corrupt
sheriffs. My heritage was crumbling quickly, and I knew of
no way to shore it up.

"Nail, boy." Shad had to say it twice, and even then it
pulled me only halfway out of the valley of resentment into
which I'd sunk. The nail I handed him was deemed inadequate for the task.

"Damn, boy," Shad snorted as he threw the bent and
rusty nail out the open window. "Couldn't drive that nail up
a fat hog's ass."

"Who the hell do you think you are?" I exploded, with
all the malice of an heir to nobility stripped of his birth-
right. "I don't have to take no orders from no goddamn
nig—"

Before I could finish my oath, Sam had me by the neck
and britches and headed toward the bedroom. My feet
didn't even touch the floor. He kicked the door shut behind
us and proceeded to read me the riot act.

"Listen hard, Tom." Sam's voice was low and firm. "If
you're going to spend time around me, remember this: you
owe respect to *everyone*. Forget color or age, forget man or
woman. You treat any passed-out drunk on the street just
like you'd treat the governor of Texas until he proves that
he doesn't deserve it. Then you just leave him alone. You

have no right to insult *anybody*. If it happens again, we're through with each other."

Sam's face was just inches from mine, and each word stung like bird shot. I felt as if it took him an hour to say those few sentences. If he had stood across the room and shouted at me, I'm sure I would have yelled back. But there was no arguing with him on this. With the emptiness of the week that I'd spent exiled from *Plain Talk* still fresh in my mind, I realized I had no choice but to accept his conditions. Still, it wasn't my nature to give up without a fight. I searched frantically for a way out.

"Damn it, Sam," I sputtered, "I nearly got my arm broke for you. Shad didn't do nothin' but watch 'em beat the hell out of you."

Sam backed off a step to give me a little room. "You and I got kicked around a little," he said slowly. "They would have gladly *killed* Shad."

He gave me a little time to think about that. I was still angry and resentful, but I wasn't ready to give up the newspaper over it. What the hell. I could think whatever I wanted to; I just had to watch my mouth.

"Are you ready to apologize?"

I nodded and we walked into the office. I mumbled a vague, insincere apology in Shad's direction. He grunted an indifferent acceptance. No one was satisfied, but new lines had been drawn and we all knew what they were.

Sam broke what was becoming a long, uncomfortable silence. "When did you leave Tascosa?"

And it was on again. Shad rambled on about the "Cowboy Strike" of 1883 that lasted about a month before the cowboys got beat up and starved down to the point where the union folded. He claimed he got shot in the shoulder a few years later when the big landowners called in Pat Garrett to put together a "police force" to push out the small ranchers and the independent cowboys. Sheriff Pat Garrett was a hero to every boy in the Bowery and revered far and wide as the killer of Billy the Kid. Of course, Billy the Kid was every bit as big a hero to us, and nobody acknowledged the contradiction. Shad talked as if Garrett were just another debased hired gun, willing to sell out to the highest bidder.

According to Shad, "cowboyin' " was long, hard, mostly boring work, and the big landowners kept the pay so low that you couldn't afford to quit. One night on the town could eat up a month's wages, and the cowboy would be forced to go back to the only job that offered food and a bunk.

"Most did it because it was all they knew how to do," Shad said. "Some did it to keep from settlin' down. Scant few of 'em walked away from it without a limp or a stoop. And no more'n a handful had anything but dust in their pockets when they quit." Shad allowed some pride to sneak into his voice here. "I saved my wages and paid down on forty acres outside Amarillo."

Shad was up to his ass in pestilence relating the grass-hopper plague of 1893 when Sam stopped him. "Would you mind if I wrote this up in the paper?"

I spun around to see if he was serious. Surely Sam didn't intend to plaster a colored man's life all over the pages of *Plain Talk*. And from what I'd heard, this particular colored man's opinions varied substantially from the accepted view of our proud history. If Sam thought he had troubles now . . .

"We don't have to use your name, if you'd rather not," Sam continued, "but this is a side of the Panhandle that I haven't heard before. You're one of the few people around here that's seen this area move from Indian country to civilization."

"Civilization," Shad said grimly, driving a nail with excessive force. "Civilization damn near ruint my life."

Sam didn't identify the "old-timer" who was the subject of his lead feature; he didn't have to. The article infuriated the citizenry of High Plains regardless of source, and it took all of about five minutes after the paper hit the street for everyone to identify the "Buffalo Soldier."

In one sense Sam had managed a feat that many had considered impossible: he had united virtually everyone in High Plains in a common attitude. New Towners and

Boweryites alike were indignant about the assault on their mythic past by an uppity old darky in league with a two-bit print hack. I don't know whether Sam didn't realize that he was poking the mean dog with a sharp stick, or just grossly underestimated the intensity of reaction. In either instance, it can safely be declared that he drew as much heat as his struggling newspaper could stand.

Perhaps Sam anticipated the controversy and considered it a price worth paying. While the immediate effect of the Buffalo Soldier article was apparent to all but the most distracted in town, the enduring legacy was that thereafter the townsfolk, and Tommy Greer, now saw a black man walk the streets where once a shadow passed.

As might be expected, that issue of *Plain Talk* proved to be the best-selling edition to date. The irony of journalism was, and remains, that newspapers derive little of their revenue through paper sales, depending instead on advertising for the bulk of their income. Even though our circulation had risen steadily, very few reputable businesses wanted their names associated with Sam's paper. We were left with the saloon trade, a couple livery stables, and a few marginally respectable Bowery businesses—a rooming house, an undertaker, and a barber.

Sam hated it, but we were forced to run a lot of ads for patent medicines of dubious effectiveness and questionable decorum. PILES–PILES–PILES! shrieked regularly from a banner headline on an interior page. The accompanying quarter-page advertisement revealed a startling medical breakthrough from Germany that promised instant relief from this tragic affliction. Another favorite was FORTUNE TELLER–LIFE READER, THE GREAT KALOHI. Kalohi could straighten out your life and rearrange your stars ("Your Astral Governors!") using only your birth date and a sample of your handwriting. The price for this remarkable service was a mere dollar donation to his New Jersey foundation. Flea powders, horse laxatives ("Good for large humans too"), and assorted tonics for "female distress" were standard fare.

Finances had become so critical that Sam had to resort to a traditional ploy of failing newspapers: he sponsored contests. "Free Year's Subscription for Tastiest Canned Good," was one week's offer. That was followed by contests for the largest potato, or the sweetest corn, or the tastiest loaf of bread. All entries were devoured by the judges—Sam and Rebekah—and the wolf was kept on the street side of the door for another week.

"Have you settled on a church yet?" I asked Miss Rebekah. We had the office to ourselves that morning, but she had been unusually quiet. I knew religion to be a subject that she couldn't resist.

"Not yet," she said, holding the composing stick in her left hand as she chose type from the case. She touched a finger to her cheek and left a dab of ink under her powder-blue right eye. I found it hard not to stare at it. "Your mother has taken me on the Cook's Tour of every Protestant church in town, but none seems quite what I'm looking for."

My job that day, and seemingly every day, was "throwin' in." I tossed the jumbled type into appropriate compartments, taking care to sort out old and unusable type into the "hell box" to be disposed of. It was a job that you could teach a monkey to do, except that you would have to pay the monkey a decent wage.

"The Baptists always seem to draw a good crowd," I offered. I had once been the pride of the Baptists, winning prizes regularly for memorizing Bible verses, but I'd been earnestly backsliding for the past two or three years.

Miss Rebekah laughed lightly. "The Baptist church was interesting, but perhaps a bit too . . . lively for my taste."

Good point. The Baptists would occasionally get wound up tight by Preacher Simon and take to jabbering in tongues, grabbing red-hot stovepipes, and tossing babies in the air. I offered a more sedate alternative. "The Methodists don't go in for all that 'holy roller' stuff. A lot of the high mucky-mucks in town go there."

"From what I saw there, they don't let the worship service get in the way of their socials and ice cream suppers," she said, her gentle though thickened *s*'s weaving merrily through the sentence like a sprinkling of daisies through a spring meadow. "I had hoped for something more substantial . . . more devout."

"I'll bet ol' Brother Nicholas would welcome you with open arms. He's pushin' for the Panhandle to secede from Texas and become a state on its own. All the counties north of Fort Worth. 'No whiskey, cars, Catholics, or Coloreds'! is their motto. His people got real excited about it till Nicholas said that even part of Oklahoma might wanta join up. Most folks felt like that would ruin it."

We were still talking religion when Rebekah dropped a loaded composing stick, scattering the contents across the floor. We were both on our hands and knees gathering up the type when Sam bounded in the door. He was in fine fettle, having just sold a half-pager for the opening of a New Town drugstore. The pharmacist was fresh off the train and unaware of our reputation as a pariah.

Sam helped his wife to her feet and gave her a peck on the cheek, but he could tell she had her mind on something else. "What's the matter, Bekah?"

She reclaimed the composing stick and moved to the type case. Her voice, always soft, was now hesitant as well. "I've been talking to the Widow Greer . . ." she began.

That couldn't be good.

"And she says that she could use some help sewing and embroidering, and such. It'll be piecework, Sam, but I can make a fair wage, I think."

She just let it hang there for a minute. Sam didn't say anything, but I could see his back bow up at the idea. In High Plains a working wife was a flat admission to the world that a man couldn't support his family. Sam was a free-thinker by Texas standards, but his expression indicated that his liberality didn't extend in that direction. He would also be giving up a good worker. I felt that I would be losing even more.

Rebekah attempted to soften the blow. "It would just be mornings, Tuesday through Saturday. I could still work here most afternoons and on Sunday and Monday."

Sam rubbed the back of his neck and walked over to the copy desk. Distractedly rearranging the scissors, paste pot, and half-finished articles, he reconciled himself to the inevitable. Sam was a smart man, but he shared a trait endemic to newspaper editors: he had a distorted sense of money. All that mattered was whether there was enough cash to put out the next issue. If there wasn't, he assumed that something would turn up. A good businessman would never have gone into journalism in the first place.

"We're not doing so badly," Sam said. He stared vacantly at some proofs on the table. "We can get a couple more issues out before we need to start worrying. Circulation is up . . ." He let it die when he found that he couldn't convince himself.

Miss Rebekah slipped her hand through his arm. "We've used up nearly everything that we brought with us," she said softly. "I can work till the paper gets on its feet."

Sam gave her a good strong hug. "I suppose it wouldn't hurt if you tried it for a week or two."

Miss Rebekah gently tendered another alternative. "Unless you want me to write my father for a loan—"

Sam pulled away from her as if she had just sprouted horns. His eyes narrowed to slits so thin that you couldn't slide a dime between them. Words were unnecessary.

"I'm going to check on the Lamour ad, Sam," I said. We all knew that the hotel never paid until Sunday, but a little fresh air wouldn't hurt me.

I talked to Doc and Zack for a few minutes, giving the situation time to defuse before walking back to the office. Inside, Sam and Miss Rebekah were both laughing, so I figured everything was jake. When I took a step inside, I could hear the next statement all too clearly.

"I guess my big problem now," Sam said, "is getting Tom to show up for work when you're not around." They both laughed.

I turned on my heel and left without being seen. Since I had never mentioned my feelings toward Miss Rebekah to anyone, I'd assumed that no one suspected my infatuation. Now that my love had been recognized, it was robbed of its magic. My feelings were no longer unique and had to be judged objectively. I could only come up wanting: she was a married woman, and I was a kid.

I walked around awhile and ended up at the swimming

hole. I sat on the bank for about an hour adjusting to the new order. Rebekah was my first love. I felt that I would never have another.

After lunch I went back to work, and never let on that I'd heard them. But it was a long time before I could look Rebekah Adams in the eye.

Chapter Thirteen

On the last Sunday in April, I rolled out of bed bursting with reasons why I could not attend church with Mama, but I could find no one to deliver them to. On the kitchen table, Mama had left two boiled eggs and a note informing me that she had "church business" to attend to, and that my presence there would not be required. Never one to stare down the gaping maw of a gift horse, I dressed quickly and set out for *Plain Talk*. Sam Adams and I had big plans for the morning, and, though it would have shocked my mother, church attendance was mandatory.

During the past several weeks, Brother Nicholas had been casting about for affirmation of his Halley's Comet/Doomsday revelation. Although never at a loss for a cause to champion—Panhandle secession, book-banning, immigrant-stoning—none of those even remotely rivaled the drama and majesty of World Destruction. The growth of the True Vine congregation had slowed to the point where it was apparent that Brother Nicholas needed something both specific and compelling in order to regain his momentum. The word on the street was that he might just have it.

> *"Surely I will, surely I will,*
> *If anyone makes it, surely I will,*
> *Surely I will, surely I will,*
> *If anyone makes it,*
> *God knows I will!"*

There was neither man nor dog in sight on the Bowery street as Sam Adams and I walked toward the off-key hymn leaking from the True Vine Church of Divine Salvation. After rounding the side of the building and leaning in a window, we observed that the store had been scoured down and cleared of all counters and shelves. Handmade benches were shoved tightly together and packed with freshly scrubbed worshipers. The singing was being led by Horace "Baldy" Guthridge, a bitter ex–bank clerk who had been sucking up to the preacher since the first prohibition rally.

When I scanned the congregation, I nearly fell through the window. On the far side of the room near the front of the church, my mother and Lily Barkley were sharing a bench and a hymnal. Mrs. Barkley had been hovering on the fringes of Nicholas's movement since his first temperance rally, but I had no idea that my mother had started attending the True Vine services. It was Mama's custom to switch churches at the drop of a prayer book, but she had always stuck with major denominations. Seeing her paired off with R. N. Barkley's wife was a real boot in the rear. Many is the time I had heard Mama and her cronies pick the beautiful Lily's bones clean for her scarlet past and "money-bought respectability." I nearly choked when I saw them raising a joyful noise together. Sam's only response to the incongruity was, "It appears that apocalypse makes strange bedfellows."

Colonel Hedgman sat at attention in his wheelchair in front of the first row of benches. His impatience with all this folderol was evident; he was ready to join the battle. Nicholas's congregation reflected a few additional inroads into the middle class, but his primary constituency remained the old and the alienated, the emotionally and physically infirm. But we were still weeks away from the preacher's target date, and anything could happen. A couple weeks earlier, Nicholas had reportedly eased away from his flat pronouncement of world devastation, and there was a consequent drop in True Vine attendance. Sam pointed out that that was the sort of trend that did not bode well for cheerful prognostication.

When "Surely I Will" mercifully ended, the congregation remained on its feet. The serenity of sanctuary was clearly absent as a congregation of pinched faces and shuffling feet waited anxiously for Brother Nicholas and his latest grim announcement. The rumor of dark prophecy had sprung up Saturday evening and spread through the town faster than pinkeye through the first grade. It hung like a smothering cloud over the cramped gathering. I could see that these folk were stretched tighter than Maggie's garters, and I had to duck away from the window and grab a headful of untainted air lest I lose my perspective.

After an inordinate wait, the door behind the podium opened and Brother Nicholas emerged. He was dressed, as always, in wrinkled black coat and pants, with frayed white shirt; his hair was uncombed, and he looked like he'd missed a week's sleep. "Eaten by a coyote and shit off a cliff," was the schoolyard expression that sprang to mind. The preacher stepped up on a two-foot-high box behind the rostrum and stared down at the assemblage. In his wake, two aides carried a large upright chalkboard and set it to the left of the podium.

Nicholas motioned for everyone to sit down. If he saw us leaning in the window, he showed no sign of it. He stared straight down the middle of the aisle and forced a thin-lipped smile.

"I would like first to welcome everyone to our services. Each week I have seen our congregation grow, and it continues to make my spirit soar. I take no pride in this," he reassured us quickly, "for all I say or do is for the glory of God and in His name."

The congregation signaled agreement. "Amen."

"Today I will forego our opening prayer and appeal for healing, since supplication and consolation must give way to matters of universal consequence. Since my initial prophecy some weeks ago, I have searched my heart and the Scriptures to establish the legitimacy of my pronouncement. I wrestled with my soul and prayed to Almighty God to direct me to a resolution. For three days and nights He drove my mind and body through a fathomless pit of misery and self-doubt before ripping the scales from my eyes." Nicholas lowered his head and shook it emphatically side to side, reliving the battle. "I will now share my findings with you."

Two aides began passing printed two-page pamphlets to everyone in the church. Sam tipped his hat to the old woman nearest our window, and she gladly passed us a copy.

While the pamphlets were being distributed, Nicholas acknowledged a benefactor. "I would like to thank Mrs. Lily Barkley for her assistance in printing up these sheets."

Lily smiled and nodded her head modestly, never raising her gaze from her lap.

Sam whispered to me, "Guess whose arm got twisted on that deal?"

I smiled. R. N. Barkley had never volunteered free paper and labor to anyone.

"Please follow closely," Nicholas instructed. It was amazing how his voice filled the room. He sounded like the brawniest man in town. "In calculation number one we establish the *base* number. From the Commandment to Rebuild Jerusalem in 457 B.C. to the Crucifixion of Christ in A.D. 33, we have four hundred ninety years."

Baldy Guthridge wrote 490 on the chalkboard. Even though we had the information on the sheets in front of us, Baldy copied the numbers as Nicholas called them out and performed the calculations.

Nicholas continued: "From the Crucifixion of Christ to the taking away of the Daily Abomination of Paganism, 475 years.

"From the taking away of the Pagan Rites to the setting up of the Abomination of Papal Civil Rule, thirty years.

"From the setting up of the Papal Abomination to the end thereof, 1260 years.

"From the taking away of the Papal Civil Rule to the First Resurrection and the End of the World in 1910, one hundred twelve years. Now add these numbers together."

Baldy was striving mightily to do so, and after several erasures and a withering look from Brother Nicholas, he arrived at the number on our pamphlet.

"Two thousand three hundred sixty-seven," Nicholas intoned with leaden gravity. "Two thousand three hundred sixty-seven is our base number.

"From the base number, subtract the 490 years between

the Commandment to Rebuild Jerusalem and the Crucifixion of Christ. Your answer is 1877.

"Now add the term of our Savior's life—thirty-three years."

Nicholas paused as Baldy did the calculation. His voice deepened when he announced the result. "The answer is *1910!*"

A murmur ran through the crowd as Baldy drew a circle around 1910. Everyone followed the calculation on the blackboard, ignoring the printed sheets in their hands.

Nicholas paused a moment to let the emotion run its course. "There is much more," he said grimly. "From the base number 2367, subtract the date of the Commandment to Rebuild Israel in 457."

The congregation held their breath as Baldy pulled down each ensuing number. A second before the final digit was etched on the blackboard, Nicholas shouted: "The answer is 1910!"

It drew an audible gasp from the crowd.

Nicholas pressed his advantage. "Leviticus Twenty-six states that the House of Israel is to be punished seven times for their sins. This means seven years of 365 days. This equals 2555.

"Subtract the date of the First Captivity of Babylon in 678.

"Add our Savior's life span of thirty-three."

Everyone knew what was coming. Heads shook mournfully in the pews, and trembling parents embraced frightened children. The only sound in the building was the harsh squeak of chalk on the blackboard.

"Nineteen ten!"

Words of alarm and distress passed among the congregation as numerical determinism sunk in. After a few moments of barely controlled hysteria, Nicholas raised his hands, palms out. Silence descended.

"The conclusion our Lord has visited upon me is indisputable," roared Brother Nicholas. "On May eighteen, the tail of Halley's Comet will envelop the planet and all life will cease. The year 1910 will be the *End*."

As the wave of rending, wailing, and gnashing swept

through the church, Sam and I backed away from the window to take stock.

"I wouldn't have believed it if I hadn't been here," Sam said grimly. "Nick ran a numbers game on them, and they bought it."

I could see how they fell for it. If Sam hadn't been there talking sense, I'd have been a mite uneasy myself. I wouldn't confess that to Sam, though. I decided to approach the subject from a professional stance.

"Is it front page?" I asked.

"Not in my newspaper. I figure one column interior, sandwiched between a laxative ad and the Poetry Club news." Sam grinned. "Maximum exposure."

We listened to the rest of Nicholas's sermon. He called for twice weekly comet vigils, and increased proselytizing, culminating in nightly revivals the final ten days. Every member was charged with converting nonbelievers, which would thereby ensure the member's own salvation. When the service broke off into committee meetings, Sam and I abandoned our window.

"Nicholas has sawed his own legs off," Sam reassured me as we walked toward Derby's Silver Dollar saloon. "He didn't leave himself a way out. Numbers are inflexible. He'll pick up some converts and ride high for a few weeks, but when the world doesn't end—and you can bet gold pieces to goat shit it won't—there are going to be some outraged people looking for somebody to blame." Sam chuckled at the thought of the preacher's comeuppance. "And there's nothing more dangerous than a group of people who have been humiliated in front of their neighbors. Mark my word, Tom, come May nineteenth, Brother Nicholas will be laying track for parts unknown."

I felt better after hearing that. The whole experience had been unnerving, particularly seeing my mother there. As we walked, I managed to convince myself that it was just another stop in Mama's spiritual odyssey, a brief sojourn of no more consequence than any of a dozen others. Sam's attitude reassured me momentarily, but I still found it impossible to dismiss the vision of my mother's face as she watched the doomsday figures appear on the chalkboard.

Chapter
Fourteen

In the month since the big fire, Derby's place had been rebuilt and painted and looked sharper than ever. If an arsonist existed, he remained at large. Derby's handbills offering the five-hundred-dollar reward hung futilely from virtually every wooden post in town, but no one expected resolution of that crime. Each passing day decreased the likelihood of either evidence or witness appearing. Even Derby had ceased to talk about it.

"Hello, Belle," Sam called through the open door. The madam nodded to us from behind the bar. She had the place to herself except for Harlow, the sweeper, and the "Perfesser," who had passed out over his piano. Derby had rewarded Harlow for his vigilance in reporting the fire by hiring him on as an odd-job man. Harlow showed up when he was sober enough to feel guilty, and Derby let him sleep on the saloon floor instead of in the alley. Success hadn't changed the drunk much; he asked for nothing more than sufficient liquor to addle himself and to be left alone to drink it. Most folks were more than glad to ignore Harlow since he had fallen onto bad times.

Harlow, like damn near every pilgrim doomed to wander this worrisome land, trailed a tragic past behind him. He had been a hard-riding cowboy until three years back, when one bright clear spring day he had been thrown while breaking an outlaw horse. He hadn't stopped falling yet. Out of work for six months while his broken leg healed, the wrangler discovered that life could be easier than daybreak to dusk on horseback. Harlow found that he could slide through life on cheap whiskey, and it would cost him nothing more than the right to look another man in the eye. Dr.

Reeves had done his usual slipshod job of setting the leg, so the cowboy dragged around a ready-made alibi with him. Of course, we all knew working cowboys who were stove up worse than the sweeper and never missed chuck at sunrise. I suspect that Doc Moss hit the nail on the head: "Ol' Harlow was given a golden opportunity to be worthless, and damn few men will pass up the chance."

"How's that leg coming along, Harlow?"

The sweeper nearly dropped his broom when Sam slapped him gently on the back. Sam was about the only person around who talked directly to the drunk. The Bowery Wisdom was that you cut your ties to the Harlows of the world and saved yourself the pain of watching the slow, inevitable tragedy that is man without will.

"It's knittin' up right well," Harlow mumbled. He seemed both grateful and embarrassed by Sam's attention. "I 'spect by brandin' time, I'll be ready to get back to it."

Acres of cowhide had been burned since Harlow had first used that dodge, but Sam smiled and nodded as though he expected to see the sweeper throwing a lariat from horseback the next morning.

At the bar, Belle was taking inventory of the liquor. She always assumed that her barkeeps were stiffing her, and measured volume consumption against income on a daily basis. Consequently, the Silver Dollar had trouble holding on to bartenders.

"Is Derby around?" Sam asked pleasantly.

Belle dropped her foot ruler and tossed Sam an envelope across the counter. "He said he'd take out a half-page ad if you'd put it on a sheet by itself—no other saloons. Otherwise, leave it a quarter-pager."

"I think we can work it out." Sam counted the money in the envelope. "Derby taking the day off?"

"He's over at that goddamn ball field." She shook her head in disgust at the thought of all that effort expended without turning one red cent of profit. "He'll be gone all day, drunk tonight, and sore for the rest of the week."

The baseball field, strategically located a half mile west of the Bowery, was within walking distance of both sides of town, but distant enough so that the constant flow of profanity and frequent brawls could be ignored by decent folk. Baseball had been orphaned by respectable elements of High Plains for the past two years owing to the distressing tendency of the games to end in free-for-alls. Just last season, games with Wishbone, Bramlett, Amarillo, and Skankton had all been called on account of blood. Local pulpits and rostrums rang with condemnations of the national sport, and the town board voted to remove the town's name and monetary support from the team. Delighted by the stripping of any pretense of respectability from a sport that he suspected society sought to emasculate, Derby gladly picked up the financial slack and renamed the team the Blind Mule Skinners.

Under pressure from the churches, R. N. Barkley had struck his blow for decency by removing the major league box scores and team standing from his newspaper. One of Sam's first editorial decisions filled that void; *Plain Talk* carried all the professional baseball news that we could get our hands on.

The ball field was in good shape. The boys had dug up the buffalo grass and uprooted the mesquite and other scrubs that had gained a toehold over the winter. Fresh lime marked the foul lines, spanking new feed-bag bases were anchored by railroad spikes, and a shiny stretch of chicken wire reinforced the backstop. The players' benches and the scoreboard were shuttled back and forth from the Bowery on Derby's wagon along with the keg of beer he provided for players and fans at the end of practice. Even allowing for the absence of an outfield fence and grandstands, the baseball field was top-notch.

Around twenty-five or thirty spectators had shown up for the first practice of the season. The Skinners had split into two teams and were only an inning into a game when Sam and I got there. The players were a ragtag and bobtail lot, with no man wearing a complete uniform. Work boots were the common footgear, though a few players had spikes, and about half wore caps.

Practice was supposed to be a low-key and good-natured affair, to work the kinks out of a long winter's layoff. There are, however, those true sons of Competition and Free Enterprise who resist all entreaty to pare back effort or moderate achievement. Slabfoot Olson was one. He would—regretfully, though inevitably—trip his crippled grandmother to win a footrace.

Sam and I had just settled down on the ground along the left-field line when Slabfoot came charging around third base like a field ox fleeing a swarm of hornets. Big Mike was the hind catcher for the opposition. He had the throw from center field firmly in hand before Slabfoot was half-way home. A sensible man would either have attempted to retrace his steps to third base or surrendered peaceably to the blacksmith. Slabfoot took a third course that was dictated by his size (very large), his nature (very hostile), and his intelligence (very slight). He attempted to jar the ball from Big Mike's grasp.

The collision left both men stunned and prone just long enough for the umpire, Derby, to jump between them. When the two giants rose in combative posture, Derby grabbed a handful of each man's shirt—he looked like a dram bottle squeezed between two demijohns. He was mightily overmatched, but Derby had a presence that men seldom challenged. (On two separate occasions, witnesses had seen him verbally disarm men who had come to his saloon for the express purpose of killing him.) He spoke to Slabfoot as though the hulk were an errant schoolboy.

"You dumb sonuvabitchin' Swede," Derby shouted, "you better grab your mitt and get your ass to first base before I throw you off this team and knock you colder'n a snake's tail to boot."

Slabfoot snorted and pawed the earth, but he backed off. The antagonists separated while exchanging mutual threats of showdown on a neutral site in the near future. Derby yelled at the players who had gathered around in anticipation of a clash of the titans. "Everybody change sides. This is a practice, goddamn it. See if you can keep from killing each other. Rooster, you're the batter."

We watched a couple of innings of rough, ragged base-ball grounded in strength rather than agility, skill deferring to aggressiveness. Base runners were tripped and occasion-

ally tackled as they rounded the feed bags. Every close play
bore potential for violence—and this merely an intrasquad
game. Sam spoke to the point when he said, "Some of
these guys should be wearing a ball and chain instead of
baseball spikes."

Pretty soon Sam got antsy and started pacing the foul
line. "Can you catch a baseball?" he asked me.

"I can catch any damn thing you can throw." I was one
of the best ball players in school.

Sam rounded up gloves and a ball, and we went to it. It
wasn't long before I could see I was in over my head. Sam
was burning me up, and he hadn't even reached back for
his hard one yet. I was mighty relieved when Big Mike ambled over with a catcher's mitt to relieve me.

And did Sam ever throw some smoke; you could hear
Mike's mitt pop at fifty yards. After he got loosened up,
Sam started mixing in some breaking pitches that the
catcher had trouble getting his mitt on. Pretty soon all
the spectators had abandoned the game to take a look at the
new pitcher. Between innings Derby walked over to check
out the excitement. Three pitches was all it took.

Derby said, "You wanta pitch?"

Sam tossed the ball into the air a couple times and
caught it in his bare hand. He thought it over longer than
he had any reason to. Finally, he nodded his head like a
man who had just agreed to his own execution. His attitude
made not one whit of sense to me. If I could throw a baseball like that, I'd be damned if I'd ever set another line of
type. They wouldn't be able to chase me off a pitcher's
mound with a handful of rocks.

"Take the mound," Derby said. He jerked his thumb at
the pitcher on the field. "Dago, go to left field."

After throwing six or eight pitches from the mound, Sam
was ready. Lantern Jaw stepped to the plate. (Yes; everybody on the team had a nickname. Derby had a lousy memory, but he had a knack for hanging a monicker on a man
that would stick. Slabfoot, for instance, shuffled around on
a set of size fifteen dogs, while Lantern Jaw had a chin that
you could do a buck-and-wing on.)

The guys on the bench were riding Sam hard, calling

him "Newsboy," "Rag Arm," and "Inky." Lantern Jaw waved his bat at the pitcher as though he intended to decapitate him with it.

Sam's first pitch was a fast ball right down the pipe. I swear it was in Big Mike's mitt before Lantern Jaw swung. The bench jockeying slowed considerably as the batter stepped away from the plate, spat on his hands, then dug back in.

Sam wound up and threw an outdrop that looked like it fell off the edge of a table. It was over the plate, but Lantern Jaw was so alarmed by its trajectory that he made no attempt to hit it. Big Mike got enough mitt on the ball to slow it down, but it rolled to the backstop. When the catcher retrieved it, he took a good hard look at the ball, then offered it to Derby and Lantern Jaw for inspection. No nicks, cuts, oil, ink, or other foreign substances were found. Derby smiled. He didn't care what Sam used so long as it wasn't detectable.

A slow sidearm curve left the batter with his foot in the bucket and swinging like the proverbial rusty gate. The bench jockeys were struck silent. I've never seen so many heads shake in unison in my life—you could hear the rattle clear across the field.

"Unbegoddamnlievable!" wheezed a spectator behind me.

Big Mike believed it. He fairly danced away from home plate with the ball held high in his right hand. "Bring on them pussies from Wishbone," the catcher whooped. "They ain't got a Chineyman's chance of hitting big Sammy."

Sam snatched me out of the beer line before I got a drop and aimed me toward town. "Holy damn, Sam," I complained, "it's impolite not to stay around for the celebration. These guys would like to congratulate us."

"We've got work to do," he said, striding hard toward the Bowery. "We've already burned up more time than we can spare."

Even after four innings of pitching, Sam didn't appear winded. He had mowed down High Plains's best ball players without giving up more than a loud foul. After his first time at bat he got untracked and knocked one of Gummy's

fast balls about halfway to Oklahoma; he had enough time
to walk around the bases on his hands. He was the star of
the show and the best thing to happen to baseball since
Derby had started providing beer at the games. Everyone
on the team was in great spirits. They would gladly have
done anything for the new ace pitcher—anything, that is,
short of buying a newspaper and reading it. Sam had to assure Derby that he would pitch in the game against Wishbone before the manager allowed him to leave.

Sam's triumph was unequivocal; he had every right to
feel that he had the world by the ass on the downhill drag.
But something had him by the neck and wouldn't let go.
He walked so fast I could hardly keep up. When we got to
the Bowery, he finally spoke. "Tom, you've got to be sure
to never say a word about this around the office. Rebekah
is never to hear the word 'baseball.' Understand?"

"Sure, Sam, I'll keep a lid on it."

We walked to the town pump, took off our shirts and
washed up. I had to ask. "Did you ever play pro ball?"

"No," he said as he splashed water under his arms. "But
a lot of people thought I could have."

"You're the best I ever saw."

He smiled the smile of a man recognized for a singular
talent long suppressed.

We dried off the best we could and struck off toward the
office. "What if she asks me where we've been?" I knew
I couldn't look Rebekah straight in the face and lie.

"Don't worry about that. She won't be home till suppertime," Sam said. "Those Methodist folks don't leave the
church until the last dog is hung."

Chapter
Fifteen

Langston Harper was thumbing through the current *Plain Talk* when we walked into the office. He'd been gone for better than a week, and he looked like hell on the hoof. His tie hung loosely over a shirt that begged to give way to a successor. His coat and pants had apparently been slept in, and his proud Stetson had picked up several creases that it would never recover from. I'd seen Langston three sheets to the wind scores of times, but I'd never known him to walk a public street looking so bedraggled.

"Greetings, noble members of the fourth estate," he called to us. He started to rise from his chair, but his wobbly knees quashed the impulse.

"What's the matter, Langston? You sick or something?"

The lawyer smiled expansively. "Not a bit of it, Thomas. Never been better."

Sam grabbed a fresh shirt from the bedroom and asked his question through the open door. "Things go badly in Amarillo?"

"Fort Worth this time, Sam," Langston corrected. "Things are as they have always been, now and ever shall be." He snorted out a laugh. "World without end, God forbid."

Sam started to say something, but Langston plowed on. He stared straight ahead, his voice distant, hollow, detached from mind and body. "Old friend of mine found his wife making the beast with two backs with a delivery boy. It had been going on for a year or more, and everybody that could possibly give a damn—including my friend—knew about it long ago, months before. But the woman got careless or vengeful or tired . . . something." Langston took a long pull from his hip flask, closed his eyes and continued. "She was banging away at this kid one afternoon on the living room floor when my friend brought his business partner home for a drink. The boy grabbed a handful of himself and ran out the back door. The wife just sat on the floor and waited. My friend walked upstairs, loaded a shotgun, and blew her head off. His partner stood at the door and never said a word." Langston rolled his head in a circle. "It was as if no one had any choice."

When he opened his eyes, he seemed almost surprised to find us still in the room. He offered Sam the flask. Sam refused.

"Did you get him off?" Sam asked.

"Certainly," the lawyer said. He sounded surprised that the question could even be asked. "Unwritten law. If I'd given them my best shot in summation, I think I could have talked the jury into giving him a medal." Langston's voice was cold and sardonic. It made me uncomfortable, and I tried to change the subject.

"Brother Nicholas has—"

"But you know who the real murderer was?" Langston pulled himself out of the chair with discernible effort. He walked to the front window and stared out on the street. "It was the partner. If he hadn't been there, there would have been no need to kill her."

There was a long silence before Sam spoke. "What happened to the boy?"

"Hasn't been found. I hope he had enough sense to get out of town. If not, I might have to go back and play another part in this never-ending folly."

Langston took another shot of liquor and shook his head like a man waking from a deep sleep. "Now, tell me what ol' Brother Nick is up to."

"You shoulda been there, Langston," I said. "Nick threw a bunch of numbers together and proved that the world's gonna end."

Langston chuckled. "Proved to whose satisfaction?"

"Tom and I haven't signed up for the Glory Train yet, but the passenger list is growing," Sam said as he pulled a pamphlet from his back pocket and passed it to the lawyer.

Langston shook the dust from the folded sheets and scanned the calculations. When he attempted to sit down in the rickety old chair next to the printing press, it nearly threw him to the floor.

"Whoa, big fella," Langston said, as he regained his balance with the shambling grace native to mountain cloggers and habitual drunks. I was always amazed at how sober he sounded long after his body had ceased to be an ally.

He winked at me. "Just lost stirrup there for a minute."

Langston pulled out his reading glasses and put on his grim lawyering face. It didn't take him long to come to a conclusion. "What we have here, gentlemen, is a numerical shell game. No matter which shell you look under, there's no pea. Take, for instance, this 'Final and Absolute Overthrow of Papal Civil Power' around ..." Langston did some quick mental addition. "Eighteen hundred A.D. That would probably come as a shock to the Pope and millions of Catholics who have not been apprised of it. And I'm not entirely convinced that paganism was wiped out completely by the sixth century. I recall that China is overflowing with devout souls that Christians have labeled 'pagan' for years." He handed the list back to Sam. "Arbitrary dates affixed to imaginary events."

"So you figure nobody is going to fall for this?" I asked.

"I surely didn't say that," the lawyer objected. "It wouldn't surprise me at all to see this tally sheet pull in converts by the netful. If there's anything that scares the human race more than the wrath of God, it's arithmetic. Bind them together, no matter how tenuously, and you have a formidable weapon."

Sam nodded and quoted, "There are lies, there are damned lies, and there are statistics."

"A sentiment worth drinking to," said Langston, and he did. "When I came to this town twelve years ago, the people here would have thrown Nicholas out on his ear before he had a chance to thump that Bible a second time. They could spot honesty in a man's eye. I left Kansas because of people like him. But they always manage to find you." Langston leaned back in the chair and closed his eyes again. "The price of civilization, gentlemen, is paid in the coin of hypocrisy."

The sound of fast-moving steps pulled everyone's eyes to the door. Rebekah Adams strode into the office, her cheeks flushed and her face drawn. My first guess was that she had somehow found out about Sam's baseball game.

When she saw Langston, she did her best to hide her distress.

"Good afternoon, Mr. Harper." She extended her hand. "How are you today, sir?"

Langston turned away briefly to knot his tie, then rose gracefully from the chair. "Couldn't be finer, ma'am. And you are passing well, I trust?"

Rebekah nodded amiably, but I detected a timbre in her voice that I'd never heard before. "Very well, thank you," she said. She turned toward Sam. "I hope you will excuse us, Mr. Harper. I need to speak to my husband."

Langston pulled his pocket watch from his vest and shook his head. In fulfillment of his role in the charade, he appeared almost shocked by the reading. "I appreciate your calling my attention to the hour, Mrs. Adams. I have business with Judge Derby that must be attended to immediately. It was a pleasure seeing you." He tipped his crushed hat.

Rebekah smiled and nodded, then walked into the bedroom.

"I'll be right in, Rebekah," Sam called after her. He looked uneasy too.

"Langston," he said, "about this month's rent. I'm not sure—"

Langston cut him off with a wave of his hand. He grabbed a jar of pickled turnips off the "contest" shelf and slipped it into his coat pocket. "Call it even," he said as he weaved through the open door.

Sam didn't bother closing the bedroom door, but it didn't matter. The walls were so thin you could hear someone scratching himself from anywhere in the building. The Adamses had never tried to keep anything from me anyway. I was always around, and they trusted me.

I went about the business of running off a proof of the

front page galley. The piece was a good strong one about the disparity between the water and sewer services in New Town and in the Bowery. The upshot being that they had the services and we had the promises. I liked all the stuff that Sam wrote raising hell with the powers that be. After the big fire, he wrote a scorcher on the failure of the New Town fire department to show up until the blaze was extinguished. People still talked about that article.

The voices from the bedroom were clear.

"Sam, it was just horrible." Rebekah's words spilled out in a torrent. "The minister talked about you in his sermon, the whole town is gossiping behind my back, and the leader of my missionary circle took me aside and asked if there was anything that *I* could do about *you*. I've never been so embarrassed."

Sam's voice was almost too low to hear. "What's my sin?"

"They say you only write about what's wrong here. That you drive people away and keep the town from growing. Don't you see these people don't want to hear about the past? They want to hear about their progress. They want to feel proud of their town."

"That's not journalism, Rebekah, that's advertising. They've already got a paper for that."

"But it looks like you go out of your way to offend people and . . . stir things up. You never did that in Kansas."

"I was just a reporter in Kansas. I'm the editor here."

There was a long silence, so I ran off a proof and banged around some to reassure them of their privacy.

Rebekah lowered her voice. "If we're going to live in this town, you're going to have to mend some fences. Get involved with the community. Coming to church would be a start."

"If I'm a member of the church or the town board, then I can't be objective about how it's run or where it's headed. I have to stay separate."

"I know that you can't fight half this town and keep a business running, Sam. Could you just try to be *positive* for a week or two, write something that will lift people up.

Maybe then you'll pick up some subscribers ... and some *decent* advertising."

Things got quiet for a while, so I moved over to the far side of the room and rearranged the chases under the imposing stone. When Sam walked out of the bedroom, I could see which route we were taking.

"Break down page one, Tom. The water and sewer article is out."

"Aw, hell, Sam, it's already set up. And it's a damn good piece."

I guess he understood my reluctance since he didn't chastise me for cussing. Still, it was sinful to throw out a full page of set type and a good article besides. I fumed and snorted for a while—for show, I suppose, since I knew it wouldn't have any effect. Damn such foolishness.

While I broke down the page and resorted the type, Sam wrote the short piece on Nicholas's numbers sermon for page three. I set that article while he wrote a lead feature called "The Glory of a Panhandle Spring." It was as blatant a piece of town-boosting propaganda as I've ever seen darken the pages of a responsible newspaper.

If I was angry about all the extra work, Sam was clearly miserable. Rebekah's attempts to lighten the atmosphere were met with stony silence; she quickly retreated to the bedroom and her sewing. I'll bet that Sam and I didn't exchange more than a dozen words throughout an evening that dragged way into the next morning. By the time we had the paper ready for Monday's printing, we could hardly look at each other without growling.

I didn't leave the newspaper office until well after midnight, and the last thing I wanted to see on my way home was a collection of twenty-five or thirty "Nickites" planted in the middle of the street, their necks contorted toward the sky like ducklings scanning for hawks. I had stumbled onto one of Brother Nicholas's twice-weekly "Comet Vigils."

The brethren were facing east as I approached unnoticed from the opposite direction. When I lifted my gaze, I was amazed at the sight. The last time I had seen Halley's Comet was the night the Adamses arrived in town, months back; then it was a dot on the horizon with a short, stumpy tail. Now the comet was a burning mass brighter than any star I had ever seen. Its tail fanned out behind it, about ten degrees wide and stretching halfway to the Milky Way. For the first time I understood the fascination and furor that historically had attended the spectacle. I stared for a long time before my reverie was interrupted by a too-familiar voice that sent a shudder through my soul.

"I'm proud that the good Lord has honored us with the privilege of witnessing the Judgment Day. No one can deny that His prophecies are being fulfilled."

My mother was standing next to Lily Barkley, and her voice carried over the low buzz of the group. Mama had never mastered the intricacies of the whisper.

Mrs. Barkley concurred. "That Japanese tidal wave wiped out whole cities, and the plague in Africa has killed millions . . ." Lily cited other examples of global devastation, but her voice was too soft for me to pick up. I didn't dare move any closer for fear of being discovered.

Mama had no problem with amplification. "The heathen will be the first to go," she agreed, "but God only knows how many people it will kill before it leaves."

"Oh, yes, brothers and sisters—"

At the first sound of Brother Nicholas's voice, I fled the scene, shaken by the experience. Brother Nicholas didn't impress me—at least I wasn't ready to admit that he did—but it was impossible to deny the power of that glorious and horrible vision that hung like a scimitar over the earth. Even more troubling was my mother's presence, once again with the Scarlet Lily, at a convocation of Nicholas's most faithful. I had not mentioned seeing her at the True Vine Church, and she had said not a word about joining the Brother's movement. She had, however, been conspicuously vague about the church meetings she was attending at peculiar hours. The realization that my mother had been slipping out of the house while I slept was so disconcerting that I stopped briefly in the street to consider the irony. The issue was too puzzling, the stakes too high, for us to avoid talking about them. I could see a showdown looming, but it was neither my place nor inclination to call her out. The best I could hope for was that by avoiding the subject a while longer, things might straighten themselves out.

In bed I tried to conjure up serene memories of baseballs run down and caught, sunny afternoons basking on riverbanks, a horseback ride through summer rain—the reassuring memories and fantasies that often led me into the whirlpool of unconcern and disconnected thought that induced sleep. My attempts to summon reverie were smothered under a cloud of amorphous fear, and my sleep was fitful and wracked with dreams of death and destruction.

I woke up early, sore and tired, and eager to quit the bed that had betrayed me. While Mama slept, I ate two boiled eggs and cold biscuits with molasses, then struck off toward the office. It was my habit to stop by before school to have a cup of coffee and talk over the news. After last night's ordeal, I considered passing it up, but I enjoyed the ritual of reading Barkley's paper cover to cover and lambasting every paragraph.

The office was dark inside, so I sat down on the sidewalk and unrolled the *High Plains Citizen-Advocate*. Sam had originally chosen to print *Plain Talk* on Monday since Barkley's rag had always taken that day off. Two weeks after Sam's debut issue, Barkley introduced his Monday edition "at no extra cost to subscribers." The Monday *Advocate* was, for all intents and purposes, a weekly newspaper. "In this way," Barkley editorialized, he "offered the reader both a daily and a weekly newspaper, and never a day need dawn when a High Plains citizen would be deprived of the privilege of reading a *first-rate* newspaper."

Barkley's lead was another piece on the possibility of luring another railroad line into town. He ran one of these every few weeks to keep the issue alive. The latest candidate was the New Mexico Railroad Company, which was "optimistic" about running a spur down to us. Fat chance. Amarillo was fast cornering the market on tracks running through the Panhandle, and everybody save Barkley freely admitted it.

Nicholas's numbers prophecy took up a good bit of page two. It was a fairly straightforward listing of all the calculations, but you could see from the slant that Barkley was backing away from his sponsorship of the True Vine preacher. The evangelist was great copy, and many people bought a paper just to see what he was up to, but as his message became more strident even Barkley recognized the threat to the town's reputation.

My eye was drawn to a familiar name above an obituary on page three. With sinking heart I read the article that I knew would grieve Sam Adams. I was halfway through it when the office door opened.

"Morning, Tom. I didn't think I'd be seeing you for a while." His voice was friendly. "Did you get any sleep?"

"Not much," I said. "Got some bad news in here."

Passing him the paper, I pointed to the article titled "Mark Twain Dead."

Sam let out a long, sad breath. "He said he'd die when Halley's was in the sky."

As he read silently, Sam's sadness shifted swiftly to anger. " 'Sprightly old gentleman known principally as a writer of juvenile fiction.' Bullshit! Who wrote this? Some old maid schoolteacher?"

He didn't wait for an answer.

"Can you skip school today?".

"Maybe." Depended on the proposition.

"Good. Break down page one—"

Sam's order fell on me like a load of hogs. "Again?"

"Lose that 'Panhandle Spring' thing. Reset the sewage article—we'll run it in two parts—and leave me three full columns for an obituary."

I could see that this meant a whole lot to him, or I would have told him to go straight to hell. When I didn't follow him into the office, he walked back outside and sat down on the sidewalk.

"Tom," he said, looking me square in the eye. "I understand how crazy and tiresome this must seem to you, but this paper is my life. If I do it any way other than the very best way I possibly can, then I'm betraying everything I believe in, and I'm cheating myself and everyone who knows me or reads the paper.

"I admit that I wasted a lot of our time yesterday, and I'll promise that never again will I put you to work on something I don't think is right. I'll try to make that up to you somehow.

"I understand if you want to take today off. You surely deserve it." He squeezed my shoulder and then walked into the office.

I sat for a few minutes cussing myself for not going straight to school and avoiding this whole damn mess. I walked around, sat outside Hayes's store and threw rocks at a passing dog, all the while considering my options. It took me a good fifteen minutes to figure out that I had none. I'm not sure that anyone ever does.

When I walked into the office, Rebekah rushed quickly past me. She looked neither right nor left and didn't acknowledge my "Good morning."

"What's eatin' her?" I asked Sam.

A shrug was his only reply. I started breaking down the front page knowing that I had received all the explanation, apology, or gratitude that I was likely to get that day. In the last few weeks—ever since the election—Sam's mood had paralleled the declining fortunes of his paper. He never got angry or abusive; he just worked harder. And when Sam was working full bore, he had a tendency to forget that not everyone craved labor sixteen hours a day, seven days a week. Sometimes hours would pass in the office with Sam taking no notice of Rebekah or me, other than to parcel out work to us. The only relaxed breath I had seen him draw lately was during the baseball game, and that lasted only as long as he was on the field. The moment he crossed the foul lines, he was tight as a clinched fist again.

It took us until mid-afternoon to reset the front page. Rebekah came in around five o'clock with an armload of sewing and walked straight to the bedroom speaking not a word. Sam sent me over to Hayes's to buy some cheese and crackers and canned peaches for supper. That was our only break all day.

It was around nine o'clock before we finally got the newspaper to the street. I was exhausted and resentful. Sam paid me my fifty-cent weekly wage for the first time in a month. He thanked me and said that I didn't have to come in the next day if I didn't want to.

I sure as hell didn't.

Chapter Sixteen

"**T**here," Mama said, holding up a pair of pants with a patch on its seat wider than a hand's span. "Nobody'll ever notice it from the back of a bucking mule."

I shook my head in despair as I pulled on the scarred trousers. Almost everyone in school had a patch on some garment or another, but Mama would mend a piece of clothing until there was no trace of the original cloth. Her grim frugality had its roots in her family's, the Ikards, grueling trek from Georgia shortly after the Civil War. Mama, often holding her baby brother on her hip, had walked behind a loaded flatbed wagon driven by her mother all the way to Beaumont, Texas, subsisting on little more than bread, water, and whatever they could gather or kill on the way. The story had been related to me so often as reprimand that resentment had long since replaced sympathy. It took me many years and some hardship of my own before I garnered any real insight into my mother's temperament and thrift. As is so often the case, my understanding would come too late to afford solace for either of us.

I buttoned my pants with one hand and tried to finish my breakfast with the other to expedite my escape.

"Don't use your bread to sop up with, and don't you dare leave a drop of that milk. It hasn't been that long since we've been able to get fresh milk." Mama tossed off orders like a drill sergeant as she padded around the kitchen in her old robe and slippers. She sewed for a living (*Stitches Fine as Fairy Fingers*, promised the sign on our front door), but never considered spending ten minutes to mend her tattered housecoat. I figured it was part of her penance.

144

"And don't forget to empty the ashes from the stove if you expect me to cook your supper tonight."

Her instructions slid off me like rain off a pitched tin roof. When she walked out of the kitchen, I took my best shot at a getaway. I wrapped the egg jerky in a piece of butcher paper, figuring I could chew on it all day for nourishment and diversion. I had one foot out the door when she nailed me.

"Thomas!"

I froze—only a door slam from freedom.

"It's time we had a talk," she said, with a finality I could not defy. The accepted rule of order in our house was that I could slip around any regulation or prohibition short of a direct command, but when confronted head-on, I had no choice but to stand and deliver. She summoned me into enemy territory.

The front room was Mama's domain. She did her sewing there, surrounded by as many as five or six Bowery dowagers—depending upon who was nursing a running grudge against whom that particular day. All those middle-aged women shared a common problem: each was trapped on the wrong side of town with insufficient means to escape to the respectability that a New Town address would confer. In retribution, they took great pleasure in vilifying the notables of High Plains. I rarely glanced into the room, for fear of finding mixed puddles of blood, snuff, and venom collected around the legs of the chairs.

The room was pin neat and white-glove clean in a part of the country where dust was as common as air; Mama kept a handkerchief tucked into her left sleeve and wiped everything within reach whenever she moved from her chair. The wood floor was bare and had paled to gray from hundreds of hours of Mama's stooped familiarity.

An Aryan cross-carrying Jesus appealed for mercy from a faded old painting on the wall. The gilt-framed photograph of my father in his Rough Rider uniform stared, severe and unblinking, from a corner table that he shared with a Sears Roebuck catalogue and a tattered copy of John Bunyan's *Pilgrim's Progress from This World to That Which Is to Come*. A couch and two chairs formed a semicircle around Mama's rocking-chair throne. At her right hand an end table supported a kerosene lamp and an over-worked King James Bible.

I avoided the parlor, feeling I could do nothing there but disrupt. I entered and left the house through the kitchen and confined my home activities to eating, sleeping, and bathing—the last every Wednesday and Saturday night.

Mama assumed her inquisitor's position, and I pulled one of the stiff-back chairs around to where I was almost facing her. She motioned for me to straighten my chair up and pull closer. I moved it a degree nearer center and about an inch and a half closer. I was determined not to submit to the morbidity that Mama had assumed like a sackcloth shroud the moment we entered the room. A speedy escape was my only hope.

"I'm sure you're aware of what's going on in this town"—Mama searched for words on the ceiling—"and in the world."

I nodded to speed things up.

"It seems that the time has come when great changes will come about that will"—she referred to the ceiling again—"change everything."

Good Lord, get on with it. "Are you talking about the end of the world?" I asked.

She sighed with relief to have it out. "Yes. And I believe that it's time for you to make a commitment. We don't know exactly how much time we have before the . . . change comes, but it could be any time, so—"

"I thought Nicholas said it was going to be the night that we passed through the tail of the comet."

"*Brother* Nicholas believes that is the correct date, but there's no way that anyone can know for sure. It could be sooner, so that makes your commitment even more important."

"What commitment?"

"You need to start coming to church with me, and spend more time getting ready. . . ."

"Ready for the world to end?"

"Yes."

Let's get this out and over with. I groped desperately for a loophole.

"You had me baptized, didn't you? When I was a kid?"

"I most certainly did! You were baptized twice."

I resisted asking why it took a double dunking, for fear of clouding the waters and prolonging the agony. "That covers me, don't it? Once you're baptized, you're cleared, aren't you? Unless you kill somebody, or . . ." I reached for another commandment that I could deny. After rejecting several outright, the one that sprang to mind was the one all us boys used to laugh at: ". . . or covet your neighbor's ox or ass."

Mama shook her head wearily. "That's not enough, Tom. You have to keep *all* the commandments, and truly repent your sins, and only then can you be born again. If you don't . . . I shudder to think."

She was so sad and serious it was beginning to get to me. Rather than be dragged into the pit of despair I struck back.

"Not everybody believes this end of the world stuff, anyway. A lot of people think ol' Brother Nicholas is just a crackpot preacher trying to make a big name for himself."

Mama's back stiffened and her eyes widened to the size of mule shoes.

"People like Mr. Sam Adams, I suppose you're referring to."

"Sam's one of 'em, but lots of people think this stuff is a bunch of hooey. Most of the town is laughing behind your back—"

"Thomas!" Her voice was a mixture of anger and desperation. Mama took a deep breath. She leaned forward and spoke in a slow, steady voice. "I know this is hard for you to understand, son. It's very important that you try, for my sake. If Reverend Nicholas is right—and *all the signs* indicate that he is—then you are risking an eternity in Hell if you continue on the path you're walking now. If Reverend Nicholas is wrong, and you live a good life for the next month or so, you haven't lost anything except maybe a few sinful indulgences that would only make you feel guilty anyway."

The way Mama laid it out there, it didn't sound like such a bad deal. Maybe we could strike some sort of bargain that would ease her mind without turning me into a holy roller. I'll confess that reassuring my mother wasn't my only motive for hedging my religious bets. There had been times, usually when I woke up real early in the morning, when I'd feel so lonely and empty that Nicholas's predictions no longer seemed the laughable ramblings of a deluded prophet. In the fragile stillness before dawn, terrifying images of Nicholas's Armageddon would merge with the manifold anxieties of adolescence and feast on my skinny, naked form. Then the end of the world seemed as inevitable as the screaming preacher claimed. My fears would fade with the morning light and street sounds, but a residue of dread was always left as seed.

"What exactly would it take to save my soul?" I asked.

Mama's eyes brightened. "It wouldn't be hard, Tom. You'd have to give up a few things like tobacco, and those awful flicker pictures."

I could handle that. I'd pretty much sworn off tobacco when I saw Rebekah Adams's reaction to my chewing, and I hadn't been to the movie house since they patched up the hole in the back wall where I used to sneak in. Newspaper wages had a way of enforcing virtue as well; vice cost money.

"Of course," she continued, "you'd have to spend more time at home reading the Bible, and you'd have to go to church with me. It's very important that you spend as much time as possible with the Lord's word in these last days."

"How about if I just go to the outdoor meetings. They're not quite so ... wrought up." Brother Nicholas's services were fast outstripping the Southern Baptists for zealousness. Talking in tongues and spontaneous dancing can be entertaining when viewed from a distance, but it made me damned uncomfortable to be shut up in the same room with it. I figured Sam would be covering most of the outside gatherings anyway, so they'd be relatively painless.

"You can begin with our open air meetings," Mama conceded, "but I'm sure that very shortly you will open your heart, and gladly attend our Sunday services."

Not likely. I stood to leave, spieling like a carnival barker. "I'm glad we had this talk, Mama, it's done me a world of good, but we've got a big test at school today, and I'd like to get there early so as to—"

She pointed a stern finger at the chair. I sat down.

"The path to Heaven is not so easy, Tom. You're going to have to make a few sacrifices and change some of your . . . associations."

"What do you mean?" The only association I knew of was the Cattlemen's, and I wasn't a member.

Mama chose her words carefully. "Reverend Nicholas has compiled a list of people who are harmful to the town. Their influence could stop a number of people from joining our cause. And many innocent people will be robbed of their chance at salvation."

Mama took a deep breath and leaned back in her chair. I resisted the urge to thumb through the Sears catalogue at my right hand and tried to look as serious as she did. I knew what was coming.

"Sam Adams is at the very top of that list," she finished grimly.

Raising her hands in front of her, she shook her head as if to repel the protest that I had no intention of making. I was quite familiar with her opinion of Sam and his newspaper, and attempting to change it would be as senseless as arguing with a mop. Besides, after the last couple days of sweatshop labor, I wasn't eager to champion Sam's cause.

"I realize," she said, wringing her hands in her lap, "that you've spent a great deal of time and effort learning the journalism trade, but I truly believe, Tom, that your immortal soul is in grave danger as long as you spend time with that man. It pains me to say so. . . ."

It clearly did; she was distraught. My stomach began to churn.

"I have the highest regard for his wife, as fine a Christian woman as I know, and I'm willing to believe that Sam Adams does what he does without understanding that it is the Devil's work. In the end it doesn't matter. His soul is bound for Hell."

She grabbed my hand and pressed her face to within

inches of mine. She whispered urgently, "Thomas, you are the only thing in this world that matters to me. Promise me that you won't let Sam Adams drag you to Hell with him."

At that moment, staring into her watery gray eyes, I remembered all those icy winter mornings when she brought hot food to my bed so that I wouldn't have to walk the frigid floors; the all-night vigils she'd spent rocking me when I had the croup; the thousand times that I could have made her heart soar by saying simply, "I love you, Mama." But I had never said it. I could make all this up to her now.

"I promise, Mama."

Chapter
Seventeen

I stumbled from the house still dazed by my conversion. Religious ecstasy wasn't entirely to blame for my confusion, as Mama had hugged me so tight that I thought ribs were going to crack before I finally wrenched free with excuses about school and tests.

The bright spring day introduced a flood of doubt over the promises that I had just made. Some, like the half oath to avoid Sam Adams and the newspaper office, I had no intention of keeping (I'd promised that I would not let him drag me to Hell, not that I wouldn't see him); others like the commitment to lead a "better" life, I was serious about, but unsure where to begin or what it might entail. One thing was apparent from the outset: I was going to have to live two separate lives. Mama must be kept blissfully unaware of my work with Sam, and the editor need not be apprised of my newfound orthodoxy. The beatific relief that is supposed to follow acceptance of the Way and the Light was sorely missing from my experience; all I could see were the complications and duplicity that I had introduced into a life that was already too perplexing by half.

I was nearly to school before I regained my mental bearings. I retreated, stashed my books at Hayes's store and set off for Langston Harper's house. After the way the day had started, I needed a charge of Langston to straighten it out.

The lawyer had built his house equidistant from the Bowery and New Town and to the west of both. Recognized as the best defense lawyer north of Dallas, Langston could make a living anywhere he chose to locate. Amarillo would have been the obvious choice, it being the largest, most prosperous city around, and even Wishbone offered a larger population and a more varied court docket than High Plains. But Langston liked what he called the "ambiance" of the Bowery and chose to settle within stumbling distance of it.

Since Langston spent only about half the year in his house, usually in four- or five-day stretches, the upkeep was left to Shad and Shad's daughter, Mary. The old man kept the house and yard, stable and tack in good repair, and the horses fed, while Mary cooked and cleaned inside. Neither job was taxing, and both father and daughter were paid well. The lawyer was as generous with his wages as he was with his affection, liquor, and opinions.

When I arrived, Shad was tending Langston's vegetable garden with buckets of water that he had carried from the well. The plot looked better than most, but needed, in Shad's words, "a three-day soaking rain" instead of well water to bring it around. We talked for a couple minutes about Langston and Sam and the weather. I believe that was the first time Shad and I ever spoke to each other for any reason other than to pass necessary information.

I knocked once then walked through the front door— folks rarely locked doors in High Plains and burglary was unheard of. Langston was sitting at the kitchen table drinking coffee and reading *Plain Talk*. He looked a little rocky, but that was not unusual; mornings were tough on Langston.

"Good article on Mark Twain," the lawyer said as Mary poured me a cup of coffee. "I know it must have pained Sam to write it."

"It pained me every bit as much," I said, then related the circumstances of the last two gruesome days at the newspaper.

Langston chuckled in sympathy. "It is your blessing and curse, Tom, to suffer employment under a man of principle. You never knew how easy you had it when you worked for a lawyer."

As Mary warmed his coffee, Langston recalled his first buggy ride with Sam following the Gem Scott case. "I figured Sam Adams would bust a gut to avoid an argument. Now it looks as though he wants to take on every scoundrel in the territory and half the crowd that shows up to watch the fight. I've never seen anyone offend so many people, so fast, just by telling the truth."

"Nothin' like a good pistol-whippin' by Texas Rangers to change your editorial policy," I said.

Mary wanted to finish cleaning, so she wordlessly maneuvered us out of the kitchen. Mary rarely spoke, but there was no question as to her influence in the house. She was invisible but omnipresent.

"Why aren't you in school today?" Langston always asked, but he would accept any answer I cared to give.

"Good behavior time. Got any work for me?"

"I think I can keep you busy for the better part of the day."

I delivered some papers to the courthouse and picked up some others at the sheriff's office. Messages needed to be dispatched from the Western Union and a couple days worth of mail waited at the post office. I was always amazed at the amount of paper that flowed through the lawyer's hands. There were always three or four piles stacked on Langston's desk.

After Mary cooked us a good lunch, Langston took his nap, leaving me free run of his library. As always, I spent a few minutes admiring the intricate ship in a bottle that testified to Langston's dexterity before booze had gained ascendency over his nervous system. The *Sea Witch* was a three-masted nineteenth-century clipper ship that could make the trip from New York to San Francisco in a little more than three months—record time until surpassed by the inelegant but brutally efficient steamships. Langston, who spoke sadly of the passing of the schooner, had passed on to me the dream of skimming the water under a flying cloud of sail, undistracted by the clang and moan of metal on metal. But the clipper ship, like the buffalo, was a long time gone.

I selected *Treasure Island* from the wall of catalogued books. I'd started it about three months back, but the newspaper left me little time to indulge in fiction. I would have taken it home, but Langston didn't lend out his books. Sam, on the other hand, practically twisted your arm to take his.

Langston's books were like new, while Sam's were ragged and sometimes lacked a crucial page.

About two o'clock Langston sent me out to help Shad in the barn. At three-thirty the lawyer tossed me a fifty-cent piece and gave me the rest of the day off. He thanked me for my hard work and offered me a ride to Nicholas's revival that night. I accepted. Since I had promised Mama that I would go, I figured I might as well go in style.

As I walked back to the Bowery flipping my half dollar, I pondered the fact that it had taken me three weeks to earn that amount at the newspaper. I couldn't help but marvel at the disparity between journalism and law. It had lately been on my mind.

Langston worked pretty much when he wanted to, and would take off weeks at a time when the mood struck him; Sam worked fourteen to sixteen hours a day, six and a half to seven days a week—he sometimes took off Monday evening if we got the paper out early.

The lawyer never lifted anything heavier than a fountain pen or law book and rarely allowed the seat of his overstuffed chair to grow cold; the editor wrestled with heavy machinery and spent the shank of every day chasing news and advertising.

The lawyer accepted generous commission from whomever agreed to his fee, only occasionally considering guilt or innocence, vice or virtue; the editor weighed every issue for fairness and would not countenance printing a word of news or editorial that he did not believe to be true and just. Sam cut no corners.

And, crucially, Langston led a dissolute life and enjoyed the respect, at least publicly, of virtually the entire town; Sam led an exemplary life and was castigated by nearly all who considered themselves respectable.

Once I had grown out of my dreams of being a cowboy, an Indian fighter, or a train engineer, I settled, through the influence of Langston, on lawyer. I'd only taken up with the newspaper to spend time around Rebekah Adams, but that pretext was gone now. Although I thought regularly about quitting the paper, and complained about it constantly, I kept showing up for work. I liked the excitement

of being involved with everything that happened in town
and the feeling that it was all my bailiwick. Even at that
tender age, I felt the stirrings of the bedrock emotion common to reporters: the feeling that the exposure of wrongdo-
ing or misfortune holds within it the key to righting it.
There were lots of things that I would change about it—the
pay and hours being foremost—but journalism was fast
seeping into my blood.

Langston picked up Sam and me at the newspaper office
and ferried us the several hundred yards to Brother Nicholas's revival meeting. The evangelist had set up his platform
between New Town and the Bowery to encourage attendance from both camps, and shrewdly scheduled his
meetings for Tuesdays and Fridays to avoid conflict with
traditional Sunday and Wednesday night services at established churches. Of course, no night was devoid of some
church activity, but Nicholas wasn't really concerned with
trampling a Campbellite choir practice or a Methodist Missionary Society. It would not be long before all the
churches were adjusting their schedules around Nicholas's
meetings.

"The louder he shouts 'Apocalypse,' " Sam explained to
Langston, "the faster people flock to him. The crowds grow
bigger and crazier, and that reinforces Nick's belief that his
prophecy is inspired and inevitable. It's a vicious circle that
I can't see breaking down till the whole shootin' match
blows up in his face, May nineteenth."

"May eighteenth," I corrected.

"Ol' Nick won't be around for that," Langston objected.
"He'll have his mammon and be gone. I've never heard of
one of these guys hanging around for the 'Grand Finale.' "

Sam shook his head. "If it's money he's after, I sure wish
he'd get to it. It would make it a lot easier to get a handle
on this whole sorry business."

It was windy, cool, and dusty as we neared the revival
site. About fifty yards off and headed our way, Gem Scott
was riding his old swayback mule toward the "Reservation," the black settlement that housed the mortal remnants

of a failed cotton-growing experiment some ten years back. Langston guided our carriage so that our paths intersected.

"Howdy Mistah Langston, Mistah Sam, Mistah Tom," Gem said, pulling his mule to a stop.

"Evening, Gem," Langston said. "You going to pass up the big party?"

Gem eyed the revival, then nodded toward the setting sun. "No time. 'Sides, I got to get these home for my suppertime." He reached into the burlap bag that was slung across his mule's back and pulled out a stringer with four stunted sunfish.

Langston and Sam nodded encouragingly at the meager catch. Gem wasn't proud of it, though.

"I had a devil of a time finding a hole deep enough to wet my hook. It don't rain soon, I 'spect the fish gwan have to learn to swim in sand."

We all shook our heads in despair. Darkness was falling, and Gem was anxious to get home. There was an unwritten law in High Plains that colored people weren't allowed out after dark. They couldn't be jailed for it, but the law showed a marked lack of concern about any harm that might befall a Negro so foolhardy or improvident as to be wandering around at night. Shad was the only exception to this stricture; he had walked this land well before streets were laid out, and no one in town had the guts to tell him to stop.

"You reckon there's anythin' to talk about that star fallin' on us?" Gem asked.

"Not a snowball's chance in Hell, Gem," Sam reassured him. "You tell all your folks there's nothing to worry about. It's just white folk's foolishness."

Gem nodded but didn't look much relieved. He nudged his mule then thought better of it. "Mistah Langston, I ain't forgot our 'greement. I'll take care of it straightway."

Langston looked puzzled for a moment before recalling his settlement after Gem's trial. "Don't fret about it, Gem," the lawyer said. "Just be damned careful when you decide to settle up."

"I jes be waitin' for the right time," Gem said knowingly.

Langston laid the reins lightly on the horse's back. "I've

always been fond of fried chicken for Sunday dinner," he
said, and winked at Gem.

As carriage and mule went their separate ways, I would
have bet that none of the four witnesses to the conversation
gave it a second thought. Sam and I knew it was none of
our business, Langston had weightier matters to consider,
and for Gem that type of transaction was a way of life. He
was no more inclined to analyze the morality or ramifica-
tions of his act than a fox or a hawk might. With the end
of the world being trumpeted from pulpit and street corner,
just how important could a twenty-five-cent chicken be?

> *"When the roll is called up yonder,*
> *When the roll is called up yonder,*
> *When the roll is called up ya-han-der,*
> *When the roll is called up yonder*
> *I'll be there!"*

While the crowd was somewhat larger than either Sam or
I had expected, Langston was overwhelmed by the size and
tenor of the gathering. In the two weeks since the lawyer
had last taken measure of the movement, it had doubled in
size and multiplied geometrically in fervor. Nicholas was
pulling in converts from neighboring towns and across
county lines. Since the drought had brought farming and
ranching to a grinding halt, people with time and despair on
their hands found the Comet Revival a natural outlet. Nicholas's "Numbers Sermon" had been awarded front-page
coverage by several Panhandle newspapers, thus conferring
a legitimacy upon the revivalist and his theory that angered
the more conservative elements of High Plains and surrounding territory.

As Langston tied his horse to a mesquite tree, I walked
off on my own to survey the situation. The speaker's platform was probably smaller than the one used for the temperance rallies, but it looked bigger since there was not a
soul or a stick of furniture on it. The only adornments were
the four unlit torches tied to the corner posts, and the banner heralding BROTHER NICHOLAS'S COMET REVIVAL suspended about ten feet above the stage. In front of the

platform two benches had been pushed together so Nicholas's right-hand man, Old Baldy Guthridge, could lead the crowd in hymn. There were no accompanying instruments to offer distraction, or melody, to the singers.

After considerable searching, I spotted Mama off to the right of the platform and about a third of the way back into the crowd. She was standing with Mrs. Lily Barkley. When I finally managed to forge my way through the dense crowd to her side, she embraced me as though I were a child rescued from the grave. After wresting free, I lied about my whereabouts all day and apologized for not walking to the rally with her. She was eager to believe my lies and forgive my sins. We shared a verse of "Beulah Land," and she beamed with pride down on my undeserving form. Lily Barkley, sharing Mama's elation at my redemption, smiled benignly and patted my head.

I felt like a miserable faker.

After Old Baldy made some introductory remarks in a voice so high and squeaky that it confused the bullbats that were chasing insects drawn to the torchlight, I told Mama that I wanted to move toward the platform so I could be closer to the message. I could see that she would rather have me standing tall at her side, but I couldn't bear to prolong the deception.

As I pushed my way through the crowd, I picked up a copy of a printed circular that Nicholas's flunkies were handing out. The preacher had obviously been cheered by the effect of his "numbers" handout, since every sermon thereafter was accompanied by printed matter. It apparently added credibility and gave the crowd something concrete to take home and discuss. I scanned the handbill as I stood on the front row. On the right half of the sheet there were biblical references to stars and comets; the left hand held "scientific" warnings gleaned from various periodicals of dubious veracity.

The crowd released a long sigh as Nicholas assumed the stage. He wore the same rumpled, black suit he had worn when he walked off the train several months earlier, but now the suit looked better than the man inside. The preacher was tired, pale, and cadaverously thin; he had dropped weight from a frame that couldn't spare an ounce. The large black eyes that had frozen me that first night at the railroad station were still alert and piercing, but they stared out of deep, dark sockets that looked like two burn holes in a blanket. Only his voice remained vibrant.

While Nicholas greeted the "brothers and sisters," reminding us all that "time is short and the day is nigh," I made my way back to the camp of the infidels; the front row of a doomsday convention was standing too close to wildfire for me. Even along the outer fringe of the crowd Nicholas's voice rang like a chapel bell.

"Tonight I will supplement our scriptural evidence with a magazine article by a noted professor of astronomy at one of our nation's most prestigious universities. Dr. J. P. Conley of the Hoover Institute of Law and Economics has outlined the scientific evidence that convinced him that Halley's Comet will destroy the Earth."

A voice from the crowd took advantage of Nicholas's brief pause. "How come hit never destroyed us before? Hit's been comin' aroun' for better'n a thousand years."

The crowd growled in unison and moved in menacingly around the heckler. Nicholas raised his hand in restraint. "As Professor Conley points out, *sir*, this is the *first* time that the Earth will pass *through* the tail of the comet. The tail of Halley's Comet consists of poisonous cyanogen gas. Cyanogen gas, when combined with hydrogen—which is in the very air we breathe—cyanogen and hydrogen form *prussic acid*. A single drop of prussic acid placed on the tongue of a whale will kill it instantly! Prussic acid will fall from the sky like rain!

"That is only one of the ghastly tortures that await the unrepented on that very last day. When the cyanogen gas unites with the nitrogen—also contained in the earth's air—cyanogen and nitrogen form *laughing gas*. As you are being pelted by rain that will strip the hide from your bones, you will be dancing deliriously, laughing and crying."

As the gape-mouthed crowd shuddered at this prospect, Nicholas proceeded to outline Dr. Conley's argument as capsulized on the handout. The preacher reeled off several other equally deadly by-products (explosive hydrogen, reversal of magnetic poles, impact of countless meteorites), all certain and fatal manifestations of the comet's visit. He linked these "scientific" findings with appropriate Bible passages to mold an argument that was cogent, persuasive, and—

"Horseshit!" snorted Langston Harper as we rolled back toward the Bowery. The sheer volume of nonsense provoked as strong a reaction as I'd ever seen the lawyer display. "Pseudoscience and quasireligion! The next time I'm in Dallas, I think I'll put out some tracers on ol' Nick. It wouldn't surprise me if the little fellow was trailing some very interesting history behind him."

Chapter
Eighteen

Mama sounded fresh and chirpy Thursday morning, when she woke me, so I knew something was up. Quick as I got my clothes on she directed me outside to take a look at the sky. Way off to the north a solid bank of black clouds was massed and rolling straight toward High Plains. I nearly whooped in delight. It was our best shot at a decent rain in months, and from the look of those angry clouds it could be a gully-washer, a real frog-strangler.

The rain clouds that followed me to school looked like a huge wave building, ready to crash on the parched earth and wash away six months of dust. The wind had picked up, and you could feel the moisture in the air sticking to your skin like honey. Gleefully, I swung the half-gallon Mammy's Cane Syrup can containing my lunch in wide circles, releasing it high into the air and catching it before it hit the ground.

All through the morning's lessons the kids were excited and kept chattering and staring out the only window in the room, waiting for the downpour. Mrs. Hardy got disgusted with us and let us out for recess early. I shot some marbles and tossed baseball, all the time keeping one eye on the sky. In the distance lightning flashed and thunder rolled from the northwest, promising a storm, O Lordy, what a storm.

I was eating lunch out by the swings when the first drops fell. The rain was so gentle and welcome that the girls didn't even run for cover. I stood up so quickly I dropped my ham biscuit in the dirt, but I didn't mind. The feel and smell of rain was so sweet, I wasn't hungry. The thunder and lightning drew closer, and we all braced for a deluge.

The "rainstorm" lasted less than fifteen minutes and amounted to about half a teacup of water. It didn't even settle the dust. We all stood staring up into the treacherous sky as the rain clouds skirted High Plains and blew off to parts obscure—probably to Wishbone, damn their eyes. When the sun broke through, hot and angry, the playground turned mean. Within ten minutes four fistfights had broken out; the girls even did some hair-pulling. The principal cut lunch short to staunch the mayhem.

The rest of the day was miserable. The students were sassy, and Mrs. Hardy resorted frequently to the paddle. I got my fair share of licks and was assigned the punishment of filling the coal and water buckets every morning for a week. I spent most of the afternoon warming the dunce bench and thinking about that ham biscuit lying out on the playground, or, more likely, resting in some mangy dog's belly. My stomach growled for an hour before the final bell rang.

Usually I headed straight to the newspaper office after school, but not that day. Mama had baked a cobbler from some peaches that she had put by last summer, and it had been hollering to me all afternoon.

I snuck in the back door, soundlessly. Out in the front room the conversation rolled on, unaware of the alien in the kitchen. I suppose I'd always had a weakness for eavesdropping, but lately the rewards for indulging my curiosity had risen; a Nicholas-inspired snuff ban at our house had rendered the tenor of discussion increasingly waspish, and, consequently, entertaining. As I crept to the pie cabinet, I sorted out the voices.

Gertie Fox speculated that Lily Barkley had worn lipstick to Brother Nicholas's last meeting. Emma Bogan quickly seconded the rumor. Mama put a cap on the subject by stating flatly that Lily had denounced all blasphemous makeup and just had naturally red lips, or perhaps a rash. Once they had become partners in faith, Mama wouldn't let anyone lay a glove on Lily. Some of the older women occasionally forgot Mrs. Barkley's promotion, since she had been a favorite target of opportunity over the years. A momentary hush fell.

Silence being the only condition that everyone in the group distrusted, they fell back on a subject that they were all comfortable with: bad health and misery. As I scooped out a generous portion of peach cobbler, the conversation turned to the woefully inadequate health care offered in High Plains. Everyone had a favorite horror story.

"In March of 'ninety-five," Emma Bogan chirped, "my least boy came down with the whoopins cough, and there wasn't a doctor in the territory who could do a blessed thing in the world about it. Doc Reeves said prayer was all he could perscribe. I told him outright I didn't need no doctor to tell me that."

Gertie Fox concurred. "I'd as soon turn a child of mine over to an Indian medicine man as that old hacker."

"Dr. High-and-Mighty Rathbone won't even touch a child if it's sick," Clara Clark complained. "He makes enough money from sore throat gargles and nose drops that he don't have to worry about sick folks."

"And his wife uses a sewing *machine*," trumped Emma Bogan.

Mama wasn't about to be left out. "There isn't a doctor in this town I'd trust a child with since old Doc Moss took to the needle. When I brought Thomas through the diphtheria, I didn't get a bit of help from a doctor. I walked the floor with him for twelve days and nights till the fever broke. It was just mother's love and prayer that did it."

Gertie Fox brought the sad state of medicine in High Plains up to date.

"It's no better now. I heard yesterday that the Haig baby—you know she was a Thorpe from Deaf Smith County, married into them worthless Haigs from around Bramlett—that child has dysentery so bad they don't expect it to live. They lost one less than a year ago, you recall? Likely something in the water."

A new voice: "I'm sorry. Please excuse me. I just remembered something I have to . . ."

It was Rebekah Adams. I heard footsteps and mumbled words of understanding from the older women. A brief silence followed the shutting of the front door.

"Poor child," my mother said finally, "she's much too frail for this part of the country."

Rebekah's steps were quick and unsteady as she walked into the newspaper office. I had followed at a distance and made no attempt to catch up with her. Within seconds of her arrival, Sam hung the Out sign on the door and closed it. The sign wasn't meant for me, but I had no desire to intrude. Overhearing an argument while working was one thing; walking into a situation that I knew was sensitive, perhaps painful, was quite another.

I pulled a chair in front of the Lamour Hotel, avoiding the Raglars, who were cussing politicians and fickle cumulonimbus clouds across the street at Hayes's store. I needed time to think.

I was sure that at that very moment Rebekah must be pleading with Sam to take her away from a town that must have seemed to her, by turns, frivolous and absurd. My heart sank at the prospect. I'd been working hard to cut my emotional ties to Rebekah for the last month or so, to little avail. She was far and away the prettiest woman I had ever seen, and the kindest. Of course, I really didn't have much to compare her to. The girls at school were just silly, giggling kids. I'd had a crush on Callie for a while, but it didn't take long working at Derby's for her to lose the soft edge of her rural charm. Her brazenness scared me now, and I avoided talking to her. But Rebekah was both beautiful and sweet; she threatened no one, and sought only to comfort.

I knew my suit was futile, but my heart never failed to jump when Rebekah smiled at me. Still, I was working my way out of it. The hurt was slow fading, but it was fading.

Even as I attempted to make peace with unrequited love, I could see that Rebekah was growing more miserable by the day. When the Adamses had first come to High Plains, Rebekah tried hard to fit into the community. The local churches, with their preoccupation with personal salvation and social gathering, fulfilled few of the needs of the High Church–Good Works Episcopalianism she had left in Wichita. Rebekah made the rounds of social clubs the town offered, but I sensed that she found them little more than pretext for gossip sessions.

Forming relationships was tough since Sam's absorption with work left Rebekah a mate short in socializing with other young couples, and her lack of offspring deprived her of the preoccupation of most married women in town. The fact that her husband was castigated by pulpit and press and the object of vituperation by much of the "respectable" element in town further isolated her. When I looked back over the events of the last couple months—the temperance vote, the Rangers' mauling of Sam, Nicholas's Doomsday movement—it became apparent that High Plains had not smiled down on the Adamses with its most charming countenance.

Lately, Rebekah had begun to spend an increasing amount of time in her bedroom leafing through her photograph albums and reading the books that she'd brought in her trunk. Once, she had shown me the photographs of her father's house and grounds; hereabouts only Colonel Hedgman's estate could compare. Now she was forced to cook on a wood stove in a shanty of a house without running water or plumbing. She had given up home, family, comfort, and religion to marry a man who worked incessantly for unpopular causes in a desperate attempt to break even. Even Sam's lot was superior to Rebekah's: he had Rebekah and his work; Rebekah had only what was left of Sam after a sixteen-hour work day.

After an hour's wait the Out sign remained untouched, and I abandoned my vigil. Sam had loaned me a dog-eared copy of *A Connecticut Yankee in King Arthur's Court* that I wanted to finish. If I told Mama that I was going to read my Bible in my room, she wouldn't bother me.

Chapter
Nineteen

On Sunday mornings I always tried to be out of the house before my mother got up. If I lingered in bed too long, there was no way around a long and wearisome battle over church attendance. This ritual had gone on for years but had peaked since the arrival of Brother Nicholas. I climbed out of bed and pulled on my "everyday" clothes in the hope that I might be able to sneak or brazen my way out of the house. I knew that my chances of avoiding That Old Time Religion today were slim, but I had to try. The rattle of pans in the kitchen crushed all hope of flight, and my heart sank as I recalled that the High Plains versus Wishbone baseball game was to commence at high noon.

Nodding to Mama, I sat down at the kitchen table to eat my breakfast. While I sifted through possible plans for avoiding Nicholas's ordeal by sermon, I went to work on my fatback, eggs, biscuits, and gravy. I was making sparks with my knife and fork when I noticed the clatter of Mama's spoon inside her coffee cup. She had been stirring her coffee and staring at the wall ever since I'd sat down.

"You all right?" I grunted between mouthfuls. One of the few things we shared was a hearty appetite. Mama was an indifferent cook, but luckily it was years before I discovered the fact. We would both normally eat anything put in front of us. However, this morning she hadn't even dulled her knife on her egg.

"Oh, yes," she said, lowering her eyes to her plate. She laid her spoon down and raised the cup to her lips. "I was just letting it cool off."

I poured myself another cup of coffee. Mama's attempts to give it up for the church had proved futile. Snuff had been proscribed from the premises, but caffeine had prevailed. Coffee was cheaper than anything else you could drink except water, and the well we shared with two other families was about played out. It was all you could do to choke down a mouthful of straight water from that sinkhole.

I was mulling over my next line of attack when Mama spoke up. She began slowly. "I'm not feeling so well today, and I'm not sure that I'm going to be able to make it to the eleven o'clock service. I don't want to put you in a position of promising to go alone when you might have trouble keeping that promise."

Well-spoken.

"So, if you assure me that you will accompany me to some of Reverend Nicholas's meetings next week, as well as the May eighteenth final meeting, you don't have to go to church this morning."

An eleventh-hour pardon from the governor! It was all I could do not to yell and run out the door. I harnessed my joy and kept a straight face and a level voice.

"If you think that's a good idea, Mama, I'll just wait for the outdoor meetings. I hear the Sunday services are so crowded that half the people have to stand up anyway."

I carried my plate to the sink. "Are you feeling real sick?"

"Oh, no," she was quick to reassure me. "Just a touch of the grippe. I'll be all right with a little rest."

I was out the door before she could change her mind. I hadn't walked far before an air of suspicion eclipsed my sense of relief. My victory had come so easily that it demanded scrutiny. I'd seen Mama go to church when she was so virulent that the bulk of the congregation had pleaded with her to go home; how could a little grippe stop her now with only eleven days till Armageddon? She had looked more preoccupied than sick anyway.

Maybe she just wanted a day off. She had attended a dizzying round of indoor services, outdoor rallies, and middle-of-the-night Comet Vigils for a solid month; perhaps the pace was wearing her down. With the all-out, pull-no-punches, final push starting the middle of next week, maybe she had just decided to avoid the crush of people who jammed into the storefront church on Sunday.

Not likely. I'd never known Mama to back away from a crowd—or anything else for that matter. Her behavior was puzzling, bordering on troubling. I couldn't see any way around sitting down and thinking about it for a minute or two.

I lowered myself to the sidewalk in front of Hayes's store and took stock of Mama's behavior over the past couple weeks. She had been like two different women. On the way to and from her spiritual duties and while in the company of other True Viners, she could entertain no thoughts other than those of Nicholas, the comet, and impending Armageddon. Rejecting morbidity and despair, Mama marched toward May 18 as a Christian general mobilizing manpower and matériel for a final, glorious assault. She brooked no doubt—often upbraiding her closest friend for innocent slips or honest questions—and entertained no possibility of prophetic errancy; her public posture of surety was exceeded only by that of the oracle himself.

When she was at home, Mama rarely spoke of the coming firestorm and ran her house as she always had: floors were scrubbed, meals were cooked, and garments sewed and mended. Conversations within the sewing circle still centered on minor scandal, pain and illness, and the indignities of life in the Bowery. I found it hard to reconcile the Old Campaigner who ceaselessly shouted "Apocalypse" with the woman who continued to save "for a rainy day," tend a feeble garden, and collect string.

While I was sorting through the contradictions, I saw Rebekah Adams walk up the sidewalk on the far side of the street. Although the Bowery was almost deserted, she didn't appear to notice me. When she started to cross, I decided to walk over to say hello.

"Morning, Miss Rebekah. You headed off to church?"

She jumped as though I had just laid the lash to her back. Her face was pale and her dark, puffy eyes looked as though a good night's sleep was a distant memory. Everyone in town seemed edgy and off feed—like a town full of suspects.

"Oh . . . good morning, Tom," she said. The only polite thing to do was to stop and talk, but her body continued to shimmer slightly, like a motor car idling high. "Later . . . I'm going to church later. I've got some errands to take care of first."

"Anything I can help you with?" I volunteered. I had some time on my hands and nothing much to do. If I went by the office, I figure Sam would have me throwin' in type right up to game time.

"No, no," she said quickly. "They're just some things I need to take care of . . . personally."

I tried to prolong the conversation. "Has Sam made his rounds in New Town this morning?"

"Yes, I believe so, Tom. He was running off proofs when I left. He looked like he could use some help."

No surprise there. I'd have liked to talk more, but Rebekah was edging away from me. "It was nice to see you, ma'am. I hope you have a good day at church."

"Thank you, Tom," she said, touching my cheek. "You're very sweet."

And then Rebekah Adams did the damnedest thing: right out in the middle of the street on the Sabbath morning, she hugged me, then kissed my cheek. She was gone before I could say anything, but I couldn't make any sense out of it.

Unable to fathom the strange behavior of either my mother or Miss Rebekah, I resorted to the solace of an old friend that had never failed or mystified me.

"Good mornin', Mr. Hayes," I said as I walked into his store. "I think I'll have a plug of Bull Durham."

Hayes's eyebrows rose at my request. Tobacco sales had fallen substantially in the last couple of weeks, and I was a known member of the sect that forbade the weed.

"It's for a friend," I said, tossing him a quarter. "You going to the game today?"

"No," he answered, handing me my change. "If I wanted to see people fighting, I coulda stayed home."

As I left the store, I scanned the streets for prying eyes before unwrapping my plug. Just as I was ready to bite off a chaw, I beheld a sight that multiplied my quandary. About fifty yards away, their backs toward me and walking stride for stride, my mother and Miss Rebekah Adams marched toward New Town. You could have knocked me over with a handful of dust. I walked directly to the newspaper office. Maybe Sam could offer some insight into these women.

"Beats the hell out of me," Sam admitted, pulling his ball glove and spikes out from behind the type case where they'd been stashed. "Maybe your mother just needed a slow, boring Methodist sermon to catch her breath. Nicholas has been selling doomsday so hard she probably wanted a little shelter from the storm.

"As for Rebekah," Sam continued, "your guess is as good as mine. We talked for two hours on Thursday, and I never did figure out what was really bothering her. She's become a mystery to me."

That was all I could get out of Sam on the subject. He wasn't the kind of man who talked about his feelings or his personal life. The worse things got—with the paper, the town, Rebekah—the less he had to say.

When we left the office, Sam was standing taller and walking faster than I had ever seen him. I was glad to see that he was pumped up for the game. He hadn't had much to feel good about lately.

"Tell me what you know about this Wishbone team," he said as we struck off toward the ballfield.

"Ain't much to know. They're big and ugly and mean as an outhouse full of rattlesnakes. Their big stick is a guy named Hoolihan. He played for the St. Louis Browns but couldn't stay off the hooch. Had a couple homers last year. They got a pitcher named Blackie can throw a baseball through a stone wall. They say he got tossed out of pro ball for gambling. He hit our first two batters, and we had a brawl lasted about fifteen minutes. They were beatin' us three to two in the seventh inning when a real knock-down-drag-out started. They fought for a solid hour before the umpires even tried to separate 'em. Neither team had enough players left fit to play so they called the game off."

Sam whistled between his teeth. "I suppose I ought to be thankful that the players don't carry guns."

"Don't worry," I reassured him. "The umpire searches everyone before the game."

Chapter
Twenty

The biggest crowd I'd ever seen turn out for a baseball game was gathered at the field. Spectators sat on the ground half a dozen deep along the foul lines and behind the backstop. Behind them, in relative comfort, were the fans who'd had the foresight to haul a chair or bench with them. Of course there were no women to inhibit or distract the warriors and witnesses.

The bulk of the crowd were Boweryites, out in force on a glorious Sunday in May. Some New Towners were sprinkled through the crowd, with more expected after church let out. Wishbone had carted along a substantial and profane contingent; they had staked out the better part of the first-base foul line behind their team's bench. I scrambled through the crowd on the third-base side and sat down in the front row between Doc Moss and Zack.

Each team provided one umpire. Both were big cusses who looked rough enough for the job. They huddled together briefly before announcing to teams and crowd that the game would be immediately suspended upon the first punch thrown by any player from either team. Some of the fans were indignant about this assault on the sacred warring code; a few of them decided that a baseball game without the possibility of a riot wasn't worth their time and they left. All in all, though, I think both teams and the heft of the crowd were relieved by the injunction. Now there was a chance that we might get to see a whole ball game, rather than five or six innings followed by a series of one-round fights.

Most of the Wishbone team were the crew from last year. Hoolihan still played first base and batted cleanup, and

Blackie still threw bullets from the mound. Over the winter, Blackie had developed a wicked sidearm curve that had our right-hand hitters bailing out on most any pitch on the inside half of the plate. I stood behind the backstop and eyeballed that pitch from the batter's vantage. Even with a hitter, a catcher, an umpire, and three layers of chicken wire between me and that sidearm curve, it was still damned scary. Blackie's pitch was even more effective since he didn't hesitate to mix in a chin-high inside fastball. If you waited for *that* pitch to break, you could wake up in the middle of next week wondering what your name was.

Once the game started, it was apparent that Sam was every bit as sharp as Blackie that day. Neither team got a man as far as third base in the first five innings, but with two out in the top of the sixth, the Boner center fielder (Swifty) hit a wicked grounder to shortstop that took a bad hop and nearly dehorned Rooster. Swifty was a demon on the base path and stole second on Sam's first pitch to Hoolihan. The Wishbone slugger fouled off a couple of curves before nailing a fast ball to left for a single. Dago came up with it cleanly and fired a bullet home to Big Mike. Ball and runner arrived within a heartbeat of each other. The crowd came instantly to its feet. The High Plains fans yelled "OUT!" with conviction and volume matched only by Wishbone's screams of "SAFE!"

When the dust cleared, the Wishbone umpire hesitated, apparently weighing the dangers of an unpopular call in hostile territory against the possibility of a lifetime as an outcast in his own town. Hearth and home carried the day.

"SAFE!"

Fights broke out along the first-base line, and the entire Skinner team and half the home team fans converged on the Wishbone umpire. I believe a full-fledged, eye-gouging, head-busting, blood-running-uphill donnybrook would have broken out if Derby hadn't thrust himself between the umpire and the raging horde. "Get your asses back on that field and play ball, goddamn it! It's my job to argue and yours to play goddamn baseball!" Derby railed. "We can still beat these cheatin' bastards!"

Big Mike was incensed at the call, but he lent his substantial bulk and influence to the manager's cause. Sam was behind the plate, backing up the throw from left field, and he planted himself in front of the quaking ump. Confronted with Derby's moral authority and the physical mass of the pitcher and catcher, the players and fans stopped in their tracks, then retreated. With order restored, Sam retired the side without further damage. Wishbone 1—Mule Skinners 0.

Blackie mowed us down in order in the bottom of the sixth, seventh, and eighth innings. The one-run lead loomed like a mountain in a land of pissants. Sam, meanwhile, was struggling with every pitch. His arm was not used to the strain of a nine-inning ball game, and the zip had deserted his fastball. By the eighth inning he was grimacing every time he threw a breaking pitch. Sam was left with only his control and the insight he had garnered into the weaknesses of the Wishbone batters; he would rather have had his hummer.

Wishbone had runners all over the bases in the last three innings. A circus catch by Frenchy in center field pulled Sam's fat out of the fire in the top of the eighth. That was why Frenchy was in the lineup; he couldn't hit a bull in the ass with a bass fiddle, but he was a jim dandy outfielder. But the ninth inning looked like curtains for Sam. The Boners had the bases loaded with two out, and Hoolihan at the plate. The first baseman had pounded the ball hard all day, and his eagerness to swing against the weakened Sam was apparent; Hoolihan looked like a starving man who had just stumbled upon a loaded banquet table.

Sam pulled the string on a slow curve that the impetuous batter was way out in front on. Strike one. Another breaking ball, low and away, was refused by Hoolihan. Ball one. Sam came high and tight with the fast ball and the Boner first baseman nearly busted a gut with his swing. The ball flew high and deep, well beyond Dago in left field . . . foul!

Doc Moss shook his head sadly. "When they pull your best fastball foul, you've run out of juice."

Sam must have agreed because he motioned Big Mike out for a conference. Pitcher and catcher talked briefly before Mike walked slowly back and settled behind the plate. Hoolihan stepped into the box and waved his bat at Sam with the businesslike assurance of an executioner brandishing an ax over a victim's head. I could hardly bear to watch.

The pitch came in chest high and right down the pipe. Sam delivered the pitch with his overhand fastball motion, and that's what it looked like. Everybody in the park knew Hoolihan was going to swing. It was his pitch.

About three feet in front of the plate the ball dove for the ground like a hungry chicken hawk. Hoolihan swung over the top of it by a good two feet. Big Mike didn't have a chance of catching it; he just shifted his body in front of it and let the ball bounce off the lower part of the doubled-up quilt that he used for a chest protector. He managed to smother it a couple feet to the right of home plate and tagged the dumbfounded Hoolihan for the third out.

The High Plains rooters went crazy, and howls of pain rose from the Wishbone side. Everyone wanted a look at the ball. The umpire, the Wishbone manager, and Hoolihan all inspected it to determine the cause for the unholy trajectory of Sam's last pitch. They could find nothing to object to.

Doc chuckled at all the brouhaha. "Those gentlemen have never seen a major league spitball before."

I sure hadn't, but Doc was glad to fill me in on it. He said few pitchers threw the spitball, even though it was legal back then. Their forbearance was not a matter of sanitation or morality, but one of ability and dependability. The spitter was a hard pitch to throw and nearly impossible to control. Since it could be thrown at high velocity and dipped so wickedly, the spitter was dreaded by catchers as well as hitters. Doc said shaking hands with a spitball catcher was like squeezing a bagful of walnuts.

With the Boners retired in the top of the ninth, the score remained one to nothing with the home team coming in for their last strokes. It was just like those nickel baseball books that the guys passed around at school, and I prayed that the resolution would be as glorious and just.

Since that day in May of 1910, I have attended scores of professional ball games and seen the finest athletes compete for the dearest prizes; none of those contests ever equaled this matchup between two amateur teams on a sandlot field with nary a player sporting a complete uniform. Nothing was at stake but the pride of the players and the honor of their respective towns—though both locales denied baseball's nobility and fought its very existence. It was damn near metaphysical in its purity, its simplicity, its intimacy.

We had the meat of our batting order coming up in the ninth. Rooster hit second in the lineup and had a knack for getting on base. Slabfoot and Mike followed with power, though neither man had shown any on that day. Sam would get another swing if someone got on base. Prospects didn't look so cheery considering we hadn't had a base runner since the fifth inning.

If Blackie was tiring, it wasn't noticeable. His pitches still popped that catcher's mitt as if it were the first inning. The weather helped; it was about seventy degrees without a trace of humidity, and the wind was blowing in from center field. If he had been pitching in August heat, he might have been running down by now.

Rooster took two pitches, a ball and a strike, hoping to work a walk out of Blackie. The shortstop then tried to lay a bunt down the third-base line. He got under the pitch, and the result was a harmless pop foul collected by the third baseman. One out.

The impatient Slabfoot unbuttoned the top two buttons of his shirt and took three good rips in a vain attempt to tie the ball game single-handedly. Idiot. Out two.

The load fell to Mike. If he couldn't get on base, it was time to piss on the fire and call in the dogs; the hunt was over.

The blacksmith squeezed Katey Dailey's handle so viciously that I swear I saw sawdust collect around his cleats. He shook the bludgeon at Blackie's head and swore at the pitcher's blighted ancestry. On the first pitch, Mike's mighty swing produced a high pop-up down the first-base line. A loud groan issued from the crowd. Hoolihan circled confidently under the ball that descended directly in front of first base. He was just about to squeeze the baseball and strangle the soul of High Plains when Big Mike's shoulder separated Hoolihan from the ball, his glove, his wits, an incisor and two bicuspids. The ball landed in short right field as Mike lumbered to second base.

The Boners, team and fans alike, howled in outrage at the brutality the home-team thugs had introduced into a game of finesse and agility. They would have jumped on Big Mike like hounds on a hambone but for the fact that nobody wanted to be the first to swing on a man with a fifty-inch chest and arms resembling the musculature of a mule's hind leg.

With Mike glowering down from second base, daring anyone to remove him, the Boners had to content themselves with baring their fangs and beating the ground in primate reaction to attack. They carried off their addled first baseman and replaced him with a huge block of granite chiseled into the shape of a slack-jawed, blond-haired throwback they called Swede.

Swede spent a minute trying to make the first baseman's mitt fit his huge hand before casting the leather aside as superfluous. You could tell by the way he hunkered around first base, knuckles brushing the ground, that baseball would never be his livelihood. He seemed more inclined toward a profession in show business—something along the lines of biting the heads off chickens in a circus.

Sam Adams stepped to the plate with two outs, a runner at second, and the team down by a run. Every Skinner fan, including the lame, the palsied, and the bedfast, was standing and cheering. Sam'd had about as much luck with Blackie's offerings as anyone; he was one for three, a hard single to center. He knocked some imaginary mud off his cleats, took a couple practice swings, then braced for the pitch.

Blackie's fastball looked low and inside to me, but the ump disagreed. Strike one. Blackie changed up with a slow overhand curve that Sam got out in front of. He slammed a blue-darter screaming down the third-base line. My heart yelled "double," but the home plate umpire responded, "Foul ball."

Foul also was Blackie's mood. He slammed the baseball vengefully into his glove. His next pitch was a sidearm fastball aimed squarely at Sam's head. Sam left the timber upstairs and got an unobstructed view of the sky above home plate. The catcher had no chance at the ball, but it bounced back quickly off the backstop. Big Mike was as slow as smoke off a manure pile so he couldn't risk lumbering to third. It would take at least a double to score the blacksmith.

The Skinner fans hurled a barrage of abuse at Blackie, who seemed to appreciate the attention. He shook the ball in Sam's direction before unleashing another sidearm fastball at the batter's head.

Sam looked a little shaky when he got up, and Lord knows he had every right to be. Few things in life are as terrifying as the sight of a small, hard projectile flung from a distance of only sixty feet, six inches at a velocity of ninety miles an hour bearing down on your frail cranium— and not only frightening, it could be fatal.

With the count two balls and two strikes, Blackie had a decision to make. He could take two more shots at Sam's head and walk him, then pitch to Dago; or he could pitch to Sam and try to end the game immediately. The smart move was probably to pitch to Dago, who had struck out his last two at bats.

Sam stepped in, defiantly dug his cleats into the loose dirt in the batter's box, and pointed the barrel of his war club at Blackie's head—an action tantamount to urinating on Blackie's ancestral burial plot. The pitcher snorted and spat the dregs of his tobacco chaw in the direction of home plate. I tossed up a quick prayer to whomever might be listening that Sam would escape with an injury to something other than his head. For the moment, I had no thought of winning or losing.

When Blackie came in with his sidearm pitch, my blood froze. It was high. It was inside. Every man in the crowd groaned. As it neared the hitter, the curveball broke sharply toward the plate. Sam stood his ground and hit a frozen rope to left center that you could have hung your wash out on. The ball rolled wild and free toward the Oklahoma border. It was left to Swifty, the center fielder, to chase it down.

I was screaming, the crowd was jumping up and down, fights were breaking out all over the right-field line, Big Mike was ambling home with the tying run, and all was right with the world.

But Sam's odyssey had just begun; there was a gauntlet to be run. The Wishbone team had reached agreement by consensus that Sam would not score the winning run. Even a free-for-all in enemy territory was preferable to the outright loss of the baseball game.

Down at first base Swede adopted a stance more befitting bear wrestling than baseball. He stalked down the first-base line toward Sam with the halting step of a primate unused to the balance demands of bipedal locomotion. When Sam took his eye off his base hit, he was less then ten feet from Swede's outstretched arms. Sam had a choice: death by asphyxiation, or evasion. Sam feinted to the left, slid under Swede's lunging grasp, bounced off first base, and ran like a scalded dog for second.

The second baseman disappointed his comrades by making only a halfhearted attempt to trip Sam as he approached the bag. The runner leaped aside, kept an eye on Swifty, who had just reached the ball, and sped toward third. Approaching the shortstop, Sam used a broken field move and a stiff arm that any Ivy League halfback would have envied. The shortstop picked himself up and continued in hot pursuit. Swifty made a strong throw to the left fielder, who relayed the ball on a single unerring bounce to third. The shortstop made his lunge for Sam's back just as Sam slid in, and the third baseman was bowled over by the double team. The baseball skipped over the pile of bodies draped around the base and landed in the crowd. A High Plains fan grabbed it and gave it a mighty heave across the prairie in the direction of the county seat.

Sam scrambled to his feet, kicked free of the shortstop's grasp, and began limping the last ninety feet to victory, glory, and—dare I say it?—immortality. The Wishbone catcher was no obstacle; Slabfoot had him pinned facedown in the batter's box. Swede was anchored to first base; he had been told to defend it as though it were the tribal watering hole, so the excitement on the other side of the diamond didn't interest or concern him.

Only Blackie remained.

He charged off the mound on a line that would intersect Sam's path about ten feet in front of home plate. Blackie's course was interrupted about five feet short of destination by two hundred and fifty pounds of irate blacksmith. Big Mike caught him in classic ambush fashion: full speed from the blind side, utilizing the combined momentum of aggressor and prey in a bone-crushing tackle that very nearly tore the pitcher's head off. Blackie was left writhing in pain within spitting distance of home plate while Sam scored the winning run.

I don't think I've ever been happier than I was at that moment. The entire High Plains team and the home crowd, every man jack of us, closed ranks around Sam, slapping him on the back and pumping his hand like he'd just been elected president. He was a flesh and blood hero. Sam Adams was my boss, my best friend, and, I admitted for the first time, the closest thing to a father I'd ever known.

Chapter
Twenty-one

Within minutes the kegs were tapped and beer flowed to the joyous partisans. Everyone wanted to touch Sam; he had become a totem whose back received flat tribute from every home team hand in the crowd. Sam was glad to see me, but I resisted the impulse to hug him, settling instead for a manly handshake.

Along the first-base line the Wishboners licked their wounds, loaded their wagons, and started their long, sorrowful trip across the prairie. Their parting obscenities were as gratifying to us as the sound of harps to a dying man. They had lost, they knew that they had lost, and they resented it mightily. I know no sight more satisfying than the limping retreat of a vanquished foe from the disputed field.

Sam drank a beer and turned his head while I drank one, as he talked with all who wanted to bask in his glory. It wasn't long, though, before I saw a veil of concern pass over his face. The worried Sam was back. Once he changed his baseball spikes for brogans, the metamorphosis was complete. Sam and I were the first to leave the celebration. I couldn't help but ask why.

"I need to break this to Rebekah," Sam said on the walk back. "It won't stay a secret for long."

The plan was to go back to the office, drop off Sam's baseball gear, and clean up before heading for the Methodist church in New Town. Rebekah was never home before four-thirty or five on Sunday, but Sam figured that this was the sort of scandalous news—Town Heretic Wins Unholy Baseball Game—that would swiftly end up in the ears of those people who would enjoy it most. Namely, every church and social group in town.

The plan went to hell in a handbasket when we walked through the door of *Plain Talk* and found Rebekah Adams sitting in a chair in the middle of the office with two packed suitcases flanking her. Rebekah had a plan of her own.

I took a feeble shot at covering for Sam. I reached for his ball glove and spikes. "I appreciate your carrying my stuff, Sam, but I reckon I best be getting home."

Sam refused my ploy and held onto his gear.

Rebekah said, "Sam, we have to talk."

"I was going to tell you, Rebekah."

"It's too late."

Neither Sam nor Rebekah acknowledged my presence. I guess I should have walked out the door, but I didn't. I just stood there.

Sam said, "It's the only thing I enjoy—"

"It's not baseball," Rebekah interrupted. "It's much more. *Everything* is wrong here. People avoid us. We owe money. We don't even have a bathroom. It's not a fit place . . ." Rebekah couldn't finish. She was nearly crying.

"What can I do?"

"Nothing," Rebekah said quickly. "I think that we should both recognize that . . . we made a mistake . . . start over again."

Rebekah stood up and lifted her suitcases. Sam and I both made a move to help her, but the shake of her head backed us down. She was miserable but determined.

"I'm going to stay with Mrs. Greer and help with the sewing till I have enough money to go back to Kansas."

When she reached the door, Sam touched her arm.

"Please don't go, Rebekah," he whispered. "I need you."

Right then I thought she would falter. Her knees buckled and her shoulders sagged. "You've told me many times that I must make my own decisions. *This* is my decision."

"If you go back to your father, you'll never have to make another."

"Will you come with me?" she asked.

Sam did not answer.

"Good-bye, Sam."

She walked through the door and didn't look back. I could hear her shoes clomp down the wooden sidewalk. Sam took a step toward the door, then a step back. His jaw was working and his mouth twisted into an angry snarl. He leaned out the door and shouted at Rebekah's back.

"Why don't you ask your father for the money? He'd buy the damned railroad for you."

I couldn't tell if Sam's vengeful words had any effect on Rebekah, or if she even heard them. She walked quickstep up the sidewalk, square-shouldered, resolute.

Sam spun around and in two long strides lurched through the kitchen door, nearly knocking it off its hinges. I followed him, reaching all the time for something to say. He pulled the top off the cookie jar and shook it. Two dollar bills and some change hit the counter. He jammed the money into his pocket and pushed past me without a word.

I stayed about four paces behind as he crossed the street. I couldn't believe my eyes: Sam walked into the Panhandle Prince, the lowest, vilest dive in town, a dirt-floor gin mill with the cheapest liquor and ugliest "girls" to be found this side of an oil boom ragtown. I'd sneaked inside the Prince once—goaded by a dare and the quality of perverse curiosity that compels one to stare into the carnage of a motor car accident—and had been quickly seized and tossed out. One visit was a gracious plenty for a sty like the Panhandle Prince; I saw nothing there but vermin of various leg count—the four-legged looking more charming than the two.

Sam could have bought a drink in any decent bar in town and been welcomed with a free shot or two thrown in by a bartender hoping to encourage new trade. Even better, he could have walked back to the field of recent triumph, drunk beer till he floated, and relived that glorious ball game pitch for pitch to boot. Sam had staked off that particular blind-pig saloon with a purpose, and it wasn't to celebrate or sell advertising.

As I waited outside the Prince, I got the uneasy feeling that lately I had spent the better part of my life sitting on sidewalks trying to figure out what the hell was going on. Only a few months before, I had this town under control; I knew what was happening, and usually why. But a comet, a preacher, and a newspaperman had turned my small world on its side and rolled it to the brink.

I leaned against a post and tried to shove the world away. I thought of steady spring rains, and the smell of the flowers that bloomed afterward. Soon I was splashing in hundred-foot waterfalls and basking in the tropical sun. Baseballs sprang from my bat in booming trajectories and landed in my glove after long runs and spectacular leaps. I shared picnic baskets with apple-cheeked girls in calico dresses beside sparkling waters. I bathed in the images that I habitually summoned to induce sleep or impose order.

I awoke with a start when I heard Sam's angry voice. Peering into the smoky, purple gloom of the Panhandle Prince, I spotted him at the far end of the bar. Sam, Skinny Kate, and the bartender, Pinky, were arguing; Sam was in the minority. The editor gave Kate a little shove—not hard, just kind of moved her aside—and slammed his fist down on the bar to make his point. Pinky declared the subject closed by whipping a hog leg out from under the bar and waving it under Sam's nose. The knife blade absorbed every light ray in the cave and looked as large and vile as a pirate's broadsword. Sam backed off a step, unbuttoned his shirt, and pushed his sleeves above his elbows.

The damn fool was girding up to do battle with one of the rankest men in the Bowery.

Sam may have been tough—it was hard to say for sure, based on his one-punch fight with the Texas Rangers—but Pinky was the consensus light-heavyweight champion in a town busting with iron-jawed contenders. Sam must have been crazy drunk to even consider it. Pinky had never displayed reluctance to use a shank, and I knew that if he came across that bar I would likely be carrying Sam out of the Panhandle Prince in sliced sections.

"Sam!" I shouted, running to his side. "You need to get over to the office quick." I fumbled for a reason. "The place is on fire!"

Sam shook his head, confused, but still eager to press the

fight at hand. Fortunately, Pinky had nothing against Sam; if the bartender had wanted to wade in Sam's blood, he would never have shown him the knife. Pinky would simply have performed some single-incision surgery, the result being an ear-to-ear smile traversing Sam's larynx.

"Come on, damn it!" I pulled at his arm. "We gotta save the press."

Sam trailed a few slurred threats, which Pinky graciously ignored as we left the saloon. When we got outside I told him there was no fire. He stumbled across the street and looked inside *Plain Talk* to make sure.

"Damn shame. Better off rid of it," he said, spinning around with purpose recalled and renewed. "Gonna kick that sombitch's ass."

He was halfway across the street again before I caught his arm. I tried to talk sense as we lurched left to right in a drunken waltz, nearly getting run over by a farmer's wagon in the process. Sam cursed horse and driver vigorously before realigning his sights on the Panhandle Prince and, I feared, imminent mortality.

"Are you wantin' to die?" I yelled up at him. "Pinky will slice you up like side meat if you go back in there."

"Who you think you are?" He jerked away from me. "I don't need a snot-nose . . . go home . . . help my wife settle in at *your* house!"

I'd had enough. "Go to hell, Sam Adams," I shouted at his back. "Go get your goddamn throat cut."

He reeled away, listing heavily to one side and then the other, like a sailor on a heaving deck. I released a lungful of anguished breath when he took a hard left turn before reaching the door of the Panhandle Prince. Staggering down the street about twenty yards, caroming off everything that did not actively avoid him, the editor piled through the swinging doors of the Wee Chap Saloon. It was a snake pit, but at least it was a *different* snake pit.

The wobbly string of baseball fans filing back into the Bowery indicated that the beer had run out at the ball field. Since I no longer shared their victory, I avoided them. I wanted to go home, to hide in my room for as long as it

took my world to right itself, but I knew that my mother
and Rebekah Adams would be there running down men in
general and Sam Adams in particular. I couldn't bear to listen to that.

Instead, I retreated to the newspaper office, slammed the
door behind me, and sought sanctuary between the covers
of *Huckleberry Finn*. I turned to my favorite part, where
Huck and Jim meet up with the Duke and the King, and for
better than an hour the town of High Plains and all its citizens were forced to muddle through without the attention
or aid of Tom Greer.

I wanted to finish the book, but hunger and nagging
dread pulled me off Huck's raft and deposited me back in
harsh reality. My stomach was empty and bitter from ne-
glect, and I recalled that a pot of Mama's chicken and
dumplings awaited my attention. Still, I could not leave the
Bowery without learning the fate of the man who had descended from heroic triumph to dissolute agony in the
space of an afternoon.

The baseball celebration was still going full tilt at Derby's and it sounded like everyone in the Bowery was involved. Everyone but Zack Hart, who sat alone in front of
the Lamour Hotel, whittling and gazing off to the west. I
suspected that he was straining to ignore the merriment that
threatened to crowd him off the sidewalk. Everyone in
town knew that Zack used to have a bad liquor problem before he quit it cold some years back. He never talked about
it, but there were times when you could tell he wanted a
drink of whiskey worse than another lungful of air. He
could hardly keep his eyes off the party at the Silver Dollar.

"Evenin', Zack." He snorted in my direction as I sat
down beside him. "Where's Doc?" I said, figuring that almost everyone else was taking advantage of the free booze.
Doc had no stomach for alcohol.

"Ridin' the laudanum tiger."

My heart sank at the news that Zack stated as flatly as
a weather report. Doc must have walked directly from triumph at the ball field to the reward that beckoned from his
syringe. Everyone in the Bowery knew that certain occasions and occurrences—Christmas, a glorious spring day,

the first snowfall—would rob us of Doc's company for anywhere from a day or two to the better part of a week, but
with each passing season his jags flared more frequently
and dragged longer. I suppose I might have maintained an
uninformed indifference to Doc's habit if I had not burst
into his darkened office with a cut and bleeding hand the
previous summer and found him slumped and moaning in
his chair, eyes glassy and half closed, mouth slack. I called
his name, but he was unable, though his effort was obvious,
to raise his head from his chest. I backed out of the office
and spoke to no one of the experience. Thereafter, I ceased
to think of Doc's absences as chosen respite, but as forced
marches to a land as terrifying as it must have been compelling.

I talked to Zack about the ball game, the sunset, the
drought, about everything I could think of except what I really wanted to know. I got nothing in response but grunts,
shrugs, and stares. I led him across the trail several times,
but he showed no sign of picking up the scent.

"Have you seen Sam Adams?" I asked finally, straight
out.

"Down at the Chap," Zack said.

"Why ain't he over at Derby's drinkin' free?"

Zack looked right through me. "That's his business."

I thought that was all I was going to get out of him, but
he must have figured that he owed me a little more. "They
sent Shorty after him, but Adams told him to go to hell."

I hated to leave such cheerful company, but I had endured all the disillusionment I could bear in a day, and it
wasn't even dark yet. Since the Wee Chap was on the way
home, I could take a quick look in before washing my
hands of this whole sorry mess.

A single kerosene lamp hung from the Chap's low ceiling, dangling over the bar. Long, twisted shadows of hard
men stretched across the grimy floor and up the cracked
walls. The saloon was dead silent; nobody was talking any
more than necessary to get a drink of whiskey.

I slipped inside long enough to see that Sam was still capable of semivertical posture and coherent enough to order
another drink. That was all I needed to know. I'd have left

right then except that a couple of mule skinners, standing at the door comparing hoary old knife wounds, were in my way. At the bar, Sam fumbled through his pockets in an exaggerated but vain search for coin. The barkeep reclaimed the drink with a haste that offended Sam's dignity. Trouble on the way.

Sam wasted a few slurred curses on the bartender, who turned his back and walked away. But Sam craved action. He staggered to the middle of the room, flung his arms out like an opera singer hitting a climactic note, and went public with his challenge.

"All you biguns line up, and all you littluns bunch up," Sam shouted, " 'cause I'm gonna whip ever' sombitch in the house."

My stomach flipped over and quivered like a landed fish as the sombitches exchanged glances, silently deciding who would defend their collective honor. The bartender must have been curious or bored since he didn't even ask that the fight be taken outside. Tables and chairs were pushed against the walls to afford space for flying bodies and rising blood.

A little skinny fellow wearing a porkpie hat and a tattered, checked vest rose from the corner table in the back. He was a rank stranger to me, though the leather grip by his chair indicated that he was likely between trains. He tossed his hat on the table and didn't bother taking off his vest. Bad sign: Checked Vest didn't expect enough competition to warrant stripping down. He walked slowly with sort of a rolling gait, his chest thrust forward like a bantam rooster. Facing Sam, Checked Vest took the classic boxer's pose, one foot forward, wrists facing inward toward the body, fists rolling in tight circles. You could tell he was no brawler looking to throw a quick sucker punch; he was there for the duration.

Sam was in the middle of his first bob and weave when Checked Vest threw a flurry of body punches of a speed such as I had never witnessed in my years of spectating barroom fights. Sam winced, backed off a pace, and connected with a short jab. When Sam attempted to follow with a looping right hand, the little fellow stepped inside and worked over the editor's gut again. As Sam bent over to protect his ribs, Checked Vest caught him with an uppercut that snapped the editor's head back as if it were on a hinge.

Sam had weight and reach on his opponent, but he was drunk and obviously outclassed. Worse, he fought like a man who knew he was in the wrong. Sam was looking for a beating.

After another battery of body blows, Sam was defenseless. His opponent appeared disappointed by the brevity of the fight. Checked Vest threw a right hook to Sam's nose that left blood splattered on the wall a good four feet away. But the editor didn't have sense enough to drop, so the mauling had to continue.

Sick to my stomach, I turned away, clasping my hands over my ears. I didn't open my eyes till I felt the thump that I knew was Sam's body hitting the floor. When I turned around, Checked Vest had Sam by the shirt collar and britches and was running him out the door.

Sam lay like a sack of raw meat in the Bowery street. The people passing on the sidewalk, accustomed to ignoring bodies flung through saloon doors, avoided looking at the pulpy face. It was nearly dark, and they probably wouldn't have recognized Sam if they'd looked. (I'm giving those good passersby the benefit of the doubt here, since not a soul offered a helping hand to a man obviously in need of one.)

It took me a good five minutes to wrestle Sam to his feet, and I had him sitting in his office before he figured out what was going on. Quickly, I drew some water from the well and dabbed at his face with a kitchen rag, trying to get past the crust of dirt and blood. He recoiled from the cold water on open wounds, cussing everything that came to his mind, including me, Rebekah, and the newspaper. Grabbing the bucket, he scooped handfuls of water over his face, then ran his fingers through his hair. That seemed to sober him up some. I learned better when I made what I thought was an obvious suggestion.

"Want me to get Rebekah?"

Sam's right arm shot out and hit me on the shoulder, knocking me to the floor. He loomed over me and shouted.

"Traitor! Get out of my sight! You tell her anything and I'll—"

He turned his back, and I clambered away on all fours. When I got to the door, I saw him pawing through Shad's tools over in the corner. With the whole room between us, I felt far enough away to shout back at him.

"You can die for all I care! I wish you was in Hell with your back broke."

I was ready to run if he made a move my way. Sam stood with his back to me and waved Shad's sledgehammer over his head. He swung the sledge in mighty arcs, the leaden head whistling the low wind of destruction as he searched for a proper target. My body went numb when he swung the nine-pound hammer full force across the bed of the printing press. The press groaned and sagged but remained erect; it gave up the ghost when Sam unloaded on it a second time.

Sam splintered the chair easily and knocked over the type case, kicking each drawer across the room. He panted heavily as he surveyed the wreckage. I'll swear his eyes lit up when he spotted the obvious target lying horizontal and vulnerable in the middle of the room. The marble imposing stone split neatly in two from a single blow of Sam's hammer.

The editor stepped back to see what he had wrought, and, lo, it was good. He smiled as he dropped the hammer and lay down on the floor.

I didn't move for a long while. People began to sidle up to the newspaper door to see what all the noise was about, but I walked away silently. I understood nothing of what I had seen and knew but a single truth: I hated Sam Adams with a cold fury that knew no bounds. His betrayal was absolute, his treachery final.

I stomped through the kitchen ignoring my mother's call from the parlor and the chicken and dumplings on the stove. I pushed open my bedroom door with a vengeance.

Rebekah gasped and pulled her bathrobe tightly over the

thin slip that she wore. She was sitting on *my* bed sorting through her open suitcase. She was as surprised as I was.

Torn between anger and embarrassment, I didn't know whether to cuss or apologize. Mama materialized instantly with an explanation.

"Tommy, I made you a bed in the off bedroom so Rebekah could have a little more room for the few days that she's going to stay with us. I knew you'd understand—"

I twisted away from Mama's hand on my shoulder and ignored Rebekah's apology as I stomped out of my room. Off bedroom, my ass! I pushed open the closet door and saw that Mama had shoved the piles of clothing and the stacks of newspapers and magazines up against the walls, leaving just enough space in the middle of the floor for a thin, narrow, straw tick mattress. The Queen of Sheba had *my room*—the room I had grown up in—and left me this narrow cell with a pallet that looked as though it had been salvaged from the bottom of a prison junk heap.

I started to go in and raise holy hell about it, but I couldn't tolerate the sight of another human being. Lying down with my clothes and boots on, I pulled the mildewed covers over my head. I felt, if I were lucky, I might never wake up at all.

Chapter
Twenty-two

I slept for ten hours and wouldn't have gotten up then, but it had become impossible to ignore the third round of pounding on the door of my tomb. At breakfast Rebekah worked hard at cheerfulness and Mama tried to drag me into civility, but I was having none of it. I said nothing, ate quickly, and slammed the curtains off the door when I left. I still halfway blamed Rebekah for Sunday's catastrophe, so I wasn't going to be the one who told those two about Sam's debacle. I didn't know how Rebekah would react, but Mama would certainly gloat over it. Sam was an infidel, so she considered any evil that befell him divine retribution. They'd find out soon enough anyway.

I had no intention of going to school, but I couldn't think of a thing I wanted to do or a soul I wanted to see. And the last thing I wanted was to spend the day alone. I felt lonesome and ornery, no longer a part of anything; nothing I did made any difference.

Might as well go to Hayes's store, I decided, to see if anybody had a project that might yield either money or diversion. Farmers and ranchers often came by Hayes's to pick up workers for odd jobs. Despite the prediction of impending apocalypse, there were still folks planting and cultivating with the single-minded faith that a farmer had to live on in country where rainfall ranged from none to never enough. The work they offered was usually mindless labor that never paid much, but it would pass the time.

I was admiring a pair of boots in the window of the mercantile when I saw Lew Schekle, the socialist, drive his wagon up the street. Dissatisfied with the pace of his brown mare, Lew jumped down and fairly dragged the animal the last fifteen yards to a hitching post. He didn't bother tying up his rig, just bounded across the sidewalk and into Hayes's store. Odd behavior indeed for a man who was always last to get his crops in the ground and a week late getting them to market.

I walked into Hayes's half expecting to hear of a socialist overthrow of the United States and the installation of Eugene V. Debs as czar; I figured nothing less would move Lew to break a sweat. The six men and two women in the store were gathered in a tight semicircle listening intently to a man they usually ignored when it became impossible to avoid him entirely.

"The Western Union rider was running down a line, and quick as he figured out what it was, he came by my place for a witness," Lew said, nearly breathless. "I hitched the wagon and rode with him for better than a mile southwest. It was just this side of the breaks. From way off I could see it twisting in the wind, like a sack of wet wash. It was hanging from a telegraph pole.

"When we drew up, I could see it was a man, then a colored man, then . . . Gem Scott!"

O Lordy. Everyone backed off a pace, shook his head or scratched his chin. Lew gave everyone time to react before continuing.

"There was a chicken tied around Gem's neck. It had pecked all over him. It was still alive—the chicken—when we got there. We cut it free and it ran off squawking."

The silence that followed extended beyond Mr. Hayes's patience. "Spit it out, Lew."

Lew continued. "I stood on the back of the wagon and I cut Gem's body down. We judged he'd been up there better than a day. I wrapped it in a quilt and took it by the sheriff's office, but they didn't want nothing to do with it. I left it at the undertaker's." Lew shrugged. " 'Course they didn't want it either. I just pushed it off the back of the wagon onto their sidewalk."

Mr. Hayes offered an opinion. "Seems like somebody went to a lot of trouble to hang ol' Gem and make a show of it. Coulda just as easy shot him, tossed a few rocks on top, and nobody would have thought much about it."

Lew Schekle reclaimed the floor; it was his party and he wasn't about to give up a captive audience. "They did a mighty poor job of it too. Ol' Gem's neck wasn't even broken. He must have just kicked around up there until he strangled to death."

Evil business. Either the executioner was inept or exceedingly malicious. More than likely it was the latter since every schoolboy knew how to adjust a noose beside a man's ear so that his neck snapped. It was part of western lore, like keeping your back to the sun in a gunfight or shooting a buffalo without scattering the herd.

The socialist saw motive, philosophy, and moral tied in a neat bundle. "I know exactly what it is, and it bears true witness to what I've been telling you for years. It's the class struggle bred from the capitalist system and manifesting in race hatred," Lew declared.

The semicircle expanded and then broke up as everyone backed away from the thought of indicting the free enterprise system for the lynching of Gem Scott. I suspect that everyone there had a good idea of exactly who lowered the rope around the black man's neck, but no one spoke the name. I knew who did it, and I knew who needed to be told about it.

Langston was packing a suitcase when I rushed into his room. He'd already heard the news.

"I've got a case in Dallas," he said, latching his suitcase hurriedly and setting it next to another bag. "Should take the better part of a week."

He was taking a lot of clothes for one week, but I didn't say anything. I could have helped him carry his luggage down to where Shad had the buggy waiting, but I didn't. The ride to the train station was long and uncomfortable since nobody had much to say. Langston tried to act unconcerned, but we both knew better. He pressed a dollar into my hand as the train pulled away. If I'd had time to think about it, I would have refused it.

Langston Harper was running scared. We both knew that Jack Clement had strung up Gem Scott and had threatened to do the same to the lawyer. Still, I couldn't believe that

Langston would just cut and run. Killing a black man, a known thief, was one thing; killing, or even roughing up, a white lawyer was certainly another.

I don't think that anyone other than Sam and myself had actually heard Clement's threat against Langston after Gem Scott's trial, but there was a recognized history of bad blood between the two. Langston's hasty departure was already being discussed by the crew of old men who hung around the station, and would be common knowledge by noon. The lawyer's agitation was obvious even to Zack, who didn't care one way or the other how people acted.

"Nervous as a whore in church," was Zack's assessment. In less than twenty-four hours I had been betrayed by the two men whom I had admired most.

I spent the rest of the morning hanging around the swimming hole, feeling as shriveled and wasted as the cracked riverbank. Now little more than a rutted gully, the river appeared to be within days of disappearing entirely. With no rain to moderate the alkali and gypsum, the water was undrinkable, nearly toxic; fish floated on their sides, eyes glazed over, tails jerking in spasm. A horned toad thought long and hard before dipping his tongue, then backed off quickly and waddled upstream. I stayed only long enough to catch my breath and rest my legs before heading to the only place in town that offered companionship without curiosity. Langston's dollar was burning a hole in my pocket, and I knew exactly where to take it.

I was headed for the poolroom when I saw Zack and Shorty playing checkers on a table set up on the sidewalk between the Lamour Hotel and *Plain Talk*.

"Who's winnin'?" I asked, though I knew the answer. I leaned against the hitching post, figuring I wouldn't be there long enough to sit down.

"He ain't beat me in twenty years," Zack growled. "I can't see it happenin' today."

Shorty just played checkers to be sociable; it gave him something to pass the time until someone came along to talk to. "Tom, did you hear about Gem Scott? Went and got himself hung."

"Sounds like he had a good deal of help with the job. At least that's how I heard it from Lew Schekle."

Shorty looked disappointed at learning that I had heard the news from the horse's mouth. He was ready to respond when all ears and eyes were diverted by the bang and rattle fast approaching from the direction of New Town. Every horse on the street shied and whinnied as the clattering Maxwell approached. R. N. Barkley, with his son Bark riding shotgun, pulled up directly in front of us and cut off his engine, or tried to. The motor ran raggedly for nearly a minute before backfiring twice and giving up the ghost.

The gouty R.N. got out slowly and, with the help of a cane, hobbled over toward us. Bark, dressed like a magazine ad, stayed a good three paces behind him. Every other kid in town wore clothes; Bark Barkley wore outfits.

"Good automobile," R.N. said, smiling, "but nobody in this town knows how to work on it. It could purr like a kitten—" He dropped the thought when he saw that his audience had the same lofty opinion of motor cars that Brother Nicholas and the prophet Ezekiel held.

R.N. slowly waddled the ten yards to the front door of *Plain Talk*. He pushed the cracked door open with his cane and shook his head at the carnage. Bark stepped around his father to get a better look. "Damn," he said, while nodding his head appreciatively.

R.N. turned toward us. "I've known a number of men who have retired from the newspaper business, but I don't think that I have ever seen anyone do it quite so . . . conclusively."

Zack, Shorty, and I exchanged glances. If that was a cuss word, none of us had heard it before. I made a note to remember it.

R.N. turned to me. "Greer, I want you to tell Sam Adams that—"

"I ain't tellin' Sam Adams nothin' for nobody. I hope I never see the sorry bastard again." I spat for emphasis.

R.N. was impressed by my vehemence. He turned toward Shorty and Zack. "Well, Mr. Adams should be told that I am willing to purchase his"—he waved his cane at the rubble inside *Plain Talk*—" 'assets' for the price of a railway ticket to California."

As Barkley prepared to climb into his auto, he leaned on the door and spoke directly to me. "Greer, you have a long history of bad blood with my son, and it is time for it to stop. I have forbidden Richard Jr. to fight with you, and I swear that if you so much as brush up against him, I will have you removed from this town. That is all the warning that you are going to get." He put his foot on the running board and pulled himself into the driver's seat.

R.N. leaned his head out the window and added, "If you ever pull a bowie knife on another human being—"

"I didn't pull no damn knife!" I shouted, but Bark had turned the crank on the front of the Maxwell, and against the clang of the misfiring engine I might as well have been whispering into a rock crusher.

As the Barkleys pulled out of earshot, I saw Shorty eyeing me. "Did you pull a bowie knife on Bark Barkley?" he asked, an element of respect in his voice.

"Hell, no! His old man caught him runnin' away from me, and Bark lied to him about it so he wouldn't look so chickenshit. I don't even have a bowie knife."

Zack leaned back in his seat and pointed his crooked index finger at me. "If you ever decide you want to do some carvin' on little Barkley or his old man," he growled, "I got one I'll lend you."

Business was slow at the High Plains Billiard Emporium; it usually was until late afternoon. No reason to open up before then except that Shaky Ben, the rack man, didn't have anything else to do and he appreciated any company that might stop by. When I walked through the open door, Ben was brushing down the carom billiard table (pocketless)— that aristocratic, though rarely used, icon that elevated this drafty, neglected building from poolroom to "billiard emporium."

Along the rear wall a couple of loafers alternately laughed and spat tobacco on the floor as they listened to a drummer repeat tired old wheezes straight out of *Jokes for the Jocular Salesman*. Two cowboys frammed away on the back table, disregarding with every breath the NO PROFANTY ALOWED sign that stared down in illiterate futility above the cash register. That lame admonition was every bit as effective as the NO MINERS prohibition that it shared the wall with. Half the poolroom's clientele was underage, with every mother's son addicted to the four-letter Anglo Saxonisms and carnal verbs that dominated conversation there.

I was glad to see that Stick was home. He was sharpening his pocketknife and thumbing through a *Police Gazette* that had been lying around the pool hall for the last six months. Stick was about seventeen years old and had been out of school for the last decade, so reading was something of an effort for him; pool, however, was not.

Stick was placed on Earth to shoot pocket billiards. Unfortunately, he'd long ago chewed up the best shooters in town and was forced to scratch his living from drunks, fools, and cocky drummers killing time between trains. In an attempt to supplement income, while keeping honest labor at arm's length, Stick had taught his long, thin fingers to milk a deck of playing cards to yield the poker hand of his choice. Again, proximity doomed his God-given talent and honest effort. His accomplishment was negated when it was rather forcibly noted that if the cards were not cut, Stick won every hand that he dealt. The subsequent short but severe beating planted in Stick the seed of realization that a small town was not the optimum venue for a sporting man. He now fancied a future full of big-city bustle, five-dollar gold pieces tossed across green felt, and pinch-back seersucker suits, but, alas, he wasn't quite ready to leave home. Three hot meals a day from an indulgent mother, and recognition as the premier pool player in town, was not an unenviable lot for a second-grade dropout.

I wasn't in his league, but Stick didn't mind shooting with me so long as there was some wager involved. Since I had money that I didn't feel comfortable with, I didn't mind spreading it around. Stick spotted me twenty points a rack in straight rotation pool, and we shot for a dime a game. He was generous with his advice, so I always felt I got my money's worth in instruction. Usually when my money ran low, he'd back off on the wager and shoot for the game. I always wondered if that streak of compassion would be his downfall as a hustler.

The fifteen ball leaped from the spot and slammed into the back of the corner pocket. Stick absently chalked his cue and exhaled a lungful of smoke. "Stayed up all night onest tryin' to miss a spot shot," he muttered, for the third time that day.

"Rack 'em up, Ben," I shouted. "Stick got lucky on me again."

Shaky Ben was slapping his knee at one of the salesmen's rusty old japes and failed to move with the dispatch that I desired.

"Christ on a crutch, Ben, you died years ago but nobody got around to telling you," I complained.

"Boy, you orta appreciate me bein' slow," Ben said, padding up to the front. "I'm savin' ya money."

Ben pocketed my nickel and took his time collecting the balls. His palsied hands, the product of age and wood alcohol, required three passes before setting a tight rack.

Stick broke, made the eleven ball, and left himself a shot on the one. As I settled back to admire his stroke, the last man in the world I wanted to see walked through the door.

Sam Adams looked like nine miles of bad road. His left eye was swollen shut and surrounded by half a dozen shades of purple and yellow. His mouth, always off center, now threatened to fall off his face. The slow, bent, wheezing gait reflected the body punches from last night's main event at the Wee Chap. I ignored him as he took the seat next to me.

"How you doin', Tom?" he said through puffy lips that scarcely moved.

"Not so bad—breakin' about even."

Shaky Ben laughed aloud at my lie, and I shot him a hard glance. Sam and I both knew that he wasn't asking about the pool game, it was just the easiest question to answer.

Stick missed a bank on the four ball, but he left me sewed up. I had to kick two rails, and didn't make anything. I sat down and watched Stick start a new run with a four-twelve combination.

I could hear Sam breathing through his mouth; his nose wasn't working.

"I'm sorry about last night, Tom. I wasn't myself."

My voice was low but there was heat in it. "Well, who-ever the hell you were wasn't worth spittin' on. You're the lousiest hell-roarin' drunk I've ever seen."

Stick made a nice cut on the six while I listened to Sam breathe.

"Some people should never drink," Sam confessed.

The poolroom was silent but for the click of the pool balls. Everyone was eyeing Sam and trying not to get caught at it. Everyone but Stick. His attention was confined to six pockets, four rails, and painted ivory.

"Did you hear about Gem Scott?" Sam said.

"Yeah."

Sam said: "Whatever happened to me, or between us, is not nearly as important as Gem Scott. I'm going to need some help on that story. I'd appreciate it if you could forget what happened last night and give me a hand with it."

I didn't have an answer ready so I just kept quiet. The load was on Sam and I didn't mind keeping it there. But as he eased himself out of his chair in sections, each part try-ing to minimize the pain of movement, I couldn't help feel-ing sorry for him.

"If you decide you want to help me with this, come by the office just before dark. We've got some serious business to take care of." I stared straight ahead, as I had done throughout the talk. He lowered his voice. "I promise you that it will be more exciting than setting type." He walked out the door.

By the time Stick had run the table, I'd made my mind up. I'd go back to Sam and the newspaper, and it was every bit as much for the newspaper as it was for Sam. People would come and go and could not be depended upon; a newspaper was a lifetime project. And a man needs a proj-ect.

If Sam hit the bottle again, I'd hit the road. It was as simple as that. As for making a major issue of the Gem

Scott lynching, I was skeptical. The black people were as ashamed of Gem's roguish ways as the whites were hostile. Even Shad had nothing good to say about Gem. I could see no base to build a movement on.

Still, I knew Sam Adams well enough to know that he'd go after Gem's murderer hammer and tongs. Thief or not, in Sam's eyes no one had the right to kill another man. I also knew that he was going to have one hell of a tough time convincing the population of High Plains of that radical notion.

Chapter
Twenty-three

When I walked up to the office door, I saw Sam and Shad standing in the midst of the rubble contemplating a scene of wrack and despair. From where I stood, it looked like they might just as well douse the place with gas, toss in a match, and start from scratch. They both brightened up when they saw me.

In order to get in the door, I had to kick aside the fractured back of what had been the sole reliable chair in the office. I leaned against the copy desk, the last piece of standing furniture. "Where's the press?" I asked.

"I took it over to Big Mike," Sam mumbled. "He thinks he can pound it out to where we can get out an issue or two. I believe we can patch up everything else."

Shad wasn't so optimistic. "Well, if it took the Lord a week to shape up the whole world, I'd say He wouldn't have more'n three or four days work here."

Walking over to where the marble imposing stone lay in pieces, I nudged it with my foot. "You're going to play hell putting this back together."

Sam's face pinched up to what might have been a smile. He nodded outside to the gathering darkness. "That's the serious business we've got to take care of."

Lying on the canvas tarpaulin in the back of Shad's flatbed wagon, I was surrounded by a couple crowbars, a shovel, a lantern, twenty-five feet of rope, and a Johnson bar. Sam and Shad sat up front talking quietly as the mule pulled us off to the northeast on a route that would take us past Nicholas's "Glorious Assumption Crusade." The preacher's final push—subtitled "Ten Days to Rapture"—had started the night before, but since both Sam and I had been indisposed, we had only secondhand accounts of the size and temperament of Sunday's crowd.

As soon as we lost the shelter of the buildings, the north wind blessed us with the chorus of "Softly and Tenderly," sung with the loud, militant disharmony that characterized Nicholas's flock. They sang every hymn as though it were a spear rattler like "Onward Christian Soldiers."

"Looks like Nick's circus has peaked out. Three hundred, maybe three twenty-five," Sam observed as we rolled slowly past the rear of the gathering. "No bigger than last Friday."

I noticed that Shad allowed the mule to set her own deliberate pace. Apparently, he wasn't anxious to get on with the night's mission any more than I was.

The town graveyard lay about half a mile beyond the revival site, stuck conspicuously on a slight knoll that passed for a hill in West Texas. In the contorted, often whimsical reasoning that suffuses man's view of mortality, the city fathers figured the denizens of the necropolis deserved the best view in the county.

A half-moon cast just enough light down on the cemetery to throw twisted shadows through its stunted, gnarled trees. Ever since the various religious denominations had established their own burial grounds the town graveyard had become little more than a potter's field for the unmourned dead lying forgotten under an arbor of malformed hardwoods.

Shad tied his mule to the rusty iron fence that surrounded the cemetery as Sam and I unloaded the wagon. The editor lit the lantern and pushed through the broken gate as confident and unconcerned as a virgin walking into Sunday school. Shad and I both found some things that needed to be done around the wagon. Things like straightening out the canvas, making sure we hadn't forgotten any tools, checking the mule's hooves for stones . . . important things, you understand. Sam tolerated our dallying for scarcely a minute before pointedly inviting us inside. When I hesitated—the harness reins looked like they might be working loose—Sam jumped to a conclusion.

"You wouldn't be a little scared, would you, Tom?"

"Hell, no!" I said, dropping the bridle. "Let's just get one and get the hell outta here. I got better things to do than hang around a marble orchard all night."

Once I went inside, Shad had no choice but to follow. "Boy's right," Shad said, easing sideways past the gate so as not to disturb anyone. "Man's gonna spend all his time here soon enough."

Sam chuckled as he walked slowly from tombstone to tombstone, running his hand over the smooth side of each one. I turned my collar up against a wind that I swear had grown colder and stronger with every step deeper into the boneyard. The dwarf trees groaned and creaked just over my head as I watched thin cirrus clouds blow past the moon. If thunder had rumbled, owl screeched, or coyote howled, I would have jumped the fence, run home, and never looked back.

Sam bent down in front of a marker and held the lantern above the inscription.

DUKE SPANGLER

1865–1908

NEVER KNEW WHAT HIT HIM

Sam whistled low. "What happened to him?"

"Got drunk and passed out in the street," Shad said. "Got run over by the first Model T in town."

"Does he have any family?" Sam asked.

Shad shook his head. "Wife bought this marker then ran off with the man that drove the Ford."

Sam took several slow, feeble jabs with the shovel before I took it away from him. I dug hastily at the back of Duke's marble slab while Shad used the Johnson bar to wedge it out of the ground. Sam's condition, Shad's age, and my size dictated group participation in loading the stone on the wagon. It was gut-busting labor in a ghoulish environment, and illegal and immoral to boot.

I clenched my teeth to keep them from chattering and hoped that Sam didn't notice my trembling hand as we spread the canvas over our contraband and tied it down.

Shad was no less apprehensive; he fidgeted in the driver's seat, the reins twisted in his hands, ready to quit this unholy place anon.

Then the sky silently exploded.

A silver streak overhead caught my eye. Shad's head jerked around to us to confirm the sighting. Before a word could be said, the sky was filled with flaming projectiles raining from a central core. Shad laid the reins heavily on the mule's back as I dropped the rope and leaped on the back of the wagon. Only Sam remained loyal to the mission; he ran alongside, trying to complete the knot that would secure Duke's memorial to the wagon. After about twenty yards, Sam saw he was losing ground and pulled himself heavily onto the wagon bed.

It's not easy to get a mule to run. As often as not they'll stop completely when you try to whip them into a faster gait. Perhaps it was the panic that Shad's mule sensed in us, or the extraordinary meteorological conditions, whatever, she understood the gravity of the situation and lit out like a dog with a tailful of firecrackers. Aided by the downhill slope, the mule galloped away from the cemetery, leaving Sam and me to roll around the flatbed groping for a handhold. Duke Spangler's headstone bounced and slid, loosened its fetters and threatened to jump ship.

We were within hailing distance of Nicholas's rally before the mule slowed to a trot. I pulled myself around to where I could see the sky. The "explosion" had slacked off to an occasional streak, and I hadn't witnessed any tragic effects yet.

"It's a meteor shower, you damn fools!" Sam shouted as quickly as he could be heard over the rattle and rumble of the wagon. "Stop the damn wagon!"

Shad tried to stop her, but the jenny was oblivious to his command. She made straight for the mass of people huddled out on the prairie. I was afraid she might split the crowd wide open, and Lord save us all if that bunch discovered the ungodly nature of our cargo. Sam and I scrambled to get the tarp back over the tombstone.

The mule pulled up at the edge of the crowd, apparently recognizing some safety in numbers. I'll admit at that moment I didn't disagree. I'd seen shooting stars and heard of meteor storms—but never like that. I was still spooked by the uncanny timing of it all.

The crowd looked smaller, but Sam pointed out that everyone had just packed in closer—tighter than buzzards over carrion. Their fear was tangible and not a soul made note of our arrival. Every eye was trained on the man who did not share their fear.

From the platform Brother Nicholas stretched his steady hand toward the firmament and roared: "Fear not, for this is but a warning. In nine days the skies will blaze with an inferno such as no man has witnessed. It will be as foreseen by Saint John the Revelator: 'And there fell a great star from Heaven burning as if it were a lamp. And the name of the star is Wormwood, and the waters became Wormwood, and men died of the waters, because they were made bitter.' "

Nicholas continued with an analysis of the saint's prophecy so obscure that Sam couldn't make enough sense of it to write it down. The preacher roared on about a "jasper and a sardine stone" and "an angel in a church in Philadelphia" that left me dizzy. Apparently it satisfied his people; they nodded and shouted as though it all added right up. When Nicholas kicked into his appeal for converts, the crowd was boiling with the spirit, shouting in tongues, shaking, dancing, falling, rolling.

It made me damned uncomfortable. I blurred out the faces in the long line to the platform; I didn't want to know who was dropping his pants in public. If I didn't know, I wouldn't have to avoid his eyes tomorrow on the street.

The sky was placid, the world intact. We spoke hardly a word on the trip to the Bowery. I could see that the editor was in considerable pain from our bone-rattling stampede from the graveyard, but he didn't complain. Sometimes I think Sam might have been a happier man if he had done some bitching once in a while.

Since Sam was now useless for heavy labor, Shad and I served penance by carrying the slab from the wagon into the office. We inverted Duke's headstone so its smooth side was up and laid it gently on the table that was to be its home. By two A.M. we had the office in tolerable order. There was still a mountain of work to do, but the job no longer looked hopeless.

Chapter
Twenty-four

The three of us were hard at it by seven A.M., and we had a two-sheeter on the street by dark. We were short of usable type, capital letters craned conspicuously from the middle of words, and there were more misspellings and typos than you'd find in a year's worth of the *Muskogee Hog Growers Gazette*. The *Plain Talk* of Tuesday, May 10, 1910, was a proofreader's nightmare, and the best piece of journalism that I have ever been associated with.

The stacked headlines summarized the story in the journalistic fashion of the day:

lOCAL NEGRO lYNcHED
FOR cHIcKEN THEFT
KIllER REMAINS AT lARGE
ClUES ABOUND IN BRUTAl SlAYING

While the citizens of High Plains, TeXas, lose theM-selves in histeria over the mindless raMblings of a misguided dooMsaYer, ruthless vigilantisM stalks the prairie and leaves a bloodY corpse swinging in its wake.

After tying our features together with this lead, Sam used the rest of the front page to recount the life and death of Gem Scott. Shad provided the few known facts about him, and Sam shaped them into a story that very nearly broke me down when I set the type. It was a story, plainly told, of a life common to Reconstruction Negroes, "freed" after two and a half centuries of slavery to walk an alien land, their inferiority assumed upon sight. In five columns Sam sketched a life of daily humiliation as tragic as it was common. That any human would be treated that way was base cruelty; that an entire race endured it was unconscionable. But Sam spoke not of the race, but of the man.

Neither did Sam mention the name "Jack Clement," but left no doubt that he was the villain. It was so obvious that on my first reading I thought I had actually seen the offending name in print.

"In the newspaper business," Sam explained, "you'll live longer if you draw a picture of a horse and skip the label."

PREAcHER BUIIDS FIOcK
ON ROcK OF TERROR
COMET HiSTORiCAIIY iNSPiRES FEAR
SCIENTISTS REFUTE HAIIEY'S dANGER

On page two Sam challenged Nicholas and his prophecy in an argument combining a history of doomsday movements with a detailed cataloguing of the preacher's scientific and scriptural misstatements.

Sam culled nine instances of widespread apocalyptic hysteria ranging from the "Millenarians," Christians in the year A.D. 1000, who took Saint John's millennial warning literally, to the "Millerites," a nineteenth-century Massachusetts sect who projected The End to fall on the vernal equinox, 1843. The Millerite cause was given a leg up by "The Great Comet of 1843" (*not* Halley's), which set members coast to coast wailing and cringing in anticipation of the fulfillment of their patron prophet Daniel's "handwriting on the wall."

Halley's Comet was historically considered to be the catalyst for four documented annihilation movements and countless other reactive disasters. Many of the attributed events were unverifiable in fact or date—Noah's Flood, Methuselah's death—and often the dates between calamities varied so strikingly from Halley's seventy-five to seventy-nine year orbit—for example, one hundred ten years from the death of Julius Caesar, 44 B.C., to the destruction of Jerusalem in A.D. 66—that the comet's appearance at both would have been impossible. Quite evidently, *any* debacle,

natural or man-made, occurring within recent memory of a
comet's appearance was incorporated into the myth.

Sam's article also pointed out the dichotomous nature of
many historical events that a single culture might view as
tragic. King Harold's defeat at the Battle of Hastings in
1066 might well have been deemed morbid by defeated
Saxons, but victorious Normans rejoiced. Consequently, in
each war that supposedly attended the comet's visit, a victor
emerged who might justifiably have considered the Death
Star a welcome talisman. Sam noted that the human pro-
pensity toward armed conflict dictated coincidence with
Halley's appearance. Hardly a year could be picked at random when European blood was not being spilled in copious
amounts under the banner of honor, religion, national
sovereignty, or spite.

To conclude his historical overview, Sam chose an epi-
sode of obvious relevance to High Plains's current situation. In A.D. 1456, Halley's visitation coincided with a
Turkish siege of the Holy Roman Empire. The comet was
construed by the hierarchy of the Catholic Church as a
monstrous omen, and throughout the Empire church bells
were rung every day at noon, and supplicants were instructed to pray for deliverance from "the Turk, the Devil,
and the Comet." The Empire survived all three scourges after Pope Calixtus III reputedly "excommunicated" Halley's
Comet. The Pope did not provide details or explanation.
Pity.

Finally, Sam quoted and refuted a score of groundless al-
lusions and fallacious conclusions from Nicholas's writings
and speeches. The editor's tone was impersonal, his method
systematic; he hoped that this merger of historical perspective and scientific analysis would show the citizenry that all
this agitation and dread was not without precedent, and
was, though understandable in such unusual times, still un-
founded and unnecessary. Sam made a case for Common
Sense and Sound Judgment.

Frankie Gilmore was the only newsboy reporting for duty
that night. Sam said it was because it was so late, but I was
inclined to believe it was due to Sam's low estate among

the mothers of the town. Frankie's mother was dead or had run off, and his father didn't care what the boy did so long as he fed himself and didn't steal the old man's liquor.

Shad and I loaded about three hundred copies on his wagon and took them around to the few businesses that would still sell over the counter for us. We could tell from our first stop at Fat Annas's barbershop that we had a wildcat by the tail. Word of content had leaked and everyone there who could read bought a copy. The arguments started before I could even get my hands on the new *Police Gazette*, and hard words followed us out the door.

When we got back, Frankie Gilmore was dashing back onto the street with another load of papers. He'd hit the saloons with his first batch and had sold out before he was halfway up the street. Since this edition was half the size of our usual four-sheeter and we still charged five cents for it, I could see a decent profit accruing.

"We'll run off another two hundred in the morning," Sam said as Shad and I walked through the door. "We may get tarred and feathered for this, but at least we'll have a couple of nickels to rub together while they do it."

As Sam and I finished off the dregs of a coffeepot that had pulled yeoman duty that day, a voice almost too faint to hear sounded behind us.

"Good evening, gentlemen." Doc Moss, looking tired and tremulous as a newborn kitten, leaned against the doorjamb. His stability was so tentative that both Sam and I reached for the only chair in the office that could sustain even Doc's negligible weight.

Doc waved us off. "I don't intend to tarry that long. I merely wanted to tell you both that you showed a great deal of courage. Either one of those stories could get you drawn and quartered in this town. Both stories for the price of a nickel is a real bargain."

Sam smiled. "Thanks, Doc. Few of my readers have mentioned courage in their evaluation of my efforts."

"Do you think they'll put Clement in jail for lynchin' Gem?" I asked.

Doc shook his head slowly. "I would be mightily surprised if Jack Clement ever spent a night in any bed other than his own for the rest of his life."

"Yeah," I agreed. "Everybody thinks we're pissin' in the wind on that one."

"What's your reading on the town and Brother Nicholas?" Sam asked. "Did we ignore him for too long to stop him?"

"Well, Sam," Doc said, so quietly that I had to lean forward to hear, "you have the collective force of several thousand years of philosophy and science behind you. The Greeks, the Italian Renaissance, the Enlightenment—you've got all that backing you up. But I don't think it is going to be enough. You're arguing against abject fear. And I've never seen the time when folks could be reasoned out of a hole they dug in dread."

Doc was so give out that he could stand no longer, and I suspect he feared that if he sat down, he would be unable to rise. We said good-bye, and I monitored the old man's walk back to his office just to make sure that he got there. I was glad he had made it out of his office after only two days on a laudanum jag, but I knew that the battle within him still raged. Doc went back to face the beckoning needle, and in his condition, the only sanctuary might appear to be astride the tiger's back.

I had hoped that Mama would still be at Nicholas's gathering, so I could slip into bed without confrontation. When I opened the door and found the kitchen empty, I thought I was home-free.

"Thomas."

The summons from the sewing room surprised me. Mama invariably closed off the front parlor after the sewing ladies left to save heat and light and to preserve order. Our kitchen was the center of the house and was large enough to sustain any activity respectable people might indulge in after dark.

"Yes, Mama."

"Come in here, son."

Mama had the light turned as low as it would burn without flickering out, to save kerosene. Her head rested against the back of the chair, her eyes were closed, and her hands lay atop the open Bible in her lap: Revelations. A bad sign.

"How did the rally go, Mama?" I wanted to steer the conversation toward *her* activities.

"The time for rallies is past. There is time only for the Final Crusade."

"Was there a big crowd?"

"The Chosen grow in number every night. All but the most foolish or arrogant recognize the truth of the Prophecy now." She spoke as if in a trance. "It is time for you to attend *every* meeting. From tomorrow through the Glorious Assumption, you will need to be at every meeting of the Faithful."

"I'd like to, Mama, Lord knows I would, but—"

When her head snapped forward and her eyes popped open, I lost my words. She stared at me with an intensity that threatened to melt my flesh. "I will hear no more 'buts.' I fear that I have waited too long to bring you into the fold. I have never demanded enough of you spiritually. I'm afraid that now I may reap the tragic consequences of my . . . misguided love."

The following silence was oppressive, but I could think of nothing to say. Nothing.

"It is the same mistake I made with your father. I loved him too much."

In order to detach emotionally from my mother's words, I turned my attention to the portrait of my father. The flickering lamp threw just enough light on the photograph to outline the silhouette, but little more. As the silence lengthened, my eyes adjusted to the light, and my father's face emerged slowly, a feature at a time. Why had I never noticed the haunting sadness in his eyes before?

"I waited too long with your father, and now he is lost. Tell me that it is not too late to save you, Thomas. I had truly rather lose my own soul than see my son . . ." She could not continue.

I put my arms around her neck and lowered myself into her lap. "I'll go to all the meetings, Mama. There's still time."

* * *

I walk down a narrow path, mountains on my right, sheer abyss on my left. I am stark naked and ashamed since I know there are people I can't see, watching me. With each step the path becomes smaller, the ground eroding and falling into the void. I hear screams, as of distant dying horses, rising from the pit.

I stand with my face to the rock wall, my feet on the last patch of quaking ground. There is a cave at each hand. The one to my right is small, tight, only waist high. There is light inside, and I hear voices singing, "Kneel down, kneel down." The cave on my left is large and dark. When the ground gives way beneath my feet, I pull myself into the large cave and run in the darkness till I fall, out of breath. My sides ache and my hands bleed.

As the walls close in on me, I grab a stick and wedge it between them. The stick becomes a snake and bites my stomach. Snakes pour out of the wound. I crawl on hands and knees toward a light in the distance. The ground becomes swamp, I can't move. I close my eyes and wait for the walls to crush me.

I awake in the desert under a scalding sun. A burning cross stretches to the sky. At its base white-robed figures are massed facing me, singing a song I cannot understand. I rise slowly, painfully, and stagger toward them, straining to hear. My skin peels away from the bone as I reach for the fiery cross.

I tumble into a pit, falling endlessly, my screams of horror are drowned out by the chant of the white-robed choir far above. My father's face, shrunken and anguished, stares down at me and wails:

"TOO LATE. TOO LATE."

I rolled off my pallet, terrified and confused. Pulling myself to my knees, I checked my aching body for wounds and burns. My bedclothes were soaked. Blood? I ripped off my nightshirt and, running my hands over my face, chest, legs, arms, I wiped pools of sweat from my skin.

I lit the kerosene lamp and held it over my body. No

blood, no wounds. The pain remained; the fear endured. I replaced the lamp, wrapped myself in the blanket away from my sweat-soaked sheets, and shivered till dawn.

Chapter
Twenty-five

"**I**t's a goddamn outrage!"

"When the day comes that a man can't hang a thief, I say it's by God time to leave Texas!"

"I kin scarce wait till the sonsabitch heals up to where I kin kick his ass proper!"

"The good Lord has a special Hell for such as Sam Adams."

The maledictions leapt with bared fangs from the sidewalks as I walked to the newspaper office Wednesday morning. I knew that some were addressed to me, but I didn't stop to discuss them. When I was with Sam, I believed resolutely in both stands taken by *Plain Talk*; when confronted with the animosity of the overweening majority of the townfolk, I wondered if being right was worth the price. Gem Scott was dead and gone no matter what we said, and after last night's vision, I was less than eager to argue the case against Brother Nicholas.

"Don't you ever go to school?" Sam asked, pulling the press handle while I dragged the ink roller across the type. It was ten o'clock before the thought even occurred to him.

"No reason to. Mrs. Hardy took up with the True Viners, and they've been shufflin' substitutes in and out for the past week. We been chewin' 'em up fast as they can draft 'em. They can't keep up with who's there and who ain't."

Shad had paying work that day, so just Sam and I were in the office. Usually there were folks stopping by with news, or advertising, or just to talk, but not a soul ventured across the threshold that morning. I was relieved since I figured that whoever came in was bound to be dragging bad news with him.

Sam had a lot to talk about that morning. It was like the first couple of weeks when we'd worked so hard to get the first issue out. Sam compared the merits of Teddy Roosevelt to those of William Howard Taft, Socrates to Aristotle, and Mark Twain to Bret Harte. Sam gave the nod to the former in each instance and tied them together under their common attribute, Compassion. Sam often would start talking about a subject like art, or honesty, or revolution, and then just follow it across centuries and cultures. Doc was pretty good at that sort of thing, but his range had narrowed as he had grown old, and he used a lot of the same examples over and over. Langston was top drawer when he got rolling, but he was disinclined to perform unless there was liquor around and an audience of at least a half dozen. Then too, the lawyer's opinion rarely seemed grounded in conviction; he would argue either side of a case convincingly, depending on how it happened to strike him at the moment. While Sam's positions were anchored in principle, he encouraged me to ask questions and contest them. He was one of the few men I'd ever known who would earnestly dissect his own opinions and beliefs and laugh at the contradiction and paradox.

I appreciated the respite from the lynching and apocalypse, but it was a puzzle to me how a man who'd just lost his wife, was fast running out of money in a failing business, and could hardly walk the street without assault, could appear so unconcerned. It surely wasn't happiness; it was closer to fatalistic serenity. He was doing what he thought was right and he had nothing to lose. Such men are dangerous.

We caught hell from every direction as we delivered the papers to Cline's Mercantile in New Town. Everyone who spoke did so in malice, though most contented themselves with baleful stares or pointed avoidance. Since just about everybody in town bought a paper, there must have been people who agreed with Sam on either one or the other of his editorials, but they chose to keep their support obscure. The frequency of the term "nigger-lover" suggested which article the citizenry considered most loathsome, though we got our share of "heathen" and "pagan" as well. I must admit that walking stride for stride with Sam up the middle of the street (conjuring visions in the adolescent mind of the archetypal gunfighter), I'd never felt more alive or more *justified*.

My shootist fantasy was encouraged by our mission. Big Sam and I were headed to the courthouse for a showdown with the last "gunslinger/hero" that the Panhandle could boast of. With the sun at my back, I rolled the tension from my fingers. The smell of black powder smoke was in the air.

Alonzo Coffey had fixed on a career in law enforcement during his confinement at the territorial prison in Leavenworth. He had pulled two years for shooting a deputy in the closest thing to a fair gunfight that Kansas ever entertained: in the climax of a running feud over a cross-eyed whore, Lon rounded the corner of a flophouse and found the deputy leaning drunk and puking against a hitching post. As quickly as identity was established, both men drew and fired. No more than fifteen feet apart, five shots were discharged and two horses wounded before the deputy staggered into one of Lon's bullets flush in the left eye.

The town was well rid of the deputy, and knew it, but Coffey's decision to neither run away nor lie about the deed was more hubris than the local newspaper editor could tolerate. A series of indignant editorials prodded the townsfolk into convicting Lon of slaying a dissolute lawman that nobody missed or mourned.

Seven hundred thirty days on a diet of one ounce of bread and a pint of water convinced Lon that if he intended to wear a gun—and he wouldn't give it up so long as his right hand could make a fist—he would for damn sure have the law behind him. After several years as an itinerant deputy and bounty hunter, he joined Pat Garrett in the celebrated hunt for Billy Bonney. Four years later he was recruited by Garrett, who placed high value on ruthless men who never questioned orders, for duty in breaking up the short-lived Cowboy's Union in the Panhandle. It was undemanding work for steady pay and the perquisite of immunity from any law.

Coffey's life was changed and his mythology ensured when he single-handedly shot the notorious desperado, "The Slack-jaw Kid." Deputy Coffey of Blind Mule, Texas, shot the Kid twice in the back, rolled him over, and pumped four shots into his chest. Sheer arithmetic dictated a verdict of self-defense and a place in the gunfighter pantheon for "Coffin" Lon Coffey. Elevated to sheriff of Blind Mule by acclamation, Coffey settled into the job he would occupy for the next thirty years.

Of course, this is not the history that I grew up with. It was many years later before I was able to reconstruct the life of our celebrated lawman. In 1910, among the boys of High Plains, Sheriff Coffey was the hero of nickel novels and the stuff of legends. We would clear the streets and peer from the corners of buildings, avoiding eye contact with a man who might well shoot you down over a misunderstood glance. As Sam and I walked down the corridor of the courthouse, my whole body trembled at the prospect of confronting a demigod.

We walked into the large office, shutting the door loudly behind us to alert the preoccupied old man sitting behind the desk. Sheriff "Coffin" Lon Coffey, armed with a can of oil, was poised like a mantis over his firearm and apparently didn't notice our entrance. Nailed to the wall above his head was a collection of parched, yellow posters promising a thousand dollars in gold coin for an outlaw long dead, or one hundred dollars cash for a horse stolen twenty-five years back.

"What do you have on the Gem Scott murder, Sheriff?" Sam asked finally.

The lawman nearly dropped his forty-five-caliber revolver, then tried to recover control of the situation by making it appear as though he were spinning the gun on his trigger finger. The gun bounced off the top of the desk as Sam and I threw our hands up in reflex to ward off any accidental discharge. The sheriff snatched up the gun, snorting disdain at our show of fear.

"No witnesses, no clues," Sheriff Coffey said, holding the barrel up to the light and examining the bore. "Can't see how it's going no place."

"Unless you figure that chicken tied itself around Gem's neck, I'd say that was a clue." The edge on Sam's voice apparently offended the sheriff.

"That gives us an idee *why* he was killed. It don't say shit about *who* killed him."

"Did you talk to Jack Clement?"

Light from the window bounced off the quivering gun barrel and got in my eye. An old gunfighter's trick? No. He dropped the gun on the floor.

"Got four witnesses sayin' he's home all night. Can't dispute that." Coffey's voice rose, disembodied, from under the desk as he groped for his fowling piece. "No reason to think he done it anyway."

"Why did you question him, then?"

"Weren't my doin'. He come in Monday afternoon with four gents that said they been together for the past three days and didn't know a thing about that nigger that got himself lynched. I said that was all right by me, and they left." The Sheriff rose from under his desk holding his shaking gun in both hands as if it were a writhing fish, and wrestled it into his holster.

Sam whistled between his teeth. "And that cleared everything up? To your satisfaction?"

The Sheriff clearly resented the questioning from a whippersnapper who didn't know shit from Shinola about law enforcement and had likely never back-shot anyone in his life. "Ain't cleared up. This is what we call a 'going-on' case. It won't be over till we finish with it."

Hard to argue with that.

The Sheriff stood up. "Now I got work to do, and I 'spect you do too, so why don't you take your boy and get after it." His angry left eye blinked out every word in code.

I suppose it was obvious to every adult in town that "Coffin" Lon was showing the ravages of a lifetime of sleeping with a gun and a whiskey bottle, but they managed to ignore his infirmity when it came time to vote. The electorate continually chose to keep our frontier Lochinvar patrolling the quiet streets, his impotent six-gun strapped to his bony thigh, the last notched sidearm in the Panhandle. Everyone in town—save idolatrous youth—would be relieved when we buried the useless old man, but nobody wanted to throw the first spadeful of dirt on the chest of an immortal. The job was his till he died.

As we walked silently down the courthouse steps, my eye was drawn to a figure emerging from Foster's Boot Repair, about thirty yards in front of us. I nudged Sam and nodded in that direction. He stopped in his tracks.

If Rebekah saw us, she didn't let on. She took a hard right and walked crisply away. Sam didn't move. In the three days since Rebekah had left, Sam had not uttered her name. I knew that he was self-conscious about his black eye and bruises, which were fading but remained pretty gruesome. Still, I kind of wanted him to chase her down.

"We got work," he said.

By the time we hit the Bowery, Sam was pretty much back to his old self, speaking to all the gents and tipping his hat to the ladies like he was the governor of Texas instead of the town untouchable. To my discredit, I was scuffing along silently behind him trying to make it appear as though our proximity were a matter of circumstance rather than companionship. It was easier to walk tall in New Town, where Mama's hawk eye was unlikely to discover my truancy and unhallowed association.

I ducked around the window of the True Vine Church, ready to break into a sprint to *Plain Talk* and safety, when I sighted the spare form that I considered only a shade preferable to that of my mother, or, for that matter, Death on a pale horse. The midday crowd parted like Moses' Red Sea to allow Brother Nicholas the good four feet of elbow room necessary for man and aura to pass unhindered. He was on the far side of the street, and I briefly embraced the hope that he and Sam might simply fail to see each other, unlikely, or that each, upon spotting his nemesis, would have the decorum and restraint to pass without public acknowledgment.

Fat chance. Their eyes locked like a pair of meat hooks

dragging them face-to-face in the middle of the street. Horses, wagons, and the odd automobile veered around them without comment, impressed by the authority of the two men who unself-consciously preempted territory traditionally ceded to wheeled traffic. I peeled off and took a position in the second rank of the crowd that materialized quicker than you could whisper "trouble." I stayed close enough to see and hear everything, while sufficiently removed to escape detection as a partisan. The onlookers tried to appear fluid and unfocused, making small talk with each other as a pretext for remaining within earshot of the looming battle.

"Brother Nicholas," Sam shouted, in mock camaraderie, "it is a rare privilege to see you gracing our fair streets. You spend too little time out among *your people*. When we see you on your stage shouting down bogus revelations, it is easy to forget what a small man you are."

There were audible gasps as the witnesses formed a circle, forsaking all pretense of being anything but spectators to a heavyweight fight.

"I am pleased to see you walking upright and unaided, Adams. Only two nights ago I was treated to the spectacle of you lying drunken and battered in front of a saloon. One wonders where you find the time to print your blasphemies between beatings."

Sam nodded pleasantly, as though acknowledging sincere condolence. "Rest assured, Brother, I'll always find the time to print the truth about scoundrels and hypocrites, and I will crawl off my death bed, if necessary, to do it. I have tried for several weeks to talk with you, but I can't get past your henchmen. I should think that you would want to use every vehicle to convey your proclamations in these *final days*."

It would have taken a nine-pound hammer and a cold steel wedge to chisel the sarcasm off Sam's words, but Nicholas didn't bat an eye.

"I am well aware of Jesus' warning of the evil of the faithless scrivener who uses his office to subvert the will of God. I chose to deliver my message directly to the people, as befits God's vessel."

Nicholas took a step to the right, but Sam countered and they were again eyeball to Adam's apple. The spectators inched closer with each exchange, leaving the combatants little more than a ring with a five-foot radius.

"It seems, Nicholas, that you have ceased to distinguish between servant and Master. You have taken an unfortunate situation and driven it headlong toward catastrophe for your own vanity and benefit. Surely during all the time that you've spent poring over your Bible searching for curses you've stumbled over the proverb: 'Pride goeth before destruction, and a haughty spirit before a fall.' "

Good lick. The crowd nodded appreciatively, but Nicholas wouldn't back off.

"We are again reminded that the Devil can quote scripture to his own advantage, but dooms his soul by his words. The Lord might well refuse to suffer such a heretic to live for even the eight days till the Assumption."

Sam smiled grimly. "If that is a threat, Nicholas, then I would have thought you wiser than to speak it before so many witnesses."

"There is nothing *I* can do, or need do. *You* demolished your lair of iniquity, despoiled *your marriage*, brought forth the revulsion of *your neighbors* upon yourself. The disciples of Satan devour their own children."

Until that moment the contest had been conducted in measured tones and cold blood. At the mention of "marriage," Sam's face knotted up and his fists clenched and rose to his belt. I thought he was going to take the skinny preacher out with a single punch. While I wanted to see him throw that punch, I had the feeling that if he did, there might well be a bolt of lightning to dodge. That fear must have been shared by other ringsiders, since we all backed off a step.

Sam dropped all pretense of civility. "Listen here, you little tinhorn holy roller—"

WHAM!

Sam was knocked staggering by a fat lady wielding a twenty-pound sack of flour. Fortunately, the woman stood less than five feet tall and attacked from the rear, so the apex of her swing landed between the editor's shoulder blades—if she had been four inches taller, she would likely have addled him seriously. The cloth sack burst on impact, covering Sam and scattering a cloud of fine ground flour into the air. She got in two good licks before her weapon went limp, then took her fight hand-to-hand.

"IDOLATOR, BLASPHEMER, ISCARIOT, GOAT DE-BAUCHER—" she shouted, her beefy arms spanning Sam's waist—actually a little lower—from behind in an attempt to bulldog him to the ground.

"PHARISEE, BAAL-WORSHIPER, ABOMINATOR—"

Brother Nicholas, sensing that the exhibition would glorify neither God nor evangelist, spun on his heels, found a crease in the dumbfounded ring of humanity, and departed with unbecoming haste. The crowd, robbed of their entertainment, and perhaps embarrassed by the degeneration from debate to debacle, dispersed as quickly as it had formed. Only an ill-bred few stood their ground and cheered on the fat lady.

"TEMPLE DESECRATOR, PHILISTINE DOG, SERPENT DEFILER—"

I didn't look back till I got to the door of the office. Sam was still wrapped in a bear hug, but his opponent had picked up a rider as well. A bald-headed old man with a splotched face, apparently the attacker's husband, had his arms around the fat lady's chest, trying to wrench her away from her prey. The struggle, complete with shouts and grunts, reminded me of an African (some said French) mating practice that I had heard about in whispered confidence at the poolroom. Before I had time to figure out the possibilities of the formation, Sam had pulled away and was hotfooting it toward sanctuary with as much decorum as a flour-coated journalist being chased by a screaming fat lady dragging a piebald man could muster.

It took Sam a long bath and the better part of the afternoon to get over the street burlesque that had been thrust upon him. He asked me three different times if I knew who the fat lady was, and spent over an hour voicing the "I-should-have-said" arguments that he would use the next time he found himself toe-to-toe with Brother Nicholas.

By suppertime he could laugh about the absurdity of the guerrilla attack by the fat lady, and he emerged renewed in spirit. The taste of battle had invigorated us both, and we—mostly Sam—committed ourselves to a bold plan. The new marching order called for us to put out a two-sheeter every three days between now and the Glorious Assumption. The backbone of these issues was to challenge Nicholas's movement and review Gem Scott's lynching; the former taking precedence unless new evidence surfaced on the murder. After witnessing the diligence of the local constabulary, we didn't expect imminent breakthrough on the hanging.

Since local advertisers paid for one exposure a week, we would run half the ads in each edition, along with standing legal notices in five-point (very small) type that the county paid us for. The fact that the biweekly would be more work was compensated for by the sense of urgency we both felt. Articles on piano recitals at the Baptist church and little Jimmie Reeves's lost Poland China boar hog were to be supplanted by ones refuting the threat of universal destruction and prodding the investigation of cold-blooded murder. We resolved that if *Plain Talk* was going under, it would do so with brawling integrity. We saw ourselves as the last musketeers defending the fiery battlement of the fourth estate, crusaders for truth and justice in the land of fabulist and charlatan.

At the office, I gave little thought to the fears that regularly assailed me between dusk and dawn. Adrenaline and purpose sustained me through the day. Only after the air turned black did despair chase me down and taunt me that if I were wrong about this single issue—Armageddon—then it mattered not if I were right about *everything else* in the world: I was still a dead man frying in Hell come midnight Wednesday. I worked hard all day to shake last night's vision, but it would not stay buried: *"TOO LATE!"*

Begging off work around five o'clock, I headed for home. I was ready to live up to the pledge of piety made to my mother. My night terrors had convinced me that if I was going to find any peace, temporal or eternal, I would have to display sufficient reverence to fool my mother and, with luck, an inattentive God.

Chapter
Twenty-six

"**H**urry up, you two," Mama called over her shoulder, "I should have been there a quarter hour ago. They can't do a thing till I show up."

Rebekah and I were straggling behind Mama's blistering pace, reluctant conscripts swept along against inclination by an indomitable spirit. It was Rebekah's first visit to Nicholas's altar; she had caved in under the barrage of proselytizing that was now the Widder's sole vocabulary. I knew the pilgrimage was contrary to every theological precept of the devout Rebekah, but she was trying to buy a little time and silence by bending to an unceasing wind. I also knew that her token sacrifice would not appease our commander; Mama would be satisfied only when those closest to her, and ultimately the entire population, would stand as one and endorse Nicholas's belief as Gospel. Rebekah and I were hoping only to purchase a quiet meal, a variety of dialogue. And I had a nightmare to pay off.

"How was school today, Tom?" Rebekah asked as we trotted along in Mother's wake. It was the second time that I had faced the question, having ducked it at the supper table. Although Rebekah seemed sincerely interested in me, and we both looked for mealtime topics that would wrench the conversation away from Mama, there was little common ground. Rebekah didn't want to talk about the newspaper or Sam—and Mama had explicitly forbidden mention of "that man's" name in the house—and I had no interest in sewing room gossip, so school came up with distressing frequency.

"Not so bad. Nothing new. Same old stuff," I said, hoping to make it so routine as to discourage follow-up.

Mama dropped back into the pack long enough to ask a question. "Who they got teaching now that Alma Hardy crossed over to us?"

O Lordy. "Uh, different people," I replied, scrambling for names. "First one and then another." We were within thirty yards of the speaker's platform. If I could stall her for just a minute—

"Like who?"

"Uh, Miss Scotnik was there today," I muttered, merging two names that I'd spent a lot of time with lately.

"Who?"

"Uh, Miss Scotnik, she's new. Polish lady, just come from . . . Minnesota or up around there. Probably won't be here long. Leaving next week I hear."

Mama stopped in her tracks, her neck twisting to the right, eyelids dropping to half-mast in suspicion. My neck lay scrubbed and shining on the chopping block.

"I believe that I've heard about her," Rebekah interjected. "She taught up in South Dakota and is here visiting relatives."

I stumbled, equilibrium destroyed by disbelief. Mama couldn't believe her ears either. She blinked a couple times real fast as she stared into Rebekah's angelic face. Rebekah was beginning to pick up some color when a blessed voice from the speaker's platform interrupted the inquisition.

"Widder, Widder Greer. Come on over here, darlin'. We got work needs doin'," Clara Clark shouted in her high, nasal voice, granting a blessed reprieve to Rebekah and me.

"We will discuss this later, Thomas," Mama said as she ushered us through the early arrivers, bodies sliding to the left and right of us like waves off the prow of a great ship. We were nearly an hour early, so the crowd was small and porous, offering little resistance to the Old Campaigner. Rebekah was embarrassed by our discourteous ingress and lagged, causing Mama to snatch her hand and pull her along like a recalcitrant child. Rebekah and I were deposited front row center, while Mama joined the seated elect.

As Nicholas's crowds had swelled, the necessity for a firm hand on the logistics had become apparent. Second only to Nature in intolerance of a vacuum, my mother jumped in with both feet, assuming responsibility for a raft of details that no one else wanted to worry about. The demands of Nicholas's crusade fit Mama's talents as though cut from cloth she had knitted herself. The Glorious Assumption was dramatic, immediate, and definitive.

The Widder Greer was a shock trooper, the first to form the conclave, hurl the brick, go to the barricades. She was the tireless worker and fearless ideologue indispensable in building an organization or movement. And, since the Glorious Assumption was an enterprise that would not be allowed the luxury of mid-life and slow decline into bureaucracy—come Wednesday, seven short days hence, there would be resolution of one sort or another—every moment until then would be filled with demands that required my mother's attention and talents.

"I'm much obliged for your speakin' out for me," I said to Rebekah several minutes after Mama's departure. "About Miss Nikscot."

"Scotnik," she corrected. The blush returned to her cheeks.

I rushed to ease her mind concerning my truancy. "It's the end of the year and most of the kids are out for spring planting or getting ready for the end of the world. Nobody's trying to teach anything. I learn a lot more at the paper, and Sam needs the help. . . ." When I violated our unspoken agreement with the mention of that name, Rebekah's gaze snapped back to the empty platform.

"When you figure on leavin'?" I thought as long as we were trapped there, I might as well ask the questions that we all avoided at home.

Rebekah absently rubbed an ugly bruise on the back of her left hand, the self-inflicted product of a slammed door. "I should think by early next week I'll have the fare."

"If your father is rich and didn't want you to come here in the first place, why don't you get the money from him?"

"It's *my* decision and *my* responsibility."

And obviously none of my business. Rebekah must have felt bad about her clipped answer; her tone was softer when she continued. "I'd like to be gone before all this comes to fruition. There is great potential for a tragedy that I had rather not witness."

No argument there. I think that each of us wanted to put the other at ease, but I couldn't see any place for the conversation to go. So I slipped under the rope and skirted the outer edge of the crowd in order to size it up.

Folks were flocking in by the droves, and with better than a half hour until show time, it appeared that Nicholas was going to command a record crowd. New disciples from neighboring towns commuted nightly to the revival and had taken to staking out their own areas. Placards raised on tall sticks boasted that contingents from Bramlett, Skankton, Broken Spoke, even the dreaded Wishbone, had come to pay homage to the regional prophet. Well to the rear, a group of twenty Negroes stood in quiet self-consciousness, all but invisible, waiting for the crowd to complete so they could form the final rank.

I heard a lot of talk about Monday night's meteor shower along with various accounts of hurricanes, cyclones, typhoons, and tidal waves around the globe. Though citing different cases, or the same case to different purposes, all agreed the pattern was obvious, the signs unmistakable. I felt myself being drawn into the whirlpool of despair, and worked hard to keep a foot on shore. Even out there on the wide open prairie, there was an air of desperate melancholy that could sweep away the ungrounded spirit. I forced myself to view the scene through the eyes of a reporter, to describe rather than experience, think rather than feel. I patted the pencil and paper in my shirt pocket. I only had time for one circuit of the crowd and a few hasty notes before the opening hymns dragged me back into what was passing for reality in High Plains.

I ducked under the rope and moved freely in front of the mass straining against the barrier. No one tried to stop me, knowing that I was the Widder's son and above the strictures binding mortals. I could see the back of Mama's head bobbing excitedly in the front row as she talked at Lily Barkley. Colonel Hedgman's wheelchair was placed two benches away from Mama's post, reflecting the mutual disregard each felt toward the other. Mamie Greer was everything the Colonel disliked about the "new breed" of woman that had proliferated since the Civil War, and the Widder had serious reservations about the Colonel's piety, semiprivately speculating that he had *bought* his way into the movement. Both considered it a severe test of faith to share a room with the other, and at times the Panhandle seemed hardly big enough to hold both of them.

I had trouble finding Rebekah; she had failed to defend her turf and had been swept back several rows. Lacking zealotry, she likely would have ended up on the back row with the black people if I hadn't taken her hand and tugged her back to the rope. I elbowed aside a fat old lady and a surly farmer to reclaim our forward post and leaned out over the rope to watch the consequence ripple down the line: a tall, red-haired woman was caught leaning on the wrong foot and was swept back into the boiling mass.

The platform was about four feet above the ground, and was bare except for a fifteen-foot-high calendar looming from the back. The "Ten Days of Rapture" had dwindled to eight: May eleventh through the eighteenth. The final date was decorated with heraldic drawings and religious illustrations, in which I recognized the hand of my old teacher Mrs. Hardy. She wrote the book on "Show and Tell."

After another five minutes of hymn-torture, Nicholas appeared from the back of the stage. Time was short and eternity near, so Nicholas no longer opened with a welcoming statement or words of condolence. He waved a Kansas City newspaper over his head and spoke effortlessly in a voice that easily reached every ear in the crowd. "You have all read the papers and heard the news: 'King Edward of England Dead! Europe Flooded! Stock Market Continues Plummet!' Earthquakes, drought, pestilence, war! Who among you can deny this Earth is doomed?

"Scientists don't deny it! In this very newspaper a famous scientist tells us that the comet's tail is filled with *explosive hydrogen*. A single spark will ignite that hydrogen, setting off a tremendous blast that will *suffocate every human being*! It will scorch the ground, boil the oceans, and consume *all living things* on the face of the planet!"

No introduction or buildup, straight for the jugular. The crowd was silent as Nicholas flung down the newspaper and raised his Bible overhead in both hands. "It is as has been foretold in Revelation: 'The first Angel sounded and there followed hail and fire mingled with blood, and they were cast upon the Earth, and the trees were burned up and all green grass, as it were a great mountain burning with fire, was cast into the sea. *And the sea became as blood!*' "

Now that Nicholas had our attention—and all I could hear was the sound of my own breath and the cry of a baby at the rear of the crowd—he walked silently across the stage, his head bowed and shaking.

"This is not a time of sadness or weakness, but one of joy and strength. God doesn't want frightened people in His Kingdom. He has tired of seeing his followers endure this vale of tears, mocked by the heathen, punished by the sun and wind and bitter Earth. It is time for the strong to rejoice in God's love and trust in His mercy. It will take courage, but it is the courage of David who slew the giant, and Daniel who feared not the lion. God will provide the strength, if you will but open your heart and cast off the vanity that is a manacle on your spirit. God will reward the strong with eternal life; the weak will languish in the pit of despair.

"Join the battle against Satan!"

I was surprised by the appeal to valor when submission had been the standing order at the churches I had attended. Camped on the front row so close that I could count the wrinkles in the preacher's clothes and chart the bobbing of his oversized Adam's apple, I felt Brother Nicholas's power for the first time. I had to admit that I liked the talk about strength and courage and battle, too. I stowed my pencil and paper, notes forgotten.

For the next seventy minutes, excluding a short break for two verses of "I'll Meet You on the Other Side," I witnessed the most spellbinding display of personal charisma and public performance that I'd ever seen. Brother Nicholas spent little time with the comet, concentrating on the glory of salvation. He screamed, pleaded, danced and crawled across his stage, sparing no emotion in attempting to snatch my soul from the agony it was plummeting inexorably to-

ward. I was surrounded by sobbing people, and the sound
of "tongues" rambling in their desperate, clipped litany was
constant. People fell to the ground in convulsion, while others cut loose in a frenzy of dancing.

Only Rebekah appeared unmoved. She stood by my side,
her face impassive. I drew strength from her, but each draft
satisfied less than the last. It was my battle without ally or
guide.

Brother Nicholas was on one knee at the right side of the
stage in what had to be his final entreaty for souls, and I
could feel myself slipping into the gray cloud of blissful
surrender. When the strong hand of God grabbed my wrist,
I nearly fainted. My mother pulled me under the rope and
to the front. As I stumbled forward, I searched over my
shoulder, hoping to steady myself on the rock of Rebekah's
countenance. Too late. She had been swept back into the
mass by the surging penitents starved for the word.

"Come to God *now*, only hours are left. This world is
lost, but you can join me in a better one. The comet cannot
hurt you if you follow *me*. The comet will be your savior,"
Nicholas beseeched. Only ten feet separated us. I was three
steps from a life free of misery and doubt.

Brother Nicholas stood at the top of the steps and waved
for the people to come forward. The gentle strains of
"Softly and Tenderly" began off to my left and spread
slowly through the crowd. The folks who climbed the steps
were mostly townspeople, folks I had known all my life,
but their redemption had transformed them. They were softened, vulnerable versions of the people who had chased me
from their doors, or yelled at me for scrapping with their
sons. Alone on the stage Brother Nicholas had seemed ten
feet tall, but now nearly everyone he embraced towered
over him.

Mama's arm remained firmly around my shoulder as she
swayed and sang. She squeezed and smiled down on me; I
knew that her dearest wish was within my power. I had myself pretty well in hand until I saw, at the very end of the
line, Mrs. Stigman wrestling with her son Timmy. The sight
of Timmy trying to twist away from his mother so he could

ride his stick horse away from this place that clearly terrified him pulled my heart to my knees.

Timmy Stigman was my age; he was born only two days
before I was, but he was a lot smaller, and he was very different. Mrs. Stigman had tried to keep Timmy in school until Mr. Hurley, the principal, finally told her what
everybody else had long known: Timmy was "tetched" and
would never read or write or do anything much more than
ride his stick horse till he died.

After Brother Nicholas had welcomed penitents into the
fold, he saw the terrified Timmy standing at the bottom of
the steps, his head pressed deeply into his mama's skirts,
his arms wrapped around her legs. The poor little fellow
was howling like a dog with his foot in a trap. Mrs.
Stigman didn't know what to do, and searched the heavens
for relief. Everybody wanted to help, but nobody moved.

Brother Nicholas descended the steps slowly, knelt, and
whispered in the boy's ear. Timmy unwrapped himself from
his mother's stomach and, still holding his stick horse in his
right hand, turned toward the preacher. The boy must have
seen something he trusted, because his screaming choked
back to a quiet sob and he embraced Brother Nicholas.
When the preacher rose with poor Timmy on his left arm,
the crowd knew that it had witnessed a true wonder. Their
hosannas followed preacher, boy, and mother up the steps,
where Brother Nicholas displayed his prize in triumph.
Timmy loosened his choke hold on the preacher, gazed out
on the sea of smiling faces, and somehow knew that everyone was on his side. When the boy raised his stick overhead and waved it like a captured flag, the ovation was
thundering. Timmy retreated to the safety of the preacher's
neck.

In the charged atmosphere of revival, that passed for
Miracle, and I too considered it such, Brother Nicholas
turned Timmy back over to the beaming Mrs. Stigman, who
silently thanked God for revealing what she had always
known: her son was blessed, her life was justified.

Brother Nicholas's voice cut through the din, and the
crowd hushed: "And the Spirit of the Lord shall rest upon
him. The Spirit of wisdom and understanding, the Spirit of

counsel and might, the Spirit of knowledge and fear of the Lord!

"The wolf also shall dwell with the lamb, and the leopard shall lie down with the kid, and the calf, and the young lion and the fatling together, AND A LITTLE CHILD SHALL LEAD THEM!"

Overcome by helplessness and the insignificance of my own existence, I fell into an abyss of despond . . . down, twisting, I plunged in a gut-churning plummet, till, Marvel of Marvels, I felt the warm glory of our Holy Cause fill my soul. If my mother pushed me toward the platform, it was unnecessary; I was the first in line for the second wave of the redeemed. I cried in joy and relief at the strength of Nicholas's hands on my shoulders and lost myself in the golden tones that welcomed me into "the Kingdom that knows not sorrow or death."

After being guided away from Brother Nicholas, I walked over to where Timmy stood. He had his right arm around his mother's skirt and stared blankly out into the crowd. He brightened when he saw me and grabbed my hand in both of his and patted it gently. I surrendered to the emotions that would not be denied. I hugged Timmy and cried.

I bathed in the love and acceptance that washed across the platform. Before I had time to search the crowd for her, Mama was at my side embracing me with a fervor so profound I was left gasping for air. We shared a verse of "The Old Rugged Cross," before a grim usher led us off the crowded stage.

Mama usually stayed for an hour or so after the crowd cleared, but she chucked all responsibility that night, and everybody understood and was happy for her. For they all knew that the Widder's most cherished prayer had been answered; she would ascend to her heavenly reward attended by her only child.

Rebekah was nowhere to be found when we started our walk back, but I wasn't disappointed by her absence. I was exhausted and content beyond words; Mama and I sailed back to the Bowery on a cloud of serenity that would not have accommodated an additional passenger. We held hands and hummed hymns all the way home.

The light under the door in my—Rebekah's—room indicated that she was safely home. Mama and I shared a last hug before I stumbled off to my pallet. I wanted time to rejoice in solitude, to luxuriate under the light of comfort and security. From the moment of my conversion till nestled in the downy bosom of sleep, I do not recall a single challenge to my bliss. The name that could have brought my newly constructed world crashing to the ground never touched my consciousness. But it was a cocoon that would not tolerate the light of day.

Chapter
Twenty-seven

Jesus Christ! What am I going to tell Sam?

My eyes had not yet opened when the horrible question exploded in my consciousness and sent a shudder through my body like a frigid chisel pounded by a steel driver's sledge ripping a course from my cranium to my coccyx. The thought must have festered in my subconscious all night, waiting patiently for the erosion of the stone wall that I'd thrown up around my conversion. Gone was the heady excitement of life begun anew, purified and resolute to do battle for the One True Cause. Now all I could think of was how to explain to the man whose respect I coveted above all others that I had betrayed our common philosophy and, consequently, our friendship. The sun wasn't up but the tentative light of false dawn speckled the small window above my mattress. There would be no rest till I came to some decision.

The first alternative—dumping Sam—I rejected immediately, though I knew that was the action dictated by Mama and my new colleagues in the Lord. I needed Sam for reasons I could not, and dared not, analyze.

Deception would be tough—no, impossible—since the names of new converts were common topic on Bowery streets, and Sam, by nature and profession, was on top of the local gossip. I didn't want to take the low road anyhow, since it would be not only a betrayal of my religion, but craven cowardice as well. I was a soldier, not a frightened, mealymouthed scripture mumbler.

The only reasonable course was clear: I would have to convert Sam. I didn't delude myself as to ease of accomplishment. Granted, he was the foremost heretic in town, and I had only one week to accomplish a feat not unlike the conversion of persecutor-Saul to missionary-Paul. I also recognized that I could not depend upon a heavenly light to strike Sam to the ground and blind him into compliant humility.

I immediately rejected the "end of the world, save your soul" approach; Sam would not be converted through intimidation. I would have to show Sam, by example, the overwhelming sense of joy and belonging that followed commitment to the Higher Power, the ecstasy of being allied to a blessed group who loved and nourished you and would help you through times and decisions that could overwhelm a mortal. Times like next Wednesday night, and decisions like choosing between everlasting bliss and eternal torment. Things like that.

Now that my course was charted, I closed my eyes, settled back into the fetal position, and summoned the feelings that I had gorged on last night. They came, but in a diluted form that did not cheer me as I had hoped. I had to content myself with a pale shadow of the glory that had been mine. The realization that religious enchantment was no more constant and enduring than the worldly variety depressed me. Little more than eight hours had passed, and already I was besieged by doubt and disappointment. Even though I had been warned that this was the Devil's modus operandi, to be expected by all who had exorcised Satan's fangs from his flank, I couldn't help but take it personally. And though it had been one of the first things that I had forsworn in post-Rapture resolution, I craved a chew of tobacco with all my soul.

I spat out my chaw and peeked around a rain barrel to confirm my privacy. I wasn't proud of myself—it was hard to be when crunched between two barrels in an alley, with a shallow, foamy pool of tobacco juice yelling "hypocrite" up at me—but I felt decidedly better, more relaxed.

I stood up and slipped what was left of my plug in my right front pocket and patted it for reassurance. Due to my elevated status, I could no longer walk into Hayes's and order another cut across the counter, so this slender two fingers of tobacco was going to have to last me through Wednesday. I shuddered at the thought.

I started whistling before I hit the sidewalk in front of the office and was well into the chorus of "Danny Boy" by the time I walked through the door. Sam's head jerked up from his desk, where he was hunched over a layout. He was unaccustomed to jocularity at this time of the morning, so my attitude sparked the desired response.

"Morning, Tom," he said. "You're sounding mighty spry today."

"Top o' the morning to you, Sammy," I chirped, sounding like a pocket-sized version of Big Mike. Since the Irishman was the only man in the Bowery who smiled before noon, I patterned my behavior after him. "I never felt better in my life."

I tossed my cap into the corner and rolled up my sleeves. "Isn't it a glorious day?" I added, to make sure that he noted that there was indeed a difference between the drab, dispirited Tommy Greer of yesterday and the new, dynamic model standing, grinning, shining before him.

Sam raised a wary eyebrow but didn't respond immediately. "Got a good bit of type to set if we're going to get a two-sheet out tomorrow," he said finally. "You can start with that copy sitting on the case. If you're ready to begin."

"Indeed I am, Sam." Rubbing my hands together, I bent over the type case, the very model of unbridled industry. Somewhere back East, Horatio Alger was smiling in his grave.

Sam walked over to the stove and filled his cup. "Coffee?" he offered.

I threw my hands up and backed away like a vampire confronted with a cross. Only this morning, Mama and I, in a fit of masochistic piety, had sworn off the use of that poison. Pollute my sanctified body with caffeine! I'd rather die.

Sam had had enough. "Damn it, Tom, could you just forget the horseshit. I've heard about your conversion, and that's your business, but if you're going to work around here, I'd appreciate it if you'd act like a human being and not some . . . self-righteous prig."

I did the only thing a man could do when his honor and religion are ridiculed: I grabbed my cap and stomped out. It took only one circuit of the Bowery to remind me of my meager options. If there were only seven days left on the planet, I'd be . . . durned if I was going to spend them in school. Mama had suggested that my presence would be most welcome down at the church, but there was a limit to my piety, and spending all waking hours with my mother was well to the far side of it. I could just kick around town for a week, but the thought of trying to fill up all those hours with the specter of Armageddon hanging over my head made me cringe. I needed to work and I needed time around someone who wasn't hollering "Doomsday" every minute. What choice did I have?

Sam hardly looked up from his desk, but his eyes smiled when I walked through the door. I tossed my cap in the corner. "I'll take that cup of coffee now."

My state of grace demanded a few concessions that Sam and I worked out that morning. It was apparent that I could no longer work on stories that defamed Brother Nicholas or the church; Sam would have to write, proof, and set them up himself. I tried to draw the line on saloon and whiskey ads, but Sam's notched eyebrow warned me away. I conceded the point, knowing better than to try to win every skirmish on the first day of the war.

"Care to take a walk uptown?" Sam asked after lunch. He checked the progress of his black eye in the mirror; it was still a sickly yellow with red tributaries snaking in and around the orb. Improving but still grim. He carefully dabbed a little flour under it. "We've got some business that will get us out of the office for a while."

"I don't know, Sam, I'd like to finish this column. . . ." Since it was my habit to leap at any chance to escape the tyranny of the type case, Sam saw through my hesitation.

"Tom, you appear to be sincere about your conversion, but you're still going to have to make up your own mind about how you run your life. A man makes his own decisions on how he earns his living, who his friends are," he paused to look me straight in the eye, "and who he can walk the streets with. *You* have to do what *you* think is best." Sam turned around to shuffle some papers on his desk, for the purpose, I believe, of giving me some time to think.

No amount of analysis was going to make this decision any easier. How long can you hunt with the hounds and run with the rabbits? I resolved my quandary in a fashion common to those who are forced to fight the battle between Desire and Reason: I did what I wanted to do and rationalized away the inconsistency.

I grabbed my hat and we left.

Perhaps all the looks that Sam and I drew on the street were not scornful, and I'm willing to believe that every remark whispered in the vicinity was not derogatory, but many of them were pointedly so. Sam tipped his hat to the ladies and spoke to every man we encountered; he wouldn't give an inch. By the time we got to the post office, I had developed some backbone myself.

After collecting our mail, we picked up a new ad commission from old Peg Foster at the boot shop. She had never advertised *anywhere*, but now she had decided that Sam deserved some encouragement for the guts he had shown in the Gem Scott articles. Sam had convinced himself it was the first of many New Town accounts that would soon swamp our paper.

After checking for news at the depot and the usual shops and stores, we headed back to the Bowery. Sam had talked my ear off on the way up, but had fallen silent when we left New Town. "Would you expect Rebekah to be at your house now?" he asked when we reached the Bowery.

"I reckon. She generally sews by herself now that Mama's drug everyone else off to the church."

Sam nodded. "You can proof the Scott follow-up. I'll be back directly." He peeled off in the direction of my house.

I whistled brightly all the way back to the office, encouraged by Sam's acceptance of my new faith and his pursuit of Rebekah. I wanted to see them back together again, and I didn't mind working alone for a few hours if it furthered that end. I'd barely started running off the proof before Sam came steaming through the door.

"What's wrong?" I said.

"Your mother. She wants to talk to you."

"HOW COULD YOU?"

You could have fried bacon on the white heat of Mama's indignation.

My hand squeezed the doorknob as I considered flight. I had known confrontation was inevitable; I just hadn't expected it so soon.

"How could you walk the streets with *that man* in broad daylight, and *lie* to me about school. I should have *made* you go with me to the church today." Mama was pacing the length of the kitchen and twisting a foot-long piece of thick string in both hands while she vented her rage.

"Have you no shame, no . . . understanding of what you're giving up by consorting with this demon *now*? These are the final days, Thomas! Every action you take is being studied and weighed against your everlasting soul. Can't you go even a day without sacrilege?" She steadied herself on the kitchen table, head bowed, eyes shut. The string that had been pulled tight into an aggressive garrote she unconsciously twisted into a hangman's noose.

"It's my own fault," she said, the anger metamorphosing abruptly into tortured self-reproach. "I'm being punished for my failings. Things I shouldn't have done, or things I should have but couldn't get around to. I could have been a better mother, I know it. . . ."

Oh, God. I could bear up under the most searing frontal attack, but I melted like May snow under her self-flagellation. I suppose that Mama knew it as well.

"No, Mama," I said softly as I moved up to the table. "It's not your fault. You see, I was tryin' to save Sam Adams from himself. The only way I could do it was by workin' with him, so I could bring him along slow." There was enough truth to that so that I didn't look over my shoulder for a lightning bolt.

"Don't lie to me, son. Don't pile sin upon sin."

But I could tell that she wanted a way out too. "I'm not lying, Mama." Technically. "I figured if I could pull Sam Adams into the church, my spot in Heaven would be sure.

It's kinda like you're doin' with Lily Barkley. I know for a
fact I've got a lot of history that needs to be put right, and
I figured Sam Adams's conversion would be enough to set
me straight with the Lord." With some change.

"Beelzebub himself could be redeemed by converting
Sam Adams. But it's not a job for a boy with only one day
in the Lord. A man like Sam Adams can twist you around
to where you can't tell what's right and what isn't." Her sad
eyes stared across the table and seized mine like a tired old
cobra transfixing a wounded mongoose—looking for an alternative to a pitched battle. "You must promise that you
won't associate with that man or that newspaper again."

I nodded.

"Say it."

"I won't associate with that newspaperman again."

"Under penalty of my eternal soul."

"Under penalty of my soul."

Though I could barely squeak out the words, the relief
that spread over my mother's ancient gray face made my
heart swell. I walked around the table and we met in an
embrace that gladdened us both. Feeling her tears falling
into my hair, I vowed to live up to my pledge.

"It's only a week, son," she said, behind barely contained
sobs, "and I promise to do everything I can to keep you on
the path."

I nodded my head as much as her hug would allow and
fought back the tears that threatened to reduce me to self-
less desperation.

"Would you like something to eat?"

"Yes," I said, though food was the last thing on my
mind. It was the least I could do for someone whose only
desire was to nourish me, body and soul.

The old True Vine Church—now re-christened The Church
of the Glorious Assumption—hummed like a new Pope-
Toledo Touring Automobile hitting on two dozen calibrated
pistons. Urgency crackled through the room; no one sat, no
hand was idle. I had never encountered that level of focused intensity short of a crap game or cockfight.

The second we hit the door, Mama turned from concerned parent to confident straw boss. She introduced me loudly to the room, then posted me to a project run by Mrs. Hardy, my old schoolteacher. I cringed at the irony. "Sister Alma" was painting the lettering on three sheets that had been stitched together to be hung from the base of Nicholas's platform. She smiled at me and nodded vacantly as though she didn't recognize her old nemesis. She hummed "Jesus Loves Me" while filling in the legend that had been outlined in pencil: *And a Great Red Dragon Fell from Heaven and the Earth Became as Bottomless Pit.*

It was my job to keep the sheet pulled tight and to hand Sister Alma whatever supplies she asked for. I could handle it. And it left me plenty of time to size up the field and the players.

Horace "Baldy" Guthridge was obviously the ramrod; he had a large oak desk at the head of the room and looked annoyed whenever one of his underlings came slinking up in petition. Baldy's years as a bureaucrat back when High Plains was the county seat served him admirably now. When our regional primacy was stolen, Baldy and a small band of county workers had been supplanted by Wishbone politicos and cast adrift in the anarchic waters of the free enterprise system. The best Guthridge could manage was to latch onto the flotsam of a bookkeeping job at Barkley's First National Bank. Though the wage differential was not significant, the bitterness of his plummet from title and prerogative was chiseled into Baldy's long face and across a mouth that had long ago swallowed up any memory of lips. Immediately after Brother Nicholas's first doomsday prediction, Baldy had quit his job at the bank and took his place at the good Brother's side.

Baldy's desk was stationed two feet to the right of a door that led to what had been the stockroom when the building functioned as a dry goods store. Twice during the long afternoon, Baldy rose, straightened his shirt and tie, brushed off his coat, and pulled himself to attention in front of the door. After one hard knock he entered the room, now Brother Nicholas's office.

The second layer of hierarchy was filled by the four men who reported to Baldy, and by my mama, who certainly did *not*. The air of hostility between Mama and Baldy would have been obvious to me even if I hadn't been treated to several weeks of dinner-table disparagement of Brother Horace. Mama's faction held sway over most of the north wall of the church and was responsible for production of banners and signs as well as the handouts distributed each night at the rallies. The Widder's sect had absorbed a crippling blow just days before when Lily Barkley announced that her husband refused to print another word of Brother Nicholas's material. Reduced to hand-printing hundreds of leaflets and posters, Mama had drafted every literate woman she could scare up. Off to my left the sisters leaned over makeshift tables and, with the single-minded ferocity of medieval monks, scribbled their way into the Kingdom.

Everyone was overtly pleasant, smiling and working hard toward a common consecrated goal, but after several hours of listening to Mrs. Hardy hum "Jesus Loves Me," I was ready to run through the wall. Around five-thirty, when the casual obscenities of Maude's Parlor House began leaking through our walls, we closed our temple with a prayer. By that time I was ready to volunteer to attend school the next day—and actually *go*.

Chapter
Twenty-eight

Friday, May 13, was the warmest day of the spring. I was making my second trip of the morning to the general store when I noticed the clouds stacking up way off to the southwest. The sight cheered me, as it did the six or seven people who stood in the street, nodding approval. "Could still save the wheat," was the consensus.

"Back so soon, Tom boy?" Mr. Hayes was glad to see me, since the church paid hard cash every Saturday. Most all the stores had to carry the farmers and ranchers through the planting and growing seasons and wait until harvest for their pay.

I handed Hayes my list and waited at the counter. I'd been designated "runner" after Baldy Guthridge had grown annoyed at my presence in the church. Mama had rejected outright my offer to go to school, but she lacked the power to countermand Brother Baldy's order. That suited me fine. After a day of sheet-pulling and "Jesus Loves Me," I felt like a rope-burned prisoner cut loose from the gallows. I kept a grim face, though, knowing that Brother Horace would likely strip me of any job that I liked. I signed Hayes's book, made some small talk about the weather, and retraced the path—soon to be a rut—to the church.

Upon my return, I was given some insignificant work to do assisting Sister Alma Hardy. I quickly managed to kick up a row sufficient to irritate Brother Baldy. Sure enough, I was dispatched to New Town with a short list of unnecessary purchases and the understanding that my return need not be hurried.

I stopped by the house for a quick lunch so as to avoid sharing the meal with my churchmen. When I walked through the kitchen door, Rebekah was gathering up her sewing, getting ready to leave. She tried, but couldn't conceal her relief that it was me at the door rather than Mama.

"Howdy, Miss Rebekah, you're lookin' a little better." She had been feeling dizzy this morning after bumping her head on the kitchen table. Rebekah had always been a trifle clumsy, but she had become even more prone to injury as of late. I knew wild bronc busters who sported fewer bruises and cuts than Rebekah Adams did during her separation from Sam.

"Thank you, I'm feeling better," she said, touching an angry-looking knot on her temple. "How are you doing?"

"Not so bad. Looks like it might rain out there."

She smiled at the thought. "That would be a blessing."

"I'm going to warm up the stew," I said, ladling a portion into a pot. "You want I should make you a bowl?"

"No, thank you. Jennie Robinson is expecting me shortly."

"I don't see how you can get much sewin' done with those babies bawlin' all the time. You can hear them from one end of the street to the other. I don't think they ever sleep." Alf and Jennie Robinson had a set of twins that were fast becoming legends in the town. Ol' Joe Clark said as far as the level of peace was concerned, he'd rather live next to the Panhandle Prince than beside the Robinsons.

"They both took a little touch of colic, but I think they're just about over it. Poor little guys." She stopped at the door. "Could you tell your mother that I won't be back till after supper?"

Understandable, since that would be after Mama and I had left for the nightly revival. Now that I had been collected into the fold, Rebekah was the sole target of Mama's relentless proselytizing. Poor Rebekah was far too genteel to yell "Halt, enough" at a woman who was providing a roof over her head, and Mama took her lack of protest for softening to the Message. The young woman often shared only breakfast with us before fleeing to a neutral household to do her work.

"Still figurin' on leavin' before the Glorious Assumption?" I didn't grasp the irony of my asking a question that presupposed an "after" the Apocalypse. In the company of my brethren, I played by Brother Nicholas's rules; when speaking with nonbelievers, I generally accepted the "heathen" reality. Confusion and fear resulted when I accepted wholly the tenets of one or the other camp or compared the two. There were few even among the movement's inner circle who had not let slip a random thought on plans for a fall trip or concern for the summer harvest. The end of the world is not a concept easily integrated into one's consciousness.

Rebekah's hands were full, so I helped her with the door. "I intend to leave High Plains by Wednesday," Rebekah said sadly. "I'm afraid there will be a great deal of suffering and disappointment . . . a lot of people hurt through no fault of their own." Her voice trailed off to near inaudibility. "And there is nothing I can do about it."

I spent the shank of the afternoon in Langston's library following the adventures of King Arthur and his gallant knights. I needed an old friend from a far country, a nobler epoch to help me through this somber time. I had hoped that Langston might have slipped back into town overnight, but the house was dark and locked. I used the key over the transom and helped myself to romance.

I kept my eye on the gathering clouds through the open library window and shelved the Age of Chivalry when the skies appeared ready to fulfill their promise. I wanted to get back to the Bowery and share the weather with folks who could really appreciate it.

It was hot and the air was gloriously humid. I admired the cloud bank that now covered the southwest quadrant and rolled faithfully toward us; my heart rejoiced at the sound of robust thunder approaching steadily, inexorably. I joined the knot of people gathered on the sidewalk at the Lamour Hotel. Zack, Doc, and Shorty sat and talked amicably to the folks who paced back and forth in anticipation. Dark cumulus clouds blacked out the sun, and at four-thirty roosters crowed in the distance, fooled by the premature dusk. The wind picked up, blowing cool and wet.

As soon as the first fat raindrops kicked up puffs of dust

on impact with the parched street, the sidewalks filled with shopkeepers, fry cooks, clerks, livery hands, bootblacks— even bartenders and courtesans turned out. Within minutes the sky was surrendering water at a rate, described graphically by Zack, "like pouring piss out of a boot." Whoops and wild dances broke out in pagan gratitude as months of frustration were relieved by that simple, profound act.

It wasn't the slow, steady rain such as populates the dreams of farmers, but nobody complained. The ground was flat and parched, so nothing short of Noah's deluge could be a drop more than we could handle. The sky was black as far as the eye could see to the southwest, and even a trace darker to the northwest. The consensus was that we could depend on at least a couple of hours of intense rain, and, with luck, considerably more.

After fifteen or twenty minutes, most of the working folk moved back inside, leaving the sidewalks to the men who habitually attended them. With the lightning drawing closer and the thunder often drowning out their words, the Raglars discussed great storms of yesteryear. The disagreement over the severity of the April 1898 downpour as opposed to the October 1904 deluge was interrupted by the clatter of hail-stones on tin roofs.

Hail was another natural enemy of the farmer, but I couldn't see much problem, the crops being so stunted to begin with. I was still too caught up in the rain to piece together the threads of wind direction, rain, hail, and season. Doc and Zack exchanged an uneasy look as they left their chairs and edged down the sidewalk. They peered hard off to the southwest. Suddenly, I could feel something bad wrong. . . .

"TORNADO!" somebody shouted from behind Derby's saloon across the street. "TWISTER OFF TO THE WEST!"

The street filled with people running and shouting. Hail-stones the size of walnuts poured down from the bitter sky.

Doc grabbed me by the shoulder and I followed the three old men around to the back of the general store. Quick as we turned the corner, we saw a mass of terrified people trying to scramble into Hayes's shelter. Zack hollered "Mercantile" and we were halfway there before I realized what I had to do. I waved a denial to my comrades and struck off toward home.

The Church of the Glorious Assumption had no storm shelter, so all those folks would be seeking sanctuary wherever possible. Mama's first concern would be my safety, and the first place she would look would be our dugout shelter.

Hail pounded my body, and the blowing sand stung like buckshot, so that I had to cover my face as I ran toward our house. I expected to see Mama waving from the house, or the storm shelter, or . . . somewhere. I made a pass through the house to see if she was inside. She wasn't. On my way out, the wind tore the back door out of my hand, off its hinges, and sent it cartwheeling across the prairie.

I jumped into the storm shelter and started to pull the door over me, but I couldn't shake the vision of Mama wandering lost out there, searching for me. I stood at the top step and shouted in every direction. That was when I first saw the twister. It was hard to draw a bearing on it with the sand and rain lashing at my face, but it appeared to be about halfway between the Bowery and New Town. I couldn't tell which way it was moving. The funnel was black as pitch and stretched to the ground, though it appeared to hop up and down and side to side.

Way up in the clouds, sheet lightning provided a dull yellow background for the flashes of forked lightning that were outlined in green and blue. The thunder was constant, so that I ceased to notice it till it stopped for ten seconds, then began again.

As the twister moved away from us, toward New Town, I interjected a prayer of thanks into my ongoing plea for survival and ducked into the shelter to wipe the sand from my eyes. I popped up long enough to see the water tank from the Gatewood Hotel tumbling toward me, tossed like a straw in the wind. It was chased by a pitch-black funnel no more than fifty yards away and bearing down fast. I jerked the door down, barred it, and prayed passionately to live forever or die quickly.

* * *

I prayed for seconds, minutes, hours—I don't know how long—as the cellar door rattled like it was being pounded by a railroad gang.

Then it was quiet.

I waited for as long as I could stand it, but the fear of being buried alive grabbed me by the throat, and I threw open the door. The rain fell, though not so hard; the thunder rumbled on, but had moved off to the east and no longer threatened.

Slowly, I crawled out of the bunker, wary of an adversary that could strike so quickly, so devastatingly. Our house was still standing, apparently undamaged except for having lost the back door and every window on the west side. Inside, the furniture had been shuffled around, turned over, but I couldn't see anything more serious than broken dishes. I hoped to find Mama in her bedroom, safe and sound, but she wasn't there.

I ran toward town looking for Mama. From our house you couldn't see much damage; it appeared that the town had weathered the storm pretty well. Since we were just east of the Bowery, all I could see were the backs of the buildings that lined the street. There was a lot of debris lying around: tin from roofs, wooden beams, tree limbs, a chest of drawers, a kitchen chair, and, finally, a chicken with no feathers walking in a confused circle trying to get her mind right.

I wasn't ready for the vision that awaited me as I raced through the alley and saw the damage done to the west side of the street. It looked like everyone in town was gathered around the rubble that had been the Wee Chap Saloon and Maude's Parlor House. There wasn't enough left of the Chap to start a decent campfire. The tornado had split Maude's place like a giant cleaver, ripping the roof off, gutting both stories while leaving the south wall intact; not a stick of furniture, throw rug, or wall hanging remained. The player piano lay in pieces on the sidewalk of Lolly's Cafe at the far end of the street. The building to the south of Maude's, separated only by a six-foot alley, was untouched: The Church of the Glorious Assumption had survived intact.

I found Mama standing with the brethren around the debris. I ran up and hugged her. "All you all right?" I asked.

"Oh, yes. We stayed in the church and prayed." Her voice was flat, detached. "It wasn't His plan to hurt us."

"I waited for you at home. The house is fine. Just a door and some windows broken."

"I knew it would be all right."

I was infuriated by her calm. I'd risked my life to get back to the house and had worried myself sick about her. "Weren't you worried about *me*?" I begged.

She looked down on me with a countenance incapable of fear or surprise. "It wasn't His plan to hurt *us*."

The only Bowery fatality was a Wee Chap patron who had passed out in the john behind the saloon, never to awaken. There were cuts, bruises, and a broken bone or two, but we had had sufficient warning, so that almost everyone found shelter of one sort or another. In this neck of the country it is universally understood that nothing in the world is going to save you if a tornado wanders across your path, so a good deal of thanksgiving was tendered to a benevolent Deity who had deemed that one derelict was sufficient reckoning to exact from the south end of High Plains.

For the rest of the afternoon I wandered both sides of town surveying the damage, listening to the stories. From what I could piece together, the funnel had passed directly over the ball field, proceeding on a north-northeasterly heading. The first casualty was Langston Harper's house; there was hardly a piece of wood big enough to pick your teeth with in the ruins. Books were strewn for miles in every direction. Most had not been mangled outright, they looked as if they had just fallen off a shelf, but of the half dozen that I thumbed through, all were missing pages. Their shells were intact, but their meaning had been gutted. It made me feel sick and I had to move on.

The funnel had lifted, sparing Langston's barn and horses, and hovered for several minutes before taking on New Town. The top floor of the Hallman Butcher Shop, rented by the High Plains Free and Accepted Masons, was wrenched off and distributed throughout the plains. The storm swept up R. N. Barkley's Maxwell and flung it over four hundred yards to the east; the seats, engine, and two wheels were never found. Fifty yards of railroad track were ripped up before the twister exited town through Reese's Bakery Shop, killing old Georgia Reese, who had been confined to her bed for the last two years, and her husband, Samuel, who refused to leave her side. The pouring rain helped put out the fire that broke out in the bakery, sparing New Town additional tragedy. A number of other homes and businesses were heavily damaged but repairable. Every windmill in New Town had been toppled.

Turning south, the funnel cut a direct path to the Bowery, where it had dismantled the Wee Chap and dissected Maude's Parlor House, before abruptly backing off and leaving the area on a zigzag northeasterly path. All in all, the Bowery had been mighty lucky to have escaped with so little damage. Even Maude lofted a few hosannas when she found her steel safe, locked and secure, leaning delicately against the cracked—but not broken—plate-glass window of the millinery shop down the street.

No one missed a chance to thank God for his mercy; the citizens praised His infinite wisdom in selecting Georgia and Sam Reese, and thus ending the vale of tears that they had dwelled in for many years. By the end of the day every detail of the tornado's visit had been examined, catalogued, and shaped to conform to God's Plan as interpreted by the children that He loved so dearly He had sent them a lethal storm.

That evening I joined a group of men who gathered at the courthouse to compare stories. We stood under an oak tree that was to serve as a totem to the Tornado of 1910. A two-by-six plank had been swept up by the storm and slung with such force that it was embedded a good five inches into the oak; little kids jumped up and down on it as if it were a diving board, till reprimanded for the sacrilege. The men exchanged tales, amazing but, for the most part, true.

Abe Richard's Jersey cow, Gertie, was picked up, moved 257 yards, and gently placed down, with no ill-effect other than turning her hide snow-white. At Muff Langer's farm a piece of broom straw had pierced a pin-sized hole through a window; Muff invited everyone out to see the straw still dangling on both sides of the glass. Raining mud had covered Hen Warlick's house so tight that you couldn't scrape it off with a hammer and chisel. A bedroom dresser was yanked out an open door at Rob Nowotny's house and discovered a half mile away. The clothing was still neatly folded in drawers, and the mirror unbroken. An additional casualty was the "Anti-Comet" rally that was to be held at the Methodist Church that night. Nobody showed up, and the event was not rescheduled.

All accounts voiced under the oak tree were steeped in the awe appropriate to survivors of a wondrous and terrifying act of Nature. There was, however, an established and vital body that neither feared nor revered the storm: its appearance had been prophesied, its timing inevitable, its casualties preordained. The tornado unleashed a windfall of credibility and a deluge of converts upon Brother Nicholas's movement. Friday, May 13, was the critical date in the life of the Glorious Assumption and in the demise of reason in High Plains, Texas.

Chapter
Twenty-nine

"**T**he Lord's angry hand has descended upon this wicked town, and just as with Jonah, He sent a great wind and mighty tempest so even the blindest of men can see, the most callous can feel the will of God and know His powers!

"Does any man here believe that this majestic storm was simply a freak of Nature, a random event unconnected to the specter that at this very moment is speeding toward the Earth to fulfill the ancient biblical prophecy of Revelation?

"If you believe this, I instruct you to go to view the ruin that was the most venal of public saloons. It is only a pile of rubble with each bottle of Satan's acid broken and soaked into earth newly christened by God's hand.

"If you believe this storm to be *natural*, I direct you to the home of a noted attorney, a manipulator of *man's* law! A man who often scoffed at the law of God! His home now shelters only spiders and crawling vermin.

"There is a motor car sitting broken and useless in the middle of the prairie. A Devil's chariot owned by this town's richest citizen, a man who mocked God! He was a *man* many thought to be *powerful*.

"*Only God is powerful!*

"I invite any doubter to visit the remains of the secret society that placed its faith in the fellowship of men and obscure symbols and writings. Their meeting place was snatched away and crushed in the unforgiving fist of God!

"If there be anyone so blind as to deny the divine will of God in this *natural* storm, I will take him by the hand and lead him to the wreckage that is the only earthly remains of the most odious and chancrous whorehouse ever to despoil the plains. I will then direct his unseeing eye to the adjacent building—a church of God! A temple intact and spared the wrath righteously vented only a few feet away. My church survived untouched! Is that the work of a capricious storm? An indifferent God?

"If you refuse to see this undeniable sign for the omen that it so clearly is, then you deserve the horrible fate that will soon befall you!"

There were no blind men at Nicholas's Friday night meeting, no one needing further evidence that there was a bad moon rising. I certainly did not. Nor did the hundreds of pilgrims who swarmed our borders within hours after the tornado's augury.

Chapter
Thirty

As near as I could figure at the time, High Plains's attitude toward Brother Nicholas—before the tornado—could be broken down roughly into thirds. About one-third of the citizenry was actively involved in the Glorious Assumption, attended the services, and prepared daily for their eternal assignation; another third was vaguely sympathetic, or shared a common fear with the movement, but was either too lazy, indecisive, or embarrassed by the fervor of the meetings to attend; and the final third was openly hostile and often projected visions of Brother Nicholas consigned to the hottest corner of Hell with the encumbrance of two broken legs.

After the tornado it was "Katie, bar the door."

The twister blew most of the undecided off the fence and into Brother Nicholas's camp; it even siphoned off a sizable chunk of the hard-core anti-Nickites. Of the folks who refused to answer Brother Nicholas's clarion call, very few now berated man or mission publicly. The Winds of Destiny had blown squarely at the back of the Glorious Assumption Crusade and its prophet.

In addition to the local constituency, High Plains was soon mobbed by a flood of immigrants from neighboring towns, counties, even states, intent on riding to glory on Brother Nicholas's coattails. With only five days till judgment, many another pilgrim considered it worth the long dusty trip to join the ragtown that had sprung up around the ball field—ground now sanctified by the tornado's path. The first wave of proselytes scavenged the wood from the storm's wreckage to set up shanties, which were soon surrounded by acres of canvas tents and lean-tos. The influx would undoubtedly have been greater if the tornado had not torn up the railroad tracks into town; even so, the run on food, water, flour, and other staples emptied our stores within a day. Cars and wagons brought in supplies from Amarillo, Lubbock, Abilene, and Wichita Falls. Prices inflated wildly, since the value of money was decidedly finite: in five days the man with a pocketful of it would have a heap of explaining to do to the Keeper of the Celestial Books.

The emotional balance of High Plains, reeling and lurching in the best of times, was knocked further askew by an invasion of cowboys, railroad men, and assorted transients who had quit jobs, drawn pay, and come to exploit the charms of the Bowery on a final fling before the whole damn ball of wax exploded. Predictably, that hardiest of human scavengers—the small-time grifter—showed up in droves to feast on the carcass of fear and debauchery. The Carnival of Despair had begun.

"I prophesied the San Francisco earthquake in 1906. I predicted the death of Queen Victoria and the assassination of President McKinley! You can look it up in the book! And just as sure as the last visit of Halley's Comet inspired our gallant Texas forefathers to name this great territory the *Lone Star State*, you good folks will never live to see the sunrise on May nineteenth if you fail to buy Dr. Carswell's Guaranteed—or Your Money Back—Comet Pills. Taken every hour on the half hour, they will . . ."

The fat, braying huckster was doing land-office business in front of Kerley's Livery Stable, blocking my path to the general store. I skirted the crowd and had one foot in the door of Hayes's when I heard the voice that made the hair on my neck stand and genuflect.

"Hey, Tom. Can I talk to you a minute?"

I ducked quickly into Hayes's store but backed right out again when I considered that the voice, and its host, might follow me in and turn the encounter into public business. I marched quickstep down the sidewalk and slipped into the alley. He was right behind me like bad luck on a beggar.

"Tom, I want to ask a favor."

Just what I needed. Not only would I go to Hell for talking to him, he wanted a favor too.

"Sam, damn it, I swore to Mama I'd never talk to you again."

He nodded quickly, concerned. "I don't like putting you in this position, but you're the only person who can help. I have to see Rebekah, alone. It'll have to be at your house."

"Forget it! *Nobody's* ever alone at my house. Lily Barkley moved in last night, and anytime we're not in church, they're holding some kind of meeting in the parlor. Why don't you just catch Rebekah on the street and talk her fool head off."

"I have to see her alone, inside. There must be a time when you folks are all at church and she stays in."

I drew a cross in the dirt with my left shoe as the noonday sun beat down on my spinning head. I tried to recall the exact words that I had sworn to Mama. "I won't associate with that newspaperman again." Okay. Sam, at the moment, was not a newspaperman; he was just a friend who needed a favor. And we weren't really associating; this was just a brief conversation in an alley. Associating, to my mind, took longer and required sitting down, propping your feet up—

"What do you say?" Sam's voice was edged with desperation. I hated it when grown-ups started breaking down.

"Sometimes, after supper, Mama and I have to get to a meeting in a hurry, so Rebekah stays behind to wash the dishes. Then she usually goes visiting. That's about the only time you could do it."

"Good. How will I know?"

"I'll tie the curtains in the front window in an X if she's alone."

"Thanks, Tom." We shook on it.

When he walked back into the street, I took a quick look around to see if we'd been observed. Apparently not. Of course, the surveillance that really worried me could not be deflected by the inch-thick slat walls on both sides of the alley. Overhead, the angry sun beat down on my unworthy frame like an omniscient, unforgiving eye offering a sample of the fire yet to come.

"Oh, no, I forgot my Bible." I stopped in the middle of the street, slapped my forehead with the palm of my hand for effect, and laughed at my own foolish incompetence.

Mama was not amused at my burlesque. "You were in such an all-fired hurry to get us out of the house, I'm not surprised," the Widder barked, slowing only a half step before regaining her stride. Lily Barkley and I had to trot to catch up. "I'd have appreciated a chance to put something cool on my feet and digest my meal before rushing out the door."

"You can borrow mine." Lily offered me her illustration-packed Deluxe Improved King James. "I don't use it once the service begins."

"No, thank you, ma'am," I said. "I think a man ought to have his own Bible, one he's used to, so he can find his place quick and follow along. It means more to you then." O Lordy, would there ever be an end to my duplicity? I stopped in the street again. "I'm going back to get it. I'll catch up to you shortly."

Mama wasn't pleased, but she didn't forbid, so I ran toward home. I cracked the front door and listened for kitchen sounds before entering. Rebekah was still washing up, unaware of my intrusion as I tied the curtains—a signal that Son Bob and I had used back in the good old/bad old days—and walked back to my room for the Bible. I had planned to get it and leave, but I decided to wait for the main event. After taking quick stock of the indiscretions that I would have to explain to Saint Peter shortly, I figured eavesdropping would hardly rate a mention.

Within a minute there was a knock out front. Putting my right eye to the cracked door, I could see Rebekah wipe her hands on the dish towel as she crossed the room. I heard her gasp as she opened the door.

Sam said: "I'd like to talk to you, Rebekah. If you'll hear me out, I promise to leave whenever you ask me to."

Rebekah stepped back a pace and Sam entered. They

stood in the middle of the room looking around and past each other, both uncomfortable.

"Can we sit down?" Sam said.

Rebekah nodded but stood fast. Sam made a motion toward a chair, then backed away, refusing to cede the advantage of higher ground.

Get on with it, I mumbled to myself. Mama would be getting impatient.

"We need to talk about ... what your plans are," Sam said, fingering the brim of his hat with both hands.

"I'm going back to Wichita." Her voice was low, her eyes downcast.

"Will you tell me why?" He scrambled for words. "If it's the baseball, I'll never touch—"

Rebekah threw up her hands and interrupted, "It's something I have to do for the good of us all."

Sam took a deep breath. "It's not for *my* good. I want you to come home with me and work this out. I'll do anything you ask. I'll work less, spend more time with you. Whatever you say."

"Will you come back to Wichita and take your old job back?"

"Yes ... maybe," Sam said, hedging as quickly as he heard the sound of his words. "I can't leave right now, but as soon as this Nicholas thing is over, we can see if there's an editor's position in Kansas ... around Wichita."

A tight cheerless smile passed quickly over Rebekah's face. She moved her body so she no longer faced Sam. "You'll never leave this town," she said flatly.

"I would if it were the only way—"

The front door flew open and the Widder Greer stood with hands on hips, loaded for bear. "What's *he* doing here?" she demanded, her right fist jabbing toward Sam.

Sam squared up with her. Mama was about a foot shorter than Sam, but she gave up little in poundage and nothing in grit.

"Listen you old battle-ax," he said, "this is my wife and I'll talk to her wherever I choose to."

Mama didn't back off an inch. "Not in my house you won't. I'll have you thrown out for trespassin'."

"I'm not moving unless Rebekah asks me to go."

The combatants stared at Rebekah, who looked as if she might collapse under the load. "You'd better go, Sam," she said softly, without looking at him.

Sam looked as though he wanted to mix it up with Mama, but he unclenched his fists. "This is the last time I'm going to chase you, Rebekah." He edged toward the door as though he expected to be back-shot if he turned around. "If you have anything to say, you can come see me."

Rebekah was silent, and Sam left with a slam of the door. Mama opened the door just so *she* could slam it; every window in the house rattled. Rebekah sat down on the couch and began to sob.

"There, there, honey, don't you worry," Mama consoled. "You know you're doing what's best on the long road. You can't just think of yourself at times like this."

I shut my door soundlessly and pushed a chair under the window. I wiggled through the tight space with agility and speed bred of fear, and raced across the plain toward the revival. I knew that I had to be there standing tall and looking righteous when Mama arrived, or I had no chance of denying complicity in Sam Adams's dastardly visit.

Chapter
Thirty-one

T hough man is often dogged by bad fortune unde-
served and unexpected, occasionally a slender
measure of justice is restored when he is spared the long-
dreaded consequence of an admitted impiety. Mama
mentioned not a word of the meeting between Sam and
Rebekah that night and posed no questions as to my whereabouts or connivance. I believe that she ignored the possibility of my treachery in order to spare me the lies that
inevitably would have followed. She was bending over
backward to give me the benefit of every doubt in hopes
that any malfeasance that she did not acknowledge might
also pass undetected On High.

"Conjure Bags! Getcha Comet Conjure Bags right chere!
The only way to be guaranteed protected against the killer
comet!"

The barker shook his sack in Mama's face as we navi-
gated the packed Bowery sidewalks. Mama knocked the
"conjure bag"—actually a Bull Durham tobacco pouch
dyed red—to the ground and stomped away as the medicine
man laid a hoodoo on our backs.

Mama had slept late following a Comet Vigil that extended well past midnight, and awoke tired and grumpy.
Sleep had not come easily to anyone the night before. I
could not be sure which of the three women with whom
I shared the house was crying at any particular time, but I
heard each of them weep desperately before dawn.

We were running late by our standard, even Lily Barkley
had beaten us out the door, but we were hardly prepared for
the crowded streets and rollicking saloons that lined our ap-

proach to the Glorious Assumption Church. On the average Sunday morning you could fire a shot down any Bowery sidewalk without fear of inflicting wound; today the same shot would net you your bag limit of drunks, panhandlers, and hucksters. This motley crew obviously wasn't ready to turn loose of Saturday night.

It was all Mama, in top form, could do to elbow past the mob jammed in front of the storefront church. I heard several shouts of, "It's Nicholas!" and "Hey, that's him," from people with noses pressed against the front window of the church, but each sighting was quickly followed by disclaimer. Only after Mama thumped the door repeatedly and shouted her identity were we granted admission.

"Lord 'a mercy," Sister Alma Hardy sighed, pushing the door shut after we rushed inside. She cracked the door quickly to allow an errant finger to be withdrawn before slamming and bolting the entrance. "Have you ever seen the like of it? It's been like this for the last hour. They take spells of screamin' for Brother Nicholas, and, honey, you know he isn't even here."

Mother's eyebrows shot up a good two inches. Brother Nicholas was always in his office before seven o'clock, Comet Vigil or not.

"Where is he?"

"Haven't you heard, Sister Mamie?" Sister Alma seemed surprised and pleased that she, a lowly water carrier, could break such important news to a potentate of Mama's stature. "He's in bed with the laryngitis and can't speak a single, solitary word."

Within minutes of our arrival, Ol' Baldy emerged from Brother Nicholas's office followed by his four adjutants. He swore everyone in the room to secrecy concerning Brother Nicholas's throat ailment, then walked abruptly out the door to address the crowd that had continued to mass in front of the church.

Perched precariously atop an overturned rain barrel, Brother Horace informed the mob that Brother Nicholas had been "overcome with a vision." It was a vision of "surpassing depth and beauty" that our Prophet would continue to pursue throughout the rest of the day. There would be no

Sunday meeting, but it was the Brother's wish that the faithful should "spend the day in prayer and meditation."

The crowd dispersed quickly, eager to spread the word to a town full of abject penitents who now had a day and a half to fill before being granted an audience with the single person who might save them from an eternity of wretchedness. I suspect that very few of these folks spent the day in prayer and meditation.

Even with our leader incapacitated, the bureaucracy made a valiant attempt to churn on. We were exhausted from our labors and unnerved by Brother Nicholas's illness, but there was work to be done. Mama's priority project had become the sewing of white "Ascension Robes," in fulfillment of the report in Revelation that, "White robes were given unto everyone of them," prior to their assumption into Heaven. After some discussion about whether the robes would be provided by sources Divine or mortal, Brother Nicholas had declared that he could envision no Angel descending to Earth bearing thousands of robes, so the load fell on Mama. Everyone agreed that the labor was Herculean, particularly since Mama refused to use sewing machines and would not tolerate coarse thread or wide stitches. If the Widder's work was destined to come under Divine perusal, she would be double-damned if she would offer up anything less than "Stitches Fine as Fairy Fingers."

As the day wore on, our frayed nerves seemed to migrate to the ends of our fingertips, and only through the intercession of the gentlest elements of the movement was vicious affray averted. "Rode hard and put up wet," was how old Joe Clark described us. The atmosphere was so contentious that I practically begged Brother Baldy to dispatch me from this holy asylum into the streets of Babel, which he eventually did.

I was coming back from a run to Hayes's when I saw the door fly open and an unbroken line of True Viners file out quickstep. I've seen burning buildings that did not empty as fast as that church.

Mama explained: "Sister Alma and Sister Lily started into pulling hair, and Brother Horace *finally* told us to go home and pray and meditate. As soon as you finish delivering that, you come straight home, you hear?"

I hurried into the empty church and unloaded my burden on Baldy's desk. As I checked off the items from the master list and signed my name on the required three forms, I heard voices from inside Brother Nicholas's office. Brother Horace and his four subalterns had not bothered to shut the door, and they were speaking in tones that did not imply secrecy. I took an extra moment to double-check paperwork; Brother Horace would want it that way.

Brother Horace's voice: "It is absolutely essential that not a word of Brother Nicholas's condition escape our circle. We have enemies that would gloat over any sign of weakness in our movement and would exploit it to the Devil's benefit and delight. If either of the two heathen newspapers get hold of this, we must deny it immediately and attack them forcefully, or—"

Brother Horace's voice stopped abruptly when a large spool of thread that I had laid on the desk rolled off and hit the floor. I dropped to my chest and squeezed under Baldy's desk as I heard footsteps approach. His shoes were mere inches from my face when he turned abruptly, walked back in the office, and shut the door behind him.

I quietly snuck out of the office and ran all the way home. After an early supper I went to my room. Two hours of Bible reading and meditation on the end of the world convinced me that no matter what the chance of being discovered, or what the punishment meted out in this world or the next, I knew where I had to go, I knew who I had to warn. As soon as darkness fell, I climbed out of my window and raced toward the clamor of the Bowery.

Chapter
Thirty-two

The window was closed but unlocked, so I had no trouble gaining entrance into the bedroom. The light under the door and the familiar voices reassured me. I inched the door back and saw Sam hunched over his desk writing, and Shad's back bent over the type case.

"Sam," I hissed through the crack. "Over here."

"Well, Tom boy," Sam fairly shouted. "Come on in, son."

I waved my hands vigorously to quiet him. "The windows, the door," I whispered.

Sam winked, then pulled the shades down and locked the door. I tiptoed into the room, still leery of discovery. I shook Sam's hand, then Shad's, bonding us all in conspiracy. They sat down, but I was nervous and moved around the office, keeping my back to the wall, my exit path unobstructed.

"So," I said quietly, "how are you guys getting along?"

"Fair to middlin'," Sam said. "We've got a lot of work, but Shad's good help. We'll finish it somehow, always do."

"You gonna get a paper out tomorrow?"

Sam smiled and passed me a proof of his front page. The headline shrieked:

NICHOLAS MOVEMENT STRANGLED
BY SORE THROAT!

"How'd you find that out?"

Sam smiled. "I had it confirmed before noon."

I was amazed that a confidence held by only a handful of committed people could be compromised so quickly.

Sam said, "Three can keep a secret if two of them are dead."

"Mark Twain?" I guessed.

"Ben Franklin. And considerably more than three were privy to Nicholas's condition. It was inevitable that it would leak out. How's he doing now?"

I caught myself before answering. Even though I didn't know anything, I resented his pumping me for information. He could tell that by the way I bowed up at him.

"It's my job, Tom. The people have a right to know. If you don't want to talk about it, we won't." Sam leaned back in his chair and clasped his hands on his stomach as if he had all day to pass with me. I knew better.

I leaned against the composing stone, feeling a little better just being in the old office. The din from the streets reassured me that people had other things to do than check on my whereabouts. "Have you heard anything from Langston?"

Sam pulled a letter from his desk drawer and handed it to me.

L. Harper
May 12, 1910

Dear Samuel,

I submit greeting and best wishes to you and your lovely wife. I trust that you are well, and am pleased to report that I find myself to be both healthy and reasonably contented. I write to convey information on my situation and to pass along insight into the position that our (your) fair city has assumed in the eyes of Texas and surrounding area.

High Plains has become a major topic of conversation in Dallas. When people learn that I hail from the "Jewel of the Panhandle," they ply me with questions about Brother Nicholas and his misbegotten crew of doom-shouters back there. As a rule, they see the Panhandle as peopled by the uncivilized, inhabiting the unlivable. During times like this it is hard to argue with them, even if I were so inclined.

The denizens of Dallas take a markedly more benign

view of the Halley's phenomenon. Rare is the night that I fail to find a party organized around the Astral Hobo. At any number of posh venues, fake spiders will dangle from gossamer webs while a full orchestra plays "Trip to Mars," or some such, for the pleasure of dancing black-robed couples. Debutantes imbibe "Cyanogen Cocktails" (reputedly a frozen sphere of gin immersed in a glass of champagne) and peer woozily through telescopes till dawn. Rest assured that most of the world is weathering comet-mania better than High Plains appears to be.

The time for my presence to enliven another dinner party is fast approaching, so I will bid adieu while tendering a piece of unsolicited advice: I think that you would be prudent to let a sleeping dog lie in regard to the recent unpleasantness that preceded my departure. I can assure you that no jury could be impaneled that would convict a white man for the slaying of a Negro thief, and to press for a trial could well earn you enmity that would make it impossible to maintain a functioning newspaper. There is potential for an even more lethal repercussion that I need not spell out, but that must be recognized. You can confirm my appraisal through Shad, a man who knows the region and sees the people through eyes unclouded by illusion.

Give my regards to any and all who conceivably would care to receive them. If I decide to make my move permanent, I will inform you posthaste so that legal and financial consideration concerning the building can be ironed out. You might well consider such a move yourself; High Plains is not the place for an honest newspaperman or a good lawyer.

Yours truly,
Langston Monroe Harper

P.S. I still have several baited lines in the water concerning Brother Nicholas. I will inform you if I get a bite on any of them.

I read it twice, feeling anger, betrayal, disappointment. I wanted to rip it up and stomp on the pieces. Instead, I just sat there. Sam brought me a cup of coffee from the stove, and I turned the hot cup in my hand for a long time. Finally I said, "I guess he hadn't heard about his house and the tornado?"

"No. He wrote that on Thursday."

"I reckon we've seen the last of Langston Harper around here."

Sam nodded.

I threw the coffee cup and the letter to the floor and exploded in a fury that had been building for days. "Goddamn Langston Harper anyway, and goddamn all those chickenshit city people too. There's room in Hell for every goddamn one of 'em."

Sam's face fell into its lopsided grin. "Well said, Tom."

I was mad at Sam too, but it passed quickly. Shad picked up my cup, filled it with coffee, and handed it to me. Sam let me take a drink and get myself together. "How are you holding up under the excitement?" he asked quietly.

"Hard to say. They keep me so busy at church during the day that I don't think much. We eat supper as fast as we can get something on the table, then go straight to the crusades. When we're all together, it's the most natural thing in the world to believe that"—I could hardly say it—"the world's gonna end. I think I was feelin' better before we got this night off." I swirled the coffee around in my cup and watched the grounds gather in the center. "Too much time to think."

Sam laid his hand on my shoulder. "I'm not trying to talk you out of anything," he said slowly, "but it might help you to know that, as near as I can tell, people make a choice between a vengeful God and a merciful God, and they generally choose the one most like themselves." He let that lie for a minute, then said, "You get the God you deserve."

I couldn't make much out of that. I think that I wanted him to say that the world wasn't going to end, and that I shouldn't worry about it. I would have had to argue with him for a little bit, but it would have been good to hear. As it was, I had more to think about than I had time or mind for. I finished my coffee and stood up.

"Don't hurry off, boy," Shad said, "we got some throwin' in that'll take your mind off your troubles."

I laughed and said, "I best be gettin' back to the house before I'm missed. I just wanted to talk to someone who was figurin' on wakin' up on Thursday."

Sam walked with me into the bedroom. "How's Rebekah doing?" He couldn't help but ask.

"Not so good, I don't think. She appears to be sick a lot of the time. Sometimes I can hear her in her room cryin'." Sam looked so sad that I wish I had lied.

"Do you know when she's leaving?"

"Quick as they get the tracks fixed, I reckon. Railroad can't find anyone that wants to work."

Sam shook his head. "They're sending in a crew tomorrow morning. They'll lay track day and night till they're hooked up."

I had one leg out the window when I asked a question that surprised both of us. "Sam, can I have that letter?"

He slipped it out of his back pocket and handed it to me. He grabbed a book from the shelf over his bed. "Take this," he said, "read it when you can't seem to get your mind off all this craziness." It was *The Adventures of Robin Hood.*

"One thing, Sam," I said. "I've heard some talk, and I really don't believe it, it's just . . . I think you better be extra careful these next few days. There's a lot of people who really hate you. And that headline tomorrow is going to make you some more enemies."

"Don't worry. I've taken to sleeping in a chair in the corner with an ax handle for a pillow." Sam laughed heartily. "Big Mike offered me Katey Dailey, but I told him I didn't want to kill anybody, just bruise them up a little."

"I'd sure as hell keep this window locked," I said.

He smiled and nodded. I felt better. We shook hands, and I slipped away into the unforgiving night.

Chapter
Thirty-three

The entire True Vine work force was much gladdened to find Brother Nicholas in his office on Monday morning. In the morning prayer that inaugurated every workday, Brother Horace gave special thanks for the restoration of Brother Nicholas's "faculties" following the incapacitating "vision" that had been visited upon the Prophet on Sunday. Though somewhat reassured, the workers kept an apprehensive eye on the door to Brother Nicholas's office, in hopes that their leader would demonstrate his revived "faculty." But the evangelist, though glimpsed several times through an opening or closing door, did not see fit to set our doubts to rest.

In his Monday night address, Brother Nicholas wasted no time in displaying an instrument restored to full majesty. For an hour that passed in the twinkling of an eye, Brother Nicholas told us of the twelve Angels at the twelve gates around the city that "lieth four square." The city was of pure gold and precious stones with gates of pearl that would not be shut by day, for there was no night.

The Brother spoke not a word of the terrors that awaited the unsaved, but only of the glory that would soon be ours. After weeks of gathering a flock through dire prophecy of great destruction and pain, our shepherd offered us a vision of green pastures, flowing waters and plentiful harvest.

This revival did not end with shouts of praise, moans of despair, spontaneous dancing, or the chant of unknown tongues. It ended with quiet tears of great happiness and expectation and the heartfelt embrace of many who had been strangers but were now as one.

* * *

The tension that had enveloped the True Vine Church like a wet, choking shroud for the past fortnight gave way on Tuesday morning to quietude and acceptance. There was much work to be done, but no one argued over jurisdiction or logistics; all the brothers and sisters exchanged vague smiles and helpful suggestions.

But the streets of High Plains were a whole 'nother shootin' match.

"Comet insurance for life and personal belongings. Step this way, folks. Better get it now; tomorrow will be too late. For two dollars cash money, insure yourself against the catastrophe of annihilation. Two lines, no waiting, step to the front."

I pushed through the line blocking the sidewalk without stopping to inquire what value "insurance" would be in a world devoid of life. No one would have answered, and, likely as not, I would have received the back of a hand for asking. Someone might well have directed me across the street to where a "Certifide Lawyer" was drawing up three-dollar wills to be executed (by Lord knows who) in the event of total devastation of the planet.

Inside the general store, Hayes was dealing with a gaggle of excited people who had taken Brother Nicholas's injunction to "set their house in order" literally, and were demanding to pay off bills. Hayes, a man of exceedingly moderate generosity, was pleased with this occurrence, but clearly wished that it could be spread across a week or two rather than piling up at a time when he had no clerk and more cash customers than he could handle. Fumbling through several old cigar boxes full of yellowed bills, in search of a forty-three-cent debt, was not practical when customers planning to ride out the coming firestorm with stockpiled food and dry goods had every counter piled high and waved dollar bills in his face. The problem was compounded since each debtor demanded a dated, attested receipt, presumably for presentation to Saint Peter's accountant for entry into the golden ledger.

It was like that all over town. R. N. Barkley had to close his bank down before noon to avoid a riot by the people who had come to sell their land for a pittance or withdraw

their savings to pay off debts. Tales abounded of speculators snatching up 160-acre farms for the few hundred dollars a farmer needed to settle his debts.

I gathered up the three bolts of white cloth I had come
for and laid the correct change on the counter, where Hayes
could collect it without interrupting the debt controversy.
The manufacture of Ascension Robes—the official garment
necessary for salvation—was proceeding apace, and stacks
of robes were fast taking over the church.

I was no more than a step or so outside the door when
I ran smack into Bark Barkley. Bark and his henchman,
Leon, had come down to the Bowery to hoot at the spectacle that had drawn travelers and novelty seekers from all
over the state. It was the only time in the town's history
that we would ever have any kind of tourist industry.

"Look at this, Leon," Bark said with the sneer that rarely
left his face. "It's little Saint Tommy Greer. Whatcha got
under your arm there? Angel harps and halos?"

My impulse was to knock Bark on his ass; it would have
been a real pleasure. Of course the first thing he would do
would be to run to his father. I had a vision of being hauled
from the True Vine Church in shackles. Hardly the way to
impress a God already angry enough to destroy the world.
So I walked past Bark without a word. I was determined to
fight only the good fight of faith, and lay hold of eternal
life. Only one day left.

"When is it you folks are going to go flyin' off into
Heaven?" Bark trailed about two feet behind me like a
yippy-ass dog snapping at my heels. "I'd appreciate it if
you could sail over the town a couple times so I can take
your picture and put it in the paper. I could get you a front
page headline: 'First Known Asshole to Ascend to
Heaven.' "

I heard people laughing. It wasn't that far to the church,
but my neck was turning redder with every step. The sidewalk was stiflingly crowded so I stepped down into the
street. Bark's braying was so loud that everyone was staring
at me. I remembered the temptations of Christ and figured
that God had sent this one down with my name on it. Bark
knew that my religion wouldn't allow fighting, and he

knew he had his daddy and the law backing him up. He got louder and cockier with each step.

"Maybe when you're rising up into Heaven, you can grab up your buddy Adams and take him with you. It'll save my daddy the trouble of runnin' him out of town."

As chance would have it, Sam Adams was standing on the sidewalk interviewing one of the dozen or more itinerant preachers who had invaded the town over the weekend. Sam looked up from his notebook long enough to nod in my direction. Zack Hart, unloading a crate off the back of a wagon, shook his head in disgust as I passed. Doc Moss winked at me from the second-story landing of his old office, where he stood surrounded by goods that had been piling up all morning in payment of debts he had long since forgiven. Big Mike waved to me from across the street. I had the feeling that every eye that had ever twinkled in the presence of Tom Greer was trained on me now, witnessing my humiliation. I had just reached the sidewalk in front of the True Vine Church—

"You know what I really want to see, Leon? I want to be there when Saint Tom's fat mama flies off—"

WHAM!

I hit Bark with a roundhouse right just as he was stepping up onto the sidewalk. Off balance, he spun completely around before hitting the ground, limp as a sackful of manure. I rolled my fists in front of me Gentleman Jim Corbett–style, like Big Mike had taught me, and moved toward Leon. Leon decided that any loyalty he had toward Bark stopped short of a fair fight. He turned his back and walked away, whistling, toward New Town.

Bark sat, one hand flat in the dirt behind him, the other rubbing the left side of his face. He shook his head as if he couldn't get focused. A trickle of blood rolled slowly down his cheek from a cut under the eye.

I stood over him and said, "If you get up, I'll knock you down again."

The crush of people who had been rushing past on all sides pulled up to watch the fight. I didn't care who or how many were there, I wanted to whip Bark's ass once and for all. If I was going to jail, I wanted to wade through Barkley blood to get there. But he shook his head and started backing away on all fours like a crab. He'd had enough.

I turned to pick up the cloth, and he did exactly what I expected: he attacked. Charging with his head down, he tried to tackle me, but I sidestepped to the left and got my weight behind a left uppercut that caught him on the side of the mouth.

Stunned, he held a handful of my shirt and tried to steady himself. I had enough room to throw a right uppercut to his stomach, and I could smell his breakfast as the air rushed from his body. He dropped to his knees and then fell forward.

I wanted to stomp hell out of him, but I didn't. Big Mike had taught me better.

Keeping my eye on the sonofabitch, I picked the soiled bolts of cloth off the sidewalk and turned toward the church. Several faces were pressed against the window: one was Mama's; another was Brother Nicholas's.

Behind me Bark Barkley had regained enough breath to croak the obligatory, empty threat of the vanquished. "I'll get you for this, Tom Greer. You'll pay."

I ignored Barkley but trembled at the thought of walking through the door to face Brother Nicholas.

I entered the church warily expecting the roof to fall in on my profane head. Brother Nicholas stood in my path and motioned for me to follow. I did so through a roomful of downcast eyes and a silence that threatened to crush me. He closed the door and then sat in a stiff wooden chair behind a rough table. There was no place for me to sit. I prepared myself for excommunication.

"Thomas, I saw everything that happened out there," he said, spreading his hands flat on the table. That was as high as I could lift my gaze. "I am sure that you are aware of our Lord's directives on the subject of physical violence. Aren't you?"

I waited long enough to establish that the question required an answer before I mumbled, "Yes sir. He was agin' it." O Lordy. Not only blasphemous, but ungrammatical.

"That's true. That's why he was called the Prince of

Peace. We must always remember that the way of the Lamb is the way of peace."

He didn't say anything for a long time, and I waited for the ax to fall. My body was soaked in sweat and I itched all over. Now that the rush of battle had passed, both of my hands throbbed in pain. I could tell from his breathing that he was getting ready to say something, and if it was loud or angry, I was ready to cut and run.

"Nevertheless, there are times that a man must pick up the sword and defend himself, his family, and his religion. Ecclesiastes declared that there is a time for war as well as peace. I heard what that boy said in denigration of your religion, and I know that his father is an enemy of our people. In light of this, I must say that your action, while regrettable, was in this instance justified."

I heard his chair squeak as he stood up, and I saw the hand extended toward me. His firm handshake turned me around and steered my body through the door. In front of the entire staff of the Glorious Assumption Church, Brother Nicholas placed his hands on my trembling shoulders and said, "There is still room for the Christian soldier in this world, Thomas. Your performance reflected proudly on our faith."

That was the last we saw of the Brother until the service that night. I was roundly congratulated by every kinsman, clasped to every bosom for a deed that I customarily got a whipping for. They did, however, take the precaution of keeping me inside to avoid a recurrence of my heroic feat. I didn't mind. By the end of the day even I was convinced that I had smote the evil mocker in defense of my religion and not because he had called my mother fat.

Brother Nicholas's address on the penultimate night of the Glorious Assumption Crusade was brief and reassuring. There were no threats of fire, suffocation, explosion, earthquake, flood, or pestilence, no visions of sinners in agony, their lamentations rending the angry sky. That had all been said, had been insinuated into our marrow, and there was no need to repeat it.

"Tomorrow night we will assemble at the north rim of

the Mentirosa Canyon for the event that we have prepared for these many days and weeks. For we are the ones who have come out of great tribulation and have washed our robes and made them white in the blood of the Lamb. Our ascension into Heaven is assured. It is time for our rest and our reward."

And it was easy to see that these people needed rest. They had been led to the river Jordan repeatedly, but denied drink. People were aging perceptibly before my eyes. It was time for resolution.

Brother Nicholas made no great effort at this time to persuade newcomers as to the legitimacy of the movement; the size and devotion of his flock bespoke the fact more eloquently than could even the man who inspired it. After leading us in hymn, we were instructed to return to our homes for prayer and meditation. The following day, Wednesday, May 18, 1910, we were to assemble at Mentirosa Canyon by sundown for final preparation. At the stroke of midnight we would ascend to Heaven.

Chapter
Thirty-four

If I slept at all that night, it was so fitful that it served no purpose. Every sin, real or imagined, grew in stature and solemnity and gnawed at my bones till I felt like screaming. After hours of agony, I lit my lamp and dug *Robin Hood* out from under my mattress. Mama had attempted to purge the house of all worldly books and magazines so we could concentrate on our sacred texts, but I couldn't bear another word of King James English.

I read until dawn chased away the terror. I eased the book down on my chest and caught the few precious minutes of sleep that would have to suffice for the next thirty hours.

Awakened by whispers—those urgent hushed tones that you know viscerally are meant to conceal information from you—I leaned against the thin wall and listened with an ear sharpened by hours of silence.

Mama, pleading: "Don't let your worldly pride rob you of salvation for you and—"

Rebekah, steady: "I appreciate your concern, Mamie, but you know my feelings on this. If you'll give me a hand with this latch, I'll be able to leave—"

Mama, indignant: "You are not leaving this house without breakfast, I forbid it! You have plenty of time and you'll not get a decent meal on that train."

Rebekah: "I'm not hungry. I still feel like—"

Mama: "I know *exactly* how you feel. Every woman who ever had a baby knows."

BABY!

I pulled away from the wall as though I'd been lashed

with a bullwhip. Things made sense now, clues that had sailed right over my head for weeks snapped to mind with the finality exclusive to hindsight.

But what could I do? Sam had to be told. Did I have any right to interfere? There was no one to tell him but me. If I didn't get to him before the train left, he would never see Rebekah again. Would they both be better off if he never found out?

And the Big Question: What did any of this matter if the world was going to end today?

The whole time that I battled these thoughts, I crawled around on my mattress as if looking for answers in the straw tick. I ended up with my back in the corner and my head in my hands. The questions were too hard, the issues too big. I wanted to lie down and sleep for a day, or however long it took for everything to straighten itself out. A knock interrupted my reeling confusion.

"Thomas, time to get up now, son. We've got a full day ahead of us."

"I'm up, Mama."

"It's a glorious day, son. The most glorious day in the history of the world."

"If you folks don't eat a little something, I'm going to have to assume I'm a failure as a cook," Mama said, with flirtatious despair in her voice. It was a strange time for the Southern Coquette to assert herself, but then, it was a strange time all round.

Mama had fixed a sumptuous breakfast using every scrap of food in the house. Unfortunately, her dining companions were not eager to avail themselves of the ham and eggs, home-fried potatoes, biscuits, fried chicken, and hominy. Rebekah toyed with her scrambled egg, looking all the while as though she were ready to bolt to the outhouse. She kept a hard eye on the clock on the wall. I could usually be depended upon to pack away a thrasher's breakfast, but a biscuit and half a chicken leg was the best I could do. Lily Barkley always looked ragged at breakfast, sleepy and indifferent to food. There was snippy speculation at the church that Lily's salvation was doubtful if her presence at the Pearly Gates was expected before noon.

Mama cooed and smacked her lips as though trying to engage the appetites of a trio of infants. "This hominy is sooo good. Why doncha have a couple of spoonfuls." Mama poked it in Rebekah's face. "It'll stick to your ribs through the long, hot . . . day." Rebekah shied away like a skittish colt. Attention was turned to me. "Eat up, Tom, we've got to get along to the church now, and no telling when we'll get another chance to—"

Lily exploded. "How in bloody hell can you worry about eating when we're all going to *die*? You think God will deny you because your stomach's empty?" Lily began crying and running her hands frantically through her red hair. "How can you act like this is some kind of damn . . . picnic? What's going to happen to us?"

Rebekah put her arms around Lily and patted her back. I didn't know what to do. I wasn't that far from tears myself, so I just sat there trying to keep from breaking over.

Mama walked around the table and pulled Lily from Rebekah's arms. "Lily, Lily, look at me." Mama swung her around so that she had no choice. "Now, listen, we've done everything that we've been told to do, and we have no reason to worry. By this time tomorrow, why, we'll be walking on streets paved with gold and meeting our loved ones who have passed over—"

"What about everyone else?" Lily said, avoiding Mama's eyes. "What about R.N. and all the people who haven't even heard of Brother Nicholas? The ones that don't believe because they don't know or haven't heard?"

"I'm sure that God will take that into consideration," Mama said. "It's just the ones who had a chance and denied him."

"What about *Rebekah*?" Lily's breathless question filled the room, robbing it of air. No one knew what to say about that. Mama and Lily rocked in each other's arms, Lily crying all the while.

Rebekah looked my mother squarely in the eye and stated flatly, "The world is *not* going to end today!" She then walked into her room and picked up her suitcases.

I could stand it no longer; I ran out the door and down the street. The train whistle drowned out my mother's voice as she called my name from the kitchen door.

"Sam, Sam," I shouted as I ran down the sidewalk and slid in the open door of the newspaper office. Nobody there. I checked the bedroom, the outhouse. Empty.

I raced out, leaping over one of the dozen sleeping derelicts who warmed the sidewalks. I caught a scent of Sam at the general store, where he had stopped a good half hour before; Hayes didn't know which way he was headed.

I tried the restaurant at the Lamour Hotel, then nearly ran over a lightning rod salesman who was coming out of Lolly's Cafe. Lolly said she'd fixed Sam some eggs, but he'd shoveled them down in a hurry and left. Didn't say where he was going.

I sat down on the sidewalk to catch my breath, tired, frustrated, feeling sick to my stomach. The streets were just beginning to fill up, the hucksters setting up their displays, briefing their shills in the alley, getting ready for what promised to be a red-letter day for the Sons of Artifice. I asked people who walked past if they had seen Sam Adams; most didn't know who he was. I was a stranger in my own town.

I had checked every place in the Bowery that was open. If Sam was uptown, or if he was in someone's office or home, I'd never find him in time. I jumped at the sound of a single blast of the train whistle—boarding. I was within one deep breath of heading for New Town when I glanced across the street to Derby's saloon. The windows, usually shuttered at this time of day, were open. I could see a shadowy figure moving inside.

"Sam, Sam! You gotta get to the depot quick!" I shouted, scaring hell out of the three guys passed out around the faro table. Belle, who was counting the night's receipts, turned white; she figured she was getting robbed after the most profitable night of her life.

"Whoa, Tom." Sam laughed down at me. "You got a fire to report?"

"You gotta hurry. Rebekah's leaving on the train. She might already be gone."

Sam took two steps toward the door, then stopped. He rested his hand on a table and rubbed his chin. I was halfway out the door and had to come back.

He shook his head. "There's nothing I can do, if—"

"You damn fool, she's gonna have a baby!"

His head snapped back like he'd been hit between the eyes with a two-by-four plank. He shook it once to clear it, then ran out of the saloon. The train whistle signaled final boarding just as I hit the sidewalk.

I was young, lean, and fast, but I couldn't keep up with Sam. When he was about fifty yards from the depot, and I another twenty-five behind him, I could see the train slowly pulling away. Being the first train to serve High Plains since the tornado, it was a long one. He had a shot at it.

Sam had to dodge in and out of the long, sluggish stream of immigrants filing toward the Bowery, while avoiding the cars and carriages that swarmed the street. He ran up the tracks toward the caboose, which accelerated slowly, steadily away. Sam drew within ten feet, then five, before he stumbled over a cross tie and fell to the cinders in front of the depot. The mass of new arrivals interrupted their search for baggage long enough to stare down in curiosity at the man lying prone and panting on the tracks. The train blew its whistle and sped off to the eastern prairie.

I wanted to cuss out everyone on that platform for witnessing the sorry spectacle. I'd reached Sam's side, was helping him up—his hands and knees were bloody—when I heard the voice, soft as rose petals falling on snow. "Sam. Sam."

He heard it too. On the corner of the platform, pushed aside by the mob, Rebekah stood, small and uncertain. It was the kind of vision that you surely distrusted because you wanted so bad for it to be real.

Sam reset his hat and beat the dirt from his clothes before taking slow, measured strides over to the depot. Since the platform was raised three feet, Rebekah held the high ground.

He looked up at her, coughed out a long deep sigh, and

turned away. He stood there, looking at the ground, looking at the sky, until I was so mad that I had my right leg pulled back to kick him. Say something, damn it!

Finally he turned around to face her. "Why didn't you tell me?" He wasn't so much angry or demanding, more hurt, puzzled.

"I couldn't tell you." Her every word was laced with misery. "You wouldn't leave, and I couldn't bear the thought of raising a child here." She nodded toward the chaotic street scene, which must have appeared to her to be the realization of a torturous nightmare. "The poor little thing wouldn't have a chance."

Sam stepped up on the platform. They stood about four feet apart, not quite facing each other, while people jostled and shouted all around them. At the far end of the depot a "comet pill" salesman hawked his wares; pills had tripled in price since the weekend.

Sam moved a step closer. "Why didn't you leave?" he asked quietly.

I didn't think Rebekah was going to answer. She twisted the handle of her handbag, and stared into the open prairie. "I couldn't leave *you*." Her right arm rose in front of her as though levitating without her knowledge.

Sam swept her up in a hug so ardent and prolonged that it embarrassed me. The platform was clearing, but the folks who remained looked pretty disgusted by this display of sensuality in a town that they'd journeyed to for salvation.

"I'll find some other work," Sam said. "I'll quit the newspaper."

"No!" Rebekah said, so forcefully that it startled me. "You were the only person to stand up to Brother Nicholas from the very beginning. I'm ashamed that I didn't. I don't know what I can do . . . or where to start, but if I'm going to raise a child here, I want to help straighten this town out."

After another embrace, Rebekah took a step back. "Your drinking?" There was iron in her voice now.

A shudder ran through Sam's body. "Never again, I swear it."

I reassured Rebekah. "I don't think anyone in this town would sell him a drink anyway."

"Will you set aside some time for the baby . . . and me?"

"Oh, God, yes." Sam raised both her hands to his mouth and kissed them. I'd never witnessed that cavalier gesture before, and I was impressed. I later incorporated it into my courting ritual, and have always been gratified by its effect.

"Will you come home now?" Sam asked.

Rebekah nodded with a smile so beatific that its memory warms my soul. Sam glanced around the depot. "Where are your bags?"

"On the train to Kansas."

Sam treated the pregnant Rebekah as though she were made of crystal. He tried to flag down a cab to ferry us back to the Bowery in style, but none of the automobiles or carriages that crowded the streets was interested in short hauls or exclusive fares; every vehicle in the territory had poured into town to transport as many pilgrims as it could carry to Mentirosa Canyon. (It proved to be a lucrative route. The six-mile trip cost two dollars per passenger before noon and rose steadily thereafter. By six o'clock people were paying the price of a good plow horse for the honor of being stacked three high in a rolling, rattling bucket and delivered to the canyon ahead of sundown.)

When we walked through New Town, I saw that the majority of businesses had been shut down by their owners. Many, like Wallace's Grocery and Cooper's General Store, having sold virtually their entire stock, had taken the day off. Others, like R. N. Barkley's bank and the High Plains Real Estate Company, had closed down to stop the fevered run on buying, selling, and withdrawal that had convulsed the town. In response, speculators had set up temporary offices in deserted buildings and alleys and bought animals, tools, and large parcels of land at fire-sale prices. As always in times of desperation, the vipers feasted.

As we walked past Coffman's Drugstore, Sam pointed toward the two huge balloons that soared fifty feet above the street. Coffman was a sharp businessman who often used the tactic on special occasions like Founder's Day,

Fourth of July, and elections. The balloons' message: OXY-GEN SOLD HERE.

"What in the world . . . ?" Rebekah said.

Sam motioned toward a man who was loading a heavy, four-foot-tall metal canister onto the back of his wagon. "You get a mask with it, so that you can breathe the oxygen tonight when the air turns to poison," Sam explained. "The kicker is that the Baptist preacher, Simon, bought four tanks this morning."

I broke away from Sam and Rebekah when we turned toward the Bowery. On the way to the church, I made up my mind that if Mama were to ask what I'd done that morning, I would not lie about it. I was sick and tired of lies. I knew that I had done the right thing, no matter what Mama, or Brother Nicholas, or anyone said. If my entry into Heaven was to be refused, or even delayed, by my part in the Adams affair, then God was not just. If He is kind and forgiving, He will understand; if He is not . . . then all assumptions were fallacies, all promises were lies, and life was meaningless.

I walked into the church with steely eyes, braced for combat. Mama grabbed me from behind, hugged me, and assigned me work without ever questioning my deeds or whereabouts for the last hour.

For the next several hours I heard no one speak of anything more abstract than the task of moving disciples and materials to the canyon rim. It was a blessing that those who were most intimately involved in the Armageddon only hours away should have worthy labor to distract them. We worked and sang hymns and treated each other with the respect and courtesy that humans rarely display. Our work was steadfast and efficient, though I could not help but notice that no eye strayed far from the office where Brother Nicholas remained sequestered, unseen and unheard.

It was mid-afternoon before the final contingent of disciples (Mama, Sister Alma Hardy, Sister Lily Barkley, and me) and the last stack of Ascension Robes were readied for the trip. Hundreds upon hundreds of the garments had been sent ahead, though we all realized there would not be enough to outfit the constant procession of pilgrims that had filed past our windows since early this morning. Time and material had simply run out.

We piled into the flatbed wagon that Old Joe Clark had been driving back and forth from Mentirosa all day. He looked as tuckered as his old chestnut horse. When we left, only Brother Nicholas and Brother Horace remained in the church.

None of us had a word to say as we rolled very slowly down the familiar street for what we all assumed was the last time. Ahead of us, we could see an unbroken line of humanity stretching toward Mentirosa Canyon and eternity.

Chapter
Thirty-five

The north rim of Mentirosa Canyon was an ocean of white sheets set against bare scorched earth and scattered scrub trees. The site, a long flat plain capable of holding the huge assemblage, offered both geographic splendor and a prevailing wind to disseminate Brother Nicholas's words. The speaker's platform had been transported, board by board, after Tuesday night's crusade and rebuilt overnight at the canyon's edge. Beyond the rim the walls plummeted hundreds of feet to where a small stream trickled almost imperceptibly through a maze of ditches and gullies. Spirals, pinnacles, and arches carved from the multi-colored rock and soil by millennial rains and winds erupted from the canyon floor. Mentirosa Canyon was an awesome spectacle and an altogether proper place to meet one's Maker.

The Indians who had been driven out of Mentirosa Canyon considered it a place of magic. I did too. Often when I could not sleep, I conjured up a vision of myself flying over the canyon like an eagle in the sun, then diving to the bottom, wetting my chest in the stream before pulling up to glide between the pinnacles and soar above the rim. It relaxed my mind and gladdened my soul.

There was little at the canyon to relax or gladden on this day. Long before Mentirosa came into view, an air of travail grabbed me by the throat and smothered my senses like the stench of three-day-old carrion. Hard work and fellowship had sustained us until then, but the long, slow wagon ride left us no alternative to grim reflection on imminent death. Lily Barkley had grown thin and pale in the last weeks and now seemed to wilt noticeably with every turn of the wagon wheel. Alma Hardy, her eyes clenched tight as a baby's fists, hummed "Jesus Loves Me" so slowly that it sounded like a dirge.

When we reached the fringe of the huge crowd, anxious worshipers descended on us from all sides to get at the final cache of sanctioned Ascension Robes, leaving their home-made ones in payment. Everyone asked questions about Brother Nicholas. How was he feeling? When would he arrive?

"Feeling fine, coming soon." We answered on faith, since we hadn't seen him and really didn't know.

Old Joe Clark pulled the wagon as close to the platform as he could before unharnessing the animal and chasing it away to graze with the hundreds of horses that were roaming free. We donned our robes. Red crosses had been sewn over the heart, marking us as original disciples and affording us access to the cordoned-off section in front of the platform. My cross was unearned, but Mama defied anyone to contest the right of her son to wear the emblem that ensured precedence. The wind that never ceased whirled bitterly through the canyon and multiplied in ferocity, shaking the wooden stand.

Mama was immediately immersed in work, so I slipped away to walk off some of the tension piling up in my gut. From the look of the sky, we still had about an hour before sundown, and that was far too long to sit and wait. Most of the folks were standing, talking quietly, although there were pockets of excited preaching and singing, hand-holding and shouting.

Though it was my intention to observe the crowd, my robe marked me as a person close to the inner circle and privy to the information upon which the masses could only speculate. The attention frightened me at first, but it took only a dozen paces or so before pride swallowed up humility, and judgment. O Vanity!

Twice I was consulted on points of interpretation:

"Will we go to Hell for riding out here in a motor car?"

No . . . but it wouldn't be a waste of breath to pray for forgiveness.

"Can we wear our hats?"

Yes, but take them off before sundown. The boots had better go too.

I was cut down, mid-swagger, by a toothless woman in a ragged sheet that showed every sign of having been lived in for the last several days. The humility carved into her face by fifty years of subsistence living had given way to desperation. Her bony fingers bit into my shoulder blades as she begged for reassurance.

"Have you seed him? He's acomin', ain't he?" Her thin voice clawed at me. "He wouldn't leave us now, not now."

Her grip paralyzed me. I stared into blue eyes turned to chalk by years of crushed hope and listened to myself, as if from the bottom of the canyon, say: "He's comin', ma'am. I saw him not more'n an hour ago, and he said he'd be right along. Don't you worry none."

A gaunt man in a dirty bed shirt tipped his hat to me and pulled the woman away. She fell to her knees, heaving sobs of relief as she wrapped her arms around the man's legs. I reached but could not bring myself to touch her for fear that her melancholy might attach itself to me.

As I moved away from the crowd, I placed my hand on my heart to conceal the badge that I had not earned, could not live up to. I joined the Negroes who had gathered off to the side of the main body, and listened to their preacher's rolling, rhythmic promises of the glory soon to come. Word had apparently been spread through many channels, since there were at least three times the number of blacks present than had ever lived on the Reservation. I stayed for two hymns, both joyous anthems promising a Paradise both pastoral and vigorous, and left feeling a little better.

Skirting the crowd, I spotted, a good fifty yards to the rear, a small group who had staked off territory in anticipation of the coming spectacle. About fifteen young, gaily-dressed "smarts" from New Town had come to picnic and observe the show that they fully expected to delight in. They had sufficient presence of mind to stay far enough away from the devout so that their laughter could be ignored. Standing, laughing, right in the middle of them was Bark Barkley. A reporter from the *Citizen-Advocate* also shared their meal and recorded their witticisms.

The sun was falling, and a high bank of black clouds rolled swiftly from east to west in pursuit. I was getting real nervous. The undercurrent of fear that had pervaded this crowd was fast turning to panic. People began screaming and chanting and dancing in circles and it was spreading.

Eternity was at hand and Brother Nicholas was not among us.

Although I had reassured everyone who'd asked me, I had no more reason to believe he would come than anyone else fool enough to stand out there in the middle of this wasteland waiting for a free ride to Heaven. Maybe it was some kind of horrible mistake, or, more likely, there *really was* some money in it somehow, and Brother Nicholas was on a train to California, laughing at us while running his hands through a bag full of loot.

But if that were true, then maybe the world wasn't going to end.

Another look at the raging sky and the chaos that was multiplying by the minute, and I *knew* that the world had to end. This was how Armageddon had been described; this was how it *felt*! My legs would not stand, I could not swallow.

Where is our shepherd? Why has he forsaken us? I was on my knees praying when I heard the shouts.

"HE'S HERE!"

"PRAISE THE LORD!"

"IT'S BROTHER NICHOLAS!"

I was deeply ashamed of myself and begged forgiveness for the doubt that I had succumbed to. How could I have ever questioned the rectitude of a saint who desired only to serve? Father, forgive me.

The cheering crowd surrounded the carriage, forcing Brother Horace to rein the horse in well short of the platform. Both men wore long, flowing robes, though Brother Nicholas's was much whiter; it was silk, sewn by my mother's hand. The evangelist's face was emaciated and pale as wax, the angular bones threatening to gouge through the tissue of skin. He stood up in the buggy and stretched his hand out. The crowd fell silent.

"MAY THE LORD LOOK DOWN UPON US AND

BLESS THIS FINAL MEETING IN HIS NAME. ALL WHO ARE GATHERED HERE TODAY WILL BE REWARDED WITH THAT MOST PRECIOUS OF GIFTS: ETERNAL LIFE!"

When I saw the crowd's response to his arrival, I cut around the outside and scrambled back toward the front. Within seconds of finding Mama and digging into a defensible position, we felt the crush of "lesser" humanity, which would not be denied. All barriers between the "twenty-four" and the rest of the flock were forgotten in the rush toward the platform. It was every supplicant for himself.

Then, at what I judged to be about thirty minutes before sundown, Brother Nicholas ascended the platform amid cheering that would have gratified a Caesar. After a single sweeping wave of his right hand, he sat down in the elevated chair, leaned forward, placing his head in both hands, and went into a soundless trance. We waited breathlessly, in fear and confusion, as storm clouds gathered and thunder approached.

Brother Nicholas did not move.

Chapter
Thirty-six

*"Have you been to Jesus for the
cleansing power,
Are you washed in the blood
of the lamb?*

*"Do you rest each morning in
the crucified,
Are you washed in the blood
of the lamb?*

*"Are you washed in the blood,
in the soul-cleansing blood
of the lamb?*

*"Are your garments spotless,
are they white as snow,
Are you washed in the blood
of the lamb?"*

The thunder to the east rumbled out ominous counter-point to the hymns that we intoned in abject fear. Black clouds were moving in quickly and threatening to overtake the sun, which now plunged headlong toward the horizon. We sang to reassure ourselves, for we were adrift without rudder, sailing directly into a storm that we could not survive unprotected. Brother Nicholas had made neither sound nor signal since assuming his throne. He sat in rigid silence—unwilling? unable?—to lead us from the watery waste to the Other Shore.

We hoped that Brother Horace's lighting of the four torches on the platform corners would rouse the sleeping prophet. It did not. We sang to keep from screaming.

> *"Lay hold on the lifeline,*
> *lay hold on the lifeline,*
> *someone is drifting away.*

> *"Christ can hold the perishing*
> *from sinking 'neath the waves,*
> *Yes, Jesus Christ—"*

The second verse broke down under the weight of terror and confusion.

"Speak to us, Brother Nicholas!"

"Don't forsake us!"

"We are lost! All is lost!"

Shouts and wails of despair poured from every sector. Mama and I held each other and cried the tears of the un-redeemed. The crowd was only seconds from riot and pandemonium.

Brother Nicholas leaped to his feet and stretched his arms to the sky. His voice overwhelmed all others. "THE TIME IS AT HAND! ASSUME YOUR POSITIONS!"

A tidal wave of humanity fell to its knees. I dragged Lily Barkley down by her robe. She rambled on in fear and supplication, unaware that we had been snatched from the pit. Our savior had taken charge and would lead us home.

Brother Nicholas pointed to the scarlet sun on the western horizon, larger, redder, than any I had ever seen. "AND I BEHELD WHEN HE HAD OPENED THE SIXTH SEAL, AND THE MOON BECAME BLACK AS SACK-CLOTH OF HAIR, AND THE SUN BECAME AS BLOOD!"

The clouds swallowed the sun and the sky was a black hole. Insects and birds fell silent, and the only sounds that I heard were the snorts and low whinnies of the horses, which had grazed quietly until now.

Brother Nicholas screamed: "AND THE HEAVENS DE-

PARTED AS A SCROLL WHEN IT IS ROLLED TO-
GETHER AND EVERY MOUNTAIN AND ISLAND
WERE MOVED OUT OF THEIR PLACES. AND THE
KINGS OF THE EARTH AND THE GREAT MEN, AND
THE CHIEF CAPTAINS AND THE MIGHTY MEN HID
THEMSELVES IN THE DENS AND IN THE ROCKS
OF THE MOUNTAINS, AND SAID TO THE MOUN-
TAINS AND ROCKS 'FALL ON US AND HIDE US
FROM HIM THAT SITTETH ON THE THRONE AND
FROM THE WRATH OF THE LAMB.' "

Brother Nicholas threw his arms open in appeal and
stared up into the void. I followed his eyes, knowing that
the end was near.

A dark specter floated high above the preacher's head
and swept toward the crowd. Hardly more than a shadow,
it seemed to be rising and moving toward us with a darting
motion. When I pointed it out to my mother, she fell back
in fear. I could not remove my eyes.

"AND THE GREAT DAY OF WRATH HAS COME
AND WHO SHALL BE ABLE TO STAND!"

The specter exploded and the heavens roared as sheets of
fire rained down on our heads. Streaks of orange, yellow,
silver—every imaginable color coursed the gray sky and
showered the unholy earth and the wretched forms thereon.
The pilgrims ran in every direction, screaming, trying to
beat out the fire that burned their skin, their robes, the
parched grass.

Brother Nicholas mocked their efforts. "FOOLS! YOU
CANNOT SUBVERT THE WILL OF GOD! 'FOR THE
FIRE HATH DEVOURED THE PASTURES OF THE
WILDERNESS, AND THE FLAME HATH BURNED
ALL THE TREES OF THE FIELD.' "

I beat out the fire that burned the cloth from my leg. I
clutched my mother in fierce desperation, but I could not
tear my eyes from the spectacle of people running, crawling, rolling, terrified, falling over their wounded brethren
while rending their garments and ripping flesh from their
own bodies. The horses stampeded through the crowd, their
screams merging into the cacophony of horror that must
surely be the hour of wrath—the Dies Irae for mankind.

Chapter
Thirty-seven

The sun had set behind the low, smothering clouds hours earlier. The faithful had regrouped around the platform, still nursing their wounds and burns as they prayed. The cold wind whipped sand in our faces as Mama and I clutched each other and awaited the fulfillment of Prophecy. Brother Nicholas had not uttered a word since the explosion; he sat in his chair with head bowed. Dead? Ascended? We didn't know. The four torches on the corners of the platform had sputtered and died.

Once the panic had run its course, the faithful had nothing to do but await the resolution. There were many people who needed care; scores had been burned by the explosion or trampled by man or animal. In front of me, I could see Colonel Hedgman slumped in his wheelchair, his body twisted grotesquely. Many were torn between a desire to ease suffering and the feeling that those who were enduring pain were doing so for a reason—God's will. And we believed that God was making his choices, that Ascension was imminent. We awaited the earthquake, the tidal wave, and the explosion of the sun; the End that was undeniable.

A continual, low undercurrent of moaning ran through the crowd, and I tried to block it out of my mind, for I knew it would drive me mad. Mama sang "Beulah Land" to me as I laid my head in her lap, my very being praying for the sleep that would renew.

Brother Nicholas did not move.

"MIDNIGHT HAS PASSED! WHERE IS ARMAGED-DON?"

The shouted question roused me from sleep. I shook

295

Mama awake, and we both rose to our feet. The sun was rising, the world was intact, the landscape was unchanged. The night had passed without Assumption, and the sound of angry betrayal rolled through the crowd up to the platform. Everyone who was able seemed to be standing and demanding answers. But Brother Nicholas remained seated and still. When the crowd surged forward now, it was in anger.

At that moment the rain that had threatened all night began to fall. When the first raindrop hit my face, I recoiled as if it were acid.

Suddenly, Brother Nicholas leaped from his chair and shouted, "I SEE THE TEAR IN GOD'S EYE!"

The mass that had pressed forward in anger now stopped dead.

"I SEE THE TEAR IN GOD'S EYE!" Brother Nicholas stood on the edge of the platform and shouted again. He walked quickly from one end of the platform to the other, talking to himself and waving his arms wildly. He stopped at the right corner, thrust his arms to the sky, and shouted: "GOD WAS GRAVELY TROUBLED BY THE HUMAN RACE. EVIL WAS WORSHIPED AND REWARDED WHILE RIGHTEOUSNESS WAS PERSECUTED AND HIS PROPHETS WERE VILIFIED! SO IT WAS IN NINEVAH WHEN JONAH WAS TOLD THAT THE GREAT CITY WOULD BE DESTROYED, MEN, WOMEN, AND CATTLE IN FORTY DAYS. BUT THE PEOPLE OF NINEVEH *HEEDED THE WARNING* OF JONAH AND COVERED THEMSELVES WITH SACK-CLOTH, AND LET NEITHER MAN NOR BEAST TASTE OF FOOD OR WATER, AND THEY TURNED FROM THEIR EVIL WAYS.

"AND GOD SPARED THEM!"

Every pilgrim within earshot was listening intently to the man who had brought them on this long strange journey, hoping he would show them the meaning of it all. The rain fell harder upon us.

"GOD SENT A COMET TO DESTROY THIS WORLD. MAKE NO MISTAKE ABOUT THAT. BUT HE LOOKED DOWN ON THE GREAT PLAINS OF TEXAS

AND SAW A GROUP OF *TRUE CHRISTIANS* AND A
TEAR CAME TO HIS EYE.

"I SEE THAT TEAR!"

Brother Nicholas was never stronger, more vital, than he
was at this moment, speaking to the confused, exhausted
remnants of his once great army. He was inspired, and I
could feel his conviction pour over us. Bodies pressed in
beside me, anxious to hear, to believe again.

"GOD SPARED THE WORLD BECAUSE *WE* HAD
THE FAITH AND COURAGE TO TRUST HIS DIVINE
PROPHECY. WITHOUT EACH AND EVERY ONE OF
YOU, THIS PLANET WOULD BE A SMOKING CIN-
DER, DEVOID OF LIFE!"

He danced across the stage, his hands hugged to his
chest in ecstasy. "WE MUST NOT LET THIS MIRACLE
PASS UNNOTICED BY A WORLD WHO OWES ITS
VERY EXISTENCE TO US! WE MUST BUILD A
MONUMENT—A TEMPLE—A *TABERNACLE* THAT
WILL SURPASS ANY IN THIS STATE. THE PEOPLE
OF THE WORLD MUST KNOW THAT *THIS SMALL
BAND OF DISCIPLES* HAS RESCUED THEM FROM
THE WRATH OF AN ANGRY GOD. THE FOUR COR-
NERS OF THE GLOBE MUST HEAR, AND *WE SHALL
CARRY THE WORD!*"

"Hallelujah!"

"Praise God, we were right!"

"We saved the world!"

The shouts were continuous, rising from all corners.
From the rear came the chant: "CARRY THE WORD!
CARRY THE WORD!"

I watched in amazement while people locked arms and
swayed as they shouted: "CARRY THE WORD! CARRY
THE WORD!"

I resisted the arms that sought to include me. The canti-
cle rolled like a wave over the multitude. My mother
shouted:

"CARRY THE WORD! CARRY THE WORD!"

At that moment I knew that no matter what Brother
Nicholas, my mother, and the hundreds of zealots
screamed, all of this was absurd. I had spent a torturous

night amidst misery and pain, terrified of a phantom that did not exist. I had been a damn fool!

I pulled away from Mama, shoved through the crowd, and stomped through the driving rain toward the Bowery. I never looked back.

Chapter
Thirty-eight

The world did not end on May 18, 1910, an insight apparent, no doubt, to the perceptive reader of this history. As nearly as scientists could tell, the Earth's orbit, rotation, magnetic poles, and atmosphere were unaffected by its passage through the tail of the great Comet Halley. The town of High Plains did not fare nearly so well.

Four people who attended the Glorious Assumption at Mentirosa Canyon died. Colonel Hedgman and an elderly woman from Skankton perished from exposure to the cold winds of the canyon and the bitter rain that fell throughout the long trip back to town. A Wishbone man died when he either fell or flung himself into the canyon. Danita Olson, the cook at the Lamour Hotel, was trampled by what most folks preferred to believe were horses; she fell to the ground after the explosion and did not survive the chaos.

More than fifty other people were injured or afflicted with illness that night, with burns, fractures, and exposure predominating. Clara Clark nearly died of pneumonia and was bedfast for a month afterward. Harlow Foley broke his left arm when he fell/jumped/was pushed into the canyon. He was spared a long descent and an abrupt stop by a ledge about twenty feet below the canyon rim that broke his fall, his ulna, and his radius.

Immediately following The Glorious Assumption, many citizens of High Plains resembled the refugees of an artillery-shelled city, with the walking wounded conspicuous in number and tragedy. Some considered their wounds to be an even greater burden spiritually, since it incriminated them in a folly that they would rather have denied.

There was, however, a segment of the wounded who

wore their injuries like medals handed down from God. Not only would this vocal minority not deny involvement in the Glorious Assumption, they would chase down a scoffer in order to convince him that *Brother Nicholas's* presence at Mentirosa, *his* piety in the face of Armageddon, had saved *everyone's* life, and the planet Earth as well.

That phenomenon, so unlikely and perverse that no one in town anticipated or fully understood it, appended a wretched coda to the Great Comet Fiasco of 1910. From the putrid ashes of the Glorious Assumption, Nicholas gathered sixty disciples who believed aggressively and indisputably that their deluded vigil on the edge of a canyon had actually saved the world. And it was precisely the people who had sacrificed the most—the wounded, the ranchers who had sold land and stock to settle debts, the farmers who had liquidated property or refused to plant crops, the workers who had renounced job or deserted family, the people who had every right and reason to want to nail Nicholas's hide to the shed—*those people* were his staunchest adherents. And my mother's voice soared above all others in championing Nicholas's new mission.

Nicholas's flock had been cut back sharply, but those who remained were the most devoted and passionate workers that a movement could ever hope for. Nicholas kept them isolated so they could feed off each other's faith with minimum exposure to the skepticism—nay, ridicule—of the public. A majority of the "Three Score," as they called themselves, had forsaken all possessions to join the Comet Crusade, and were now dependent on the food and shelter that Nicholas and their brethren were eager to extend. Cots filled the True Vine Church, and members who still had homes cheerfully housed those who were destitute. Daily meals were served at the church, where the adherents gave repeated and heartfelt thanks for the thin stew and hard bread. Though the coffers were nearly empty, Brother Nicholas's confidence that God would provide satisfied the parishioners. The alternative was spiritual desolation.

My mother housed six strangers in our home, while I slept on the floor of *Plain Talk* and took my meals with Sam and Rebekah. Mama made several attempts to lure me back to the True Vine fold, but I met her entreaties with anger and harsh words. I missed her desperately, and the only compromise in all the world that I would not make to have her back was succumbing to the vow that her faith demanded.

Chapter
Thirty-nine

GLORIOUS ASSUMPTION PROVES
PRESUMPTUOUS!

Sam, Rebekah, Shad, and I had the special edition on the street by mid-morning Friday. People chuckled over the headline and grunted approval over the two-page account that had been written and printed in a feverish twenty-four-hour stretch. Rebekah Adams worked tirelessly on the gamut of newspaper tasks and proved singularly adept at interviewing the veterans of the Glorious Assumption. Witnesses, who clammed up resentfully under Sam's questioning, showered emotion and detail upon the sympathetic Rebekah.

We also found that many townspeople who had not attended the sojourn at Mentirosa were anxious to express their contempt for the fools who had followed that crazy preacher to the edge of madness, though I could remember few being so vocal just two days earlier. Outside of the zealots still holed up in the True Vine Church and the demonstrably wounded, it was damn nigh impossible to find a citizen who would admit to having walked that final mile with Nicholas.

Sam took a short nap after we got the paper on the street, but bounced right up around one o'clock, anxious to get out to the canyon to work on the overriding mystery of the explosion, which remained unsolved, and, as near as we could tell, uninvestigated.

It was no mystery to me. I explained it, once again, to Sam and Rebekah on the buggy ride out of town. "Ol' Nick put someone up to it so it would look like the end of the world, just like he'd predicted all along. He probably had Ol' Baldy rig up some kinda deal that would explode and scare the ... the *bejesus* out of everyone there. Who else could it be?"

"I don't know," Sam said, laying a little soft leather to the back of the lazy horse that he'd rented from Kerley's livery. "But if Nick really believed that the world was going to end, and I believe he did, then there was no reason for two-bit carnival fireworks."

"Nobody else had anything to gain," I said, exasperated by Sam's naiveté. "I tell you Nick was behind this whole thing. He knew the world wasn't going to end, and he had to have some kinda show or else the crowd might get mad and toss his sorry ... toss *him* into the canyon."

Rebekah shook her head grimly. "Brother Nicholas believed everything he said. All those poor, desperate people would have been better off if he had been dishonest, rather than ... deluded."

We tied the horse to the platform, and Sam and I established as nearly as possible where the explosion had occurred. All three of us paced off the area, foot by foot, looking for anything odd. The rain and mud and countless footsteps had churned up the ground so it looked like a recklessly plowed field.

Rebekah found it. She had stumbled and fallen to her knees, only to discover a piece of rubber about the size of a silver dollar. It had been painted black on one side and had fallen across the limb of a low scrub bush. We scoured the area for another half hour, finding two more similar pieces, before redirecting the search. The wind had blown out of the east-northeast on Wednesday, but the swirling winds of the canyon were unpredictable. After we had trampled the area over an hour, I spotted a leather pouch lying behind a low mound. It wasn't the pouch that interested me; it was the yellow powder inside it. Sulfur. I found it a good two hundred yards away from the platform, on a plateau that was higher than the rim of the canyon. Some brush had been piled up so that there was room for a person, maybe two, to approach from the east and move around without being seen.

We ate the picnic lunch that Rebekah had packed as we hurried back to town. We had planned to spread the food out on a clean tablecloth at the edge of the canyon and really enjoy the scenery, but now that we had a hot lead, food was of little importance to any of us.

After we returned horse and wagon to Kerley's livery, Rebekah confessed that fatigue and nausea would prohibit the involvement she clearly desired in the next phase of our investigation. After expressing our concern and disappointment to her, Sam and I took our pocketful of clues up to New Town.

"I pulled them down and deflated them around three o'clock, when I closed up," H. W. Coffman said, draping his arm protectively over his cash register. "I packed them both away in the storeroom. We still had goods to sell—lots of goods, I stocked up heavy—but I was tired of dealing with all the lunatics on the street." The druggist's voice lowered as he leaned forward to speak in confidence, "Money isn't everything, you know." He spoke as though it were something that he had just learned but wasn't sure everyone should be told.

"Would you mind checking to see if they're still there?" Sam asked casually.

Coffman rolled a cocked eye warily over the patrons of his store as though half expecting to find a masked desperado bent on rifling the register if he removed his arm. " 'Spect I could," he said grudgingly, waving to a clerk who was trying to look busy rearranging the patent medicines. "Mr. Cedric, could you attend my station while I walk to the back with these gentlemen?"

Mr. Cedric walked wordlessly over to us and replaced Coffman's arm atop the money box with his own. Reassured, the druggist unlocked a heavy oak door and led us through a maze of barrels, kegs, canisters, and oversized apothecary jars to the back wall. The storeroom was dark, with only one north window to afford us daylight, but I knew Coffman wouldn't light a lamp until circumstances demanded it. He was tight even by Presbyterian standards.

Coffman reached down to a shelf that was about knee

high and pulled out a collapsed balloon that still bore the hand-painted legend OXYGEN SOLD HERE! His hand scrambled around on the shelf for a full minute in search of the second balloon before he finally lit a match to confirm his loss.

"Do you know who stole it?" he asked, his voice rising at the thought of his own vulnerability. "Did they get anything else?" His eyes darted around the room, blinking quickly, trying to register every possession or its absence. He rattled the lock on the back door. It held.

"Do you keep sulfur?"

"Certainly." Coffman lifted the lid of a barrel. "Someone's been in here. My scoop has been moved."

"Dynamite?"

"Haven't stocked any in the last three months."

"Gunpowder?"

Coffman opened the top of a small keg. "I'd venture I'm short a little better than two cupfuls."

Sam wrote it down. "Thank you, Mr. Coffman," he said.

"Who was it? How'd he get in?" Coffman said, anger and fear fighting for precedence in his voice. Finally. "Who's going to pay for it?"

"I don't know yet," Sam said, walking to the door. "But I'll find out, and you can read about it in *Plain Talk*."

"Black paint?" Ronny Baines chirped. "Yes, indeedy. And we're the only store in town that carries it. We order it special from Dallas, takes two weeks to get here. How much do you need?" Ronny waved his gold pen with a flourish, eager for our order.

Sam waved his hand to slow the clerk down. Ronny was always very enthusiastic, and he had a way about him that put a lot of people off. Men who shopped at the mercantile ignored him just as surely as their wives sought him out for advice on cloth pattern and style.

"What I need to know, Ronny," Sam said pleasantly, "is whether you sold any of it on Tuesday or Wednesday?"

"I surely did. Wednesday, right before we closed up. I sold our last gallon." Ronny was nearly breathless as he reached for a piece of paper and scribbled out a note. "I've

got to tell Daddy to order some more." Ronny's father, Jack
Baines, owned the mercantile.

"Do you remember who bought it?"

"Yes, indeedy." Ronny placed his pen neatly back in its
holder, then wiped some dust from the counter with the
back of his hand. "It was Bark Barkley. It was the first time
in my life that he ever treated me with civility."

"I know how Bark got into Coffman's storeroom," I said to
Sam as we walked the New Town sidewalk. "There's a
hole above the window latch. You can see it better from
outside. All you gotta do is bend a piece of wire and loop
it around the lock. Late at night you can get in and out
without anyone knowing."

Out of the corner of my eye I saw Sam shake his head.
"I'd appreciate it if you could forbear from nocturnal visits
into areas where discovery might cost me my best reporter."
His voice was not harsh, just serious.

"I gave up all that already. It was just candy and tobacco.
Kid's stuff." After a short silence I was ready to change the
subject. "Where we headed now?"

"Well, there's two ways we can go about this thing."
Sam laughed and shook his head. "There always seem to
be two ways, doesn't there? The first way is to work our
tails off chasing down every lead that might connect Bark
to the explosion, and interview anyone who might have
seen him with the balloon or around the canyon. That's accepted journalistic practice. It's slow, and methodical, and
the way the law ought to handle it. If we had any doubt
that Bark did it—"

"The S.O.B. is guilty as Judas with a handful of silver."

"Well said. I'm inclined to agree, and seeing as how we
want to crack this forthwith, I guess we'll take the second
option. Bark Barkley appears to me to be the kind that
would break down and convict himself if we could confront
him. If we can't get to him, then we may just spread the
word around that we suspect Bark. I'll bet that folks will be
beating our door down with information."

"You think somebody saw him?"

"Tom, in this town you can't lower yourself to the bottom of a well and drop your drawers without someone admiring your rear end."

"So where do we start?"

"Right at the top."

Sam and I had just stepped up on the plank sidewalk of the depot when we caught sight of R. N. Barkley and son Bark crossing the street toward the First Cattlemen's Bank. They were a good fifty yards ahead of us, but R.N.'s gout slowed him, so we were able to make up the ground before they reached the door of the bank. When Bark saw us approaching, he attempted to pull his father along at a faster clip and received a rap from the old man's cane for his impatience.

"Mr. Barkley! We want to talk to you," Sam called as we approached. We stopped a couple steps shy of the sidewalk, about ten feet from where Barkley was fumbling with the keys. There was a sign on the door: CLOSED BY ORDER OF THE TEXAS STATE BANKING BOARD.

R.N. turned toward us and shook his head. "I have nothing to say to you, Mr. Adams. Good day." He turned again toward the door but dropped his keys.

"We have evidence that your son was responsible for the explosion at Mentirosa Canyon Wednesday night," Sam said. "A lot of people were hurt. Do you have any comment?"

I had my eye on Bark, and I saw the fear that seized his face. Guilty! Guilty! Guilty!

Sam's question sounded way too respectful to me. While Barkley groped for his keys on the sidewalk, I presented my assessment of the situation.

"Listen, you fat old sonuvabitch," I shouted, "your chickenshit son exploded a balloon bomb and damn near killed a lot of people. He's goin' to get his ass thrown in jail. If he don't get strung up first."

Barkley managed to snare his keys, and when he straightened up, he found himself staring into a crowd that had gathered instantly at the sound of contention. His tone was now conciliatory. "If you would like to step into my office, Mr. Adams, I believe that I can disabuse you of this fable—"

"That's not necessary, Mr. Barkley," Sam said, "we're confident of our facts. Bark stole a balloon from Coffman's storeroom along with gunpowder and sulfur. He painted it black with paint he bought from Ronny Baines and set it off over the crowd."

"That's a goddamn lie," Bark shouted. "I was home all night. I was with my daddy." Bark looked beseechingly to his father for confirmation. R.N. couldn't meet his eye.

"I seen him at the canyon," yelled a voice in the crowd. "He was in his old man's buckboard pulled by a dun horse."

WHAM! The first rock hit the window about a foot above Bark Barkley's head. When I turned around to see where it came from, I was amazed to find at least thirty people gathered behind us; half the crowd held rocks, and the other half were searching the ground for ammunition. A volley of stones fell on the Barkleys as R.N. attempted to jab his key into the door lock. I couldn't tell whether most of the projectiles were aimed at the older or younger Barkley, but most folks seemed to be satisfied with which-ever one they hit. The two ultimately made it inside before meeting a fate more befitting a Christian martyr than a scoundrel and his loutish son. The crowd didn't stop chunking till every window was broken and free of even large shards.

By the time Sheriff Lon Coffey ambled over to break up the riot, everyone had pretty well lost their enthusiasm for the sport anyway. Sam talked to several people who could place Bark at Mentirosa Canyon or add some corroborating evidence to our story. We lost no time in getting back to the office and setting up the story that we knew would be "ex-clusive."

R. N. Barkley had his son on the first train out of town af-ter the sun set that night. Bark Barkley never set foot in High Plains again and was never legally charged with det-onating the explosive in Mentirosa Canyon that injured dozens of people and contributed to the death of two. Within a day his culpability was common knowledge, his motive assumed. His contempt for his stepmother was well-known, as was his disdain for the movement that she had come to devote her life to. And everyone in town recognized Bark as a spoiled and willful child whose delinquency would ultimately pass the bounds that his age and his father's position could extricate him from.

Although the townspeople were satisfied that Bark's act was simply the product of mendacious destiny, a bad seed come to flower, I knew Bark well enough to know that his rage had been directed at me. The realization, the responsibility, was slow to descend into my consciousness, delayed by my loathing for him. I did not set match to fuse, but it doubtless would never have been lit had I not knocked Bark Barkley on his ass in front of a street full of witnesses.

Chapter
Forty

On the Tuesday following the Glorious Assumption, there were six of us—Doc Moss, Zack Hart, Old Joe Clark, Shorty Carter's brother Jap, and some layabout I couldn't place off to my right—sitting in front of the Lamour soaking up the afternoon sun. Sam and I had put out an abbreviated issue of the paper the day before just to get back on our Monday schedule, and he had taken the day off. Rebekah had him working in the kitchen and bedroom, doing some odd jobs that he was ill-suited for. I've known few men as dangerous as Sam Adams with a carpenter tool in his hand.

The Raglars had settled in silence after spending a good deal of time and wind discussing Bark Barkley's flight from town and the anticipated exodus of Brother Nicholas. Most folks figured that the second incarnation of Nicholas's church would stagger along on inertia for a week or two—long enough for the membership to wean themselves from the excitement of battle on the heightened plane of universal combat—before fading back into the community and the wan existence of wind, flat land, dust, and people getting by as best they could. The only wager that you could strike up was whether Nicholas would last out the week and whether his exit would be public or veiled in darkness and deceit. Smart money favored a moonlight getaway.

Doc Moss spat a long brown stream across the sidewalk and into the street, signaling that he was ready to take the floor. "I heard that up in the wilds of Oklahoma last week a group of some forty religious folk, headed up by a gentleman calling himself 'Harmon the Freethinker,' took it upon themselves to avert the end of the world by sacrificing a sixteen-year-old virgin."

Every eye rolled up a notch at that announcement. Joe Clark shifted heavily in his seat so that he faced away from Doc and whittled double time on the stick that must have represented the accumulated sins and foolishness of his life. Old Joe had eased back into the group after the Glorious Assumption, but was often moody and quiet; he grew visibly uneasy at any mention of the painfully recent debacle.

Doc spat again to give us time to conjure up the scene: beautiful maiden staked hand and foot on a wooden altar, robe pulled aside to afford access to the dagger poised over her heart by a double-fisted priest/assassin.

"The sheriff and posse broke up the ceremony just minutes before it was to be consummated," Doc finished.

I whistled appreciatively, a habit that I'd picked up from Sam.

"That's a black lie!" Zack said firmly, not even bothering to look up from the cigarette he was rolling.

Necks were rubbed, clouds studied, and cracks in the sidewalk examined as we considered the challenge. Doc's veracity was one of the few things in our small universe that was virtually unassailable. I, for one, would rather have spat in the eye of the governor than contest Doc's word.

The doctor leaned back in his chair, his hands folded across his stomach, serene as Buddha. "There's a newspaper article in the *Tulsa Dispatch*." He reached into his vest pocket. "I have the clipping right here for your examination."

Zack shook his head so hard I was afraid that it might fly off and roll down the street. "I'm sure you got a clippin'," Zack said, lighting his cigarette, "but I'd like to know how in hell you're going to find a sixteen-year-old *virgin* in Oklahoma."

Doc leaned forward and stroked his chin. "I suspect they imported her from Ioway for the occasion."

We laughed about that for a while, but the image of the Virgin Sacrifice lingered with me for considerably longer. I borrowed the clipping to show to Sam and barely had it tucked away when I saw Shorty Carter walking our way.

His head was bowed and he was talking to the ground so
hard he walked past without seeing us. We hollered him
back and waited for the news that couldn't be good.

"They read the will," Shorty said, in a slow, confused
growl. "Colonel Hedgman left it all to Nicholas. Money,
land, stock. Everythin'."

Any one of the five old men around me would rather
chew off his own tongue than express surprise or alarm at
anything; no one seemed to interrupt a knife stroke or even
alter his breathing. I was ready to yell at them when Doc
finally spoke.

"God deliver us," he said, "from deluded men with capital."

Colonel Hedgman's will was airtight and quickly escaped
probate, following a challenge by the Colonel's son and
daughter. Their father's bequest of one dollar apiece seemed
inadequate compensation to children who had borne the
abuse and tyranny of an autocrat conditioned by years in
the military feudal system. Colonel Hedgman's last will and
testament was his ultimate acknowledgment to the chain of
command, a soldier's final salute to an indifferent Commander in the hope that a gesture of servility would bring
a reward worthy of the Colonel's sacrifice of time, independence, and humanity. Nobody knows if the salute was returned.

When the court challenge was denied, the money and
land surrendered to the original beneficiary, Brother Nicholas and his lieutenants launched full-scale plans for a commune housed in the Hedgman mansion and centering on
farming, dairy cattle, and handcrafts. The Colonel's twenty-
five-hundred acres was the finest spread around, made more
precious by the river that once again flowed within a
stone's throw of the mansion's high front porch.

The men immediately began construction of Brother
Nicholas's temple, the "Tabernacle to Surpass All," but
completion would be delayed until arrival of another train-
load of lumber from Colorado. Even half built it was an
imposing monument, with a pulpit floor constructed with
the wood from Brother Nicholas's crusade platform. Rumor

had it that, when finished, it would house over six hundred worshipers while affording all the living and meeting space that the commune would need.

New Jerusalem, in those first halcyon weeks of its founding, showed firm indication of becoming a functioning cooperative sufficient in leadership and resources to provide a welcome alternative to people who deserved a better shake from life than the bone-grinding poverty that had been their lot. Left to its own destiny, it is hard to say what might have become of the collective experiment conceived so auspiciously, or the man who was its guiding spirit. The history of utopian communities is shot through with joyous commencements that soon staggered under doubt and hardship, only to collapse in failure and acrimony. Dating from the initial experiment in the Garden of Eden, the human animal has a woeful record of maintaining peace and prosperity under even the most Elysian conditions. Still, New Jerusalem's bulging coffers eliminated a common obstacle to survival, and the dustbowl mentality of its members gave the commune a leg up on communities founded on the vagaries of artistic consensus, philosophical thought, or youthful idealism.

Nevertheless, New Jerusalem showed promise of stability and longevity, and that prospect galled a substantial portion of High Plains. Sam Adams counseled patience, but I, for one, would have gladly laid torch to every vestige of New Jerusalem if I thought it would free my mother from her folly. There were many who felt as I did, and I heard much talk about vigilante action against the collective. It came to nothing. Soon all but the bitterest of the townsfolk had reconciled to the presence of an autonomous kingdom within shouting distance of our town.

Chapter
Forty-one

It had been a bad day all around. The press had broken down twice, throwing us way behind, and even Rebekah was showing wear around the eyes and mouth from internalizing the irritation that Sam and I openly vented. We maligned the town council, the governor of Texas, the St. Louis Browns, President Taft; it was open season on anyone not covered in ink and grease and knee-deep in misprinted newspaper. We suffered from fatigue and familiarity; we all needed time apart, time alone.

After taking a stack of papers up to New Town, I decided to stop by my mother's house to pick up some clothes. I had been home only once since Mama had deserted it—me—for New Jerusalem, and had been so overcome with dread that I had failed to take half of what I had come for and needed. I had walked through my home like an enemy soldier inching through a mine field, afraid to look either left or right.

I had seen Mama only twice since our break, both times from a distance as she walked into New Town shops with an armload of sewing. She was attended by two "sisters," since Jerusalemites were not allowed in town in groups of less than three. They walked Indian file by rank, Mama in front, and wasted neither word nor glance on the people that they had known all their life. I stayed out of sight and vowed to myself that I would not cry the next time I saw her, or ever again.

The kitchen door was unlocked; I don't think there was ever a key. The dust was thick and the air stale and heavy as a dungeon's. Everything was as I had remembered it except for the envelope on the kitchen table.

Dear Tom,

Come join us . . . I pray for you every day . . . my life is joyous . . . save your immortal soul . . .

I tore the letter in two, threw the pieces on the floor, and backed away from the table and out of the house.

Returning to the newspaper, I walked into the office with my head down, awash in misery. It took several blinks for me to recognize the lean, gray-haired figure sitting with his back to the door. I'd never expected to see him again. Another ghost.

When it looked as though I wasn't going to move out of the doorway, Sam motioned me inside. Langston turned in his seat and smiled up at me. "How you doing, Tom boy?"

I nodded curtly, my eyes thin slits leaking contempt. I crossed the floor on leaden feet and leaned against the type case, too tight and angry to sit. My attitude seemed to make them both uncomfortable, which didn't bother me at all.

Sam said, "Langston was telling me that the people of Dallas treated the comet's visit as justification to throw one long party."

The thought of a bunch of big city swells waltzing in tuxedoes while hundreds of people thrashed miserably in the chaos of Mentirosa Canyon infuriated me. "If he had been where he was supposed to be, he woulda seen people goin' crazy and dyin' instead of gettin' drunk and dancin'."

Sam gave me a scalding look, and I stared right back at him.

"I couldn't have done anything about that, Tom," Langston said, no apology in his voice. "It was too big."

"Maybe if youda been here instead of hidin' from Clement, some of us might not'a got involved, not so deep anyway. You coulda talked sense, helped Sam, stood up for something, for Chrissakes."

Langston shook his head. "That was the last thing anyone was going to listen to around here. Sam's lucky he didn't get run out of town for talking sense." He paused. "Everyone did what they had to do for their own reasons."

My head was boiling with anger and frustration that I

could not articulate, knowing that if I tried, I would be washed away in feelings I could not control, lost in words that would not mean what I felt. I bit my lip and concentrated on the pain, clawing my way back into control.

Sam nodded to the leather briefcase at Langston's right foot. "I'd like to see that information."

Langston drew two folders from his briefcase and spread letters and clippings into several piles as he talked. "In Dallas I met a vice-president of the Kansas City Zephyr line. In return for cancellation of a sizable debt he had incurred across a cribbage board, he made inquiries into railroad schedules and passengers riding south on and around the end of February. Particularly small, weasely, black-suited passengers waving Bibles. We were able to trace one such passenger back into western Kentucky. A county sheriff in Fort Palestine responded to our circular with information on a certain 'Reverend Augustine' who had kicked up a lot of sand during a prohibition campaign before fleeing the town, leaving an unhappy mob behind." Langston smiled like a cat chewing a mouse head as he handed Sam a letter. "It seems that a saloon was burned down on the night before their referendum, and the folks with the tar and feathers suspected that Reverend Augustine might have soot on his hands and ash in his hair."

Sam smiled quickly, grabbed his notebook off his desk, and paced as he asked questions. "Did you get a description? Is there a warrant out?"

Langston leaned back in his chair and scratched his head. The hair that I remembered as a shining gun-barrel-silver mane now appeared lank and pale, fading to a tired gray. "No warrants. The only description the sheriff provided was that Brother Augustine was, quote, 'not much bigger than a good-sized hard-on,' unquote."

Sam threw his head back and laughed. "I'll write the Fort Palestine newspaper. This is all circumstantial," he said while leafing through the correspondence, "but very compelling."

Langston spoke with the light sarcasm that always cloaked his words concerning Law and God and Man. "I'm glad that I could lift your spirit, but I can't see how any of this will make a difference to those folks holed up in Colonel Hedgman's house. You print what we've got, Nick will deny it and attack you, and you'll be lucky if your office—my office—doesn't end up in smoking cinders." Langston rubbed the eyes, once vital, clear and dark, that now hid pale and hesitant behind puffy lids. "The law doesn't want him, and his people won't surrender him anyway. The only way you'll ever get him out of this town is shoot him, kidnap him, or scare him out. You don't have much time. Once they finish that temple, he'll be entrenched."

Sam paced the length of the office as Langston organized the paperwork and laid a folder on Sam's desk. When he closed his briefcase, the lawyer offered an alternative to weeks of correspondence and months of capricious judicial proceedings. "From a legal perspective, I'm not encouraged. However, if you could develop a course of action to use this information quickly and judiciously, you might be able to drive old Nick out without committing a felony or getting cremated."

Sam's pacing stopped mid-stride. He lowered his foot slowly to the floor as if taking the initial step into alien territory or onto a tightwire. His face sagged under the weight of grave decision, his head twisting slightly to the right, then left, as if studying different aspects of the problem.

Langston's voice was rueful. "I recognize the irony of my counseling bold action, Sam, but this may be a situation best handled directly." Langston pulled himself heavily to his feet and placed his Stetson on his head with a waxy, shaking hand. "I've got a train to catch."

Sam put his hand on the lawyer's back as they walked toward the door. I held my ground, leaning against the type case, still angry. Any elation that I felt over the possibility of ridding the town of Nicholas was secondary to the loss and disappointment I felt in the presence of a man whom I had once idolized.

"Where are you bound?" Sam asked. "Dallas?"

"Oh, no!" Langston shook his head vigorously, as though Hell were preferable. "I have a friend who says Arizona is a tolerable place and should remain so, at least until they make it a state. Then I suppose there's always Alaska. Did you know that's where Derby made his money?" Langston winked as he pulled a handkerchief from his vest pocket and wiped sweat from a forehead grown mottled and furrowed. "America has run out of frontiers."

"Write when you get settled," Sam said, "so I'll know where not to send the rent."

Langston's laughter, for the first time since his arrival, was genuine. "I've put everything but this building up for sale. Pity I didn't do it last winter, back when it looked like another railroad might come through. It'll be hard to give away land in this town now."

"Tom." I tensed at the sound of my name. "Take care of yourself."

I nodded but didn't move from the type case.

And then he was gone. I never saw him again, but he was never far from my thoughts. A day rarely passed that I didn't regret my refusal to shake his hand.

Chapter
Forty-two

Brother Nicholas,

I have evidence concerning your previous existence under the name "Reverend Augustine," in Fort Palestine, Kentucky. If you would like to negotiate for suppression of this information, I will meet you at midnight Wednesday at the True Vine Church. Failure to appear will result in disclosure to the law and to the public. Come alone.

A Friend

We pushed the door open and surveyed the interior of the True Vine Church by the sparse light leaking in from the street. The room was bare but for one broken-legged chair and a rough table, furniture deemed unworthy of moving to New Jerusalem. Sam pulled the shades before lighting our lantern and placing it on the table. He ran his hand over the bulky foot-long piece of mesquite wood that he had packed along as he walked toward the closed door of Nicholas's old office. I waited at the front door, my hand on the knob, ready to run for help if the office proved to be full of Nicholas's henchmen. I checked the streets for enemy. None visible.

Sam kicked in the office door and stepped back quickly, making great diagonal swipes with the mesquite club splitting the air with the sound of potential mayhem. The office was empty. I slipped out the back window into the alley and climbed onto the roof, where I could keep an eye on most everything that moved in the Bowery. I stared off to the east over the top of the barbershop to where, under the light of the half moon, I could make out the main house of New Jerusalem. No lights, no movement.

For thirty minutes or more I saw nothing more interesting than a drunken cowboy falling off his horse. Nicholas was late or wasn't coming at all, leaving me with the conclusion that either he wasn't Reverend Augustine from Kentucky and had no idea what the letter was all about, or that he figured he could deny any accusation and gut out the consequences. Neither case augured well for the prospect of getting him out of town quickly and bloodlessly.

When the Panhandle Prince tossed the last besotted cowboy onto the sidewalk, I pulled myself up and beat the dust from my seat and knees. I had one foot on the makeshift ladder when I saw movement about fifty yards to the rear of the barbershop. I waited long enough to establish that it was a single limping man before abandoning my post.

"Nicholas! Alone!" I whispered into the dim room. I left the office door open a crack and pressed my eye to it. Sam sat in the broken-legged chair, using the wall for support, as he rested his feet beside the pale lantern on the table.

In less than a minute the door swung slowly open. Nicholas stood framed in the threshold, allowing his eyes to adjust to the light before stepping inside. "Adams," he hissed with disgust. Nicholas checked behind the door before shutting it firmly.

"We're alone," Sam said. "This is between you and me."

Nicholas ignored the lie and walked directly toward the office door and me. He used ten paces in crossing the room, and I took advantage of the five "thumps" his bad leg made to slide quietly beside the door and flatten myself against the wall just before he flung the door open. The frame was out of plumb, and the door snagged on the uneven plank floor, stopping inches from my back. I could hear Nicholas breathing hard on the other side. As he limped away, I nudged the door with my heel; it swung back far enough so that I could see through the crack below the hinge.

Nicholas stood in front of the table like a prisoner in the dock while Sam leaned back, relaxed and in charge. The lantern threw light up under the preacher's head, making his thin face look skeletal, his features bleeding off into the shadows. He stood rigid, his hands behind his back, chest thrust forward like a fighting cock.

Nicholas said, "I came only to see who the vilifier was and to warn him of the danger inherent in his attack. I have never heard of any Reverend Augustine, and I have never set foot in Kentucky. If you spread this slander or print it, I will take appropriate action."

"Appropriate legal action, I assume," Sam said, his voice mocking.

"I have alternatives. If this speculation is printed, I'm sure that my disciples will conclude who the enemy of the Lord is."

"Let's leave the Lord out of this, Nick. He's taken a hell of a beating lately." Sam lowered his feet to the floor and leaned across the table. "There are warrants out in Kentucky, and I have descriptions and news stories due any day. We both know what they're going to say, and I'll have a paper on the street within hours. What I'm trying to do here is give you the chance to be gone before your sins catch up with you."

"I am not Reverend Augustine, there are no warrants for *my* arrest. If you print otherwise there will be serious consequences." Nicholas spun around and was nearly to the door when Sam played his trump card.

"I may not print this at all, Nick. I might just turn it over to the man who had *his* saloon burned down a few months ago. I know Derby will be struck by the coincidence, and I'll get a five-hundred-dollar reward to boot." Sam laughed and leaned back in the rickety chair. "And Derby is not the kind of man who will pursue this through the courts. He's more likely to beat you into bad health and then shoot you between the eyes."

Nicholas took a single step and reached for the doorknob. My heart leaped when I saw his shoulders sag and his head tilt forward. He opened the door about a foot, but I knew he would not walk out. His steps back to the table were those of a man reporting for a noose-fitting.

"I can do so much for my people." I was barely able to hear Nicholas's low sob. "They have nothing. I can give hope and order to their lives. They need guidance. What will happen to *them*?"

"They damn sure don't need a self-righteous little jackleg messiah to worship. They'll get by."

"Don't you see that I'm a different man? The Lord has changed me."

"What matters is that I will have no trouble convincing Derby that you are the same man that torched his saloon. If you're not out of this town in twenty-four hours, or if you try to take one dollar out of the bank, I'll lay all this out to Derby. And no matter where you hide, he'll find you."

Nicholas slouched forward, his hands on the desk, a routed soldier. "Money was never my object."

" 'The desire for power in excess caused the angels to fall,' " Sam quoted. "I advise you to get out of town, or the fall will prove fatal."

Chapter
Forty-three

Before the sun rose on the following morning, Brother Nicholas was gone. Sam, Rebekah, Big Mike, and I spent a long, anxious night at castle watch expecting that we might have to defend the newspaper office against gray-robed arsonists, but they never came. Instead the dawn was greeted with shouts of celebration from New Jerusalem proclaiming the miracle of the bodily assumption of Brother Nicholas into Heaven. The Sainted Brother, we were told, had lain down in his bed that night and was never again beheld by mortal eyes. A miracle by any standard.

The exodus from New Jerusalem that began within days of Nicholas's "ascension" accelerated when the manor came under siege. The *Plain Talk* article exposing Brother Nicholas's previous existence in Kentucky (and Arkansas, we discovered) solidified the town's hostility toward the cult, as well as creating additional internal doubt. Predictably, the last members to join were the first to leave. Each morning a diminished host would arise, the defectors frequently availing themselves of food or the Colonel's housewares upon leaving. The remaining seventeen members of the "Twenty-four," the bedrock of the Glorious Assumption, had broken into several conflicting sects. They could not agree on theology, on leadership, on tactics, on anything, but they would not give up the dream mined in the passionate defeat of the prohibition campaign, melted in the crucible of the Comet Crusade, fused and forged in the pain and revelation of Mentirosa Canyon. To abandon the cause that had been their blood and sinew for months was unthinkable; on three occasions the torch carriers met, made peace, and swore fidelity. Within hours they had crossed swords anew over interpretation of scripture, delegation of work, wording of prayer, personal slight.

New Jerusalem did not explode in heat and passion over issues of vast scope and surpassing depth, as would befit a movement founded upon the most profound concerns that obsess the human soul; it crumbled under the insidious assault of envy, vanity, greed. The spring of 1910 sowed in my soul the genesis of realization that the heavens are indifferent to our existence, and it is Man that makes life so much harder than it need be.

When Sheriff Coffey padlocked the doors and posted No Trespassing signs on the Hedgman property, the last person to leave the mansion was the Widder Greer. Head high and carriage erect, she silently pushed through the small knot of onlookers gathered at the front gate. She ignored the comfort offered by old friends as she walked impassively to the home she had so joyfully abandoned. She looked older than I had ever seen her.

I followed at a distance. I didn't know how she would greet me, and I had erected a wall of resentment that I was not sure I could pull down. I counted to twenty before following Mama into our house. She sat at the kitchen table in her gray robe, the last material vestige of her long, painful journey through faith, bliss, and betrayal.

"Hello, Mama," I said as I took a single step into the kitchen.

When she raised her head and saw me, years fell away from her face. She moved across the room and swept me up in the ardent bear hug that never failed to reduce me to a helpless child. I could feel her warm tears falling on my head and neck. "Oh, Tom, how I missed you. Are you all right? Have you been eating properly?"

"I'm all right." My resentment ebbed under the cascade of her tears. But I couldn't surrender that easily. "Why did you go with *him*?"

Mama shook her head in apparent disbelief as she led me by the hand to a kitchen chair. She pulled her chair so close that our knees were touching. Then in a torrent of words that would not tolerate interruption, she proceeded to explain the inexplicable: "Tommy, we both know that you pulled me into Brother Nicholas's movement!"

What?

"I admit that in the beginning, I had sort of a . . . curiosity about his interpretation of the Bible, but you must remember how you first fell under the spell of that Adams man, and then switched your allegiance completely to Brother Nicholas. What kind of mother would I have been if I had let you get into that alone. I had to go along to look after you."

"Mama, that's—"

"Oh, it's nothing to be ashamed of, son. You're just a boy. And you *must not* feel guilty. We can put all this behind us now. I certainly never expected the world to end, and I've taken these last several weeks to rest up and put things in perspective. I've done a lot of thinking and it's obvious that all the causes I've worked for, all the clubs I've started, and the people I've tried to straighten out—it was all for nothing. It's hopeless trying to fix this world, or even this little town. These people aren't ready yet; they're too pigheaded to listen. I can see now that you have to start a whole lot closer to home. You have to straighten out yourself and those closest to you."

Look out!

"And since I've gotten so old, what's left is shaping the young folks. You're the hope of the future, son, and from now on I'm going to spend every moment preparing you to finish the jobs that I started."

Whoa, Nelly!

"I think you're giving up too quick, Mama. You've made a good start on a lot of things in this town, and folks are expectin' you to jump right back into the fight now that all this Nicholas stuff is over. There's a lot of things that needs to be set right." My brain scrambled for an example. "Uh, for one thing, I don't think I'll rest easy so long as women can't vote. Now that's real injustice! And ain't a thing I can do about it."

"No, Tom. All the people my age have already made up their minds about these things, and nothing or nobody is going to change them. The only hope we have is the young

people. And I think you're the best of the bunch. You can
lead the way!"

So I became the Widder's sole project. Mama spent the
years preceding the World War subjecting me to a regimen
of mental, physical, and spiritual conditioning that would
have crushed a lesser human. She employed resources ranging from the Classical Greek to the most outrageous con-
temporary craze—often in improbable combination—in a
headlong, devil-take-the-hindmost attempt to impose nobility on my unworthy form.

Mama's only concession to my wishes was her acceptance of my work at *Plain Talk*. I suppose she understood
that that was the price she had to pay to keep me from running off to join the circus. For seven years Sam, Rebekah,
and I printed the best weekly in the state of Texas and
eventually generated sufficient profit to purchase a new
printing press. The only time I ever saw Sam look prouder
was when his daughter was born.

Epilogue

I was discharged from the Army on December 12, 1918, one month and one day after the Armistice. They rushed me through processing because my mother was sick with Spanish influenza.

I arrived in High Plains two days after she was buried.

The town was smaller. The main street of the Bowery, a memory that I had conjured up regularly in the trenches, in the barracks, on the troopship, had shrunk from a grand boulevard throbbing with buckboards, cars, and horsemen, to a rutted cattle path barely capable of sustaining two wagons abreast. Over half the storefronts were boarded up, the saloons having been closed in 1912 in a last-ditch attempt to impose respectability on a town that had never recovered from the folly that became synonymous with its name. The only thing that had separated us from dozens of other Panhandle towns was free-flowing liquor, but it was a distinction that the town could ill afford after the comet fiasco.

After the Dallas-Overland Railroad bypassed us for Wishbone, the town had plummeted in a tight spiral. R. N. Barkley pulled out in 1911, leaving the town without booster or benefactor. Son of a bitch or not, a town needs an engine, and Barkley drove High Plains. Merchants moved down the tracks to towns that held promise of growth and prosperity. When shopkeeper died, no son stepped forward to assume the business.

The long hours and hard work at *Plain Talk* were continually relieved by the joy I felt as I watched my goddaughter grow—a child rescued from the curse of being too beautiful by inheriting Sam's whimsical, off-center smile. Although Sam occasionally, in the heat of editorial controversy, railed at himself for abetting Rebekah's independence, the newspaper profited in style and content from the input of her conscience and voice. Curiously, the clumsiness that had seemed to plague Miss Rebekah since her arrival at High Plains abated as she assumed more responsibility at the newspaper.

Unfortunately, *Plain Talk*'s primary mission in the second decade of the twentieth century was chronicling the town's erosion. After Doc Moss died following an eight-day laudanum binge, and Zack Hart, shortly thereafter, lay down on the railroad track in time to catch the 9:11 mail train, there were no Raglars left to lend insight and continuity to the sidewalks. The Hedgman property was awarded by the state court to the state government and then left to deteriorate. The only remnant of New Jerusalem and Brother Nicholas was the charred foundation of the Great Tabernacle burned by vandals on New Year's Eve, 1910. About once a year Sam would review the Gem Scott affair, but nothing ever came of it. Jack Clement died old, in bed.

For several long years following the Glorious Assumption, my mother remained true to her vow and ignored the problems and politics of our town, concentrating instead on perfecting the character of her only child. She found it to be a task comparable to Sisyphus and his rock attaining the top of the hill; I consider it a tribute to my spirit that it failed categorically. Fortunately, for me, the Widder Greer entered the Great War in 1914, three years before President Woodrow Wilson saw fit to commit American troops to the conflict. She filled numerous scrapbooks with newspaper and magazine articles on the battles, collected scarce relief materials for shipment overseas, and corresponded regularly with British pen pals (mothers all) arranged through the Red Cross. With my mother's attention diverted by "the war to end all wars," I was able to return to a somewhat "normal" life.

When Son Bob Suggs and I determined that we should be the first volunteers from High Plains to fight the Bloody
͟ ͟n, it freed Sam and Rebekah from an obligation that nei-
͟ ͟ ͟uld confess to. There was no future for a newspaper
͟ ͟ ͟lains, hadn't been since the Glorious Assumption,
͟ ͟ ͟stayed, I am sure, for my sake. I would not

leave my mother, and they would not leave me. Throughout my enlistment, whenever the inept military mail system managed to locate me, I received bundles of letters from the Adamses. Each letter implored me to join them in California, where Rebekah and her child were happy, and Sam was, as always, optimistic about his newspaper's prospect for turning a profit.

I knew that High Plains had changed little in the nineteen months that I was gone, but thousands of miles and centuries of innocence removed from my home, knee-deep in the mud and death of the trenches, I had chosen to recall the town the way it appeared to a twelve-year-old on a payday Saturday night, before Nicholas, before the comet. Confronted with this pale and stunted version of a scene that had sustained me through countless hours, I felt a freedom that is the domain of a mind stripped of a primary layer of illusion.

I stayed in High Plains only as long as obligations demanded; I had learned the lessons that it could teach, and I would store and value the memories. Freed from the military, granted reprieve from the past, there was much to anticipate. I would see Sam and Rebekah in California, but there was no hurry. There were many choices to be made and each was to be savored.